SPARTACUS:
THE GLADIATOR

ALSO BY BEN KANE

The Forgotten Legion Chronicles

The Forgotten Legion
The Silver Eagle
The Road to Rome

SPARTACUS:
THE GLADIATOR

BEN KANE

 ST. MARTIN'S GRIFFIN ⚏ NEW YORK

This is a work of fiction. All of the characters, organizations, and events portrayed in this
novel are either products of the author's imagination or are used fictitiously.

The Library of Congress has cataloged the hardcover edition as follows:

Kane, Ben.
Spartacus : the gladiator / Ben Kane.—1st U.S. ed.
   p. cm.
 ISBN 978-1-250-00116-0 (hardcover)
 ISBN 978-1-4668-0266-7 (e-book)
 1. Spartacus, d. 71 B.C.—Fiction. 2. Gladiators—Fiction. 3. Rome—History—Servile
Wars, 135–71 B.C.—Fiction. 4. Rome—History—Fiction. I. Title.
 PR6111.A536 S67 2012
 823'.92—dc23

2011279125

ISBN 978-1-250-02156-4 (trade paperback)

First published in Great Britain by Preface Publishing

First St. Martin's Griffin Edition: February 2013

D 10 9 8 7 6 5 4 3 2

For my brother Stephen

Republican Italy in the first century BC

ALPS

CISALPINE GAUL

R. Padus
Mutina

ITALIA

Pisae

Apennines

ETRURIA

PICENUM

ILLYRIA

Adriatic Sea

CORSICA

Rome

LATIUM

Via Appia

Capua

SAMNIUM

CAMPANIA

Venusia

Via Appia

Brundisium

Pompeii

LUCANIA

Metapontum

Tarentum

Thurii

SARDINIA

Tyrrhenian Sea

Via Annia

Messana

Rhegium

Ionian Sea

MARE

SICILY

INTERNUM

AFRICA

| 0 | 50 | 100 | 150 | 200 miles |
| 0 | 100 | 200 | 300 km |

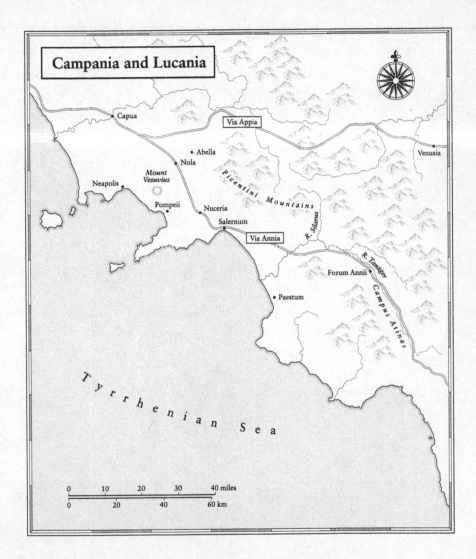

Campania and Lucania

Capua

Via Appia

Abella
Nola

Venusia

Neapolis

Mount
Vesuvius

Picentini Mountains

Pompeii

Nuceria

Salernum

R. Silarus

Via Annia

Forum Annii

R. Tanager

Paestum

Campus Atinas

T y r r h e n i a n   S e a

| 0 | 10 | 20 | 30 | 40 miles |
| 0 | 20 | 40 | 60 km |

SPARTACUS:
THE GLADIATOR

I

When the village came into sight at the top of a distant hill, a surging joy filled him. The road from Bithynia had been long. His feet were blistered, the muscles of his legs hurt and the weight of his mail shirt was making his back ache. The chill wind snapped around his ears, and he cursed himself for not buying a fur cap in the settlement he'd passed through two days prior. He had always made do with a felt liner and, when necessary, a bronze helmet, rather than a typical Thracian fox-skin *alopekis*. But in this bitter weather, maybe warm clothing was more important than war gear. Gods, but he was looking forward to sleeping under the comfort of a roof, out of reach of the elements. The journey from the Roman camp where he'd been released from service had taken more than six weeks, and winter was fast approaching. It should have been less than half that, but his horse had gone lame only two days after he'd left. Since then, riding had been out of the question. Carrying his shield and equipment was as much as he could ask the horse to do without worsening its limp.

"Any other mount, and I'd have sacrificed you to the gods long ago," he said, tugging the lead rope that guided the white stallion ambling along behind him. "But you've served me well enough these last years, eh?" He grinned as it nickered back at him. "No, I've no apples left. But you'll get a feed soon enough. We're nearly home, thank the Rider."

Home. The mere idea seemed unreal. What did that mean after so long? Seeing his father would be the best thing about it, although he'd be an old man by now. The traveler had been away for the guts of a decade, fighting for Rome. A power hated by all Thracians, yet one that many served nonetheless. He had done so for good reasons. *To learn their ways so that one day I can fight them again. Father's idea was a good one.* It had been the hardest act of his life to take orders from some of the very soldiers he had fought against—men who had perhaps killed his brother and who had certainly conquered his land. But it had been worth it. He had learned a wealth of information from those whoresons. How to train men mercilessly, until they fought as one unit. How vital it was to obey orders, even in the red heat of battle. How trained soldiers could be made to stand their ground in the most extreme situations. Discipline, he thought. Discipline and organization were two of the most vital keys.

It wasn't just the desire to learn their ways that had you leave your village, added his combative side. After its last defeat by the legions, your tribe had been thoroughly cowed. There was no chance of fighting anyone, least of all Rome. You are a warrior, who follows the rider god. You love war. Bloodshed. Killing. Joining the Romans gave you the opportunity to take part in never-ending campaigns. Despite everything that they've done to your people, you still took pleasure from waging war alongside them.

I've had a bellyful of it for now. It's time to settle down. Find a woman. Start a family. He smiled. Once he would have scorned such ideas. Now they were appealing. During his service with the legions, he'd seen things that would turn a man's hair gray. He'd become used to them—in the red heat of battle, he had acted in much the same way, but sacking undefended camps and villages, and seeing women raped and children killed, were not things that sat especially well with him.

"Planning how to take the fight to Rome will do me for a while. The time for war will present itself again," he said to the stallion. "In the meantime I need a good Thracian woman to make lots of babies with."

It nibbled his elbow, ever hopeful for a treat.

"If you want some barley, get a move on," he said in an affectionate growl. "I'm not stopping to give you a nosebag this near to the village."

Above him and to his left, something scraped off rock, and he cursed silently for letting his attention lapse. Just because he'd encountered no one on the rough track that day didn't mean that it was safe. Yet the gods had smiled on him for the whole journey from Bithynia. This was a time when most Thracians avoided the bitter weather in favor of oiling and storing their weapons in preparation for the following campaigning season. For a lone traveler, this was the best time to travel.

I've done well not to have run into any bandits thus far. These ones are damn close to my village. Let there not be too many of them. Pretending to stretch his shoulders and roll his neck, he stole a quick glance to either side. Three men, maybe four, were watching him from their hiding places on the rocky slopes that bordered the rough track. Unsurprisingly for Thrace, they seemed to be armed with javelins. He eyed the tinned bronze helmet that hung from the pack on the stallion's rump, and decided against making a grab for it. Few peltasts could hit a man in the head. As for his shield, well, he could reach that while their first javelins were still in the air. If he was hit, his mail shirt would probably protect him. Trying to untie his thrusting spear would take too much time. He'd carry the fight to them with his *sica*, the curved Thracian blade that hung from his gilded belt. They were acceptable odds, he decided. As long as the brigands weren't expert shots. *Great Rider, watch over me with a ready sword.*

"I know you're there," he called out. "You might as well show yourselves."

There was a burst of harsh laughter. About thirty paces away, one of the bandits stood up. Merciless eyes regarded the traveler from a narrow face pitted with scars. His embroidered woolen cloak swung open, revealing a threadbare, thigh-length tunic. A greasy fox-skin cap perched atop his head. He had scrawny legs, and his tall calfskin boots had seen better days. In his left hand, he carried a typical *pelte*, or crescent-shaped shield, and behind it a spare javelin; in his right, another light spear was cocked and ready to throw.

No armor, and apart from his javelins, only a dagger in his belt, noted the traveler. Good. His friends will be no better armed.

"That's a fine stallion you have there," said the thug. "A pity that it's lame."

"It is. If it wasn't, you shitbags wouldn't have seen me for dust."

"But it is, so you're on foot, and alone," sneered a second voice.

The traveler looked up. The speaker was older than the first man, with a lined visage and graying hair. His hemp-woven clothing was equally ragged, but there was a fierce hunger in his brooding gaze. For all his poverty, his round shield was well made, and the javelin in his right fist looked to have seen good use. This was the most dangerous one. The leader. "You want the stallion, I suppose," the traveler said.

"Ha!" A third man stood up. He was larger than either of his companions; his arms and legs were heavily muscled, and instead of javelins, he carried a large pelte and a vicious-looking club. "We want it all. Your horse, your equipment and weapons. Your money, if you have any."

"We'll even take your food!" The fourth bandit was skeletally thin, with sunken cheeks and a sallow, unhealthy complexion. He had no shield, but three light spears.

"And if I give you all that, you'll let me go on my way?" His breath plumed in the chill air.

"Of course," promised the first man. His flat, dead eyes, and his comrades' sniggers, gave the lie to his words.

The traveler didn't bother answering. He spun around, muttering

"Stay!" to the stallion. Even as he slid his hand under his large circular shield and snapped the thong that held it in place, he heard a javelin zipping over his head. Another followed behind on a lower arc. It struck the dust between the horse's hooves, making it skitter to and fro. "Calmly," he ordered. "You've been through this plenty of times before." Reassured by his voice, it settled.

"Oeagrus, stop, you fool!" shouted the leader. "If you injure that beast, I'll gut you myself."

Good. No more javelins. The stallion is too valuable. Keeping his back to his mount and raising the shield, he turned. The skinny bandit was to his rear now, but he wouldn't risk any more spears. Nor would the others. Drawing his sica, he smiled grimly. "You'll have to come down and fight me."

"Fair enough," growled the first man. Using his heels as brakes, he skidded down the slope. His two comrades followed. Behind him, the traveler heard the thin brigand also descending. The stallion bared its teeth and screamed an angry challenge. *Let him even try to come close.*

When the trio reached the bottom, they conferred for a moment. "Ready?" he asked mockingly.

"You whoreson," snarled the leader. "Will you be so arrogant when I cut your balls off and stuff them down your neck?"

"At least you'd be able to find mine. I doubt that any of you scumbags have any."

The big man's face twisted with fury. Screaming at the top of his voice, he charged, pelte and club at the ready.

The traveler took a couple of steps forward. Placing his left leg behind the shield, he braced himself. He tightened his grip on his sica. *This has to be quick or the others will be on me as well.*

Fortunately, the thug was as unskilled as he was confident. Driving his shield into his opponent's, he swung a wicked blow at his head. The traveler, rocking back slightly from the impact of the strike, ducked his head out of the way. Reaching around with his sica, he sliced the big man's left hamstring in two. A piercing scream rent the air, and the bandit collapsed in a heap. He had enough sense to raise his pelte, but the traveler smashed it out of the way with his shield and skewered him through the neck. The thug died choking on his own blood.

He tugged the blade free and kicked the corpse onto its back. "Who's next?"

The leader hissed an order at the skinny man before he and the cap-wearing bandit split up. Like crabs, they scuttled out to either side of their victim.

The stallion trumpeted another challenge, and the traveler sensed it rear up on its hind legs. He stepped forward, out of its way. An instant later, there was a strangled cry, the dull *thump, thump* of hooves striking bone, and then the noise of a body hitting the ground. "My horse might be lame, but he still has quite a temper," he said mildly. "Your friend's brains are probably decorating the road. Am I right?"

The two remaining brigands exchanged a shocked look. "Don't even think of running away!" warned the leader. "Oeagrus was my sister's son. I want vengeance for his death."

Unobtrusively, the traveler lowered his shield a fraction, exposing his neck. *Let that tempt one of them.*

The man in the fox-skin cap clenched his jaw. "Fuck whether the beast gets hit," he said, hurling his javelin.

The traveler didn't move from the spear's path. He simply raised his shield, letting it smack directly into the layered wood and leather. Its sharp iron head punched two fingers' depth out through the inner surface, but did not injure him. Swinging back his left arm, he threw the now useless item at the thug, who scrambled away to avoid being hit. What he wasn't expecting was for the traveler to be only a few steps behind his flying shield. When the bandit thrust his second javelin at his opponent, it was parried savagely out of the way.

Using his momentum to keep moving forward, the traveler punched his opponent in the face with his left fist. The man's head cracked back with the force of the blow, and he barely saw the sica as it came swinging back around to hack deep into the flesh where his neck met his torso. Spraying blood everywhere, and looking faintly surprised, he fell sideways into the road. Keeping time with the slowing beats of his heart, a crimson tide flooded the ground around him. *Three down, but the last is the most deadly.*

The traveler turned swiftly, expecting the leader's attempt to stab him in the back. The move saved him from serious injury, and the javelin skidded off the rings of his mail shirt and into thin air, causing the man to overreach and stumble. A massive backhand to the face sent him sprawling backward onto his arse, losing his weapon in the process.

He stared up at the traveler, frank terror in his eyes. "I have a wife. A f-family to f-feed," he stammered.

"You should have thought of that before you ambushed me," came the growled reply.

The bandit screamed as the sica slid into his belly, slicing his guts to ribbons. Sobbing with pain, he waited for the death blow. But it did not fall. He lay there, helpless, already passing in and out of consciousness.

A few moments later, he opened his eyes. His killer was watching him impassively. "Don't leave me to die," he begged. "Even Kotys wouldn't do this to a man."

"Kotys?" There was no response, so he kicked his victim. "You were going to cut my balls off and feed them to me, remember?"

He swallowed down his agony. "P-please."

"Very well." The sica rose high in the air.

"Who in all the gods' name are you?" he managed to whisper.

"Just a weary traveler with a lame horse."

The blade scythed down, and the brigand's eyes went wide for the last time.

†

Ariadne scraped back her hair and carefully pushed a couple of bone pins into her long black tresses, fastening them into place. Sitting on a three-legged stool by a low wooden table, she angled the bronze mirror that sat there so that it caught the watery light entering through the hut's open doorway. The shaped piece of red-gold metal was her sole luxury, and using it occasionally served to remind her of who she was. This was one of those days. To the vast majority of the people in the settlement, she was not a woman, a relation or a friend. She was a priestess of Dionysus, and revered as such. Most of the time, Ariadne was content with this prestige. After her harsh upbringing, her elevated position was better than she'd have ever dreamed possible. But it didn't mean that she didn't have needs or desires. *What's wrong with wanting a man? A husband?* Her lips pursed. Currently, the only person showing interest in her was Kotys, the king of the Maedi tribe. Unsurprisingly, his interest had put paid to any other potential suitors. Those who crossed Kotys tended to end up dead—or so the rumor went. Not that there had been any before that, she reflected bitterly. Men with the courage to court a priestess were rare beasts indeed.

Ariadne did not want or appreciate Kotys' lecherous advances, but felt powerless to stop them. He hadn't yet tried to become physical, but she was sure that was because of her vaunted status—and the venomous snake that she kept in a basket by her bedding. Her situation was complicated by the fact that she had to remain in the village. She had been sent here by the high priests in Kabyle, Thrace's only city, which lay far to the northeast. Extraordinary circumstances notwithstanding, hers was an appointment for life. If she returned to Kabyle, Ariadne could expect to be performing menial duties in the main temple there for the rest of her days.

There was no question either of returning to her family. While she loved her mother, and prayed for her everyday, Ariadne harbored two feelings for her father. Hate was the first, and loathing was the second. Her emotions stemmed from her brutal childhood. Ariadne's existence had consisted of beatings, humiliation and worse, all at the hands of her father. A warrior of the Odrysai tribe, he had despised her because she—his only child—was not male. During the long years of misery, her sole means of escape had been praying to Dionysus, the god of intoxication and ritual ecstasy. It was only when communing with him that she'd felt some inner peace, a state of affairs that still prevailed.

To this day, Ariadne believed that Dionysus had helped her to survive the unending abuse.

Other than through marriage, the concept of escaping her father had never entered Ariadne's mind. There had been simply nowhere for her to go. Then, on her thirteenth birthday, things had changed utterly. In a remarkable intervention, Ariadne's downtrodden mother had persuaded her father to allow her to attend the Dionysian temple in Kabyle as a prospective candidate for the priesthood. Once there, her burning determination had impressed the priests and allowed her to remain. More than a decade later, she still had no desire to return home. Unless, of course, it were to kill her father, which would be a pointless exercise. While Ariadne's position as a priestess elevated her above that of ordinary women, a patricide could expect but one fate.

No, her best option was to weather out Kotys' attentions—*Dionysus, let some doe-eyed beauty catch his eye soon*—and establish herself here. It had been a mere six months since she'd arrived at this, the main Maedi settlement. Not long at all. Ariadne's chin lifted. There was another option of course. If Kotys were deposed, a better man could take his place. She'd been here long enough to sense the seething discontent with his rule. Rhesus, the previous king, and Andriscus, his son, weren't especially missed, but Sitalkes, the noble who might have replaced them, had been a popular figure. They were careful not to do it within earshot of Kotys' bodyguards, but plenty of warriors spoke nostalgically of Sitalkes and his two sons, one of whom had been killed in battle against the Romans and the other had gone to serve the conquerors as a mercenary, and never returned.

If only someone would step forward and harness the simmering rage against Kotys, thought Ariadne. A short, sharp fight and the bastard would be gone forever. Not for the first time, she cursed the fact that she'd been born a woman. *No one would follow me.* She studied the familiar reflection in the bronze mirror before her. A heart-shaped face, with a straight nose and high cheekbones, framed by long black ringlets of hair. A determined chin. Creamy white skin, most unsuited to the blazing sun that bathed Thrace every summer. A swirling design of dots tattooed on both her forearms. Slim but muscular shoulders. Small breasts. What does Kotys see in me? she wondered. I'm no beauty. Striking perhaps, but not pretty. As ever, the same answer entered Ariadne's head. He sees my wild spirit and, being a king, wants it for his own. It was the same fieriness that had often got her in trouble during her training, and which had also helped her to become a priestess sooner than might have been expected. Ariadne valued her tempestuous nature greatly. Because of it, she could enter the maenad trances easily, and reach the zone where one might encounter Dionysus, and know his wishes. My spirit belongs to no man, Ariadne thought fiercely. Only to the god.

Standing, she moved to her simple bed, a blanket covering a thick layer of straw in one corner of the hut. It was the same as that used by everyone in the settlement. Thracians were known for their austerity, and she was no different. Ariadne donned her dark red woolen cloak. In addition to marking her position in life, it served as her cover at night. Picking up the wicker basket that lay at the bed's foot, she put it to her ear. Not a sound. She wasn't surprised. The snake within did not like the chilly autumn weather, and it was as much as she could do to rouse it occasionally from its torpor and wrap it around her neck before performing a rite at the temple. Thankfully, this simple tactic was enough to inspire awe in the villagers' minds. To Ariadne, however, the serpent was but a tool in maintaining her air of mystery. She respected the creature, indeed feared it a little, but she'd been exhaustively trained to handle it and its kind in Kabyle.

With the basket under one arm, she headed outside. Like most of the others in the settlement, her one-room rectangular hut had been constructed using a lattice of woven branches, over which a thick layer of mud had been laid. Its saddle roof was covered with a mixture of straw and mud, with a gap at one end to let out smoke from the fire. To the hut's rear stood part of the rampart that ran around Kotys' living quarters. It was a defense within the circular settlement's outer wall, reinforcing the king's elevated position and serving against treachery from within. Other huts lay to either side, each surrounded by a palisade that kept in their owners' livestock. The dwellings followed the winding paths that divided the sprawling village. Like the regular dungheaps and mounds of refuse, they had evolved over centuries of inhabitation. Ariadne was eternally grateful that her hut was a reasonable distance from any of these necessary, but stinking, piles.

She followed the lane toward the center of the settlement, acknowledging the respectful greetings of those she met with a grave smile, or a nod. Women with babes at the breast and the old asked for her blessing or advice, while all but the boldest of the warriors tended to avoid her gaze. Children tended to fall into two camps: those who were terrified of her and those who asked to see her snake. There were far more of the former than the latter. There was little to leaven the loneliness of Ariadne's existence. She forced her melancholy away. The god would send her a man, if he saw fit. And if he didn't, she would continue to serve him faithfully, as she had promised during her initiation.

The crowd in front of her parted, revealing a group of richly dressed warriors. Ariadne's heart sank. It wasn't just the men's swagger that told her who they were. Their red long-sleeved tunics with vertical white stripes, elaborate bronze helmets and silver-inlaid greaves shouted stature and importance. So too did their well-made javelins, *kopis* swords and long, curved daggers. Ariadne mouthed a silent curse. Wherever this many of his bodyguards were, Kotys wouldn't be far behind. Glancing to her left, she greeted an elderly woman whose sick husband she'd recently treated. A torrent of praise to Dionysus filled Ariadne's ears. Smiling, she moved nearer to the woman's hut, turning her back on the path. With a little luck, the warriors wouldn't have seen her. Perhaps they weren't even looking for her?

"Priestess!"

Ariadne cursed silently. She continued listening to the old woman's patter, but when the voice called again, it was right behind her.

"Priestess."

†

The traveler didn't linger at the scene where he'd been ambushed. Of course, the brigands had nothing worth taking. All he'd had to do was clean his sica, snap off the javelin that had skewered his shield and re-tie the shield to the pack on his horse's back. Leaving the bodies where they'd fallen, he set out for the village. At this rate, they'd be lucky to reach it before dark. That eventuality did not bear thinking about. Banks of dull yellow clouds overhead promised an early fall of snow. His luck was in, however. Whether it was the adrenaline pumping through his mount's veins, or an intervention by the Great Rider, he did not know, but the stallion now seemed to move more easily on its bad leg. They made good progress, coming within sight of the settlement just as the first flakes began to fall.

Loud bleating carried through the air, and the traveler looked up. Aided by a pair of dogs, a small boy was herding a flock of sheep and goats onto the road just ahead. "We're not the only ones seeking shelter," he said to his mount. They halted, giving the lad space to usher his resentful charges onto the stony track. "Some bitter weather coming. You're wise to head for home now," he said in a friendly tone.

The boy made no move to come down off the slope. "Who are you?" he demanded suspiciously.

"Peiros is my name," he lied. Even this close to his home, he did not yet feel like revealing his true identity.

"Never heard of you," came the dismissive reply.

"You were probably still crawling around on a bearskin rug at your mother's feet when I left the village."

Some of the wariness left the boy's eyes. "Maybe." He began urging the last of the sheep and goats onto the road with sharp cries and waves of his arms. The dogs darted to and fro, ensuring that there were no stragglers. The traveler watched, and when the entire flock was safely down, he began to walk alongside the young shepherd. *I wonder what I can find out.* "How's Rhesus?" he asked.

"Rhesus? The old king?"

"Yes."

"He's been gone these four years. A plague took him."

"His son Andriscus should be king then."

The boy threw him a scornful look. "You really have been away. Andriscus is dead too." He glanced around warily before whispering, "Murdered, like Sitalkes." He saw the flash of horror in the traveler's eyes. "I know, it was terrible. My father says that the Great Rider will punish Kotys eventually, but for now, we have to live with him."

"Kotys killed Sitalkes?"

"Yes," replied the lad, spitting.

"And now he's the king?"

A nod.

"I see."

A silence fell, which the boy did not dare break. He wouldn't admit it, but the grim traveler scared him. A moment later, the man halted. "You go on." He gestured at his stallion. "I mustn't make him walk too long on his bad leg. I'll see you in the village."

With a relieved nod, the boy began chivvying the flock along the road again. The traveler waited until he was some distance away before closing his eyes. Guilt nipped at his conscience. *If only I had been here, things might have been different.* He didn't let the feeling linger. *Or they might not. I too might have been slain. Father's decision to send me away was a good one.* Somehow he knew that Sitalkes also would not have changed what had transpired. It was impossible to deny his sadness at the news of his father's murder, however. He thought of Sitalkes as he'd last seen him: strong, straight-backed, healthy. *Rest well.* All he'd wanted was to come home. For his service with his most hated enemies to end. To hear that his father was dead was bad enough, but if it was true that he had been murdered, there would be no warm homecoming. No rest. Yet to think of turning away from the settlement and retracing his steps was not an option. Vengeance had to be obtained. His honor demanded it. Besides, where would he go? Back into service with the legions? *Absolutely not.* It was time to return, no matter what reception awaited him. *I do not question your will, Great Rider. Instead I ask you to protect me, as you have always done, and to help me punish my father's killer.* The fact that this meant slaying a king did not weaken his resolve.

"Come on," he said to the stallion. "Let's find you a stable and some food."

†

Ariadne turned slowly. "Polles. What a surprise." She made no attempt to keep the ice from her voice. Polles might be Kotys' champion, but he was also an arrogant bully who abused his position of authority.

"The king wishes to talk with you," drawled Polles.

Despite the veneer of courtesy, this was an order. *How dare he?* Ariadne forced her face to remain calm. "But we spoke only yesterday."

Polles' thin lips twisted in a travesty of a smile. Everything about him from his striking good looks to his long black hair and oiled muscles smacked of self-importance. "Nonetheless, he desires ... the pleasure of your company once more."

Ariadne did not miss the short but deliberate delay in his delivery. Judging by the other warriors' chuckles, neither had they. Filthy bastard, she thought. Just like your master. "When?"

"Why, now," he replied in a surprised tone.

"Where is the king?"

Polles waved languidly over his shoulder. "In the central meeting area."

Where all the people can see him. "I'll be there in a moment."

"Kotys sent us to accompany you to his side. At once," said Polles, frowning.

"He may well have done, but I am busy." Ariadne indicated the fawning old woman. "Can't you see?"

Polles' face flushed with annoyance. "I—"

"Are the king's wishes more important than the work of the god Dionysus?" asked Ariadne, lifting the basket's lid.

"No, of course not," Polles answered, retreating.

"Good." Ariadne turned her back on him.

Angry muttering broke out behind her. "I don't know what you should say to the king. Tell him that we can't find her. Tell him that she's in a trance. Make up something!" snapped Polles. Ariadne heard feet scurrying off and allowed herself a small smile. Soon, however, her conversation with the old woman petered out. It wasn't surprising. Having the king's champion a few steps away, no doubt staring daggers at both of them, would intimidate anyone. Murmuring a blessing on the crone, Ariadne glanced at Polles. "I'm ready."

With poor grace, he beckoned her into the midst of his warriors. They closed ranks smartly and Polles led the way forward, bawling at anyone foolish enough to get in his way. It didn't take long to reach the large open area that formed the settlement's center. The space was roughly circular in shape, and fringed by dozens of huts. Crowds of women gossiped as they carried their washing back from the river. A ragtag assortment of children played or fought with one another in the dirt while skinny mongrels leaped excitedly around them, filling the air with shrill barks. Smoke trickled from the roof of a smithy off to one side; the clang of a hammer on an anvil could be heard from within. Several men waited outside, damaged weapons in hand. There were wooden stalls selling metalwork, hides and essential supplies such as grain, pottery and salt, a miserable inn, and three temples— one each to Dionysus, the rider god, and the mother goddess. That was it.

Like their fellow Thracians, the Maedi were not a race that depended on trade for a living. Their territory was poor in natural resources. Farming provided little more than a subsistence living, so they had evolved into fighters, whose sole purpose of existence was to make war, either in their own land or abroad. The people visible proved this point: they were mostly powerfully built warriors. The majority were red- or brown-haired, with dark complexions. Varying in age from stripling to graybeard, all had the same confident manner. Clad in pleated, short-sleeved tunics that ranged in color from red and green to brown or cream, they wore sandals, or leather shoes with upturned toes. Many wore the ubiquitous *alopekis*, the pointed fox-skin cap with long flaps to cover the ears. Richer individuals sported bronze or gold torcs around their necks. A sword or a dagger—often both— hung from every man's belt or baldric. They stood around in groups, bragging of their exploits and planning hunting trips.

Polles and his men attracted the attention of everyone in the vicinity. Ariadne felt the weight of the onlookers' stares as they strode toward Dionysus' temple, a larger building than most, with a squat stone pillar on each side of the entrance. She heard their mutter- ing too, and hated it. They were brave enough to fight in battle, but not to stand up to the king they resented. It made her feel very alone.

The king was waiting by the temple doors. He was flanked by body- guards, while a throng of warriors stood before him. He cut a grand sight. Although he was nearly fifty, Kotys looked a decade younger. His wavy black hair showed not a trace of gray and there were few wrin- kles on his shrewd, fox-like face. Over his purple knee-length tunic, Kotys wore a composite iron corselet with gold fittings and twin pec- torals of the same precious metal. Layered linen pteruges protected his groin, and greaves inlaid with silver covered his lower legs. He was armed with an ivory-handled *machaira* sword, which hung in an amber- studded scabbard from his gold-plated belt. An ornate Attic helmet sat upon his head, marking his kingship.

As Polles and his men pushed through the throng, Kotys' eyes drank Ariadne in. "Priestess! Finally, you grace us with your presence," he called.

"I came as soon as I could, Your Majesty." Ariadne did not explain further.

"Excellent." Kotys made a peremptory gesture and her escorts moved aside. Reluctantly, she took a step forward, then a few more. Ariadne could sense Polles smirking. Turning her head, she glared at him. The gesture was not lost on Kotys, who waved his hands again. At this, the bodyguards withdrew some twenty paces to the smithy.

"You must forgive Polles' lack of manners," said the king. "He is ill suited to running errands."

Why send him then? "I understand," she murmured, forcibly dampening her anger.

"Good." One word was the limit of Kotys' own courtesy. "It would be easy to make more suitable arrangements," he said brusquely.

"And they would be?" Ariadne arched her eyebrows.

"Dine with me in my quarters some evening. There would be no need for Polles, no need for an escort."

"I'm afraid that won't be possible," Ariadne replied icily.

"Are you forgetting who I am?" asked Kotys with a scowl.

"Of course not, Majesty." Ariadne lowered her eyes in a pretense of demureness. "Evenings are the best time for communing with the god, however," she lied.

"That couldn't happen every night," he growled.

"No, the dreams are only occasional. Dionysus' ways are mysterious, as you would expect."

He nodded sagely. "The rider god is the same."

"Naturally, the erratic nature of their arrival means that I must always be ready to receive them. Spending an evening away from the temple is out of the question. Now, if you would excuse me, I must pray to the god." Although her heart was thumping in her chest, Ariadne bowed and gave Kotys a beatific smile, before making to move past him.

To Ariadne's shock, he seized her by the arm. She dropped the basket, but unfortunately the lid stayed on.

"You're hurting me!"

"You think that's painful?" Kotys laughed and thrust his face into hers. "Know this, *bitch*. Toy with me at your peril. I won't tolerate it forever. Remember that I am also a priest. You *will* come to my bed, one way or another. And soon." He suddenly released his grip, and Ariadne staggered away, white-faced.

What she would have given for a lightning bolt to flash down from the sky and strike him dead. Naturally, nothing of the sort happened.

She might be the representative of a deity, but so was Kotys. In a situation such as this, Ariadne was powerless. Kabyle with its powerful council of priests was far, far away. Not that they'd intervene anyway. As ruler of the Maedi and high priest to the rider god, Kotys was the one with all the power. She managed a stiff little bow. Kotys' lips twitched in contemptuous amusement. "We will speak again," he said in a grating voice. "Shortly."

With trembling hands, Ariadne carried the basket to the temple doors, where she set it down. She lifted the heavy bar that held the portal closed, letting the light flood in to the dim interior. The moment that Kotys was gone, she let out a shuddering gasp. Her knees felt weak beneath her, and she fumbled her way to one of the benches that sat against the side walls. Closing her eyes, Ariadne inhaled deeply and held it as she counted her heartbeat. At the count of four, she let the air out gradually. Dionysus, help me, she begged. Please. She continued to take slow breaths. A vague sense of calm crept over her at last, and some of the tension left her shoulders. A lingering fear remained in Ariadne's belly, however. It would take far more than prayers to stop Kotys from taking matters into his own hands. She felt utterly helpless.

A discreet cough interrupted her reverie.

Ariadne turned her head. The figure in the doorway was outlined by sunlight, preventing her from recognizing who it might be. Needles of panic stabbed through her before she regained control. Kotys or Polles would not be so polite. "Who is it?"

"My name is Berisades," said a respectful voice. "I'm a trader."

Ariadne's professional mien took over. "Come in," she commanded, gliding toward him. Berisades was a short man in late middle age with a close-cut beard and deep-set, intelligent eyes. "You've been on the road," she said, eyeing his green tunic and loose trousers, which were covered in dust.

"I have come from the east. It was a long journey, but we made it without too many losses. I wanted to offer my thanks to the god immediately." Berisades tapped the purse on his belt, which clinked.

Ariadne ushered the trader forward to the stone altar. Behind it, on a plinth, was a large painted statue of Dionysus. In one hand, the bearded god held a grapevine, and in the other a drinking cup. Waves lapped at his feet, showing his influence over water. A carved bull with the face of a man stood to one side of him while a group of satyrs cavorted on the other. At his feet lay bunches of withered dry flowers, miniature clay vessels containing wine and tiny statues in his likeness. Light winked off pieces of amber and glass. There were long razor clam shells, ribbed cockles and, most prized of all, a rare leopard cowrie shell.

Kneeling, Berisades placed his pouch among the other offerings.

Ariadne retreated, leaving him to his devotions. An image of a leering Kotys filled her mind's eye at once, and her spirits plunged. She could see no escape from him and despair overtook her. Thinking that meditation would make a difference, she closed her eyes and tried to enter the calm state that so often provided her with insight into the god's wishes and desires. She failed miserably, instead imagining Kotys manhandling her on to his bed.

"What do they call you, lady?" Berisades' voice was close by.

With huge relief, she jerked back to the present. "Ariadne."

"You weren't here when last I visited."

"No. I arrived here six months ago."

He nodded. "I remember at the time the old priest not being that well. Still, you're young and healthy. No doubt you'll be here for many years, to gladden the eyes of every grateful traveler wanting to pay his respects."

"You're very kind," murmured Ariadne, cringing inside. *If only you knew the truth.*

"It won't be long until the next pilgrim arrives, by the way."

"No?" Ariadne was barely listening. She was already worrying about Kotys once more.

"I met a warrior yesterday who was returning here. He'd have come in with us, but his horse is lame. Spent years in the Roman auxiliaries, apparently. He wants to give thanks to the tribe's gods for his safe return. A quiet man, but he put himself across well."

"Really?" replied Ariadne vacantly. She had little interest in the return of yet another tribesman who'd served as a mercenary for the Romans.

Berisades could see that her mind was elsewhere. "My thanks, lady," he muttered, withdrawing.

Ariadne gave him a bright smile. Inside, however, she was screaming.

†

As they climbed the slope to the palisaded settlement, old memories came flooding back. Hot summer days swimming with other boys in the fast-flowing river that ran past one side of the village. Herding the sturdy horses that served as mounts for the wealthier warriors. Hunting for deer, boar and wolves as a youth among the peaks that towered overhead. Being blooded as a warrior after killing his first man at sixteen. Kneeling in the sacred grove at the top of a nearby mountain, praying to the Rider God for guidance. The hours of his life he'd spent wishing that his mother had not died birthing his sister, a babe that had lingered less than a month in this world. The day he'd heard the news that Rome had invaded Thrace. Riding to war against its legions with his father Sitalkes, brother Maron and the rest of the tribe. Their first glorious victory, and the bitter defeats that followed. The agonizing death of Maron, a week after being thrust through the belly by a Roman sword, a *gladius*. The subsequent vain attempts to overcome the Roman war machine. Ambushes from the hills. Night attacks. Poisoning the rivers. Unions with other tribes that were undone by treachery or greed, or both.

"We Thracians never change, eh?" he asked the stallion. "Never mind what might be best for Thrace. We fight everyone, even our own. Especially our own. Unite to fight a common enemy, such as Rome? Not a chance!" His barking laugh was short, and angry. The first part of the task his father had set him—serving with the Roman legions— had been completed. He had anticipated a period of relatively normal life before attempting the second part, that of trying to unify the tribes.

It was not to be. The dark cloud of war with its bloody lining had found him yet again. Yet he did not try to ignore the adrenaline rush. Instead he welcomed it. *Kotys killed my father. The treacherous bastard. He must die, and soon.*

Used to both his soliloquies and his silences, the horse plodded on behind him.

Two sentries armed with shields and javelins stood by the walled settlement's large gates. They peered at him through jaundiced eyes, muttering to each other as he approached. Few travelers arrived at this late hour, in such bad weather. Even fewer possessed a mail shirt or tinned helmet. Although the newcomer's stallion was lame, it was of fine quality. It was also white—the color prized by kings.

"Halt!"

He came to a stop, raising his left hand in a peaceful gesture. *Just let me in without too many questions.* "It's an evil evening," he said mildly. "After paying respects to the Rider God, it's one to spend by the fire with a cup of wine."

"You speak our tongue?" asked the older guard in surprise.

"Of course." He laughed. "I'm Maedi, like you."

"Is that so? I wouldn't recognize you from a dog turd," snarled the second sentry.

"Me neither," his comrade added in a slightly more civil tone.

"Maybe so, but I was born and raised in this village." He frowned at their scowls. "Is this the best welcome I can expect after nearly a decade away?" He was about to say that his name was Peiros, but the first guard spoke first.

"Who are you?" He peered at the newcomer's arms, noticing for the first time the spatters of blood, and then back at his face. "Wait a moment. I know you! Spartacus?"

Shit! "That's right," he replied curtly, caressing the hilt of his sword.

An incredulous grin split the older man's face. "By all the gods, why didn't you say? I'm Lycurgus. Sitalkes and I rode together." He threw a warning look at the other guard.

"I remember you," said Spartacus with an amiable nod. The stare he gave the second sentry was far less friendly. Mortified, the warrior took a sudden interest in the dirt between his feet.

"Things have changed since you left home," said Lycurgus unhappily. "Your father—"

"I know," Spartacus cut in harshly. "He's dead."

"Yes."

He couldn't help himself. "Died in suspicious circumstances, I hear."

Lycurgus glanced at his companion. "Neither of us had anything to do with it. Polles is the one you want to talk to."

"Polles?"

"The king's chief bodyguard." The distaste in Lycurgus' voice was clear.

"What about Getas, Seuthes and Medokos? Are they still alive?" he asked casually.

"Oh yes. They've fallen from favor, but they keep their noses clean so Kotys leaves them be." Aware of the dangerous undercurrent to their conversation, Lycurgus licked his lips. "Are you . . . ?"

Spartacus acted as if he hadn't heard. "I'm tired. I've been on the road for weeks. All I want is some hot food in my belly and a drink with my old friends. The king can wait until tomorrow. He doesn't need to know that I've returned until then." *By which time, gods willing, it will be too late. Now that these two know my identity, I've got to act at once. Getas and the others will help.* "That's not too much to ask, is it?"

"O-of course not," stammered Lycurgus. He glared at his companion.

"We won't say a word to anyone."

"Not a soul," warned Spartacus. Hearing the sudden chill in his voice, the two guards nodded fearfully.

"Good." Pulling a fold of his cloak over the lower half of his face, Spartacus walked by without another word.

"You fucking idiot," hissed Lycurgus the instant that he had vanished from sight. "Spartacus is one the deadliest warriors that our tribe has ever seen! Be grateful that he was in a good mood. You do *not* want to piss him off."

"What is he planning?"

"I don't know," snapped Lycurgus. "I don't want to know. If anyone asks later, we didn't recognize him. Understand?"

II

riadne's mood was darkening. The usual ritual of burning incense and meditation had brought her nothing but a sequence of fractured, distressing images. Most of them featured Kotys, naked on a bed. Others also involved Polles, which revolted her. The more appealing—and dangerous—ones were those in which she defended herself against the king with a knife, or her snake. What use is there in killing him? she wondered hopelessly. I'd have to flee the settlement to avoid being killed by his bodyguards. Where would I go then? Kabyle? Ariadne could think of nowhere else, but she dismissed the notion out of hand. The priests in the city would not shelter a regicide. She was trapped. Alone, with no one to help her.

Cloaked by misery, she shut up the temple and headed for her hut. The sky was full of clouds threatening snow, and she wanted to gain the safety of her door before it started falling heavily. The settlement wasn't dangerous for most, but Kotys could easily have set some of his warriors to lie in wait for her. As she hurried toward the alleyway that led home, Ariadne saw a man entering by the main gate. She'd never seen him before, but his slow, self-assured carriage attracted her attention. He was of average height, with short brown hair, and wearing a mail shirt and closely fitting red trousers. A Roman soldier's belt circled his waist; from it hung a sheathed sica and dagger. The bronze helmet he was holding had a forward curving crest, and the lame white stallion following him was also clearly Thracian.

He called out a low greeting to a bunch of warriors who were standing nearby. Ariadne recognized three of them: Getas, Seuthes and Medokos. Hearing the other's voice, Getas turned his head. He frowned, and then with delighted looks, he and his companions descended on the newcomer.

So that's the traveler whom Berisades met, thought Ariadne. He must be well liked if they have not forgotten him in his absence. She kept walking. Reaching home was more important than staring at strangers. Perhaps Dionysus would visit her that night. Give her some hope. She consoled herself with that idea. A moment later, she heard a characteristic, braying laugh coming from inside the alleyway. Recognizing Polles by the sound, Ariadne reacted without thinking. She quickly angled away from the alley's entrance to approach it from the side. Poking her head around the corner, she saw the outline of at least three men a short distance inside. Their slouching posture was at direct odds with the naked weapons in their hands. Feeling very weary, Ariadne sagged against the house's cold wattle and daub. Kotys was being true to his word. The bodyguards were there to abduct her. *Curse him!* Creeping around them to reach her hut by another route would merely delay the inevitable. In that instant, the helplessness that Ariadne had felt when her father was about to assault her sexually returned. It sat in her belly as if it had never been absent, an acid pool of nausea and self-loathing.

Her indecision seemed to last an eternity, but in reality was no more than a few heartbeats. Unsure of where to go, Ariadne stumbled across the central space. It was then that she saw a second party of warriors heading toward her from the temple. Ducking her head in a pathetic attempt not to be seen, she changed direction. There was only one way to go. To the main gate. It didn't matter that it was bitterly cold, snowing, or that it was dangerous beyond the village walls. She had to get away from Kotys, and it didn't matter how.

"Priestess!" a voice called behind her.

A sob escaped Ariadne's lips, and she quickened her pace. All she had to do was reach the entrance. The guards outside wouldn't dare to stop her and the impending snowstorm would swallow her up as surely as the underworld. What she was doing was madness, but in that exact moment, Ariadne didn't care. Death was better than experiencing again what she'd endured as a child. She glanced over her shoulder and was pleased to see that the warriors were too far away to prevent her from escaping. With few other people about, this one tiny victory would not be denied her.

Totally absorbed, Ariadne wasn't looking where she was going. With a thump, she collided with someone. It was only the other's strong arm that prevented her from falling flat on her back. She looked up to find a pair of amused gray eyes regarding her. It was the man who'd just arrived with the lame stallion. Ariadne blinked. This close, he was quite handsome.

"My apologies. I don't usually make it my business to knock over attractive women."

"N-no, it was my fault," she faltered.

Noticing the tattoos and red cloak that marked her station, he released his grip. "I'm sorry, priestess, I meant no disrespect. Why the hurry?"

"I——" Ariadne glanced back. The warriors were less than twenty paces away. "I have to go. Leave the village."

"In this weather, priestess?" He looked alarmed. "You'll catch your death. If not, the wolves will have you."

"That's as may be," muttered Ariadne, "but I'm going nonetheless." She made to move past.

He threw out his arm, stopping her. "What have you done?" he asked, nodding his head at the approaching group.

"Done? Nothing!" She laughed bitterly and tried again to walk on, but his arm was immovable, like a bar of iron. Ariadne didn't have the strength—or will—to push against it.

"Something tells me that lot aren't coming to discuss the weather. Who are they?"

"Kotys' men," she replied flatly.

"Kotys?" *I haven't thought of the prick for years, but now his name is falling from everyone's lips.*

"The king."

His lip curled. "The *king*. You've crossed him, I take it?"

"Does refusing to go to his bed count as crossing him?" she spat back. "If it does, then yes, that's what I've done. Now let me go."

He lowered his arm. "So they're coming to take you to Kotys, but you won't have it?"

"Yes. I'll die before I let that bastard rape me." Ariadne stared into his eyes, and was surprised by what she saw. As well as anger, there was admiration. And hate—but not for her.

"Don't move." Dropping the horse's lead rope, he stepped in front of her.

"What are you doing?" she stammered.

"Men might act like that in war, but not in peacetime, in my fucking village," he barked. "I thought I'd left all that behind me." *I thought I could come home without discovering that my father had been murdered by a man he once called a friend.*

Ariadne watched, petrified, as the warriors arrived, four well-armed warriors with hawkish expressions and a purposeful manner. "Well met," called the first. "We're in your debt for stopping that woman."

"I didn't stop her," he replied harshly. "We collided and I prevented her from falling."

"It's of no matter how you did it." Revealing rows of rotten teeth, the warrior's leer was more snarl than smile. "She'd have escaped but for you. We're grateful. Now step aside."

"Why? What's she done?"

"None of your damn business," growled the warrior.

"She's a priestess. Hardly a common criminal. Not the type of person to manhandle either, unless you want to anger a god. Don't you agree?" His voice was low but menacing.

The warrior blinked in surprise. "Look, friend, we're just following orders. The king wants to see her. So do us a favor and piss off, eh?"

He looked back at Ariadne. "Do you want to go with these men?"

"You don't have to do this," she whispered, not quite believing her eyes and ears.

He didn't acknowledge what she'd said. "Yes or no?"

Ariadne looked at the quartet of bodyguards and shuddered.

"Well?"

"No," she heard herself say. Instantly, guilt tore at her. *Why have you involved him too?*

He shrugged carelessly. "You heard. She's not going."

"What's your name, fool?" hissed the lead warrior, raising his spear. "I like to know the name of a man before I kill him."

He ignored the demand. Drawing his sword, he pointed it straight at the man's face. "Ready to die? Because that's what is going to happen next."

Even in the poor light, it was possible to see the warrior turn pale. He glanced at his companions, who also looked far from happy.

"Shall we get this over with?" he snarled, taking a step toward them.

Ariadne couldn't believe her eyes. The bodyguard's confidence shrank like a bladder pricked with a knife. "We've got no quarrel with you," he mumbled.

"Nor I with you, but I'm not about to see you seize a priestess without good explanation," he snapped, continuing to advance. "It was my understanding that we held such people in great veneration. That we didn't treat them like runaway slaves."

Lifting his spear point into the air, the warrior backed away. His companions did the same. "This isn't going to end here," muttered the first man.

"I'd be disappointed if it was." He watched as they vanished into the gloom.

"I wish you hadn't done that. You've as good as signed your own death warrant," Ariadne said coldly, disregarding the amazement she felt at the warriors' about-turn.

"A simple thank-you would suffice," he replied in a mild voice.

"I don't want another's death on my conscience!" she said, coloring.

"My fate is mine to decide, not yours," he growled. "What kind of a man would I be if I just let a group of thugs carry off a priestess?" *It was a rash move, all the time. Thank the Rider that none of them recognized me.*

"A wise one," she snapped.

"Got quite the temper, haven't you? Seeing as you don't want my help, I'll leave you to it. The gate's still open." He picked up the lead rope and clicked his tongue at his horse. "Come on. Let's get you stabling and some food. And better company, if we can find it."

"Wait," said Ariadne, hating her fear, which had resurged at the prospect of him leaving.

He raised an eyebrow, which made him even more attractive.

"It was noble of you to intervene. Thank you."

"You're welcome. Was there anything else?" He made to move off again.

"The king's men won't leave it at that, you know. They act as they please."

"I can tell. But they'll have to find me first. The settlement is a big place to search for one man." He nodded in farewell.

"Stay for a moment," asked Ariadne. Walking out into the night now seemed utterly terrifying. So too did waiting for Kotys' warriors, alone.

"I was going to until you decided to be rude."

"I'm sorry," she replied, her voice catching. "I didn't want to see you hurt, that's all."

"Your concern is endearing," he said in a gentler tone, "but let me worry about things like that."

"Very well." Ariadne felt embarrassed, but she continued regardless. "Please accompany me home. I have a small shed where you could stable your horse."

"Is it far?" He gestured at the stallion. "As you've probably seen, he's lame."

"It's no more than a couple of hundred paces. Follow me." With her heart thumping in her chest, Ariadne led the way. By now, it was completely dark and the alleys had emptied of people. Only the occasional dog skittered by, giving them a wide berth. She caught him checking every shadow, and was relieved when he eventually relaxed a little.

Ariadne was also pleased to see no lurking shapes near her house. Polles and his men were still in the alleyway or, more likely, had returned with their cheated comrades to the king. Filling a bucket of water from the nearby well, she left him settling the horse in the lean-to. She hurried inside, noticing as she lit an oil lamp that her hands were shaking. Trying to regain her composure, she sat down on the three-legged stool. Had her situation improved in any way? In reality, she had just exchanged one set of dangers for another. He might be a fearsome warrior, but he couldn't fight all of Kotys' men and expect to win. Despite her pessimism, Ariadne could not deny the spark of pleasure that glowed in her heart. He had been under no obligation to step in. Most sane men would have turned the other way when they'd seen the king's bodyguards. Instead, at the risk of his own life, he had saved her. Weirdly, Ariadne felt a trace of hope. He had to know the odds that they faced, yet he remained calm, even unperturbed. That meant he must have a plan.

She smiled as he entered, barring the door behind him. "Is your horse fed and watered?"

"He is," he replied, looking satisfied.

"You care for him greatly."

"I do. He's been under me, or by my side, through more than five years of constant war."

"That's a long time to be fighting."

"It is. That's why I came home. To hang up my sword and settle down for a while. Instead, I've done the complete opposite." His lips twisted wryly. "To be honest, I'm not that surprised. The Rider has a habit of doing this to me. And he knows best."

"Nonetheless, I'm sorry," said Ariadne, feeling even worse.

"We've covered this ground already," he said in a reproving voice. "It was my decision to intervene." *My decision to enter the village, even when I was recognized.*

"It was," she acknowledged. Then, "I don't even know your name."

"Nor I yours," he replied, smiling.

"Ariadne." She couldn't stop her cheeks from burning as she spoke.

"It's an honor to meet you. I am Spartacus."

She frowned. The name rang a bell in her head, but she didn't know why. "How long have you been away exactly?"

"Eight years, give or take. You've not been here that long."

"No. Six months."

"When did Kotys start bothering you?"

"Practically from the first moment I got here. I've managed to fend him off thus far, but today, for whatever reason, he had had enough. Ostensibly, I was to dine with him, but it was just a façade. For him to—"

"I can imagine," he interjected. "I knew that the whoreson was a murderer, but a rapist too? The world will be a better place when he's gone." *And if the Rider wills it, my blade will end his stinking life.*

"So the rumors are true then?"

"Oh yes," he replied bitterly. "When Rhesus, the last king, died, Kotys had his son and heir slain. Sitalkes, my father, must have tried to intervene, because he was killed too."

"Your father, murdered?" Ariadne's heart went out to him. "How did you find this out?"

"I met a boy tending stock not half a mile from the front gate. It was easy enough to persuade him to talk. I wasn't sure whether to believe it all, but one of the guards was an old comrade of my father's. He confirmed the story. So did the friends I spoke to briefly."

"I'm sorry." She reached out to touch his arm, but suddenly self-conscious, stopped herself.

His scowl deepened. "Not half as sorry as Kotys and Polles, who-ever the fuck he is, will be soon."

Ariadne's breath caught in her chest. "What are you going to do?"

"I'm told that Kotys is very unpopular. That the majority of war-riors hate his guts and only his bodyguards are truly loyal. There are what, a hundred of them or so?"

Still not believing what she was hearing, Ariadne nodded.

"If I can persuade sixty or seventy men to follow me, we'll take them."

She saw the self-belief in his gray eyes, and her heart filled. *Thank you, Dionysus!* "This is what I've been praying for."

His eyebrows rose. "You've also been plotting to overthrow a king?"

"What of it?" she retorted. "He's nothing but a tyrant."

"Feisty, aren't you?" He gave her an approving look, and her stom-ach fluttered. "So you will help?"

"In whatever way I can. I will consult the god, but I have no doubt that he would wish Kotys removed from power."

"Good. With your permission, I'll tell the warriors exactly that."

She started up in alarm. "You're going?"

"Not yet. I'll stay until midnight or so. If Polles and his men haven't appeared by then, they're not going to before the morning. I'll rest until then. It's been a long day."

Ariadne caught him looking at the cupboard where she kept her provisions. "I'm sorry. You must be hungry after your journey."

"I could eat."

"Let me fetch you something." Conscious of his eyes on her the whole time, Ariadne prepared a plate of bread and goats' cheese. She added a spoonful of cold barley porridge from a blackened iron pot. "Apart from water, that's all I have."

"It's plenty," he said, reaching out with eager hands.

Ariadne crept to the door while he demolished the food. Placing her ear against the timbers in a number of places, she listened. Nothing, apart from the usual chorus of dogs barking. It was some relief. Not knowing what else to do, she found a spare blanket and tossed it to him. She saw his eyes move to her bed. "Don't go getting any ideas. You can rest on the floor."

"Of course." He looked amused. "I expected no less."

Discomfited by his confidence—was it smugness?—she lay down on her bed without undressing and pulled up the covers.

"Sleep well." He moved around the room, blowing out all but one of the oil lamps. Laying the mantle by the door, he drew his sword and placed it alongside. Then, sitting with his back against the wall, he pulled his cloak tightly around himself and closed his eyes.

Almost at once, Ariadne found herself staring at him. The flickering of the lamp's flame threw Spartacus' regular features half into shadow, giving him a mysterious appearance. His hair was cut close to the scalp in the Roman military fashion. A faint scar ran off his straight nose on to his left cheek. A heavy growth of stubble covered his square, determined jaw. It was an attractive face, as she had noticed before. Hard, too, she thought, but she could see no cruelty there, no similarity to the likes of Polles or Kotys.

Was it possible that he had been sent by Dionysus? she wondered. It was tempting to think so. If he hadn't appeared, she would currently be dying of exposure, or of injuries sustained from falling off one of the precipices that lined the road away from the village. She offered a prayer of thanks to her god. That done, Ariadne relaxed on to her bed. It was time to get what rest she could. Tomorrow was another day.

Ten steps away, Spartacus was silently communing with his own favorite deity, the Thracian Rider God. He who shall not be named. *I ask you to keep your shield and sword over us both. Let the warriors listen to me as I go among them.* It was a heartfelt plea. For years, Spartacus' life had been about nothing more than fighting, killing and learning Roman battle tactics. In the last two hours, things had changed more than he could have thought possible. His hopes of a warm homecoming had vanished.

He was now seeking vengeance for his father's murder. He was a potential regicide. Spartacus let out a long breath. Such was the way of the gods. Over the years, he'd learned to take the knocks that life delivered him, but this one was harder than most. *As always, I bow to your will, Great Rider.* He took a surreptitious look at Ariadne, and his fierce expression softened. Not everything that had happened since his return was to be regretted.

✝

Ariadne woke from an arousing dream in which Spartacus had enveloped her in his arms. Shocked, she sat up, clutching her blanket to her chest. He was by the door, sheathing his sword. "Good sleep?"

"I-I think so," she muttered, hating her crimson cheeks and racing pulse.

"You're beautiful."

Startled, she glanced at him. "What did you say?"

"You heard. The best-looking woman I've ever seen in this village, if I may say so."

"You made a habit of comparing them, then?" she asked, using sarcasm to cover her embarrassment.

"Of course," he said, grinning. "Every man does."

Disarmed by his honesty, and more pleased than she'd ever let on, Ariadne pointed at the door. "Did you hear something?"

"No, nothing. It's time for me to go."

Reality came crashing back, and her stomach clenched into a painful knot. "I see. How will I know what has happened?"

"You'll hear the fighting. It will soon be obvious who won."

Terror constricted Ariadne's throat. She wanted to ask Spartacus not to leave, but she knew that would be futile. Everything about him now oozed grim determination. She let herself take strength from that. "The gods keep you safe."

"The Rider has been good to me all these years. I trust that he will continue to do so." He fixed her with his gray eyes, and smiled. "Afterward, I would like to get to know you better."

For a moment, Ariadne's tongue wouldn't move. "I-I would like that too," she managed.

"If things go against me—"

"Don't say that," she whispered. Images of Kotys filled her head.

"Nothing is certain," he warned. "If it comes to it, take my horse and go. Even though he's lame, you're light enough for him to carry. With all that will be going on, nobody will notice that you're gone for a day at least. You'll be able to reach the next village, and seek sanctuary there."

What good will that do? Ariadne wanted to scream. All she did, however, was to shake her head in silent assent.

He lifted the beam that barred the door. "Replace this after I've gone."

"I will."

"Get some more rest if you can."

Her chin firmed. "No."

He was halfway through the doorway, but he turned. "Eh?"

"I will pray to Dionysus for your success. And Kotys' death," she added.

His eyes glinted. "Thank you." He slipped out without another word.

Gods, but she's fiery. Attractive too. Putting thoughts of Ariadne aside, he let his vision adjust to the darkness. Using all his senses, he scanned the alleyway. After a few moments, he relaxed. No one was stirring. Even the dogs had gone to sleep. Keeping a hand to his sword, he stole off through the gloom. Eight years of absence didn't stop him from unerringly making his way to Getas' house. He'd grown up here and knew every alley and path in the settlement like the back of his hand. The yellow glow of lamplight through chinks in the wall drew him past the palisade, and he rapped lightly on the portal. "Getas?"

The muffled conversation within died away. He heard footsteps approaching. "Who is it?"

"Spartacus."

There was a scraping noise as the locking bar was lifted, and then the door eased open, revealing a skinny man with a mass of tangled red hair. He grinned. "Come in, come in."

Spartacus stooped and crossed the threshold. The inside of the rectangular hut was similar to most in the village. A large fire burned in a fireplace set into the back wall. Bunches of herbs hung from the roof beams. Tools were stacked untidily in one corner; bowls, pots and pans in another. A weapons rack stood proudly by the entrance, weighed down with javelins, spears and swords. To the left of the fire-place, two small children were curled up together under a blanket, like puppies. A dark-haired woman lay alongside them, her eyes watching his every move. Getas urged Spartacus to the bench in front of the blaze, where three warriors clad in long-sleeved, belted tunics were sit-ting. They all rose, smiling, as he approached.

"Spartacus! It's been too long!" exclaimed a tall man with a shaven forehead. "Thank the gods you have returned."

"Seuthes!" Spartacus returned the embrace before greeting the two others in the same way. "Medokos. Olynthus. I've missed your com-pany."

"And we yours," replied Medokos, a barrel-chested figure with a wiry beard. Olynthus, who was older than all of them, murmured in loud agreement.

"Sit," said Getas, waving a clay jug. "Let's have a drink."

When they all had a cup in hand, he poured the wine. Raising his right arm, he toasted them all. "To the Rider, for bringing Spartacus home in one piece."

"To the Rider!" They all drank deeply.

"To the end of Kotys' tyranny," said Seuthes. "May he be rotting in hell very soon."

"Polles too," added Getas.

"And plenty of the other scumbags who follow at their heels," snarled Medokos.

They threw back the wine. Getas poured everyone refills.

"Let's be clear," warned Spartacus. "What we're talking about places all of our lives in great danger." His eyes flashed to the woman and the children. "You understand me?"

"We know the dangers, Spartacus," said Getas fiercely. "And we still want to be part of it."

"Good. I need to talk to every warrior that you three regard as trustworthy. How many do you think that is?" He scanned their faces intently. Everything hinged on the rough poll he'd asked them to conduct earlier. *Let there be enough, Great Rider, or we're all dead men.*

"I had nineteen men say 'Yes,'" said Getas.

"Sixteen," added Seuthes.

"Twelve." Medokos looked annoyed. "One of them delayed me for at least an hour. He insisted on drinking in your honor."

Spartacus smiled. "You did well." He glanced at Olynthus, who had always been slightly aloof. It was probably because of the hunting injury that had left him with a permanent limp in his right leg. Aware that Olynthus' peer group often poked fun at him, Spartacus had always made him welcome, including him in all their boyhood exploits. Nonetheless, he knew Olynthus less well than the others.

"Twenty."

Delighted, Spartacus punched him lightly on the arm. "Sixty-seven warriors. Including us, I make it seventy-two. That's good enough odds for me." He clenched his fists, which were hidden in his lap. "How about the rest of you?"

"When do you think we should do it?" asked Getas by way of answer.

Spartacus grinned. "Always the hasty one, Getas!" He eyed the others.

"I'm with you," said Seuthes.

"Me too," muttered Medokos.

"Aye." Olynthus' answer was a heartbeat slower than that of the others, but the adrenaline was pumping so hard through Spartacus' veins that he barely noticed.

"Excellent. Have you told the men to gather so that I can talk to them?"

"Yes, in three houses," replied Seuthes. "We'll take you to them, one by one."

Getas was like a dog with a bone. "How soon do we attack the king?"

"We need to do it tomorrow."

Medokos' eyebrows rose. "So soon?"

"Yes. You know what people are like with idle gossip, let alone something like this. Best strike while the iron is hot." He ignored the awe in their eyes. "We can do it!"

"Gods, but it's good to have you back. Sitalkes would be proud," said Getas, beaming from ear to ear. "Let dawn arrive soon!"

The tension eased as they all chuckled at his enthusiasm.

Spartacus let them enjoy the feeling for a moment. Then, "We'd better get a move on. There are a lot of men who need to hear what I've got to say."

"True enough," said Getas. "May the Rider watch over us."

During the course of the next few hours, Spartacus moved tirelessly through the village with his four friends. He was greatly heartened by the warm reception he received everywhere. The level of discontent with Kotys' rule proved to be huge, and his words fell on fertile ground. Men fondly remembered his father and brother, and lamented both their deaths, especially that of Sitalkes, who had been poisoned at a feast held by Kotys. They apologized for not avenging Sitalkes' death, and were happy to swear undying loyalty to Spartacus. Every single one promised to send the king, Polles and the rest of his followers to oblivion in a variety of unpleasant ways. To a man, the warriors seemed to love Spartacus' plan of storming the royal compound at dawn, when most of the bodyguards would be asleep. "The simple plans are the best," he promised them all. "There's nothing that can go wrong."

When he was done, Spartacus considered returning to Ariadne's house to sleep. The idea appealed, but he put it aside. There was no point endangering her even more than he done already. By telling so many warriors of his plan, he had opened himself up to betrayal. Yet there was no other way of doing it. If he did nothing, Kotys would hear of his presence in the village by the next day. There was no way that the king would not act. Spartacus steeled his resolve. *All will go well. It has to. By sunset tomorrow, I will be the new ruler of the Maedi.* It scarcely seemed possible. Although the idea had crossed his mind during his time away, it hadn't ever been something that he had thought would come to pass. Rhesus, the previous king, and Andriscus, his son, had been popular and courageous men. He scowled. *They're gone now, like Father. Kotys must pay for that with his life. If achieving that end brings me the kingship, so be it. I'll make a better leader than the dog who currently sits on the throne. I will be able to lead the tribe against Rome all the sooner.* Another pleasing thought crossed his mind. *What of Ariadne?* A smile spread across his face. *We shall see.*

He walked quietly back to Getas' house, bidding farewell to the others one by one. Safely indoors, his friend handed him a spare blanket. Spartacus nodded his thanks. He lay down without undressing, making sure that his sword was to hand.

Getas crept under the covers with his wife, who was now mercifully asleep.

Spartacus closed his eyes. So much had happened that day that he expected to lie awake until the appointed hour, which was when Getas' cockerel started to crow. Apparently, it was annoyingly reliable, beginning its morning chorus an hour before sunrise each day. Spartacus was more weary than he'd realized, however. Lying back, he sank into a dreamless slumber.

He woke to the sound of splintering wood. Long years of combat experience sent him leaping up, tugging at his sword. Too little sleep, and the fact that he stumbled as he rose, meant that Spartacus had no time to draw his blade successfully. Half a dozen men came charging through the remains of the door, clubs in hand. They closed in on him and Getas, who had grabbed a cooking spit from the fire, like wolves cornering a deer. "What the hell's going on?" Getas mumbled. "What do you want?"

Spartacus knew in the pit of his belly what this meant. *Someone has betrayed us.* One of the men smashed him across the head with his club. The stars that burst across his vision were accompanied by a tidal wave of agony. He dropped to the floor like a bag of rocks. As more blows rained down, he was dimly aware of Getas' wife and children screaming in the background. Rage battered the edges of his consciousness, yet Spartacus could only curl into the fetal position in a vain attempt to escape more punishment.

"Stop," shouted a voice at last. "You'll kill him."

Reluctantly, the warriors stood back.

It took every shred of Spartacus' strength to move, but he managed to uncurl himself and look up. "Getas?" he croaked.

"I'm all right."

He eyed the handsome warrior who looked to be in charge. "Motherless cur! You must be Polles."

There was a mocking bow. "At your service."

"If you lay a hand on the woman or the babes, I'll—"

"Do what?" interrupted Polles with a cruel laugh. His men smirked.

"Cut your balls off and force you to eat them," growled Spartacus. "That's before I kill you."

"I'd like to see you try." Polles stepped over and kicked Spartacus in the belly, causing him to retch uncontrollably. "Fortunately for you, the king doesn't want them harmed. At least, not yet." He sniggered.

Spartacus reached out weakly, trying to grab Polles by the ankle, but the champion just moved beyond his reach. "Everyone thought you were dead."

"Clearly, I'm not."

"You will be soon. Plot to murder the king, would you?"

"You'd know all about murdering," replied Spartacus. "You whoreson."

Polles chuckled. "Heard about your father, then?"

Spartacus threw him a hate-filled glare by way of reply. "Who's the rat? Who told you?"

Polles glanced at his men. "Shall I tell him, or let him stew in his juices for a while?"

"Leave it until he sees who it is," suggested one warrior cruelly. "I'd like to see the expression on his face when he realizes."

"Good idea," purred Polles.

"Fuck you all," whispered Spartacus. Now he remembered the

delay before Olynthus had replied to his question. Olynthus. He was the traitor for sure.

"What are you going to do with them?" asked Getas' wife in a trembling voice.

"What do you think?" Polles sneered. "These two and the other prick who is responsible will be tied up in front of the whole tribe and tortured. When Kotys is happy that all the conspirators have been identified, he'll have their throats cut. The remainder will simply be executed."

Screaming with rage, she threw herself at Polles, but the warrior guarding her stuck out his foot. Getas' wife tripped and went sprawling to the floor, coming to rest beside Spartacus. She did not try to get up, even when the children began to wail. Silent sobs racked her thin frame.

Impotent fury filled Spartacus. "Ariadne?"

"So it was you who stood up for her by the gate. I thought it might have been," snarled Polles. "Once the day's proceedings have finished, Kotys is throwing a celebratory feast. He'll bed her after that. She's to be his new wife."

Spartacus' face contorted with fury, and he tried to get up. A heavy blow from a club knocked him back to the floor. He was barely aware of being picked up and carried outside, where a crowd had gathered. Their faces were unhappy, but none dared intervene. They'll have attacked Seuthes and Medokos' huts at the same time, thought Spartacus bitterly.

Then the blackness took him.

†

When Ariadne awoke, she looked straight at the spot where Spartacus had sat. Disappointment at his absence and guilt for feeling like that filled her. Sharp realization sank home a moment later as she stared at the daylight streaming in through the chinks in the roof. It was nearly full day. She had overslept. Cursing, she jumped up and padded to the door. Why had the fighting not woken her? She was a light sleeper at the best of times. *Maybe there was no fighting. Could they have been betrayed?* The thought made Ariadne feel sick to the pit of her stomach. *Please, no.*

Throwing her cloak around her shoulders and picking up the basket that contained her snake, she unlocked the door and stepped outside. Unusually, the alleyway was deserted, but Ariadne could hear the swelling noise of a crowd from the central meeting area. Cold sweat ran down her back as she walked slowly toward the sound. Her feet felt as heavy as lead. Something had gone wrong. Spartacus had failed. She knew it in her bones.

Rallying her courage, she emerged from the alley. Practically everyone in the settlement looked to be present. They weren't happy either. The angry mutters rising from the onlookers made it clear that whatever was going on in the center was unpopular. Ariadne's dread grew as she heard Spartacus' name being shouted periodically. Other names were also being cried out, although she didn't catch them. Ariadne began pushing her way through the throng. People soon gave way when they saw who wanted to pass by, and it wasn't long before she had reached the front of the crowd. Her knees nearly buckled at what she saw. The king's entire force of bodyguards stood in a rough square around three wooden frames upon each of which a man had been tied, face down. Polles waited behind them, holding a whip. Kotys stood alongside him, a thin smile playing across his lips. To their rear, perhaps three score warriors were kneeling in the dirt, ropes tied around their necks. Their bloodied and battered appearance told its own story.

"Who are they?" Ariadne whispered to a woman beside her.

"Spartacus, Sitalkes' son. Getas and Seuthes, his friends, and the men who had sworn them loyalty."

Where are the rest? Ariadne wanted to scream. Where are Olynthus and Medokos? But she had no time to linger on the horror of that implication, that Spartacus had been betrayed by two of his so-called comrades, because Kotys stepped forward, smirking. "Priestess. You honor us with your presence. I'm glad that you will witness this."

Ariadne turned her face away in disgust. It was the only way she could resist. Dionysus, help us please, she begged silently. I'll do anything. Anything.

Kotys made a gesture at Polles.

"Before you are three traitors who planned to depose the king. Know that one of their number is not here. He was killed when my men went to arrest him."

Spartacus had just come to. I honor your passing, Medokos, he thought. At least you died well.

"Together these pieces of filth persuaded more than sixty warriors"—Polles waved contemptuously at the tied-up figures to his rear—"to join their hopeless cause. Thank the Rider, Kotys was alerted to the danger. He owes his thanks to the loyalty of a warrior whom Spartacus, the fool, trusted implicitly."

The bodyguards roared with laughter.

Balefully, Spartacus lifted his head from the frame. He caught Getas and Seuthes doing the same.

"Step forward, Medokos," ordered Polles triumphantly.

Utter disbelief filled Spartacus as Medokos emerged from the crowd to a chorus of jeers. So Olynthus is dead. Forgive me, brother, for misjudging you.

"How could you?" roared Getas. "You fucking shitbag!"

"Curse you to hell!" cried Seuthes.

Spartacus stared at Medokos with utter hatred.

His former friend flinched, but walked out to stand by Kotys, who patted him on the shoulder. "Your loyalty will not be forgotten."

Ariadne began calling down silent curses on Medokos' head. May he go blind. May disease waste the flesh from his bones. May lightning strike him down, or a horse throw him to his death. She knew that if there was ever a time to flee, it was now, but she couldn't bring herself to do it. At the very least, Spartacus and his comrades deserved someone to stand witness to their terrible fate.

"Continue, Polles," directed the king.

"The traitors are to be whipped first. Forty lashes for each man." He indicated the tools on the table beside him with an evil smile.

"Then the real torture will begin. When we're done, I will slit their throats and move on to the other scumbags." He glanced at Kotys.

"Luckily for you miserable goat-turds," the king thundered, "the tribe cannot afford to lose so many warriors. I have therefore decided that one in six of you will die. Ten men, drawn by lot. The rest of you will swear undying allegiance to me, and will provide a hostage as surety of this newfound allegiance."

The crowd's unhappiness soared, and they pressed forward at the bodyguards, who used their javelin butts to restore control. Ariadne's rage knew no bounds. She had to stop herself from leaping out at the king and trying to kill him. *Dionysus, help me, please.*

"Start with Spartacus," commanded Kotys.

Ariadne could not watch, but nor could she block her ears to the horror. There was a sibilant whisper as the whip hissed through the air. Next came the crack as it connected with Spartacus' flesh. Last—and worst of all—came his stifled groan. Within a couple of heartbeats, Polles brought the whip down again. And again. And again. It was unbearable. To stop herself from crying out, Ariadne bit the inside of her lip. It wasn't long before the metallic taste of blood filled her mouth, but rather than release her grip, she clamped her teeth even tighter. Somehow, the agonizing pain filling her head made it easier to listen to Spartacus' ordeal.

By the time that Spartacus had counted twenty lashes, he could feel his strength slipping away. He was angered, but unsurprised. During his time with the legions, he had seen soldiers whipped on plenty of occasions. By forty lashes, he'd be semi-conscious, the flesh of his back in tatters. If Polles was ordered to continue beyond that, he would know nothing after sixty strokes. From that point, he could easily die from his injuries. That thought brought a fleeting, sour smile to Spartacus' lips. Kotys wouldn't want him to die under the lash. It would end at fifty strokes. Only then would the true pain begin. He'd seen the table covered in the tools of the trade: the pliers, probes and serrated blades, the glowing brazier alongside. Still his experience didn't seem real. It felt like a complete aberration. *Beaten and tortured to death in my own village. How . . . ironic.*

Spartacus didn't hear the challenge of the sentry at the gate.

Kotys, Polles, Ariadne and those watching the gory spectacle were also oblivious.

It was when the column of men filed inside the walls that people began to notice. Heads began to turn. Men asked questions of one another. Some even broke away to go and speak with the newcomers. Ariadne craned her head, but the throng prevented her from seeing anything. Eventually, even the king became aware that something was going on and ordered Polles to cease.

With a disappointed look, the champion obeyed.

Sucking in a ragged breath, Spartacus sagged against the wooden frame. He had no idea why Polles had stopped. The short delay was welcome, however. It would give him the chance to recover some of his strength. Allow him to endure more of the pain when it resumed. He caught Ariadne looking at him, and the agonized expression on her face tore at his conscience. He tried to smile in reassurance, but succeeded only in grimacing. *Great Rider, protect her at least.*

"Let them approach," shouted Kotys.

There was a short delay as his bodyguards manhandled people out of the way to create a path leading toward the gate. Curious, Spartacus squinted to see who, or what, had halted his punishment.

The first person to come striding into sight was a shaven-headed, blocky man wearing a faded green cloak. From the belt around his waist hung a sheathed gladius. The newcomer looked as if he knew how to use it too. He resembled a Roman soldier, thought Spartacus. So did the eight similarly armed figures following him. Hard-faced, their limbs laced with scars, they had to be veteran legionaries. The men in ragged clothes who stumbled along behind, and who were chained to each other's necks, were a different matter. Even the smallest child could see that they were slaves. They were of different nationalities: some were Thracian, but others seemed to be Pontic or even Scythian. Two men took up the rear, leading a trio of mules.

Slave-trader scum, thought Spartacus savagely. Men like these—human vultures—had followed in the wake of every army he had ever served in. They usually bought prisoners captured by the legionaries, but they weren't above abducting anyone weak or foolish enough to come within their grasp. Men, women, children—they took them all. In recent decades, Rome's appetite for slaves had become insatiable. This individual was not an average slave trader, however. He only had males, which meant that his prospective clients owned farms or mines. Spartacus closed his eyes and tried to rest. This was nothing to do with him.

"That's close enough," shouted Polles when the newcomer was a dozen steps from Kotys. "Bow to the king."

Immediately, the other obeyed. "My name is Phortis. I am a trader," he said in poor Thracian. "I come in peace."

"It's as well," said Kotys acidly. "Nine of you wouldn't make much impression against my bodyguards."

"Indeed, Your Majesty." Phortis' smile was rueful.

"Why are you here?"

"My master in Italy has sent me in search of slaves, Your Majesty."

"I can see that. Agricultural slaves and the like, eh?"

"No, Your Majesty. I want men who can fight in the arena, as . . ." Phortis paused, searching for the right word before reverting to Latin. ". . . gladiators."

Spartacus' ears pricked. He had seen Roman prisoners of war forced to fight each other to the death for the amusement of thousands of cheering legionaries. The savagery of these combats had been mitigated by the fact that the victors were often allowed to go free. Spartacus doubted that that was the case in Italy. Shifting position on the rack, he shuddered as fresh waves of agony radiated from the raw flesh of his back. He closed his eyes again, breathing into the pain.

"Gladi-ators?" asked Kotys, frowning.

"Yes, Your Majesty," replied Phortis in Thracian. "Skilled fighters of various classes who battle each other in front of a crowd until one is victorious. It makes for a first-class spectacle. The practice is very popular among my people."

"You use only slaves? How can they be entertaining?" demanded Kotys contemptuously.

"It's not that simple, Your Majesty. Prisoners of war and criminals also provide large numbers of suitable candidates." Phortis jerked his head at his captives. "There's nothing wrong with using slaves either, if you pick the right ones. Scythians are savage bastards, and Pontic tribesmen fight like cornered rats. But the pick of the lot are Thracians. Everyone knows that your people are the most warlike in the world. In Italy, we say that the Thracians are 'worse than snow,' and that if every tribe were to join together, you would conquer every race in existence." He smiled at the growls of appreciation that rose up from those within earshot.

"Honeyed words from a Roman," interrupted Kotys, snarling. "So you have come looking for slaves to buy?"

"Yes, Your Majesty," said Phortis in a humble tone. "Prisoners that your warriors might have taken during raids on other tribes, and the like." His gaze moved to Spartacus and his companions and slithered away.

Kotys did not miss Phortis' interest. "Do these gladi-ators live for long?"

Phortis' eyes returned to Spartacus, appraising him. Then he glanced at Seuthes and Getas and gave a tiny snort of contempt. "No, Your Majesty. Only a fraction survive for more than a year. The rest are soon defeated; wounded and humiliated in the arena, they are executed in front of a crowd baying for their blood. When it's over, their bodies are dragged outside. Each corpse has its throat slit to make sure that none are playing dead, before being thrown on the communal refuse heap."

Ariadne could not help herself. A tiny gasp of horror left her lips.

"You don't like the idea of that, eh?" asked Kotys, rounding on her like a striking snake.

She said nothing, which told him everything he wanted to know.

"Imagine Spartacus, and his friends," Kotys lingered over the words, "being in such an arena with thousands of Romans screaming for their deaths. Hundreds of miles from home, they would be totally alone. Abandoned to their fate. I cannot think of a worse death."

Nor can I, thought Ariadne, listening to the screams of Seuthes' and Getas' wives rend the air. You evil whoreson.

Adrenaline coursed through Spartacus, and he opened his eyes. It might be fighting for the amusement of a mob of stinking Romans, but it sounds better than what Kotys has planned for me. He stole a glance at Seuthes and Getas and took heart. There wasn't a trace of fear in their faces, just a cold, calculating rage.

"How exactly are they executed?" inquired Kotys lasciviously.

"A variety of ways. In one of the most common, the loser has to kneel and lift up his chin to expose his throat. Then the winner of the fight stabs him like this." Phortis mimed the action of a sword entering the hollow at the base of his throat. "The blade slides down into the chest cavity, severing half a dozen major blood vessels. It kills instantaneously."

A quick, honorable death, thought Spartacus.

The image described by Phortis and the blood in her mouth combined to make Ariadne feel faint. Swaying from side to side, she struggled to keep her balance.

Kotys was delighted by the intensity of her distress. "What will you give me for these creatures?" he demanded of Phortis.

Dionysus, help Spartacus, Ariadne begged. A few angry shouts went up, but no one dared even to approach the king's bodyguards. Her spirits fell into a deep abyss.

"They don't look up to much, Your Majesty," muttered Phortis, narrowing his eyes.

"Looks often deceive," retorted Kotys. "Spartacus, the first one, has just returned from years of service with your legions, so he must have some skill. In his youth, he was one of the tribe's best warriors. The others are tough men too, veterans of many campaigns."

"Really, Your Majesty?" said Phortis in a disinterested voice.

"Don't fuck with me!" Kotys' face was purple with rage. "Remember that you and your men are only here by my grace. One click of my fingers and my warriors will carve new assholes for you all." He glanced at the nearest bodyguards, who grinned and fingered their weapons.

"Forgive me, Your Majesty," said Phortis quickly. "I meant no offense."

Kotys' scowl eased a fraction. "Spartacus is the perfect type of material you're after. So are his two friends."

"Indeed, Your Majesty," agreed Phortis. He cast a sly look at the king. "And the rest?"

"They're not for sale. Just these three."

To Ariadne's surprise, a tiny ray of hope shone down into the pit of her despair. Could some good could be wrenched from this situation?

"May I ask why?"

"They were plotting to overthrow me."

Phortis didn't look surprised. "What will you take for them, Your Majesty? A thousand pieces of silver?"

"You've got balls, I'll give you that! Do you really think that I'd give these lumps of dogshit away free?"

"Of course not, Your Majesty," replied Phortis smoothly. "How does fifteen hundred sound?"

"It's two and a half thousand, or nothing. I know as well as you that Thracian slaves are worth double the price of every other race."

Phortis didn't even blink. He gestured at Spartacus and the others. "May I . . . ?"

"Be my guest. Fortunately for you, only the first one has been beaten. He's escaped lightly too. My champion was just getting warmed up when you arrived."

Spartacus lifted his head from the wooden frame and gave Phortis a baleful stare as he approached. The trader ignored him, instead studying his back. "Your Majesty is correct. There's no lasting damage." He moved on to examine the two others, prodding their muscles and examining their teeth as he would a horse. He made an approving noise at Seuthes' shaved forehead. "So your enemy can't grab you by the hair at close-quarters, eh?" Seuthes glowered but did not reply.

Phortis glanced at the king. "It's a fair price, Your Majesty," he admitted.

As Kotys smiled with triumph, Phortis barked an order, and one of his men hurried back to the mules. He returned bearing two heavy purses. "There should be more than enough here," said Phortis.

Kotys motioned Polles forward. Without ceremony, the champion upended the leather bags on to the ground and with the help of another warrior, began counting the silver coins that tumbled out. "It's all there," Polles growled eventually.

"Good," said Kotys. "Then we have a deal. Release them." He directed a triumphant, malevolent glance at Ariadne. He had no idea that her heart was racing with anticipation. She had a plan at last, born of her utter desperation. Or was it Dionysus finally intervening? Ariadne could no longer tell. Her tactic might not work either, but it felt better than doing nothing.

At least I am not to die today. Spartacus summoned the reserves of his strength. When the last of his bonds were cut away, he was able to stand, knees locked, rather than simply fall to the ground. *What about Ariadne?* His eyes wandered to where she stood. He took heart. Inexplicably, her expression was no longer distraught, but determined. *She will survive somehow.*

"Get over here," barked Phortis. "You're mine now."

Spartacus and his friends shuffled toward him and allowed the trader's men to fasten iron collars around their necks. These would be attached to the other slaves by a chain. Their indignity was completed by the fetters placed around their ankles. They left no chance of escaping. This leads to the arena. At least there I'll have a fighting chance of survival, Spartacus told himself. That fate was infinitely preferable to the one on offer from Kotys. His heart wrenched again with guilt. What would happen to Ariadne? Determination would only carry her so far.

"Have you any other men like these, Your Majesty?" asked Phortis.

"It's the wrong time of year for prisoners," Kotys snapped. "It's best to come in the summer, when we're raiding other tribes."

"I told my master that, Your Majesty," said Phortis, "but he wouldn't listen. At this rate, I'll be lucky to avoid snow on the mountain passes that lead back to Illyria. With your permission?"

"You may go," Kotys grunted. He was already turning toward Ariadne.

Spartacus clenched his fists, feeling more helpless than he ever had in his life.

She was utterly terrified, but Ariadne knew that she had to act now. Rolling the blood clots to the side of her mouth, she began to speak in her harshest voice. "As his faithful priestess, I call upon Dionysus, the powerful Almighty, the god of intoxication and mania, to witness my curse upon the king of the Maedi."

A hushed silence fell over the watching villagers. Polles and the other bodyguards gave each other nervous looks. Even Phortis and his men stopped what they were doing. Kotys' face went white, but he dared not stop her.

"No one loves a tyrant or a murderer, Kotys. I curse you to an early, violent death. I curse you to die slowly and painfully, with an enemy's blade buried deep in your guts." Ariadne paused, relishing her power. Dionysus had returned to her! "Your final moments will be filled with agony, and when your miserable soul leaves your body, the gates of the warrior's paradise will be closed to you. Instead, Dionysus' maenads will carry you below, to the underworld. There, for all eternity, they will rip off pieces of your flesh and present them to the god." Delighting in Kotys' shocked expression, she spat the gobbets of blood in his face. "Finally, I mark you as one of Dionysus' chosen ones."

There were loud, reverential gasps from the onlookers. Most people looked petrified, as if they had seen a divine apparition. The king's eyes were filled with living horror. He stood mutely, with trails of scarlet running down his cheeks, as Ariadne walked toward Spartacus. "I am this man's wife. I am following him into captivity," she announced in a loud, authoritative voice.

"His wife?" roared Polles, moving to block her way.

"That's right. We exchanged our vows last night," lied Ariadne. She gripped the fabric of her cloak until her fists hurt. *Let me pass!*

"We also consummated the marriage," croaked Spartacus. "After so many years on campaign, I couldn't wait any longer."

Ariadne's cheeks flamed as the bystanders roared with laughter.

Kotys glared, humiliated anew, and Ariadne dared to feel a scintilla of hope. No king would want a woman who had given her virginity to another. "It is Dionysus' wish that I should go with Spartacus into exile," she shouted.

"Dionysus! Dionysus! Dionysus!" The villagers' thunderous roar of agreement drowned out all other sound.

Visibly furious, Polles stood aside. Ariadne hurried to stand with Spartacus.

Phortis shrugged. He wasn't about to argue with the mouthpiece of a god or hundreds of angry Thracians. "One more mouth to feed shouldn't matter."

"Are you sure you want to do this?" asked Spartacus in an undertone.

"Look at my alternative." With a tiny jerk of her head, Ariadne indicated Kotys.

"I understand."

"We will travel to Italy, and see what fate awaits us there," she intoned, trying to ignore the new fears that clutched at her. Part of Ariadne was pleased, however. *I can stay with him—for now at least.*

Spartacus was glad too. "This way, you won't be left alone."

III

"Show me again, Paccius," ordered Carbo, offering the gladius.

Refusing to accept it, the doorman—a big Samnite with a mass of curly black hair—looked uneasily over his shoulder, toward the open doors of the *tablinum*, the main reception area. "We should stop, young master. It was one thing play fighting with wooden swords when you were a boy, but you're sixteen now, and nearly a man. I'm not supposed to use a real blade unless your father orders me to. If he catches me showing you how to use one of his own weapons—"

"He won't," declared Carbo briskly. "He will be gone all day. Mother won't be back for hours either, and the only other people about are the kitchen slaves. I've given them a coin each to keep their mouths shut. Stop worrying. Our secret is safe."

"If you're sure," said Paccius unhappily.

"I am," Carbo snapped.

Paccius didn't know the reason for Carbo's father's absence. Jovian's financial situation was desperate. Carbo had learned that things had recently come to a head when Jovian hadn't been able to pay the previous quarter's arrears on his loan. They were now at risk of losing their farm, their home here in Capua, and all of their property, slaves included. Carbo only knew of the drama facing the family because he'd eavesdropped on part of his parents' worried conversation the night before. Jovian was pinning all his hopes on securing a stay of execution today. Furious at his own powerlessness, Carbo shoved the sword forward again, hilt first. "Take it!"

Unable to protest further, Paccius took a firm hold of the bone handgrip. "Grasp it so. Remember, it takes real force to stick it in a man's belly. Like this." He thrust his right arm forward in a powerful, calculated manner and pulled it back to his side. He repeated the move several times. "Clear?"

"Yes, I think so."

"Let me see you do it," said Paccius, handing the gladius back.

With grim concentration, Carbo held the sword close to his right side. With a grunt, he copied Paccius' move, imagining that he was sinking the iron blade into the guts of a Pontic warrior or a Cilician pirate. Along with the former Marian leader Sertorius in Iberia, these were Rome's main enemies. Better still, he imagined, would be to bury it in the flesh of his father's largest creditor, whomever he was. "Like that?"

Paccius pursed his lips in approval. "That's better. Do it again."

Carbo obeyed eagerly, plunging the weapon back and forth in a flurry of blows.

"Slow it down. Conserve your energy. Striking your opponent in the belly once should be enough to put him down. There are few men who'll stay standing after half their guts have been sliced apart." Contorting his face in mock agony, Paccius clutched at his abdomen and mimed falling to the ground. "That's the beauty of this weapon," he went on. "When used with a bloody great shield like the *scutum*, by a line of soldiers who stick close together, it's damn near invincible."

"That's how your people were defeated."

Paccius grimaced. "It's one of the reasons, yes."

Carbo had spent his childhood listening to Paccius' tales of the Social War, when the last of the fiercely independent Samnites had been crushed by Rome. He knew how the defeat still rankled. Once Paccius had been a high-ranking warrior among his people. Now he was but a slave. When they'd lived on the family's farm, a dozen miles from Capua, he'd been the foreman. After the move to the city, he'd assumed the role of doorman and guard. Paccius was also the person to whom Carbo went with his problems, and he cursed himself for bringing up old, painful history. "I want to learn how to use a shield too," he said, changing the subject. "Go and fetch one."

Paccius started to argue again, but thought better of it. Muttering under his breath, he disappeared into the tablinum again.

Carbo dipped a hand into the fountain that graced the center of the small courtyard. He patted his face with water several times, refreshing himself. Inadvertently touching the myriad of pockmarks that covered his cheeks, he scowled. Much of his good humor fell away. *Why couldn't the scars be on my chest or back?* It was easy to tell himself that he was lucky to be alive—after all, more than a third of those who developed the pox died, while others were left blind—but quite another thing to enter adulthood looking like a freak. The matter wasn't helped by the fact that most of those he'd regarded as friends didn't want to know him now. And what woman would ever want him? Carbo's mother kept telling him not to worry about it, that an arrangement would be made with a suitable family, but it did little to ease his self-loathing. While some of his peers were already sleeping with willing girls— merchants' daughters and the like—Carbo found it hard even to skulk into a brothel and choose a prostitute.

Apart from using his hand, his only other form of sexual release had been to bed his father's female slaves. Two or three of them were passably good-looking. In their lowly position, they could not refuse Carbo when he'd ordered them to his bed. During the months since his recovery from the pox, he'd used this power a number of times. The sex had been a real release, but he had found it hard to ignore their poorly concealed revulsion at his appearance. What Carbo really wanted was for someone to accept him as he was. He blinked. *Stop thinking about yourself. Father's problems are far more important.*

"There you are!" he cried, glad to be distracted from concerns over his father. The Samnite was carrying a scutum that Jovian had used during his military service years before. Carbo reached out an eager hand.

Paccius didn't give it to him. "Steady," he warned. "Knowing everything about your arms and equipment is just as important as learning how to use them."

He knows best. Carbo nodded reluctantly. "Very well."

Paccius tapped the metal rim that covered both ends of the shield. "What's this for?"

"At the top, it's to protect against sword strokes, and at the bottom, it prevents wear from contact with the ground."

"Good. And this?" Paccius pointed to the heavy central iron boss.

"It's decorative, but it's also a weapon." Carbo threw his left fist forward. "If you punch it toward an enemy's face, he'll often lean backward or to the side, exposing his throat." He followed through with a thrust of the gladius. "Another man down." He looked at Paccius proudly.

"Nice to know that you sometimes pay attention to what I'm saying," was the Samnite's only comment. "Let's start with the basics: how to hold the shield correctly." He reversed the scutum and proffered its inner surface.

Carbo sighed. His impatience would get him nowhere. If he was to benefit from Paccius' experience, he had to do it his way. He took hold of the horizontal grip. "What next?"

Finally, Paccius smiled. "Hold it up, so that I can barely see your eyes. Have your sword pointing forward from the right hip, ready to use."

Carbo obeyed. At once his pulse quickened and the sounds of domestic life dimmed. Despite the peacefulness of their surroundings, he could imagine standing on a battlefield, with comrades on either side of him. Yet the picture dimmed within a couple of heartbeats. Carbo scowled. It was highly unlikely that that would ever happen. Since they'd moved to the city four years before, his father had maintained that the best career for him to follow was not working the land, which is what their ancestors had done for generations, or joining the army, Carbo's dream, but politics. "The days of citizen farmers are gone. The cut-price grain from *latifundia*, and from Sicily and Egypt, has seen to that." Jovian regularly lamented the changes in agriculture that had seen family farms all but obliterated by vast estates owned by the nobility. "Your mother's brother Alfenus Varus, on the other hand, is making a name for himself in Rome. He's a new man, but look at him—one of the foremost lawyers in Rome. He is fond of you too. With the gods' help, he might take you under his wing." A lawyer, thought Carbo bitterly. He couldn't think of anything worse. Training with Paccius might be the only military training he ever received. Without further ado, he determined to absorb every word that fell from the Samnite's lips.

Before Paccius had made any serious attempt to teach the finer points of weapons training, he had Carbo run around the rectangular courtyard more than twenty times, carrying the gladius and scutum. When that was done, the Samnite began showing Carbo how to move in combat, both singly and when in formation. He repeatedly stressed the importance of holding the line and sticking with one's comrades. "Contrary to what you might think, winning a battle is not about individual heroics. It's about discipline, pure and simple," he growled. "That is what differentiates the Roman soldier from the vast majority of his opponents, and it is the main reason for the legions' success over the last two hundred years." He pulled a face. "My people could have done with more discipline."

Carbo redoubled his efforts, proudly imagining himself in the midst of any one of the armies that had variously defeated the other ethnic groups in Italy: the mighty Carthaginians and the proud Greeks. Deep down, however, his pleasure was constantly dimmed by the knowledge that it was all an exercise in fantasy. His father's debts were what mattered right now. Yet he couldn't stop picturing himself as a soldier. Paccius' martial tales had stirred his blood since early childhood.

"We had best finish now," said Paccius, glancing at the sky.

Carbo didn't argue. His arms were burning and he was drenched in sweat. Although it was still bright, the sun had dropped below the level of the house's red-tiled roof. It wouldn't be long before his mother returned and his father would not be long after her. "Very well." He grinned his thanks. "You can teach me more tomorrow."

"Serious about this, aren't you?"

"Yes. I want to be a soldier, no matter what Father says."

Paccius sucked his lip, thinking.

"What is it?" asked Carbo eagerly.

"The best way of building up your general fitness would be to use proper training equipment, not these." Paccius lifted up the gladius and scutum without effort. "New recruits to the legions use wooden swords and wicker shields that are twice as heavy as the real articles. Obviously, we couldn't practice with those here. But outside Capua, it would be a different matter."

"You mean the plain to the north of the walls?" It was used similarly to the Campus Martius at Rome. There, the young men of the city, noble and commoner alike, practiced all kinds of athletic activities. "We can't go there. Someone would see us. It'd only be a matter of time before Father heard."

"I was thinking of the waste ground to the south, where the city's refuse is dumped. No one will trouble us in a place like that," said Paccius with a sly grin.

"Good idea. And I can tell Father that you're going to teach me how to throw the javelin and discus, on the training area to the north. He couldn't complain about that."

"I know a trader who'll sell me the gear." Paccius turned to go.

"Wait." Carbo hesitated. "Thank you."

"It's nothing. Wait until tomorrow," Paccius warned. "You might not feel the same way after an hour at the *palus*."

"I will," vowed Carbo. "This goes far beyond your duty as a slave."

"Aye, well . . ." The Samnite coughed. "I've been looking after you all these years. It seems stupid to stop now."

Taken aback by the unexpected thickness in his throat, Carbo nodded. "Good. Tomorrow morning, then?"

"Tomorrow morning," agreed Paccius. He walked off without another word.

A gust of wind carried down into the courtyard, and Carbo shivered, suddenly very aware of the sweat coating every part of his skin. It was time for a wash and a change of clothes. Thinking of his father's task that day, he sighed. *Jupiter, Greatest and Best, help us, please.*

†

Carbo tackled Jovian the moment he returned. His father was a short man with thinning black hair and a kind face, which of recent days had been lined with worry. Carbo forgot all about that as he launched into an explanation of his idea. To his initial relief, his father had made no objection to the idea of Paccius training him in use of the discus and javelin. Guilt soon replaced Carbo's delight, however. It was unsurprising that he'd had no resistance. Jovian's visage had been gray with exhaustion—or worry.

Carbo was about to ask what was wrong when his mother had intervened. "It will get you out of the house. These past six months, you've hardly gone out," she'd said with an encouraging smile.

Carbo had muttered his thanks, but his good mood had gone. He turned to catch Jovian mouthing the words "Three days" and "Marcus Licinius Crassus" to his mother. Was that the deadline for paying his debts? Was Crassus, the richest man in the Republic, his father's main creditor? Carbo didn't know, but given Jovian's grim expression, and the tears that had appeared in his mother's eyes, there weren't many other conclusions to draw. Neither of his parents proffered any further information and Carbo spent a restless night wondering how he could help. Nothing came to mind, which wasn't surprising. At sixteen, with no trade or profession yet to his name, he had little to offer anyone. Carbo's frustration at this was exacerbated by the fact that his father's career choice for him—that of a lawyer—was very well paid. So it wouldn't be for years, but he'd earn far more that way than he would as a lowly soldier.

The following morning, Jovian left early, saying again that he would be gone all day. Carbo's mother was in bed, feeling unwell.

Once he had checked on her, Carbo and Paccius headed out into the city. The family's modest house was situated in a prosperous area near the forum. Self-conscious as always, and more angry than he had ever been, Carbo glowered at the people who thronged the narrow streets. He longed for the peace of the countryside, where he'd spent his childhood. Few but Paccius noticed his fury. The shopkeepers selling wine, bread, fresh meat and vegetables were more concerned with bawling at more receptive passersby. The tradesmen—blacksmiths, carpenters, potters, fullers and wheelwrights—were toiling in their workshops, too busy to stand around studying those who walked past.

Where there was space, jugglers and acrobats stretched their muscles, preparing to start their entertainment. An occasional snake charmer sat cross-legged, flute in hand, pointing at his basket and describing the most venomous serpents imaginable. It was early, so the doorways between the open-fronted shops that served as entrances to the flats above were empty of the prostitutes that usually hustled there for business. Only the lepers, scabrous and maimed, pestered Carbo. Their presence helped him to raise a sardonic smile. There were others even more ugly than he.

Paccius took him to a dingy establishment near the south gate. Carbo's excitement grew as he studied what was on sale. Rather than the usual foodstuffs, ironware or domestic goods, this place sold weapons. Wooden racks outside held swords by the dozen, mostly *gladii*; Carbo also spotted the distinctive curve of at least one Thracian *sica* and, beside it, several Gaulish longswords. Bundles of javelins and thrusting spears were propped against the shop's walls; shields of various sizes and shapes were stacked carelessly alongside.

Clutching the money given him by Carbo, Paccius went inside to talk to the grizzled proprietor. He emerged a moment later with two large wicker shields. Under one arm, he bore a pair of wooden *gladii*.

"We can hardly bring them back to the house," said Carbo. "Father will realize what's going on."

"It's all arranged. For a nominal fee, we can leave the equipment at the shop and pick it up each morning."

Paccius' ingenuity brought a grin to Carbo's face. His anger returned with the next heartbeat, however. Unless his father secured a new loan, they would have three days, no more. Three days until what? He didn't want to imagine.

Paccius led Carbo out from Capua's southern walls, past an area of open ground that was littered with huge piles of household refuse and human waste. The carcasses of mules, dogs and even an occasional man sprawled here and there, their rotting flesh adding to the acrid stench that filled the air. Unsurprisingly, the spot was deserted. Even the beggars who came daily to search the heaps of stinking rubbish did not linger unless they had to. Carbo's skin snaked with dread. Gods, could we end up picking through the filth here? he wondered, staring at the black, hopping shapes of crows pecking busily at eyeballs and body openings. Their cousins, the vultures, hung far overhead in lazy ones and twos, searching out the best morsels.

Paccius stopped by the skeleton of a dead tree, the branches of which grasped at the air like claws. "This will be your palus. We'll begin here."

Carbo knew enough of gladiator training to understand that the narrow, gnarled trunk would act as a post for him to launch attacks on with his sword. He grinned savagely, imagining that it was not a tree, but Marcus Licinius Crassus, tied to a stake. "What do you want me to do?"

With a veteran's poise, Paccius showed him how to approach the tree, shield in hand. "Treat it with respect, as if it's an enemy warrior who wants to cut you into pieces. Move lightly, on the balls of your feet. Position your head low, so that only your eyes are visible, and keep your sword close to your side. When you're near enough, thrust for the belly, or the heart." He pointed at a blackened opening in the center of the trunk, where some disease had eaten away the tree's core. "Pull back, hack the right side and then the left. Keep doing that until I tell you to stop."

Copying what Paccius had done, Carbo padded confidently toward the "palus." As soon as he could, he stabbed the gladius into the hole.

His arm jarred under the impact of healthy wood, and he pulled the heavy blade back. At once he set to, chopping at both sides of the dead tree with a vengeance. Splinters flew and chunks of rotten timber fell away, and Carbo redoubled his efforts. By the time he'd counted twenty blows, Crassus was long dead, cut into mangled chunks of flesh. Carbo's right arm had also begun to tire. He looked questioningly at Paccius.

"Did I tell you to stop?"

"No."

"Keep going then," snapped the Samnite.

Sullenly, Carbo obeyed. This wasn't what he had been expecting; it was a world away from wielding a real gladius, as he had the day before. And his target was just a tree, not the man who held his family's fortunes in the palm of his hand. Soon every fiber of muscle in his arm was screaming for rest, and the air was catching raggedly at the back of his throat with each breath. His remaining pride, such as it was, wouldn't let him glance at Paccius.

"That's enough."

Gasping with relief, he let the gladius fall. Without warning, Paccius jumped forward and drove his shield against Carbo's. He stumbled backward, away from his weapon. With a snarl, the Samnite advanced, his sword at the ready. "So that's what you would do in a real battle, is it? Drop your gladius, and leave yourself completely defenseless? That's the best example of pure stupidity I've seen in a while."

"But this isn't real. It's only practice," retorted Carbo.

Grimly, Paccius drove at Carbo again, hammering a brutal series of cuts on his shield. An occasional blow glanced off the side of his head, sending stars shooting across his vision. It was all he could do just to hold his ground. Finally, the Samnite eased his assault. "Do you understand now why you never drop your weapon?" he demanded.

"Yes," muttered Carbo resentfully. To his relief, Paccius did not belabor the point. "Go and pick it up. We'll come back to the palus later. It's time to start building up your general fitness." He saw Carbo's questioning look and laughed. "See that tree?" he asked, pointing into the distance.

Carbo squinted, making out a lone beech about half a mile away. "Yes."

"I want you to run there and back again." There was a slight pause. "Five times, carrying your gladius and shield. Without stopping."

Carbo wanted to tell Paccius where he could shove his wooden sword. *I'm here to learn.* He nodded firmly.

"Go on, then! What are you waiting for?"

Beginning to realize what he had let himself in for, Carbo took off at a fast trot.

†

Several hours passed, during which the Samnite allowed Carbo three breaks, brief affairs to allow him to catch his breath, swallow a mouthful of water and nothing more. After his five-mile run, Paccius had set him to attacking the palus again, although at a slower pace. Press-ups, stretches and more running followed; after that, there had been yet more work with the sword and shield. When the Samnite declared at last that they had done enough for the day, Carbo was on the point of collapse. He was damned if he'd admit to that, however. "How was I?" he asked boldly.

Paccius stared at him askance. "Looking for praise on your first day? Don't bother. You'd have been killed in the initial moments of any battle."

Carbo glowered.

Paccius clapped him on the back. "Don't lose heart. I could say the same of any raw recruit. To be fair, you showed a lot more passion than most."

Carbo grinned. This was high praise indeed. Then his smile faded. *Has Father succeeded?*

"What is it?" asked the Samnite. "You've been preoccupied all day."

"It's nothing," replied Carbo grimly.

Paccius' eyebrows rose.

I can't tell him. Carbo glanced at the sun. "We'd better head back."

"No point raising your parents' suspicions," agreed the Samnite.

Carbo grunted in agreement, but his mind was already fixed upon finding out what was going on with his father. He couldn't bear not knowing any longer.

They trudged back in silence. Soon they had joined the last part of the Via Appia before it entered the city. As always, the road was choked with traffic traveling in both directions. Sturdy carts full of hay or root vegetables creaked along, drawn by pairs of impassive oxen. Farmers walked alongside, using murmured encouragements and, intermittently, their whips. Merchants strode in front of their wagons, which were laden with trading goods: red Samian ware, amphorae containing wine or olive oil, and bales of cloth. Next were the bodyguards: groups of unshaven, dangerous-looking men carrying spears, clubs and the occasional sword. It was their job to protect the merchandise rumbling along the road before them. A column of slaves, each attached to the next by a neck chain, shuffled along behind their owner and his armed henchmen. Official messengers on horseback distastefully picked their way through flocks of sheep being driven to slaughter. A party of legionaries marched by, their shields slapping gently off their backs. They bawled a rowdy chorus, which their *optio* chose studiously to ignore.

Impotent fury filled Carbo. That was the kind of comradeship he longed for but would never have. Crazy ideas filled his mind. Maybe he should just run away and join the army? His conscience instantly reined him in. *You can't desert your family while it's in such dire straits.* Carbo was desperate to help in some way, and a legionary's yearly pay would be nowhere near enough to cover his father's debts. In frustration, he kicked a loose stone along the road's paved surface. It skittered away and struck the fetlock of a nervous horse in front. Rearing up in panic, it almost unseated its rider, a florid-faced man in early middle age. Curses filled the air and Carbo quickly took an interest in the landscape off to his right. *A pity that wasn't Crassus. A pity he didn't fall off and break his neck.*

"Fortunate that you weren't seen, eh?" murmured Paccius as the man regained control of his mount. "I'd say he would have shown you the business end of his whip. Sure you don't want to tell me what's going on?"

Carbo shook his head. He couldn't bear the idea of Paccius having a new master, of never seeing him again. The Samnite shrugged. "Suit yourself."

They passed under the massive archway that formed Capua's southern entrance. There were several other such gates in the tall stone walls that ringed the city. The defenses hadn't been used since the second war with Carthage, when the local politicians had foolishly decided to defect to Hannibal's cause. The punishment meted out by Rome had been severe: to this very day, the city was directly ruled by a praetor, and its inhabitants had not yet regained the civic rights accorded to the rest of Italy's population. Civic rights? thought Carbo resentfully. Will I even have any of those soon?

Soon after, they'd reached his family home. They had barely entered the atrium when the summons rang out. "Carbo!"

Gods, he must have been waiting for us. Jupiter, let it be good news.

Jovian was standing in the doorway of his office, a simply decorated room situated off the courtyard. Carbo didn't especially like the space. No swords or military mementos here, just stands displaying busts of famous Roman and Greek orators, long-dead men whose names his father had drummed into him but which he refused to remember. Carbo felt—and resented—their heavy-lidded stares on him the moment he entered.

Jovian was scanning a parchment. As Carbo approached, he let it snap closed with a sigh. "Where were you?"

"Training with Paccius, Father."

Jovian gave him a blank look.

"With the discus and javelin, remember?"

"Ah yes. Well, I hope you enjoyed yourself. There won't be much of that from now on."

Carbo's heart sank. "Why not?"

"You've probably noticed that I've been quite preoccupied of late."

"Yes."

"Are you aware of why we moved to Capua four years ago?"

Carbo's head filled with happy memories of the former family home, a respectably sized villa on their land. "Not really."

"I couldn't afford the upkeep of such a large property." Shame filled Jovian's blue eyes.

"How can that be?" cried Carbo incredulously.

"It comes down to little more than the price of Egyptian grain. It's ruinous! How any Italian farmer can compete, I do not know. It costs more to produce wheat here than it does to import it from hundreds of miles away." Jovian sighed. "I told myself each year that things would improve, that the harvests in Egypt would fail, that the gods would answer my prayers. I took out large loans to keep the farm running. And what happened? The price of grain fell even further. For the last twelve months, we have had no income worth talking about, and there's no sign of that changing."

"So . . ." began Carbo uneasily.

"We're ruined, Carbo. Ruined. My biggest creditor is a politician in Rome. Marcus Licinius Crassus. You've heard of him?"

"Yes." *I heard correctly, then.*

"According to his agent, whom I deal with, Crassus' patience is exhausted. It's not that surprising, I suppose. I haven't made a payment for more than three months." Jovian's jaw hardened. "What I can't forgive is Crassus is taking not just the farm and the villa, but this house too."

Carbo felt a numbness taking hold of him.

"Did you hear me?"

His father's voice came as if through a long tunnel.

"We're being evicted, Carbo."

Fucking Crassus! He controlled his rage with difficulty. "Evicted?"

"This is no longer our home," said his father gently. "We'll go to Rome. Varus will take us in for a little while." His lips quirked. "At least I hope he does, when we turn up on his doorstep unannounced."

Carbo felt a wave of guilt. "I'm sorry," he muttered.

"For what?"

"All I've been thinking of is running off and training with Paccius. I should have been trying to help you."

"Gods above, it's not your fault, boy," cried Jovian.

"What will happen to the slaves?"

"Crassus owns everything now, apart from our personal possessions. The slaves will go with the house." Regret filled his father's face. "I know how much Paccius means to you."

"You must be able to do something!" said Carbo furiously.

"I've been to every moneylender in the city."

"No, I mean can you not approach Crassus directly?"

"I'd have more chance of walking up to the gates of Hades and stroking Cerberus on the head." He saw his son's incomprehension. "Crassus is the personification of friendliness and jollity when he lends money. If he's decided to foreclose on a debt, however, he's a devil incarnate."

"Bastard," muttered Carbo. "I'd soon show him some manners."

"I'll have no talk like that." Jovian's voice was sharp. "We're law-abiding citizens. Besides, Crassus has done nothing wrong. Do you understand?"

Carbo did not answer.

"Carbo?"

"Yes, Father," he said, biting down on his resentment.

"Go on then," ordered Jovian wearily. "Pack your things. We have to quit the house tomorrow, and it's a long journey to Rome."

Carbo stamped off to his room, where he thumped his fists into his pillow until they hurt. He couldn't believe it. His world had just been turned upside down. From now on, he and his family would exist on the charity of his uncle. Could anything be worse? Varus was kind enough in his own way, but he was pompous and had a tendency to be overbearing. Carbo could already imagine his patronizing tone, and the years of interminably boring lessons he'd have to sit through to become a lawyer. On the spur of the moment, he decided to run away. He had his own savings, a little stash of *denarii* that sat in a clay pot under his bed. They would secure him a room of his own somewhere in Capua, and give him enough to live on while he looked for work. What kind of work, Carbo wasn't sure, but the idea was far more appealing than trudging in penury to Rome. *I'm better than that.*

Amid all the uncertainty, one thing was certain in his mind.

One day, somehow, he would be revenged on Crassus.

IV

Several weeks later...
The Illyrian coast

The sun was still climbing in the sky when the column reached the busy harbor. Most of the craft visible were broad-beamed merchant vessels or simple fishing smacks, but at the end of the stone quay was the unmistakable sharp-prowed outline of a Roman trireme. Unsurprisingly, it occupied the best mooring spot, and fully half of the area for unloading goods. Yet the warship's presence caused no rancor. In the eyes of the traders and seamen swarming about the area, it was welcome. Even the rumor of its existence would help to deter the rapacious Cilician corsairs who infested the local waters. Without the trireme's protection, they regularly ran the risk of losing their goods, slaves and even their lives through piracy.

Seagulls swooped and dived overhead, their beady eyes fixed on the catch being brought ashore by the local fishermen. They ignored the file of men that had just arrived. In turn, Phortis, the figure in charge, paid the screeching birds little heed. His only interest was in finding a ship that would carry his party to Italy. Phortis scrutinized his fifteen captives with a practiced eye. He would have loved to be taking more over the Adriatic, but a lifetime in the slave trade had taught him not to be greedy. Fifteen was enough. Thracians, Scythians and Pontic tribesmen were excellent gladiator material, but, by all the gods, they were slippery as eels. Untrustworthy. Dangerous. Consequently, every one of the new slaves had chains around his neck, but also encircling his wrists and ankles. Phortis' eight guards were all tough ex-soldiers. If he ordered it, they would slit a man's throat or toss him overboard without even blinking.

Remembering the last time that he'd had to order a guard to do exactly that, Phortis grimaced. Such losses were unfortunate, but they still happened periodically. Over the years, he'd seen numerous men abandon all reason when they realized at last the dreadful fate that awaited them. Sometimes it was when they crossed the mountains from Thrace into Illyria, and at others it was when the glistening Adriatic filled the western horizon. More often, it was when they had to embark and sail for Italy. Not this trip, though. So far, the men he'd bought during their journey had remained reasonably calm, and given little trouble. Just the short sea passage remained. With that accomplished, a swift crossing of the Apennines would bring them to the *ludus*, the gladiator school, in Capua.

There, Lentulus Batiatus, the *lanista*, would be waiting. A trainer who accepted only the best. Phortis sighed. Batiatus was the sole reason that they'd had drag their arses halfway to Asia Minor in their search for suitable gladiator material. Most lanistae were happy buying slaves off the block in their local market in Italy. Not Batiatus. Thinking of the heavy purse he'd get when they returned, Phortis relaxed. His hard work would have been worthwhile. For all that Batiatus was an exacting master, he paid well.

Phortis' gaze flickered again over the men he'd bought and abducted in the previous two months. There was a quartet of Scythians; bearded, tattooed savages whom he'd kept apart from day one. That hadn't stopped them from trying to converse with one another in their guttural tongue at every opportunity. Of course Phortis had seen it all before. They didn't plot murder and escape any longer—at least not with one another. A particularly savage beating of the last one he'd caught whispering had kept the bastards silent for days now.

Phortis had bought the three Pontic tribesmen from a lank-haired trader on the Illyrian border with Thrace. Renegades who'd been part of Mithridates' army, apparently, and captured by Thracians fighting for Rome. Phortis didn't know the truth of that story, nor did he care. The scars on the warriors' chests and arms, and their combative manner, spoke volumes. They were fighters, and that was what Batiatus wanted.

He studied the eight remaining men. As usual these, the majority of his captives, were Thracian. The most warlike of all the peoples Rome had ever encountered. Tough, intelligent and stubborn. Natural warriors, they were excellent at both ambushes and face-to-face combat. Always prepared to fight to the death. Bitter enemies. It was fortunate, thought Phortis, that the majority of Thracians had ended up as subjects of Rome. Now they provided much of the fodder for the gladiatorial games.

When the largest of the Thracians, a warrior with black hair, noticed Phortis looking, he glared back. Phortis affected not to notice. A beating at this stage would serve little purpose. It was important not to crush all of the slaves' spirit. If the fool learned to curb his temper, he would survive the first weeks of savage training. A man with any brains at all could last twelve months in the ludus. If the Thracian was lucky as well as smart, he might make it to three years, when he'd be entitled to the *rudis*, the wooden sword that symbolized freedom. And, if the gods smiled upon him, he would reach the benchmark of five years as a gladiator, and be granted his manumission. The black-haired man looked strong enough to do that, Phortis concluded. So did the short, muscular warrior with swirling tattoos on his chest. And the rest? He idly scanned the group. In all likelihood, they wouldn't last that long. Few did.

His gaze fell last upon the most unremarkable-looking Thracian, a compact man with short brown hair and slate-gray eyes. It was odd, thought Phortis, that he knew the man's name. Normally, he didn't bother with such details. It had all come out in the Maedi village, however, where he'd bought two other men as well. Kotys, the tribe's chieftain, had accused the trio of plotting to overthrow him. That was good enough for Phortis. As with the rest of his new acquisitions, the three men's guilt—or innocence—was irrelevant.

Phortis saw Spartacus staring at the little huddle of women who stood a short distance away. He sneered. Like some of the other captives, Spartacus' wife had followed him into captivity. It wasn't uncommon. The alternative, being left without a man's protection, was worse. A slender, aloof figure, Ariadne was more composed than her companions, who wept and wailed at Phortis' and the guards' nightly sexual assaults. Yet none fought back. It was part of the unspoken price of being allowed to accompany the column. Phortis' groin throbbed at the thought of Ariadne. She was striking rather than pretty but there was an inexplicable sense of the untamed, the exotic about her. It was most alluring. He hadn't touched her, though. Nor had his men. If the truth be known, Phortis didn't have the courage to. Who could forget the curse she'd placed on Kotys? In addition, the madwoman carried a venomous snake. Who would dare to try and fuck a creature like that?

Spartacus didn't look like anything special, however. Just wait until he's injured or, better, killed, in the arena, thought Phortis. We'll see how brave the bitch is then.

✝

Spartacus watched Phortis sourly. His haggling with the captain of a merchant vessel looked to be drawing to a successful close. "This is it. There's only one place we're going to now. Italy." The guilt he'd felt at the death of Olynthus and the ten others condemned to die felt heavier than ever. *Curse Kotys to hell.*

"Unless the ship sinks, and we all drown." Getas eyed the glittering sea unhappily. It extended to the western horizon. "The weather at this time of year is so unpredictable. A storm could take us at any time."

"It could. And there's nothing we can do about it except to ask the gods for their protection," replied Spartacus. "Get used to that idea."

Deep in his own misery, Getas didn't register his annoyance. "I've never been on a stinking boat before," he went on.

"Prepare to vomit constantly for the next day or two, then. You won't need bad conditions to make you feel sick either," warned Seuthes. "Just being on it is enough. You won't know what bloody way the ship is going to move from one moment to the next. Up, down, forward, backward, side to side. It's always changing."

"Thanks," muttered Getas. "I can't wait."

Spartacus wasn't looking forward to the motion sickness either. He'd been on ships when serving in the legions, but never for more than a few hours, the time it took to cross to Asia Minor from the southeast coast of Thrace. *That is the least of my concerns.* Seeing Ariadne approach, he forced a smile. "Wife."

"Husband," she answered gravely.

Because they were chained to one another, Getas and Seuthes hadn't been able to give Spartacus and Ariadne real privacy since they'd left the village. Out of courtesy, however, they had got in the habit of moving back a step. They did so now, and began talking to each other in low voices. Spartacus felt a wave of gratitude toward them yet again.

"Ready for the journey?" she asked.

"After a fashion."

She frowned, suspecting the reason for his reserve, but not wanting to ask.

"It's the finality of leaving Illyria. Not for me, you understand? I'm reconciled to my fate," Spartacus growled. "It's you I'm worried about. After I'm dead and gone, you'll be left alone. Not only will you be in an alien land full of bastard Romans, but you'll have Phortis trying to screw you at every turn. I've seen him staring at you. Wouldn't it be better to reconsider? For you to stay here?"

"It was my choice to accompany you. Don't you remember what

Kotys would have done to me?" Ariadne felt sick just thinking about it. "Leaving with you was my best option by far! Where else would I have gone—back to Kabyle, and the crusty old priests there? Or to my bastard of a father? And as for Phortis—pah! The whoreson will get a face full of snake if he tries anything. No. My place is here, by your side." Hoping that her bravado was convincing, Ariadne reached out and squeezed his arm. "It's what Dionysus would want," she lied.

He shot her an intense glance. "Have you seen this?"

"No, not as such." Her sigh was full of not wholly feigned regret. "But I cannot believe that the god would want me to have stayed there, for Kotys to abuse. What would be the point in that? At least this way, I can carry his word back to Italy. His religion has been suppressed there for generations. I will be a new emissary for him."

Spartacus thought for a moment. It wasn't as if he could stop her anyway. If the truth be told, he was glad that she was coming. "Good."

Ariadne sent up a silent prayer to Dionysus: Forgive me. I do not mean to use your name in vain. Surely the best thing for me is to travel with Spartacus? I will do my utmost to tend to your devotees, and to win new converts. Coward, screamed her conscience. You're just looking after your own skin.

†

Since their untoward passage of the Adriatic, they'd walked for nearly a week. Nothing could have prepared Spartacus for the fertile Italian countryside, and its fields that contained every crop imaginable to man. That overwhelming display was without even taking the bread-baskets of Sicily and Egypt into consideration. No wonder the bastards could raise such large armies, he'd reflected bitterly. The Romans' food supply was guaranteed, unlike that of his people, who lived in a homeland that was barren by comparison. Yet for all Italy's fertility, the narrow mountain path that had carried them through the Apennines had been welcome, because it had reminded him of Thrace. It had taken in the most stunning scenery: steep ravines, plunging streams and rocky crags inhabited only by birds of prey. They had encountered no one but the occasional shepherd.

A couple of hours previously, the column had finally emerged from the mountains and joined a wide paved road, the Via Appia. It had led them southeast toward the town of Capua, the imposing walls of which now filled the horizon. Before it, however, perhaps a quarter of a mile distant, lay a squat, rectangular building standing on its own. It was partly backlit by the rays of the setting sun, giving it a black, brooding appearance.

"There you are, fine sirs," sneered Phortis, gesturing. "The first glimpse of your new home."

Every one of the captives craned his neck to see.

"It looks like a damn fortress," said Getas in an undertone.

Somehow Phortis caught the words. "Congratulations! You're not as stupid as you look," he answered in Thracian. "That's exactly what it is. The walls are nearly ten feet thick, and there's but one entrance, which is guarded day and night by six of Batiatus' best men. With two hundred scumbags like you inside it, what else would you expect? I hope you like it there, because once you've entered, the only time you dogs will ever leave is to go to the arena. Or," and he leered, "when your corpse is being carted to the refuse heaps nearby." Phortis glared at the seven non-Thracian captives, who were regarding him blankly. "Journey finish soon!" he shouted in Latin, and pointed. "Ludus! Ludus!" He smiled as the men began muttering unhappily to one another.

"What was the first bit?" hissed Seuthes to Getas, who had a smattering of Latin. The other whispered in his ear, and Seuthes' expression grew angry. "Screw him anyway," he growled. "Gloating over us as if we were a herd of cattle going to the slaughterhouse."

"That's about what we are," replied Getas grimly. "Except it's the carrion birds who'll feed on us after we're dead, not people."

Phortis came stalking along the line, looking for someone to use his whip on, and they both fell silent.

Spartacus, who'd also understood, kept his gaze fixed on the road.

Inside, he was warning himself never to say a thing within fifty paces of Phortis. The man's knowledge of Thracian was far better than he let on, and his hearing was uncanny. He didn't relax until the Capuan had resumed his place at the head of the column. The moment he had, however, Spartacus' eyes focused on the ludus. He kept his gaze fixed on it as they drew nearer. It looked impregnable. No doubt it was the same inside. Gradually, the sound of voices and the familiar ring of weapon on weapon carried to him through the air. Spartacus' jaw hardened. The battles than he fought from now on would be much smaller in scale than he was used to. According to Phortis, the majority would probably be one on one. That didn't mean he'd approach them any differently. In fact, thought Spartacus savagely, he'd go in twice as hard. Twice as fast. Twice as brutally. With only one aim. To win. That's all his life would be about from now on. Winning.

It was that or death, which didn't appeal.

Spartacus didn't overly care about himself, but it wasn't just about him any longer. He had Getas and Seuthes to look out for. And most importantly of all, there was Ariadne. Spartacus had no real idea how he'd provide for her. He had heard a rumor that the best gladiators could earn good money, and hoped it was true. Ensuring that Ariadne had plenty of cash would mean that if, or when, he was killed, she had the resources to survive on her own.

Grant me that much at least, O Great Rider.

†

Carbo twisted and turned, trying to get comfortable. It was impossible. The filthy straw mattress beneath him was falling apart. It was also full of bed bugs. His blanket had more holes in it than a fishing net. Rats scuttered to and fro on the floor, looking for food. He'd emptied the bucket by the end of the bed the night before, but it still stank of piss and shit. Because he had no money to buy fuel for the little brazier that sat in the corner, the room was freezing. Room? Carbo scowled. It could scarcely be called that.

The cheapest accommodation that he'd been able to find, it was located at the very top of a five-story *insula*, or block of flats. There were no windows, and he rarely used his oil lamp, so the only light that came in was through the gaps in the roof tiles. Carbo glanced around the pathetic limits of his domain. It could be called a garret perhaps. Scarcely ten paces by six, it had an angled roof that made it impossible to stand upright. The door didn't lock, and the walls were so thin that he could hear every sound made by his neighbor, a rheumy-eyed crone with a hacking cough.

The old witch was at it now, as she had been all through the night, choking and wheezing until Carbo thought she'd vomit. He wanted to go next door and throttle her. Instead, he shoved his head into the excuse for a pillow and placed a hand over his free ear. It made little difference. *Gods above. I might as well get up and go out.* Because of the coughing, Carbo had had little sleep. He'd hoped now that she was up, he might get some rest. Why fare abroad anyway? It was so damn cold outside. Of course those weren't the only reasons that Carbo was huddled, fully dressed, under his blankets. He had no money, and no job. Nowhere to go. No prospects. Impotent fury filled him. Since he had run away, things had gone from bad to worse.

He'd kept his head low for several days, and then gone back to the family home. The only people he'd seen apart from a couple of the domestic slaves were an officious-looking man in a toga and several workmen. His attempt to speak with Crassus' agent had been brushed off; so too had his request to meet with Paccius. Secure—and outraged—in the knowledge that his parents were gone, Carbo had begun looking for work. It hadn't been long before the realization sank home that his whole plan was a disastrous mistake. Most of the tradesmen he'd approached took one look at his well-made tunic and soft hands, and laughed in his face. Some had offered him work, but at such a low wage that Carbo had told them where to stick their miserable offers. Unfortunately, his savings had not lasted. The cost of living was much greater than he'd realized. His few remaining friends had helped where they could, giving him food and money, but even their goodwill had started to run dry.

Carbo ground his teeth with rage. What had he or his family done to anger the gods so? He had visited all the major temples, asking for guidance. He'd heard back nothing. Nothing. Even the old soothsayer to whom Carbo given his last coins the previous day had been useless, telling him that he'd soon be married to a wealthy merchant's daughter. "Louse-ridden charlatan," muttered Carbo. "I should find him and take back my money." The idea of marriage brought his mother to mind. *Gods, but she must be worrying about me. Father too.* His pride wouldn't allow him to write them a letter, however. *I'll let them know when things have improved. When I'm making money.*

A new storm of coughing overtook the crone next door, and he gave up any pretense of trying to rest. Anything was better than this torture. Getting up, he fastened his cloak at one shoulder with the last valuable item he possessed, a silver brooch given to him by his mother the year before, when he had taken the toga. Carbo ran his fingers over it, and silently asked Jupiter and Fortuna for help. Feeling a fraction better, he headed for the stairs. Perhaps his luck would change today. Perhaps the gods would help him at last. If not, maybe he could find a way to join the army. That at least would be better than returning in shame to his family in Rome. His belly grumbled, reminding him that he'd hardly eaten in three days. Carbo's mind raced. Maybe he could steal a loaf from the bakery next door.

†

All eyes were upon the column from the moment they passed under the stone archway and into the large colonnaded courtyard beyond. They had to be. Phortis had led them straight into the middle of the circular training area, forcing the gladiators there to move out of the way. None looked unhappy at the interruption to their training. Far from it. The fighters crowded in around the new arrivals. Insults and catcalls in several tongues rained down; these turned rapidly to wolf whistles and lewd suggestions when Ariadne and the other women were seen. Doing his best to ignore the abuse, Spartacus picked out the loudest individuals and memorized their faces. A thickset Thracian with a long ponytail. A skinny Gaul who was missing his top teeth. A Nubian with one gold earring. *I'll sort out those fuckers.*

Ariadne, who had worked her way into the midst of the women, kept her eyes firmly on the sandy ground. Until men knew that she was with Spartacus, the less attention she got, the better.

"Shut it, you curs!" shouted Phortis. He looked up at the archers on the first-floor balcony, which ran all the way around the courtyard. "You there! Tell Batiatus that I'm back. Quickly!" As one of the guards scurried off, he turned back to his fifteen captives. "In a line! In a line! Face that way," he ordered. "Batiatus will want to see what kind of men I've brought back for him."

Spartacus, Getas and Seuthes had been near the head of the column, so they found themselves on the left of the line. While they waited for Batiatus, the thronging gladiators took their opportunity, jeering and throwing mocking comments at all and sundry.

"Hey, new boy!"

Instead of reacting, Spartacus scanned the dozens of hard faces arrayed before him: they were Gauls, Thracians and Germans for the most part, but there was also a smattering of Greeks, Egyptians and Nubians. There were three basic types of gladiator that he could see. Thracians, like himself, dressed in little more than a loincloth and wide leather belt, with a typical crested helmet to protect their heads. Lucky ones among them wore greaves. All carried wooden versions of the sica. Mixed among his countrymen were dozens of shaggy-haired, bare-chested Gauls in belted trousers. Clutching wooden spears or long swords, they looked every bit as fierce as he'd heard. There were men he didn't recognize too, in triple-crested helmets and with simple metal plates protecting their chests.

"New boy! I'm talking to you!"

Spartacus felt Getas nudge him. "It's that big fucker on the left, with the scar right through his mouth." Spartacus' eyes flickered sideways, taking in a blocky Gaul with long blond hair. His face had been ruined by a sword cut that would have killed most men. The result was an ugly purple cicatrice that ran from just under his right eye to the left side of his chin. Miraculously passing his nose, it had split his lips in two. Someone had stitched them back together, but, thought Spartacus, they hadn't done a very good job. When the brute talked, one half of his face moved independently to the other.

"Are you talking to me?" snapped Spartacus.

"That's right," growled the Gaul. He licked his ruined lips. "I'll see you in the baths later. You can suck me off."

There was a burst of ribald laughter, and Phortis smiled.

Spartacus waited until the noise had died down a little. "Suck off an ugly son of a bitch like you? You should be so lucky." He laughed. "Because we've just met, I'll be nice. Next time you even look at me, though, I'll send you to fucking Hades. Understand?"

Stung by the roars of laughter that met Spartacus' riposte, the Gaul took a step forward. "You dirty Thracian bastard," he hissed.

Phortis moved into his path, whip raised high. "Get back!" he bawled. As the Gaul sullenly obeyed, he rounded on Spartacus. "Unless you're asked to speak, keep your stinking mouth shut!" Flecks of his spittle flew to land on Spartacus' cheeks, who had the sense not to wipe them off.

"Phortis. You have returned." The voice was not loud, but its authority cut through the noise. "Welcome."

Phortis' evil expression vanished as he turned. "Thank you, sir." He bowed to the short, portly man who had appeared on the balcony above.

"Having a little trouble with the new 'recruits?'" Batiatus' eyes were already dancing along the captives, appraising them. Spartacus deliberately didn't meet the lanista's gaze. Instinctively, his comrades copied him. No point attracting Batiatus' attentions this early.

"Not at all, sir. Just a few of the usual wisecracks. You know what it's like."

"Indeed." Reaching the end of the line, Batiatus regarded the Capuan. "Your journey was successful?"

"I think so, sir, yes. I didn't have to pay the moon and stars for any of these scumbags, but they're all tough men who look able to handle themselves. I'm optimistic that you'll agree with my choices."

"Tell me about them."

Spartacus scanned the watching gladiators sidelong as Phortis began exalting each of his purchases. Where were the leaders, the men he'd come up against sooner rather than later? Not far from the scarred man who'd shouted at him, he spotted another Gaul, an immense figure with bulging muscles and an arrogant look smeared across his broad, handsome face. *That bastard's one. I hope he's not as skillful as he's big.* Spartacus slid his gaze onward. A moment later, it stopped on a broken-nosed German, a figure almost as large as the haughty Gaul. He didn't look that remarkable, but the two men who stood at each of his shoulders told a different story. *He's a leader. They're his bodyguards.* Spartacus didn't spot any more like the first pair he'd picked, but he knew there'd be plenty of fighters who fancied themselves as superior to him, a lowly new arrival.

Phortis finished his descriptions.

"Of course we won't know until they have to fight, but you appear to have done well," Batiatus pronounced.

"Thank you, sir." The Capuan grinned.

"Get them to take the oath, then take off their chains and get them settled in. No point in wasting any more training time than necessary, eh?" With a pleased nod, Batiatus disappeared from view.

"So the whoreson lives in the ludus?" whispered Getas.

"Seems like it," replied Spartacus, eyeing the rest of the first story. "The armory and the infirmary look to be up there too. We poor shitbags get to stay down here." With a jerk of his head, he indicated the lines of cells that ran under three sides of the portico.

"Listen to me, you miserable sacks of shit!" bellowed Phortis. "It's time for you to swear your allegiance to your new *familia*—the gladiators you see all around you." He repeated his words in Thracian and Greek. "Understand?"

One of the Scythians, a man with a thick black beard, moved forward a step. "What if . . . we . . . refuse to take oath?"

Phortis clicked his fingers, and an archer on the balcony lifted his bow. "Your journey comes to an end. Here. Now. Clear?"

The Scythian grunted and stepped back.

"Anyone else? No?" Phortis sniggered. "I didn't think so. Repeat after me, then, the words of the *sacramentum gladiatorum*, the most sacred oath that any of you wretched excuses for men will ever take!"

A silence fell over the ludus. Glancing around, Spartacus realized that the assembled fighters respected what Phortis was about to say. All of them had been through the same ritual. In the brutal world of the ludus, it gave their lives a purpose.

"Will you swear to endure being burned and being bound in chains?"

There was a heartbeat's delay.

"Yes," muttered the fifteen men.

"Do you vow to accept being beaten and flogged?"

"Yes."

"Do you commit yourself to Batiatus, body and soul, asking nothing in return? Will you swear to meet your death by sword, spear . . ." Here Phortis paused. ". . . or in any other way that the lanista sees fit?"

There was no response.

Ariadne stiffened. She'd had no idea quite how powerful the gladiator's oath was.

She could not see Spartacus grinding his teeth. *Body and soul?*

"Answer me! If you don't, the bowmen above will start to loose. On the count of three," shouted Phortis. "One."

Spartacus glanced at Getas and Seuthes. "Pointless dying over a few words, eh?" he hissed. They both gave him a tight nod.

"Two," roared Phortis.

"Yes," cried the fifteen men.

"Louder!"

"YES!"

"Good. Welcome to our familia." Phortis' smile reminded Spartacus of a wolf's snarl. Reaching into his tunic, he pulled out a chain, upon which hung a set of keys. "Time to set you arse bandits free. Free!" Laughing at his own joke, he began unlocking the iron ring that sat around each man's neck. When he reached Spartacus, their eyes met.

I'll kill you one day, thought Spartacus. Out loud, he said quietly, "Where do we sleep?"

"Have a look around. Some of the cells are empty. It's first come, first served," the Capuan growled.

"When do we get fed?" asked Getas.

"First thing in the morning, and when training finishes, in about half an hour. It's a good diet too." Phortis saw their interest and chuckled. "Barley porridge twice a day, and as much water as you can drink."

"I—" protested Seuthes.

"Yes?" Phortis' tone was silky smooth, but his eyes were full of venom.

Seuthes looked away.

"Get as much rest as you can. Tomorrow the trainers will decide which of you will fight for each of them," Phortis advised. He scowled at their incomprehension. "You stupid bastards better start learning some Latin or you just won't get on. This once, I'll explain. There are three basic types of gladiator: the Gaul, the Samnite and"—he broke off to spit on the ground—"the Thracian." With that, he moved on to the next man.

"See if you can get us a couple of cells beside each other," said Spartacus to his comrades. Rubbing at the raw flesh on his neck, he made for the group of women. He'd only gone a few steps before he was shoved violently from behind. He stumbled and fell to one knee. He knew who it was without even looking. This fight had to be fought right now. If he avoided it, his life in the ludus would be twice as hard. Yet he had no weapon, while the other probably did. Instinctively, his fingers scraped into the sand, picking up as many of the yellow grains as he could. Spartacus jumped to his feet, spinning as he did. "Did you push me?" he snarled.

"I did." The Gaul with the mangled lips shrugged. He pointed with the filed-down piece of iron in his right hand. "I was aiming you in the direction of the baths." He glanced to either side, and his two companions grinned evilly.

Spartacus focused on the leader's homemade weapon, which had probably been filched from the smithy. He wasn't surprised that one of his opponents was armed. Any fighter with a titter of wit would be. Those who weren't, or who were too weak, would end up as followers, or pieces of meat for men like the Gaul before him. Spartacus had no idea what chance he had against three of them, but he wasn't going to back down. He couldn't. "Is that so?" he said softly, taking a step forward. "Well, I don't feel the need for a wash right now."

The Gaul's gash of a mouth twitched, and he rubbed his crotch. "Who said anything about a wash?"

His companions laughed.

Crouching, Spartacus took another step. He had to get as close as possible. "You certainly need one. You stink worse than a sow in farrow!"

Roaring with anger, the Gaul jabbed the homemade dagger at Spartacus' belly.

Spartacus swung his right arm around and opened his fingers, letting the sand fly. In the same instant, he dodged sideways, out of reach. There was a scream as the Gaul's eyes filled with grit, and Spartacus spun, smashing a punch into his side. The Gaul stumbled, and Spartacus hammered home more blows, sending the other sprawling to the ground. Sensing movement behind him, he half turned, but a fist collided with the side of his head. Stars burst across Spartacus' vision and a thousand needles of pain lanced into his brain. His knees buckled, and it was only with a supreme effort that he managed not to topple on top of the Gaul. Someone grabbed at his arms from behind, trying to pinion them to his sides. He snapped his head back, catching his assailant on the bridge of his nose. Spartacus felt the crunch of breaking cartilage, and heard the man scream and fall away. Desperately, he glanced to either side. Where was the third motherless cur? Too late, he saw a blur of movement coming at him from the left. The glitter of metal in the figure's hand told Spartacus that he was in mortal danger. Too late, too slowly, he tried to get out the way. He steeled himself for the agonizing sting as the dagger slid into his flesh. By some miracle, however, the blow never landed. Instead, Seuthes came leaping through the air, knocking the third Gaul backward.

Even as Seuthes rained a flurry of blows upon the man's face and midriff, Spartacus was looking for the scarred Gaul and his other companion. To his utter relief, Getas was giving the second man short shrift, while his original attacker was still cursing and trying to clear his eyes of sand. Quickly, Spartacus scooped up the sharpened piece of iron, which was lying by his feet. A sideways glance at the archers told him that although they had noticed the fight, they were not going to intervene. Yet. No doubt this was a daily occurrence, he thought. "Don't kill them, but make a decent racket," he hissed. "I'm going to the baths."

Without waiting for Getas or Seuthes to reply, Spartacus ran in behind the Gaul. Grabbing his right arm, he twisted it up behind his back. He touched the homemade dagger to the other's throat. "Walk," he ordered. "Walk, or I'll stick this in so far that it comes out the outer side of your fucking neck."

The Gaul did as he was told, walking stiff-legged in the direction he'd pointed a few heartbeats earlier. "What are you going to do?" he growled.

Spartacus jabbed the iron into the Gaul's skin until blood ran down his neck. "Shut your trap." Behind him, he heard his comrades screaming abuse as they kicked and spat on the other two tribesmen. Spartacus grinned with satisfaction. The archers' attention was now completely on that brawl. Just what he wanted. "Move it. Faster," he hissed.

Seeing steam coming out of a pair of latticed windows, Spartacus aimed for the nearest doorway. He bundled the Gaul inside and out of sight of the guards. The warm room they'd entered was square, and tiled from ceiling to floor. Colorful depictions of fish, sea monsters and Neptune covered the walls. A low bench ran around the room; it was covered with bundles of clothing, left there by the gladiators who were in the baths through the door opposite. The air was laced with the thick, pungent smell of aromatic oils. The only other occupant of the room was a half-dressed, dark-skinned, short man with black hair. He goggled in surprise at the pair's dramatic entrance.

Good, thought Spartacus. I want a witness to spread the word. "So this is where you were going to take me, eh?"

Tense with fear, the Gaul nodded.

"To suck you off?" He spat out the words.

"Yes."

"That isn't going to happen, is it?" Spartacus wrenched the Gaul's arm up under his shoulder blade, causing him to moan in pain.

"No!"

"Sadly, I don't have the time to make you suffer. This will have to do, you fucking shitbag." Pulling back the piece of iron, Spartacus plunged it into the Gaul's neck with all his strength. There was a loud choking sound and blood spurted all over Spartacus' hand. He jerked free the iron, and a tide of red followed it, jetting sideways on to the floor.

Making a strangled attempt to speak, the Gaul tottered forward one or two steps before crashing to the tiles, face first. A lake of scarlet rapidly began to form around his twitching body.

"Who are you?" Still gripping the bloody weapon, Spartacus pinned the dark-skinned man with his stare.

"R-Restio is my name. I'm from Iberia."

"I see. Well, I am Spartacus the Thracian. In case you hadn't realized, I've just arrived. And this is my answer to anyone who wants to fuck with me." He pointed at the Gaul. "Make damn sure that you tell every man in the ludus what you've seen. Do you understand?"

"Yes."

"Not a word to Phortis, or any of the guards, though. I wouldn't want you to end up the same way as this idiot."

"My lips are s-sealed."

"We understand each other then." Wiping the iron clean on the Gaul's tunic, Spartacus shoved it into the waistband of his undergarment and sauntered outside. Whistling a tuneless ditty, he glanced up at the balcony. The guards above were showing no real interest in what was going on. He could not see Phortis either. *Good. That probably means I got away with it.* Next, he looked for Getas and Seuthes. They were talking loudly to Ariadne. What they were really doing, of course, was protecting her until he got back. She started forward at the sight of him, but he signaled her to wait.

"Where are the two Gauls?"

"They crawled off into whatever shithole they call home," replied Seuthes with a savage grin.

"One had a broken arm, and I added a few cracked ribs to the smashed nose you gave the other," interjected Getas. "What about the ugly one?"

"He'll be staying in the baths until someone drags him out of there."

Ariadne's eyes filled with horror. "Is he . . . ?"

"Dead, yes," replied Spartacus harshly. "It was the only way. If I'd let him live, everyone in the damn place would regard me . . . us," and he indicated Getas and Seuthes, "as soft targets. This way, they know that we're most definitely not."

Ariadne nodded. Killing the Gaul had more than one purpose. Spartacus wouldn't be able to watch over her all the time. It was important that every gladiator knew that she was with someone not to be trifled with. The corpse lying in the baths would send a very clear message about that.

V

It didn't take long for the Gaul's body to be discovered. A pair of Germans were next to enter the bathing area. They emerged, shouting at the tops of their voices. Footsteps clattered on the stairs as a group of guards descended in response. Crowds of fighters gathered to watch the limp Gaul being dragged outside. A broad trail of blood marked the ground all the way back into the baths. Spartacus watched the proceedings from the door of the cell he'd taken for himself and Ariadne. He was pleased to see that none of the guards looked especially surprised by what they'd found. Restio was doing his job too. Already he was getting plenty of looks from fighters in the yard. Most were respectful, but some were angry or challenging. Spartacus ignored them all. Without doubt, fewer men would now want to take him on than before. He wondered how Phortis would react. Unless Restio played him false, there would be no witnesses' accounts for the Capuan to go on. All he'd have was the gossip floating around the ludus. Would that be enough for the Capuan to act on? Spartacus wasn't sure, but he didn't think so. Murders in the baths or toilets had to be regular occurrences. Such things kept a natural order in the ludus.

And so it proved. The evil stares that Phortis was soon throwing at Spartacus clearly showed that he'd heard of his involvement, but the Capuan did nothing. Half an hour passed, and the gladiators' training finished for the day. A short time later, the dinner gong sounded. Spartacus marched boldly into the yard with Ariadne, as if he were going out to eat. Getas and Seuthes walked two steps behind them. They headed for the dining area, which consisted of sets of benches and tables on either side of the kitchen doors. A queue of men led through the portals; through the steamy air within Spartacus could see a large cauldron perched on a table with stacked bowls and piles of wooden spoons. Behind it stood a slave, ladle in hand, and Phortis, watching everything like a beady-eyed crow. Four beefy guards were present too, security against any trouble.

They joined the back of the line. The fighters immediately in front looked around. One or two nodded a greeting at Spartacus, which he returned. No one spoke to him or his companions, which suited him fine. The first day and night in the ludus were all about establishing his independence, his lack of need for friendship with others. He'd told Getas and Seuthes as much. In silence, they shuffled into the kitchen.

"Here he is! The new *latro*." Phortis' voice was mocking. "Watch out, or you might get stabbed in the back."

At this, plenty of the gladiators stared. A few guffawed. None said anything.

"I'm no bandit," replied Spartacus loudly.

"Is that so?" sneered Phortis.

"It is."

"So you'd know nothing about the body in the baths, then? The ugly bastard who died of a hole in his neck?"

"I don't know what you're talking about."

"That's not what I've heard."

Spartacus lifted his shoulders into an expressive shrug. "Believe what you will. Men like to gossip. Nearly all of it is horseshit. Have you got any proof?"

"I don't need proof to dispense justice, you halfwit," barked Phortis. "Let's just say that any man who can best that brute of a Gaul must be a good fighter. I'll expect great things from you in the arena."

Curse him! Spartacus hadn't considered the eventuality that the Capuan would do nothing even if he knew.

Phortis wasn't finished with him. "How did a scumbag latro like you end up with such a high-class piece of ass, eh?"

Men's heads turned again. Lustful mutters passed between them as they drank in Ariadne's exotic looks.

"I am a warrior of the Maedi tribe, and Ariadne is my wife," said Spartacus with a calm smile. Inside, though, he was now raging. He wanted to leap on the Capuan and smash his teeth down his throat. But he kept his peace. He'd kill Phortis, of that there was little doubt, but the four guards would slay him in turn. A stupid way to die.

"Your king had a different story. He said that you're a lying, cheating whoreson who was plotting to overthrow him."

Spartacus could feel the muscles in his jaw working. "No surprise there," he snapped. *Kotys always was a cowardly scumbag.*

"What's that? I didn't hear you."

"Kotys would say that," cried Spartacus. "He was a weak leader. My mere existence made me a threat to his authority. Selling me into slavery was a perfect solution."

"So if you weren't standing here, you would have seized power over the Maedi?" Phortis glanced at the slave who was doling out the barley porridge, who sniggered dutifully. "Do you hear that? We have a king in our midst!"

A number of the gladiators laughed. One, the massive, arrogant-looking Gaul whom Spartacus had noticed earlier, stepped out of line and faced them. Blond-haired, mustached, and wearing only a pair of patterned trousers, he was the epitome of a Gaulish warrior. Half a dozen fighters moved to join him. The Gaul performed an extravagant bow. "Come and take my place, Your Majesty. If you can."

Phortis smirked.

Gods above. A fight with him and his cronies is the last thing I—we—need right now. "You were here first, friend," Spartacus replied, meeting the big man's gaze evenly. "So was everyone else in front of me. I'll take my turn."

"Scared of a fight?"

"No. But I won't take you on this evening. Not when Phortis is trying to set it up," said Spartacus, praying that the Gaul was as sharp as he was strong.

"Go on, Crixus! Dance to the puppet master's tune," shouted a voice.

There was a rumble of amusement from the rest of the gladiators, and Phortis scowled.

Crixus didn't miss the barbed comment, or the Capuan's expression. "Another time then," he growled. Throwing a filthy look at Phortis, he grabbed a bowl from the pile on the table and held it out. "Fill it up. To the brim!"

The kitchen slave hurriedly obeyed.

Grabbing a flat loaf, Crixus stamped off, and the next of his followers took his place.

Getas let out a long hiss of relief. "Thank the Rider! That bastard is as big as Hercules."

"Even Hercules had his weaknesses," said Spartacus. "That Gaulish prick's not popular either. Most of the fighters seemed happy enough to laugh at him. I'd wager that the six who stood by him are his only supporters."

"That's still four more than us," warned Seuthes.

"True. We need to avoid picking a fight with them for now," said Spartacus, thinking of the big German with the broken nose. How many men were loyal to him? Would he be as combative as Crixus? Would the Samnites? Spartacus hoped not. He wouldn't be able to engineer every fight the way he had the one with the ugly Gaul.

There was plenty to think about as they ate.

Spartacus was still in a pensive mood when he and the others returned to their cells. Most of his chamber, which measured little more than ten paces by ten, was filled by two straw mattresses that lay close together. There was no furniture. In fact, the only other objects visible were Ariadne's possessions: a pair of little statues of Dionysus and the wicker basket containing her snake. The concrete walls were covered in lewd or boastful graffiti, the work of previous occupants. Patches of mold grew in the corners, giving the room an unpleasant, musty smell.

"This is it. Home," said Ariadne brightly. "At least it will be when I've sorted it out."

Spartacus grunted by way of reply. Glancing idly at the basket, his heart nearly stopped. The lid was no longer properly in place. "Look!" Flipping off the lid with his foot, he peered warily within. "Gods above! It's gone." He took a step into the center of the room.

"Steady," soothed Ariadne. "It won't have gone far. Unless . . ." And her gaze moved to the gap under the door's bottom edge. "Dionysus, do not let it have gone outside," she whispered. *I need it to protect me!*

Spartacus wasn't listening. He peeled off his tunic and dangled it from his left fist. Lifting the first mattress with great care, he peered underneath. Nothing. He pulled the straw-filled sack to the far side of the room, where he leaned it against the wall. Returning, he raised the corner of the second mattress.

"There it is!" cried Ariadne, pointing at a lithe, coiled shape. "Let me get it."

But Spartacus was there before her. Heaving the mattress out of the way, he tossed his tunic over the serpent and leaped over to grasp it behind its head. "Got you," he hissed.

"What are you doing? You hate the thing!" Ariadne lifted the basket so that he could drop the snake inside.

Spartacus waited until she'd secured the lid again. "I do. But there's nothing like confronting your fear. If you think the devil's behind you, turn around and face him, as they say." He wiped his brow and grinned.

"You could have been bitten. Let me pick it up next time," Ariadne snapped, irritated that he'd had the temerity to touch her most sacred possession. She was also scared of what might have happened.

"Next time? If you'd secured the basket properly in the first place, we wouldn't even be having this conversation," he needled back.

"Leave me alone!" Ariadne retorted, flushing with anger and embarrassment.

Seeing her mood, Spartacus chose to ignore her.

The bad feeling between them lingered in the air like a bad smell, and they retired in silence. Spartacus blew out the oil light, and lay down beside Ariadne. They were close enough to touch, but neither did so. Neither spoke either. After a few moments, Spartacus turned over and inadvertently brushed his leg against hers. She turned on him before he could say a word of apology. "This marriage is a convenient pretense, you understand? Don't get any ideas."

She saw his lips twitch in the half-light. "I touched you by mistake. And I never thought our 'marriage' would be otherwise."

Ariadne was furious to feel cheated that he hadn't put up more of an argument. I'm acting like a child, she thought. But she couldn't bring herself to apologize. The last man to touch her had been her father. *Damn him to hell.* A wave of hatred toward all men swelled in her heart. *You profess to want a husband, when in reality you'll never let anyone close.* She was too frightened to do so. *Stop it. There are decent men in the world, men who do not act as my father did. Spartacus is one of them.* If he wasn't, she reflected with a guilty thrill, why did she want him to touch her?

Spartacus stared at the outline of her shape, watched her chest go up and down with each breath. *Why is the bloody woman so prickly?* Suddenly, he grinned. *She's still damn attractive. Maybe she'll come around in the end.* With that thought uppermost in his mind, he closed his eyes and fell straight to sleep.

Once he began to snore gently, Ariadne relaxed. The moon came out from behind the clouds that had masked it previously, and the cell filled with a gentle yellow light. Spartacus did not stir, and Ariadne was shocked to find herself surreptitiously studying him. Guilty pleasure filled her at what she saw. There were little laughter lines at the corners of his eyes that she'd not noticed before, and a few hairs that shone white among the others on his head. The scar on his nose and cheek had tiny dots on either side of it, marking where the sutures had sat. His face, neck and arms were a darker color than the skin that normally lay beneath his tunic. Everything about Spartacus, from his firm chin to his wiry muscles, spoke of strength. Ariadne found it most reassuring, and when an image of Phortis inevitably came to mind, she was able to shove it away with ease.

To her surprise, sleep was not long coming.

For the second time, she dreamed of being in Spartacus' arms.

†

Carbo slurped down the dregs of his wine and stared into the bottom of his cup, hoping for inspiration. He found none. Glancing around the clammy, packed tavern, he scowled. He wouldn't be finding any in here either. The place was full of lowlifes: scrawny, ill-fed men with, if Carbo were to make a bet on it, a nasty tendency toward the criminal. The only women present were a couple of gap-toothed, straggle-haired waitresses and three diseased-looking whores. The inn's sole attraction was its wine, which was the cheapest Carbo had found. It didn't taste that bad, considering its likely provenance. After a few its flavor had even started to grow on him.

"Another one?"

Carbo turned his head to find the innkeeper standing over him. He looked at the four bronze coins on the bar top by his left hand. They were all he had left of the two denarii that Paccius had given him. He let rip with a morose belch. At least he'd had the sense to pay his rent arrears first. "Why not?"

In the blink of an eye, his crudely worked clay cup had been filled; one of the coins also vanished.

Carbo nodded his thanks before taking a deep swallow. He considered his day for the umpteenth time. What had gone wrong? His plan of hanging around his former home had initially seemed a good one. An excellent one, in fact. He'd wanted to see Paccius, to have a word with the only person in the world who still had time for him. It had worked too. The Samnite had emerged not long before noon, heading out on an errand. Carbo had caught up with him on the next street, and they had walked all the way to Capua's forum together.

Naturally, Paccius hadn't had any news of his parents, but he'd been able to tell Carbo all about what was going on. How their new master, Crassus' agent, did not seem too bad—for the moment. Carbo had been glad for the Samnite, and the other domestic slaves, whom he liked well enough. He'd been mortified when Paccius had pressed the two silver coins on him, however. "You need these more than I do," he had said. To Carbo's undying shame, he'd taken the coins. Saying goodbye to Paccius had been even more poignant than the first time, when he'd crept out before his parents woke. *I took money from one of my own slaves.* His attempt to join the army had also been a disaster. The centurion he'd approached had demanded proof that he was seventeen. Carbo had stuttered that his birthday was not far off. The officer had told him in a kindly tone to come back with the relevant paperwork when the time was right. Of course he wouldn't be able to comply, because his father had all the family records. *It's all fucking Crassus' fault.* He drained his cup and thumped it savagely on to the wooden top.

Hearing the impact, the innkeeper materialized once more. "Want a refill?"

"Why not?" snarled Carbo. "I've nothing else to be doing."

An instant later, he had another full cup of wine, and only two coins. Soon after, it was one coin, and then none. Carbo was destitute once more. Before he had time to dwell on that miserable detail, one of the prostitutes sidled over and tried to sit on his knee. Carbo waved her away irritably. "Even if I wanted to, I can't afford it."

"You've got this," she purred, poking at the brooch on his cloak with a cracked, dirty fingernail. "I'll screw you every night for a week for it. Maybe even two weeks, if you're man enough." She cackled at her own joke.

"That piece is worth more than your life, you diseased bitch," Carbo growled. "Leave me alone."

Her expression soured. "Who said I'd fuck you anyway? Those scars would put anyone off."

Carbo raised the back of his hand to her, and she stepped back, curling her lip. But it was a pyrrhic victory. The moment that the whore had reached her friends, she began jeering and pointing at him. "Shame you're not a man or I'd give you a damn good hiding," he growled, making an obscene gesture. They hissed with fury. Getting unsteadily to his feet, Carbo made for the door. When would his luck change? he wondered bitterly. Making any kind of money seemed impossible. Pulling open the door, he stumbled outside. The blast of cold air that hit him restored some of his senses. *I'll feel better after a good night's sleep.* Trying to keep that thought uppermost, Carbo wove off into the narrow, unpaved alley. Despite the near complete darkness, he knew his way back to the insula atop which his garret perched. It wasn't far.

A moment later, the prostitute whom Carbo had rejected came hurrying out of the inn. She was accompanied by an unsavory-looking man. Both came skulking after him.

The first thing Carbo knew about it was when a heavy blow struck the back of his head. The explosion of light that burst across his eyes was accompanied by a tidal wave of pain, and he dropped like a sack of grain. Landing face first in the muck, Carbo was all too aware of its foul stench, and taste, but he was too weak to do anything about it, or about the fingers that were already rifling under his tunic for a purse. *Bastards!*

"Don't waste your time," said a shrill female voice. "He's got no money, just the brooch I told you about."

"It's still worth checking," growled the man. "You never know what you might find."

Carbo felt himself being rolled over, and a hand pawing at his left shoulder. "No, no," he mumbled as the fabric ripped. His reward for speaking was a blow across the face that smacked his head back down into the reeking blend of mud and human waste. Light-headed, half stunned, Carbo's strength deserted him.

"Shall I cut his throat?"

"You might as well," answered the woman. "In case he saw us coming after him."

I know who you are, and I'll kill you if I get half a chance, Carbo wanted to say, but his attempt came out as an unintelligible mumble. As his chin was shoved back, he tensed in expectation of the blade. *What a god-awful way to die.*

There was a creaking sound from above as a window opened. An instant later, a torrent of urine and feces landed on all three of them. The woman screamed. "Hades take your soul!" roared the man. "What whoreson did that?"

"It was I, Ambrosius the veteran," bellowed a loud voice. "And now I'm coming outside with three of my slaves. We're all armed with swords and spears."

Carbo felt the weight on his chest ease as the thug scrambled up. "That's it. I'm not dying just to finish off this fool."

"Leave him," muttered the woman. "Hopefully, he'll die anyway."

Dimly, Carbo heard their footsteps retreating. He tried to move but his limbs didn't seem his own. He heard a door creak open and then the orange glow of an oil lamp penetrated the darkness.

A ruddy, concerned face bent over him. "Are you alive?"

"I think so. My head hurts like a bastard."

"I'd say it does," replied Ambrosius with a scowl. "I heard the crack of the blow from my bedroom." Carbo tried to sit up, but Ambrosius pressed him back down again. "Wait." He probed with his fingers around the sides and back of Carbo's head. "I can't feel a break. You'll probably live," he said with satisfaction. "Grab my hand."

Carbo obeyed, and felt himself being pulled upright. The mud made a wet, sucking sound as it released him, and his nostrils were again filled with the rank odor of everything that made it into such a glutinous morass. He didn't care. "They took my brooch. It was the only valuable I had." He made to move after the thieves. "I have to get it back."

Ambrosius' strong arm blocked his way. "I wouldn't. Be grateful that you don't have a gaping smile around the base of your neck."

His slave nodded in mute agreement.

Reality crashed back down on Carbo. Better to be covered in shit and breathing than to be dead. "Very well. Thank you for your help."

"Don't mention it." Ambrosius wrinkled his nose and stepped back a little. "Gods, but you stink. You've got baths at home?"

Carbo's pride rallied. "Yes, yes," he lied.

"Good. You'll understand if I don't accompany you," said Ambrosius. "And as for my slave, well, I only have the one . . ." Looking shamefaced, he fell silent.

"It's all right. You did more than most people would ever do, coming out on to the street in the middle of the night. I can find my own way back." To what? he thought furiously.

"Here." Ambrosius shoved forward the oil lamp and his rusty gladius. "You'll have more chance of making it with these."

"But—"

"I insist. If you wish, return them to me in the morning. My door is the one by the butcher's. As you know, Ambrosius is my name."

"Thank you," said Carbo simply, accepting both lamp and sword. "I will come back tomorrow."

"Excellent! My wife won't have any reason to complain if I bring you in for a cup of wine then."

Leaving Ambrosius and his slave to return indoors, Carbo trudged off. The end of his all too brief contact with a decent person fueled the flames of his anger to new heights. Now he had to return to his garret, where no one cared if he lived or died. Where the crone would keep him awake all night with her coughing. It wasn't even as if he could wash before climbing into his bed. The insula had no running water, so he'd have to lie in his own filth until the morning, when it was safe to go out and the public baths were open. Carbo wished for the pair who had attacked him to appear before him. *I'd cut them both to pieces.*

Of course nothing happened. He kept walking.

Then, in the flickering light cast by his oil lamp, something caught his eye. He stopped and peered at the plastered wall to his left. On it, someone had scratched a series of crude drawings. Carbo leaned closer, making out a pair of small, almost childlike figures fighting each other and, on either side, sets of cursive characters. He read the gladiators' names and the boasts about them. "Hilarus the Thracian, never defeated, victor in fifteen fights, and Attilius the Samnite, strongest of his tribe, and killer of four men." Hope, and a little excitement, stirred deep in Carbo's heart. Here was one path left for him to follow. It might be that taken by the lowest of the low, by criminals, prisoners of war and slaves, yet occasionally it was taken by a citizen. He could become an *auctoratus*, a contracted gladiator. If he succeeded, the financial rewards could be very great indeed.

The thought made Carbo's lips twitch. Despite all that had happened that day, this seemed like a sign from the gods.

†

Spartacus was woken before dawn by the cold. His blanket had slipped off in the night. Pulling it up to his chin, he trained his ear to the early-morning sounds entering from outside. The strident crowing of a cock in the ludus' vegetable garden, which he'd seen outside the thick walls. The rattle of a sword tip along the window bars of the gladiators' cells. Phortis' nasal tone rousing them from sleep. The slap of men's feet on bare concrete floors. Throats being cleared. The distinctive noise of spitting. And from beyond the ludus, where Capua's market sprawled, the hum of normal life: the rival cries of bakers, butchers and other tradesmen. From the nearby Via Appia came the shouted greetings of travelers, the creak of cartwheels mixed with the lowing of oxen, and the ill-tempered braying of mules. It was very ordinary, and very similar to Thrace. Spartacus hated it. Loathed it. Freedom was so near, he thought bitterly, and so far. A world away. Who'd have imagined that after years of service to the Romans, he'd end up as the lowest of the low? *A fucking gladiator.* He thought of Kotys and grimaced. *At least I'm alive.*

Clack, clack, clack. Right on cue, Phortis' weapon dragged along the bars of the cell's window. The metallic sound of a key unlocking the door followed. "Stop plowing your woman, latro! Get out here while the porridge is nice and hot."

"Filthy Roman bastard." Spartacus' whisper was reflex.

"Do you hear me, latro?"

"I hear you." He sat up.

"Good. Today we'll see what kind of fighter you are to become." Phortis moved on.

Spartacus scowled.

"About last night . . ." Ariadne began.

He glanced at her, and saw the desire for reconciliation in her eyes. "I shouldn't have snapped at you," he said. "Although I'd caught the creature, I was still feeling jumpy."

"I'm the one who should be apologizing. It's my snake, and my responsibility to make sure that it stays in the basket." She paused, looking awkward. "So I'm sorry."

"Let's forget about it, and move on."

"Fine." Feeling better, she smiled.

"You look much better like that than with a frown on your face."

He likes me! Delighted but also embarrassed, Ariadne floundered about for what to say. "What type of fighter do you think they'll pick you for?" she blurted.

"Thracian, I'd assume," replied Spartacus, climbing to his feet. "I'll soon find out. What will you do with the day?"

"The first thing will be to clean this room properly. Only the gods know when that last happened," Ariadne said disapprovingly. "Then I want to find something that will serve as an altar for my statues. If I have a chance, I'll also sound out the women who already live in the ludus. Learn about how life works here."

"Stay safe. Keep away from the toilets and baths unless you're with plenty of other women," he warned.

"Don't worry." She pointed to the basket. "That's going everywhere with me."

"Good."

She nodded. "Be careful."

Her sudden thaw made him grin. "I will." Pushing open the door, he was gone.

Discomfited, Ariadne was grateful that he hadn't seen the rising blush in her cheeks.

†

The new arrivals had barely finished their porridge when, accompanied by Phortis, the trainers who supervised the different classes of fighters came looking for them. The three middle-aged, hard-faced men were each armed with a club, a whip, or both. All were former gladiators who'd earned their freedom the hard way, by winning the rudis.

Forced out into the yard, to a chorus of jeers from the other inmates, the fifteen men were lined up side by side. Spartacus, Getas and Seuthes found themselves at the far end, away from Phortis, who began at once. He threw a barrage of questions at the first man, one of the Pontic warriors, demanding to know his age, his former occupation and his combat experience. The trainers listened carefully to the stumbling answers in poor Latin. Before long, the tribesman was ordered to stand by the man who would school him as a Thracian. The next captive was chosen to fight as a Gaul, and the one after that, as a Samnite. Gradually, Phortis worked his way down the line. The other Thracians grinned as they were selected to appear in the arena representing their own kind. Hearing this, Spartacus' expectations grew. There'd be some pride to be had fighting as he had in real life.

"Ah. The latro," drawled Phortis. He smiled as Spartacus' face tightened. "This one's a Thracian too," he explained to the trainers. "Age?"

"Thirty."

"Occupation?"

"I've been a warrior since the age of sixteen. That's when I slew my first man," Spartacus growled. "He looked a bit like you."

"Ha! You're a real killer, eh?" Phortis' eyebrows rose mockingly. "You have some military experience too?"

"I've fought in every campaigning season since I reached manhood. In eight of those, I served with the Roman auxiliaries as a cavalryman. I've been in more fights and skirmishes than I can remember, and at least six full-scale battles."

"Killed many men?" asked one of the trainers.

Spartacus stared him in the eyes. "I lost count after twenty. At least half of them were Romans."

The trainer grunted noncommittally.

"I don't believe you," challenged Phortis.

"It's true. How many have you killed?" retorted Spartacus. He was pleased as Phortis waved a fist in his face. Nor did he miss the smile that twitched across two of the trainers' lips. *Good. I got under your skin, you miserable goat-fucker.*

"I've slain plenty, damn your insolence! Harder men than you too."

Really? I doubt it.

"He'll do best as a Thracian. I'll take him," said a short trainer with a well-trimmed beard. His companions murmured in agreement.

"No, you fucking well won't," snapped Phortis. "He's not to fight as a Thracian."

"Why not?"

"Because Batiatus says so," replied Phortis with smug satisfaction. "The dog is too arrogant. It'll give him ideas above his station. The same applies to his two friends."

"I'll take him on then. The others too," said the third trainer, who had the look of a Gaul.

Phortis shrugged. "Fine."

Hearing no further protest, the trainer jerked his head at Spartacus, Getas and Seuthes. "Get over here."

Spartacus couldn't help himself. "But——"

In the blink of an eye, Phortis had pulled the short club from his belt. With an almighty heave, he brought it down across Spartacus' head. "Do as you're told!"

Half-blinded by pain, Spartacus still managed to leap forward. He was prevented from getting to Phortis, however, by Getas and Seuthes. They grabbed him roughly by the arms. "Leave it," hissed Getas. "He'll kill you."

Phortis watched expectantly.

Attacking him just gives the dog what he wants. Spartacus took in a deep breath and relaxed in their grip. "All right. I'll fight as a Gaul."

"You listen to your friends. That's good." Phortis couldn't quite hide his disappointment, however. "Keep doing that, and you might survive." He glanced at the trainers. "I'll leave you to it. I'm sure you've plenty to teach these whoresons."

Amarantus, Spartacus' instructor, was a Gaul of perhaps forty summers. Although a freeborn warrior, Amarantus told them how he'd elected to stay on as a trainer after earning his rudis. His first order was for the four men he'd chosen to take each other on with heavy shields and wooden swords. He set Spartacus against one of the Scythians, and Getas and Seuthes upon each other. "Fight until one man has been disarmed, or received a 'mortal' wound," he shouted. Spartacus' opponent was strong and fierce, but his skill did not compare. Within the space of a hundred heartbeats, Spartacus had knocked the Scythian's sword from his hand and touched the tip of his own blade to the other's throat. Amarantus nodded in satisfaction, and allowed them to rest as Spartacus' two friends went at it like men possessed. Seuthes prevailed, tripping Getas and "finishing" him with a thrust to the chest.

"That's told me how good, or not, you are with weapons," Amarantus declared. "Now we shall see if you're any way fit, or just the bloated wineskins you look like." He waved his arm around the courtyard's perimeter. "Twenty laps of that, at a run. The man who stops before that gets ten lashes. If he stops a second time, I'll give him twenty. A third time, thirty. Clear?"

As Spartacus ran, he studied the gladiators who were also at their training. The yard was packed with men running as they were, or boxing and wrestling. Others lifted weights. Still more sparred against one another with wooden spears and swords, or attacked thick timber posts buried in the ground. One unfortunate was being lashed by his irate trainer, while his companions watched.

Spartacus was grateful that the journey from Thrace had not taken too much out of him. Although the food hadn't been the best quality, he'd lost little weight or condition. Twenty laps was well within his capability, and that of Getas and Seuthes too. As it turned out, the

Scythian was fit as well. Amarantus gave a satisfied grunt as they rejoined him, their faces dripping with sweat.

†

Carbo had reached his insula without further problems. He'd had a fleeting sensation of sweet revenge when his tread on the creaking floorboards had woken the crone. It had soon vanished during the coughing that followed, but Carbo had been too tired, and his head had hurt too much, to curse his neighbor. Uncaring of the layer of semi-liquid filth that coated his hair, back and legs, he'd eased on to his mattress and pulled up the ragged blanket. A few heartbeats later, he'd fallen asleep. Mercifully, he had had no dreams.

Waking to the chill of another gray dawn, Carbo had lain with a throbbing headache, wondering if becoming a gladiator was the wisest choice. He'd wrestled with the option for an age, worried that he would not be tough enough for the brutal world of the ludus. But Carbo could think of no other path to follow. Eventually, the bad smell coating every part of him had prompted him into action. At the public baths two streets over, he'd managed to cadge the entrance price from a kindly old man. Carbo had never enjoyed washing himself so much, or felt so grateful that he had grown up with the luxury of running water in his house. Once he was clean, the problem of his soiled tunic and undergarment—*licium*—became far more pressing. Wearing the drying cloth furnished by the baths attendant, Carbo had ventured on to the street, where he washed his clothes in the public fountain that sat alongside the bathing house. Donning his soaking wet garments, he had glowered at the passersby's laughter. Next, he'd gone to Ambrosius' door where he had returned the lamp and gladius to the same slave who had helped save him the previous night. Refusing the invitation to go in and meet the veteran, Carbo had headed straight for the city's ludus, which lay outside the walls to the north.

Now that he'd reached its gates, his courage was threatening to desert him. Carbo stood mutely, staring at the thick metal strips that criss-crossed the timber doors, and the tall ramparts above. The ludus looked, and felt, like a prison. From within, he could hear shouts and the dull clash of weapons. It was quite daunting.

"What do you want?"

Carbo focused on the guard, a swarthy man carrying a spear and shield. A battered helmet concealed much of his face, making the demand even more intimidating. "I've come to offer my services as an auctoratus."

"You? An auctoratus?" The three words conveyed endless contempt.

Carbo held his stare. "Yes."

"Can you use a sword or spear?"

"A sword, yes."

"Is that right?" sneered the guard.

"Yes, it damn well is, you cheeky bastard," snapped Carbo. For all his failures, he was far above this creature on the social ladder. "I demand to see the lanista."

The guard blinked at his determination. "What do I care if you want to get yourself killed?" He rapped on the timbers with his knuckles. "Open up!"

With a loud creaking noise, one of the gates began to open.

Carbo's stomach twisted, but he stood his ground. *Stay with me, Jupiter, Greatest and Best.*

VI

With a loud creaking sound, the ludus' main gate opened. This was enough to attract most gladiators' attention. The trainers, Amarantus among them, were not immune either. A guard came stumping in, followed by a tall figure in a once-fine tunic. The moment that they were both inside, the gate swung shut with a heavy clang.

"Someone looking for fighters?" wondered Getas.

"No," answered Spartacus. "He's only a boy. He can't be more than eighteen."

"Look at the way he carries himself. He must be from a good family."

"His clothes are soaking wet," noted Spartacus. "That's odd."

The young man was led upstairs to Batiatus' quarters. Rival theories about his reason for visiting the ludus rippled through the assembled gladiators.

"Back to work," cried Amarantus. "Get a move on, you lazy scumbags. We haven't got all day."

"Attention!" Phortis' voice cracked through the air like a whiplash.

Spartacus looked up to see the Capuan on the balcony beside the man who'd been escorted upstairs. The youth was sallow-skinned, with a thin, pockmarked face.

"This young gentleman goes by the name of Carbo," announced Phortis. "He has asked Batiatus if he can enter the ludus as an auctoratus."

"He looks as if he's still on his mother's tit!" bellowed a fighter.

"The prick's far too scrawny," cried another. "He'd snap in two if you hit him hard enough.

A rumble of amusement rose from the yard, and Carbo flushed with anger.

"Why is he here? Has he screwed his father's mistress?" asked Crixus.

A murmur of interest replaced the gladiator's laughter. It was rare, but not unheard of, for a citizen to join their number as a paid contractee. Some joined for the thrill of it, the taste of danger that they might never experience otherwise. Most, however, entered the ludus under a cloud. Sometimes it was because they had broken the law in some way, but often it was the likes of gambling debts that drove them through the gate.

Above them, Phortis smirked. "It wasn't that. Or so he says. I didn't like to ask further."

"What was it then?" cried Crixus. "Lost all your money on chariot racing?"

Carbo's temper flared. "It's none of your damn business."

"A sensitive issue, is it?" retorted Crixus, glowering back.

"Piss off," Carbo replied.

"Come down here and say that again," yelled Crixus. Given Carbo's request to enter the ludus, the huge difference in their status meant little, and he knew it.

Carbo cursed silently. *Why couldn't I have kept my mouth shut? I've just angered someone as big as Hercules. Even if by some miracle I win, he'll want to kill me.*

"Before Batiatus agrees, he wishes to have Carbo's ability with weapons judged," said Phortis loudly. "I need a volunteer to spar a round or two with him." He smiled at the animal sound of interest that met his words. "With wooden swords. I know what you lot are like. Otherwise, Carbo would spend his first month here in the infirmary. Who's interested?"

At least half the men in the yard stepped forward with raised hands. Spartacus regarded them with faint amusement. Thrashing a nobleman, especially a damp, beaten-down one, was the last thing on his mind. To most, however, the prospect was clearly appealing, even if it was only with a blunt-edged practice weapon.

Phortis looked down in silence, studying the fighters.

Crixus was busy hissing at every Gaul within earshot. "Stand back! Lower your hands! This is my fight." With sullen glances, some of his countrymen obeyed. Wary of antagonizing him, a number of other gladiators did the same. Plenty ignored Crixus, however.

"It seems that some want to fight you more than others," said Phortis, casting a sardonic glance at Carbo.

"Fine," snapped Carbo. "I don't care." And he genuinely didn't. He had run out of ideas, bar one: to pass the entrance test here.

"In that case," said Phortis, his tone silky smooth, "you won't mind if . . ." His gaze fell on Crixus, before moving on. He pointed to Spartacus. ". . . a fellow newcomer, as yet untested in the arena, has the honor of welcoming you to the ludus?"

Carbo eyed the Thracian. Despite Phortis' deprecating comments, he was compactly built, and looked expert at handling himself. His guts churned. "Let's get it over with," he said, trying to sound confident.

Spartacus could sense Crixus' rage from twenty paces away. Anger surged through his own veins. Phortis had done this deliberately, not to see Carbo beaten, but to set the Gaul against him—as if he wasn't already, after what had happened the previous night. He set his jaw. There was nothing to be done about it for now. "Where do I go?"

"Follow me," directed Amarantus. He headed for the roped-off square in the center of the courtyard. Already fighters were standing three and four deep around it. Spartacus and his comrades followed. So did the Scythian. They shoved their way through the throng, right up to the waist-high ropes that formed the area's perimeter.

"In you go," said Amarantus, lifting the rope.

As Spartacus entered the square, he felt a tickling thrill of anticipation. A fight was still a fight.

"Who'll back Carbo?" shouted a voice. "The boy looks unremarkable, but he wouldn't have walked in here if he couldn't handle himself."

Glancing around, Spartacus recognized Restio, who had seen him kill the Gaul. *So he's a betmaker too.*

"What odds?" asked a German.

"Twenty to one against."

"That's well worth a gamble." The German's grin was feral. "Put me down for five denarii."

A clamor of voices rained down, placing even larger wagers on the newcomer. Restio's business was only interrupted by the arrival of Phortis and Carbo in the square. The Capuan had two practice swords under one arm. Ordering Carbo to shed his tunic and sandals, he made the pair stand ten paces apart.

Spartacus stared hard at Carbo, who surprisingly held his gaze.

The onlookers were eyeing the Roman's well-muscled chest and upper arms. "Sure you should have given me such long odds?" asked the German.

"Compared to Spartacus, he looks like a plucked chicken," retorted Restio with aplomb. "Just wait and see."

Next, Phortis tossed each man a weapon: to Spartacus, a gladius, and to Carbo, a sica. Spartacus gripped his blade like a lover, and wishing that he'd been given the other sword. Unused to the wooden sica's weight, Carbo hefted his to and fro. *A damn shame that I didn't have more lessons from Paccius.*

"Helmets and shields!" Phortis bellowed.

There was a short delay before two slaves appeared. One carried a scutum, while the other bore a small, square shield and a distinctive Phrygian helmet. The first headed for Spartacus, and the other to Carbo. They handed over the items and scurried to safety.

Phortis looked up at the balcony, where Batiatus was now waiting. An expectant hush fell over the courtyard.

"The bout will last until one man is either disarmed or acknowledges defeat," said the lanista. "Begin!"

Phortis scrambled out of the way, and Spartacus moved forward at a trot.

By now, Ariadne had heard what was going on. Using a bench to stand on, she peered out of the cell window. Let it be over quickly, she prayed. Keep Spartacus from harm.

Carbo had the sense not to meet Spartacus' overwhelming attack head on. With nimble footwork, he dodged to one side. Instantly, the air filled with jeers. Spartacus spun around and went after him with deadly speed. He caught up within six strides. Clattering his shield off the other's, he thrust his gladius straight at Carbo's face. The Roman's head jerked frantically to one side, and the wooden sword's tip skittered off the side of his helmet.

Carbo's lightning-fast response caught everyone off guard, Spartacus most of all. Even as Carbo reeled backward, he thrust around the side of his shield, driving the point of his weapon into Spartacus' bare midriff. The Thracian doubled over with pain. He had the wits to pull close his shield and shuffle backward but even so, Carbo was on him like a dog on a rat. He rained down a flurry of blows, aiming for Spartacus' head. *Maybe I can win this!*

"No!" whispered Ariadne in horror. It was easy to imagine that the bout was real.

A few men began cheering for Carbo. "What odds will you give me on the Roman now?" demanded a Samnite.

Restio recovered his betmaker's poise fast. "The rookie's wasting his time. Everyone knows that Thracians' skulls are incredibly thick. Spartacus probably doesn't even know that Carbo's hitting him." He smiled as the men around him roared with laughter.

Spartacus heard none of the exchange. He was concentrating on recovering the breath that had been driven from his lungs by Carbo's first blow. The moment that the young Roman's attack slowed, he'd strike like a snake. Fast and lethal. End this charade for once and for all.

Realizing that his assault was having little effect, Carbo swung his right arm down. Trying to repeat his earlier success, he made a desperate thrust at Spartacus' abdomen. This time, however, the Thracian was ready for him. With a powerful sideswipe of his shield, he smashed Carbo's blade up and out of the way. In the same instant, Spartacus launched a massive swing at the other's head. His gladius connected with a loud, metallic clang, and Carbo staggered away, his vision blurred, and with a huge dent in his bronze helmet.

Take that, you bastard, thought Spartacus.

Many of the gladiators cheered loudly. Ariadne joined in.

Carbo adjusted his helmet and shook his shoulders. *What in Hades should I do now?* There was no possible way that he could beat Spartacus. *But I can still impress Batiatus.*

"Game over," announced Restio with satisfaction. "Why bother with swordsmanship when brute force will do?"

Spartacus sauntered toward his opponent. "Ready to surrender?"

Carbo raised his sword and shield determinedly. "No," he said, his voice muffled by his helmet. *Jupiter, help me.*

"Don't be stupid," growled Spartacus in a low voice.

"Piss off." Carbo didn't back away either, nor did he drop his weapon. Instead, he slid his bare feet across the sand, moving toward Spartacus with just as much intent as he'd shown earlier. He wasn't aware quite how dangerous the Thracian was, however.

Powering forward, Spartacus swept away Carbo's thrust as easily as he'd have swatted a fly. Dropping his right shoulder, he smashed his shield into the other's, sending Carbo sprawling to the ground. Spartacus stooped and shoved the point of his sword right under the lower edge of Carbo's helmet. "Yield!"

Carbo shook his head. *Batiatus has to see that I'm no coward.*

"What's he doing?" hissed Restio. "Does the fool want to die?"

Spartacus suspected his reason for not giving in. *His pride won't let him. Sometimes, death is preferable to dishonor.* "Yield!" he repeated.

Again Carbo shook his head in refusal.

"Finish the stupid bastard!" roared Crixus.

"*Iugula! Iugula!*" shouted many of the gladiators. "Kill him!"

Spartacus glanced up at the balcony. There was no longer any sign of Batiatus. Phortis merely shrugged. He didn't care whether Carbo lived or died.

The roar of "*Iugula*" swelled until the very walls of the ludus rang with it.

Spartacus glanced around the square, and saw the fighters' bloodlust. He felt it himself. The decision was down to him. His strength and the proximity of the strike meant that even with a wooden sword, Carbo ran a real risk of dying. He hardened his heart. *Is that my fault?* The fool had had two chances, and refused both. If he didn't follow through now, the other gladiators would see him as weak. *He's only a fucking Roman after all.* With a snarl, Spartacus pulled back his right arm.

Suddenly, Carbo realized that he might have pushed things too far. He clenched his teeth in bitter acceptance.

"No," whispered Ariadne. "You can't kill an unarmed man."

"*Iugula! Iugula!*"

Closing his left eye, Spartacus took aim at the small hollow at the base of Carbo's throat. If he drove the wooden sword in hard enough there, it *would* kill the Roman. *So be it.*

"Hold!" bellowed Batiatus through the shouting.

Spartacus barely heard. He just managed to check himself. Confused, he squinted up at the lanista.

"What do you think you're doing?"

"He won't give in," replied Spartacus. "And Phortis didn't say not to."

Batiatus rounded on the Capuan. "Idiot! I step away from the balcony for a moment, and this is what happens? Why didn't you end the fight? Carbo fought well enough for a *tiro*. He might be inexperienced, but he's no good to me as a damn corpse. Eh?"

"No, sir," muttered Phortis. He shot a vengeful look at Spartacus.

"Step away from him," ordered Batiatus.

Spartacus did as he was told.

Ariadne felt a wave of relief. The Roman would live. She glanced at Spartacus again, feeling awe, and a little fear. *Gods, but he is a tough bastard.*

Slowly, the Roman sat up. *Thank you, Jupiter.*

"I didn't expect you to fight so well, Carbo. But your inexperience was also obvious. You have a lot to learn," said the lanista. "The first thing should be that if you go into a fight looking to die, you'll probably succeed." He smiled at the guffaws this produced.

Carbo nodded wearily. With an effort, he took off his helmet.

"Return tomorrow. You'll be paid your joining fee, and you can start training at once. My lawyer will have drawn up the contract by then." Batiatus turned and was gone.

"The entertainment is over. Back to your training!" Phortis shouted. He threw another venomous stare at Spartacus, but the Thracian ignored him.

Carbo's voice broke into his reverie. "You were going to kill me."

"Of course I was, idiot. What do you expect me to do when you wouldn't give in—try to talk you out of it?"

Carbo flushed. "No." *There's no mercy in this world.*

"You were foolish not to yield when I knocked you over," said Spartacus harshly, feeling a trace of remorse. *He's only a boy.*

"I see that now. I was trying to . . ." Carbo hesitated.

"You want to die? There's no need to come here. Why not fling yourself in front of a chariot at the races? Or off a bridge into a damn river?"

"It's not that. I wanted to prove to Batiatus that I was brave enough," muttered Carbo.

"Eh?" Spartacus barked. "Well, you did that. You showed real ability too."

Carbo blinked in surprise. "Ability?" he repeated.

"That's what I said. Why not put it to some use?"

Carbo met Spartacus' unwavering gaze, and saw that he was not joking. His chin lifted. "All right. I will."

"Good." The Roman had humility as well as courage, thought Spartacus. Despite the fact that Crixus' and Phortis' animosity toward him had deepened, he was glad now that he hadn't killed Carbo. "Keep your mouth shut. Listen to your trainer. Watch men like Crixus, the big Gaul. Learn how they fight. If you can do that, you *might* still be alive in six months' time. That's all any of us in here can expect."

"Thank you."

Spartacus stalked back to where Getas and Seuthes were standing with Amarantus. From the corner of his eye, he was aware of other gladiators giving him approving nods. *Excellent.* In being prepared to kill Carbo, he'd done the right thing.

Unaware of the politics, Carbo looked around for Phortis. He needed to ask if he could stay immediately. There was little point returning to his garret, where his rent would run out again in a week. He could use some of his joining fee to pay it, but it would be a waste. His bed and board here came with his contract. It would be tough here, however. Already there were lascivious glances coming his way from a few fighters. Carbo squared his shoulders. *Screw them. I'll make a go of it.*

Ariadne also noticed the favorable looks being thrown at Spartacus. She was surprised by the sudden pride that filled her. Her husband was making a name for himself. No doubt that had been his primary motive in being prepared to kill Carbo, she reflected. She knew enough of Spartacus now to know that he was not a cold-blooded killer. His new status would make life in the ludus safer for her too. Then Ariadne saw Phortis leering at her, and her fears resurged.

Safer from the gladiators, at least.

†

Over the following few days, two other gladiators picked quarrels with Spartacus. He'd gone for the kill in both fights, battering one of the men, a Nubian, until he was unconscious, and the other, a blocky German, until he'd begged for mercy. After that, it was as if Spartacus had passed some kind of test. The fighters began to give him a wide berth. Soon after, he was approached by a number of Thracians. They came offering their allegiance. Their approach was most welcome. Spartacus had realized that survival and status in the ludus was all about being a member of a group. The oddments of the ludus, a disparate group of nationalities, were the only ones who were leaderless. Under Oenomaus, the Germans were well organized into one bloc. The Samnites were loyal to the charismatic but dangerous Gavius. Even the quarrelsome Gauls had Crixus, Castus and Gannicus. Three factions rather than one, but both were a damn sight stronger than the ten or more bunches of Thracians that had gradually evolved.

Spartacus was therefore content to accept the warriors' fealty. The knowledge that they regarded him as their leader gave him a warm feeling in his belly, like the times he'd recruited war bands in Thrace. It was only a start, but a start nonetheless. Certainly it felt better than just waiting to be killed in the arena. While word had got out that Ariadne was a priestess, making men look at her with more reverence than they had, it didn't mean that she was safe. His increased number of followers meant that he could ensure she was watched over far more closely. It also meant that Crixus, who was still clearly spoiling for a fight, kept his distance. Spartacus knew that this was putting off the inevitable, but when the time came to take on the huge Gaul, he wanted it to be on his terms. "More often than not, the general who chooses the battlefield wins the fight," his father had often said. To this end, Spartacus drove himself to new lengths with his training, continuing to run around the courtyard and lift weights long after Amarantus had finished with him for the day. While Getas and Seuthes moaned bitterly, they too stuck to his regime.

One evening, Spartacus was actually glad to call an end to his exercise. Thanks to the dark, threatening clouds filling the sky, it was growing dark earlier than normal. A bitter autumn wind was whipping down into the yard, penetrating his tunic with ease. The sweat that coated his body was being cooled even as it formed. Spartacus didn't want to catch a chill for the sake of a few extra laps. "Let's call it a day," he said.

"Thank the Rider," said Getas, purple-faced. "I thought you'd never say that."

"To the baths?" asked Seuthes.

"Where else?" Spartacus led the way.

As they neared the doors to the bathing area, he saw Carbo skulking in the shadows under the walkway. The young Roman was living in the ludus, but Spartacus hadn't seen where. A quick glance told him that Carbo wasn't faring well. He had a black eye, a cut to his lower lip, and his tunic had been ripped off his right shoulder. The flesh underneath was badly bruised. *Poor bastard.*

"Come here."

Carbo looked around in surprise. "Me?"

"Yes."

Carbo limped out into the yard, in obvious pain. "What is it?" He rubbed at the dark rings under his eyes with one hand. The other stayed inside his tunic.

"Not getting much sleep? It's tough here, eh?"

"I'm not complaining," Carbo replied curtly.

"I know you're not. The fact is, though, that you're being picked on by men who are bigger and tougher than you."

Carbo's eyes glittered, and he revealed the hand that had been residing in his tunic. In his fingers, he gripped a length of iron. "The next whoreson who comes near me will get this stuck in his chest."

"You'll get yourself killed, boy." Spartacus stepped closer. "Why don't you throw your lot in with me?"

Distrust twisted Carbo's scarred features. "Why would you ask me that?"

"Because we need good fighters." *Leave the boy his pride.* Spartacus grinned wryly and lifted his tunic to reveal the mark left by Carbo's sword. "And you're definitely one of those."

Carbo felt his worries ease a fraction. This hard man had some respect for him after all. "I'd be pleased to join you."

"Good. Come into the baths, get yourself cleaned up. You can bunk in with Getas and Seuthes for the moment." He saw Carbo's suspicion. "Neither of them will touch you. They're not like that."

A gusty sigh of relief left Carbo's lips. He'd been sleeping—more accurately, dozing—in Restio's cell. While the Iberian had not attempted any sexual assaults, as others had, Carbo didn't trust him at all. He wasn't sure of Spartacus either, but this was a better offer than he'd had from anyone else. "Thanks."

A tiny, secretive smile twitched across Spartacus' lips as they entered the baths. *Another one enters the fold.*

†

"Gods above, get off me!" Spartacus muttered. Waking abruptly, he sat bolt upright. Ripping off his thick woolen tunic, he threw it to the floor. He saw nothing. With an oath, he leaped across to the farthest corner of the cell, where he checked the wicker basket. It was securely closed. Spartacus mouthed another savage curse.

"What are you doing?"

He didn't answer.

Ariadne opened one eye, and then the other. *Gods, but he looks good naked.* "What is it?"

"Nothing. Go back to sleep," he muttered, returning to his mattress.

The tension in his voice alarmed her. "Spartacus?"

He wouldn't look at her.

"Was it a dream?"

The slightest of nods.

"A nightmare?" she asked intuitively.

"I suppose. It's probably nothing."

"Tell me. Maybe I can make some sense of it."

Silence.

Ariadne waited.

Finally, turning his head, Spartacus met her gaze.

"You're worried."

"Yes. It was awful."

Her eyebrows arched into a silent question.

"You won't leave it alone until you find out, will you?" he asked. "I'm starting to know what you're like."

"Is that so?" Ariadne's smile faded as she glanced at the basket. "You dreamed of a serpent."

He gave her a startled look. "Yes."

"What was it doing?"

Spartacus' hands rose to his neck and lower jaw, encircling them. "The damn thing was coiled up here. It was looking me in the eyes!"

"And you thought that it was my snake?"

"Have you forgotten the other night?" he asked testily. "I only wish it had escaped this time as well." He made an obscene gesture at the basket.

"You hate the creature," said Ariadne calmly. "Why on earth would you want it wrapped around your throat?"

"Because then my dream wouldn't have meant a thing. Now . . . the whole thing feels like a bad omen. A message from the gods. Not one I'd welcome either." Spartacus made the sign against evil.

"What else can you remember?" Ariadne kept her voice calm, but inside her heart had begun to race. *This doesn't sound good.*

"Eh?" His gray eyes came back into focus. "I was in a desolate place, with little but rocks all around. It may have been the top of a mountain."

"Why do you say that?"

"I could see nothing but sky around me, and the air was thin, as it is at altitude."

"Was I with you? Or Getas and Seuthes?"

He frowned, concentrating. "No. I was alone."

"Anything else?"

There was a short pause. "I was carrying a sword."

"What type?"

The fingers of Spartacus' right hand clenched and opened again. "It was a sica."

"You're sure?" demanded Ariadne.

He nodded.

This vision can only have been sent by the gods. Ariadne rose from the mattress without a word. She drew on her robe. Moving to where her figurines of Dionysus sat, she knelt. Her lips began to move in silent entreaty. *I place myself at your command as always, O Great One. I ask you for an explanation of my husband's dream.* There was no immediate response, which did not surprise, or worry, Ariadne. She began to breathe deeply, preparing herself to go into the trance-like state that often aided her understanding of all things arcane.

Spartacus eyed her with a mixture of reverence and suspicion. She had placed their single oil light before two tiny carvings. Both depicted Dionysus. One showed him as a half-clad, beardless youth surrounded by ecstatic maenads, his women followers; they reached their hands up to him in offering. The second statuette was of two figures, the first a mature, bearded deity, clad in a long tunic and with a fawn skin cloaking his shoulders. Ivy wreathed his entire body. Dionysus' right hand gripped that of the other figure, a majestic, elderly man whose left hand bore a scepter. *Hades.*

Spartacus shivered. He'd have been happier without a representation of the god of the underworld in his living quarters. He could take the maenads presenting Dionysus with raw animal flesh to eat, but seeing Hades always made him feel uneasy. Yet he had to respect with Ariadne's ways. Her habits. It was part of who she was. As ever, Spartacus prayed not to Dionysus, but to his favorite deity, the Rider. Finishing his own request, Spartacus watched her in respectful silence.

Time dragged by.

Spartacus knew better than to interrupt Ariadne. He fell deep into thought, worrying about what the dream might mean. In the background, he was vaguely aware of Phortis unlocking the door and throwing in his usual taunts. Eventually—Spartacus was not sure how long—he felt Ariadne's eyes upon him. "Did you see aught that might explain what I saw?"

She shook her head sorrowfully. *I can't think of anything positive to say either.*

"I see." The horror Spartacus had experienced as the snake coiled around his neck surged back. A moment before, his belly had been grumbling. Now it felt like a pool of burning acid. *So I will end my days here, as a plaything for the Romans.* Sighing, he shrugged on his undergarment, tunic and over them, a densely woven brown cloak. "Coming?" he asked without looking at her.

"Spartacus."

He dragged his eyes up to Ariadne's.

"Try not to worry. It might be revealed later." *Great Dionysus, do not fail me. I beg you.*

"Or it might not," he retorted sourly. "I could be killed at any time."

She recoiled as if stung. *Do not let his dream be about that. His life cannot be nearly over yet. Can it?*

"I'm sorry," said Spartacus, feeling instant remorse. There was no need to remind her of the dangers he faced.

"So am I." He moved toward Ariadne, but as ever, was stopped by her raised hand. "Leave me. I must try to reach the god a second time."

"So soon?" Spartacus protested. "Is it not too exhausting?"

"I'll be the judge of that." Her retort was far sterner than Ariadne had meant it to be, but she needed it to retain control. *I have to discover something positive to lift his spirits.*

Spartacus bowed his head, hiding his concern. Leave her to it. I am not her master. Think of the hours ahead, he thought. Convincing himself that his bad dream would be forgotten by sunset, Spartacus headed for the door. Like every day since his capture, this was just another one to be endured.

Ariadne's expression, however, remained troubled long after he had shut it behind him.

†

Spartacus hadn't forgotten the snake by the day's end, but he'd managed not to dwell on it too much. Amarantus had largely been responsible for that, running him and the three others ragged. The Gaul had stopped treating them as rookies. Instead, he concentrated on increasing their fitness to even higher levels. By the time the sun sank in the sky, Amarantus had finished with exercise. He had begun talking about gladiatorial tricks, things mostly alien to a soldier. "When you're about to fight, get to the weapons rack first. The best blades go fast. Once in the arena, keep the sun at your back so that it doesn't blind you. Ignore any insults that are thrown at you from the crowd, but acknowledge any praise or encouragements. Try to get the spectators to support you. Make flashy moves during your bout if you can. Lightly wounding your opponent goes down a treat."

It rankled Spartacus to hear this, but he listened closely. Amarantus hadn't got to where he was by being stupid.

Getas was much unhappier, though. "Why should I try to entertain the whoresons?" he demanded. "They'll have come to watch me fight and die, nothing less."

Amarantus' smile was world-weary. "Remember that your survival might depend not just on the goodwill of the *editor*," he warned. "The men who organize these things are always out to please the audience. If you've pissed *them* off, and then you're unlucky enough to lose, don't be disappointed when they call for you to die. *Iugula!*" Miming the gesture that meant death to the defeated gladiator, he jabbed a rigid thumb at his throat. Spartacus blinked, imagining the pain of a snake striking him there. "Whereas if they like you, they'll do the opposite." Pulling up the corner of his tunic, Amarantus waved it at the balcony, as if to catch Batiatus' attention. "*Mitte!* Let him go!"

"Bastard Romans," muttered Getas, glowering.

"Listen or not, it's your choice," said Amarantus with a shrug.

"That's how life is now. If you want to survive, pay attention," Spartacus whispered. "Think how stupid it would be to die because you refused to take in one piece of advice. It'd be like not thinking out your tactics before fighting a battle."

Getas gave him a tight, angry nod.

Amarantus' lesson came to an end soon after, and he dismissed them. Other trainers were doing the same. All over the yard, men were tugging off their sweat-drenched helmets, drinking from water skins and doing stretches to loosen their weary muscles. Idle banter, boasts and fabricated stories filled the air. A mobile food vendor who'd been allowed in worked his way around the gladiators, hawking spiced sausages, roasted cuts of meat and small, round loaves of fresh bread. Already there was a queue for the baths. It was the quietest time of the day, when Phortis was either absent or closeted with Batiatus, talking business. Even the guards were more relaxed, talking in twos and threes on the balcony.

During this period, another group of Thracians approached Spartacus. He and his companions immediately prepared for a fight. Instead of wanting to quarrel, however, the warriors asked to join with him. Pleased, Spartacus accepted. Now he could call on nearly thirty men. It wasn't nearly as many fighters as Oenomaus commanded, but it was approaching the size of the other factions in the ludus. Spartacus glanced around the yard, catching several other gladiators glowering at him, clearly unhappy that his position had grown stronger. Crixus in particular looked most unhappy. *I can't let down my guard even a fraction*, Spartacus thought. *Despite his newfound followers, it wouldn't be that hard to kill him.*

Irritated that his good mood had not lasted, Spartacus headed for his cell. Ariadne's guarded expression jumped out at him as he entered. "I've tried all day. I could see nothing," she said softly. "I'm sorry." Blinking away images of the snake around his neck, Spartacus nodded.

"Thank you for trying." *Stay with me, Great Rider.*

†

One afternoon, after training had finished, Carbo headed for the quarters he shared with Getas and Seuthes. The exercises that day had been particularly savage, and he wanted nothing more than to lie down for a while. The two Thracians were busy talking to Spartacus, but Carbo wasn't worried about entering the cell. Every fighter in the ludus now knew which faction he was in, and they left him alone. To pick a fight with him meant taking on every man who followed Spartacus. He was immensely grateful for this security, without which he would surely have already been raped several times. Wiping the sweat from his brow, he flopped down on the straw padding that was his bed. Previously, Carbo would have scorned such scratchy bedding, but now it felt like the height of luxury. He closed his eyes, and soon dozed off.

Some time later, a sound woke him. He jerked upright, reaching for the piece of iron that served as his self-defense weapon. Instead of anyone threatening, however, he saw a young female slave clutching a bucket in the doorway. Her free hand rose to her mouth. "S-sorry. I was coming in to take out the slops. I didn't know there was anyone here." Ducking her head, she made to leave.

"Wait."

She glanced around at him shyly. Surprise filled Carbo that she did not react to his scarred appearance. He studied her features with great interest. "Are you Greek?"

She nodded.

It was usual for Greek women to wear their hair up. This girl didn't. Instead, her long black tresses fell around her face to her shoulders, concealing her from the world. She was very striking, possessing a delicately boned, round face. Her fearful brown eyes regarded him from under slightly arched eyebrows. Her typical Greek nose was not too straight, and he thought he could spot a dimple in her left cheek. Carbo's groin throbbed as his gaze dropped lower, taking in the swell of her breasts beneath the coarse fabric of her dress. "I haven't seen you before. Have you been here long?"

"No. Only two days."

"That must be why I haven't noticed you."

Her eyes rose to his. "I know who you are."

"Eh?"

"You're Carbo, the auctoratus. One of Spartacus' men."

"How do you know that?"

There was a careless shrug. "Everybody knows you."

Carbo's pride soared. He found her immensely attractive. "What's your name?"

"Chloris."

"Your Latin is good," he said awkwardly.

"Yes. I had a private tutor..." She hesitated, then added, "...before."

"Before you were enslaved?"

"Yes. My father was a wealthy merchant in Athens. After my mother died, he began taking me on his voyages to buy goods." She smiled ruefully. "He took me on one too many."

"Pirates?"

Chloris' face twisted. "Yes. Father was killed in the initial attack and I was taken prisoner. Sold in Delphi to a Roman slave trader, who took me to Capua, where Phortis bought me."

Carbo shook his head at life's randomness. "In another life, we might have met socially, when you visited Italy."

"Chloris!"

She started at the summons. "I'd better go."

"Who's calling you?"

"Amatokos. He's one of the Thracians."

"I know who he is." *One of Spartacus' best warriors.* "Is he your..."

"Yes. I need someone to protect me in here."

Carbo scowled as she left the cell. He'd lost all desire to rest.

VII

The nightmare became part of Spartacus' life, recurring every week or so. For all that he did his best not to dwell on it, he was unable to dismiss it from his mind entirely. Frustration gnawed at him over its possible meanings, but he didn't ask Ariadne about it again. He had come to the conclusion that it probably meant his death in the arena. Frustrated by his powerlessness to change that fate, he did his best to bury his concerns. Ariadne knew that Spartacus was still having the dream—he woke her up every time with his thrashing about. Things were complicated by the fact that he'd taken her reassuring touch one night for more than it was, and come on to her. Ariadne had leaped away from him as if he'd poured a pot of scalding water over her. Spartacus' instant apology had produced nothing but a muttered curse. It had taken days for her frigid disapproval to thaw. He hadn't tried it on with her again. His memories of rape from his time with the legions were too dark, too savage. Ariadne would consent to sex, or it wouldn't happen at all. And yet the yoke of his unfulfilled lust was less troubling than his dream of the snake. Spartacus was damned if he would do anything about it again, however. If Ariadne came up with some explanation about it, she could approach him. Angered that both avenues seemed to be dead ends, Spartacus got on with his existence, such as it was. He trained hard. Bound his followers to him. Existed.

The flavor of his reality over the subsequent few months was unvarying. Nightmares. Training. Recruiting men to his cause. Fights. Pressed by Phortis, Amarantus began entering him into single combats in the local arena. He won his first bouts with ease, and the Gaul responded by putting him in against more skilled opponents, often from the *ludi* in Rome. Spartacus beat them too, learning with each to gain the crowd's approval from the first moment he walked on to the circle of sand, the gladiator's world. With each victory, his following within the ludus increased. His status was also augmented by Ariadne's efforts. She had begun accepting offerings to Dionysus and making requests of the god on behalf of a good number of the school's inmates.

Spartacus' successes made it inevitable that he would eventually be forced into a contest to the death. His opponent was a strapping German who belonged to another lanista. The fight had been hard, but Spartacus had prevailed. Phortis' hope that he died in the arena had been firmly set aside by Batiatus, who was delighted by his new fighter's success, and the amount of money he'd won as a result. The sea change in Spartacus' situation was made evident by the size of the purse he was thrown afterward, and by Batiatus' approving looks. Instead of feeling pleased, he felt increased resentment toward the lanista. *I'm no prize bull, to be paraded whenever you choose.* His anger was fueled to new heights by his abiding memory of the whole episode, which was not burying his blade in his opponent's throat, but the bloodthirsty roar of the crowd that had followed. While he knew intimately the adrenaline thrill of killing a man, and a primitive part of him took pleasure in the sensation, Spartacus loathed the way random people could pay to watch him commit the act and enjoy that feeling vicariously. Let the whoresons come down on to the sand and do it for themselves, he had thought savagely. I'll wager that few could actually shove a sword into another's flesh the way that I can. His eyes had drifted to the guards. The way that I could kill every one of you.

From that moment, Spartacus' troubling vision of the snake had been interspersed with a regular dream about freedom. For all that it seemed impossible, the idea would not go away.

†

Carbo's life, had definitely improved. He had won his first two fights, and with them, small sums of money, which he carefully salted away. These steps encouraged him hugely. If the gods kept him safe from injury or death, he would save until he had a decent amount of cash to send to his father. Sometimes he dreamed of gaining retribution on Crassus. It was pure fantasy, but enjoyable nonetheless. Carbo found dealing with his attraction to Chloris more troubling. He couldn't stop himself eyeing her up at every opportunity, and resenting Amatokos, her strapping lover. Yet it was common policy for the female slaves in the ludus to pair off with a gladiator. Without a guardian, they fell prey to every fighter who felt like sex. Unsurprisingly, Batiatus cared not a jot about such violations. If the women became pregnant, nine months later he would have either a boy child who could be reared as a gladiator, or a girl who could be sold in the slave market when she was old enough. Knowing this did not ease Carbo's frustration. He'd tried talking to Chloris, but Amatokos kept a close eye on her, and he'd been lucky to avoid a beating from the Thracian on one occasion.

Carbo wasn't sure, but there was something about the way that Chloris slyly returned his stares that told him not to give up all hope. While Amatokos was around, however, nothing much would happen. The warrior was tough, fast, and had won more than half a dozen fights in the arena, including one mortal bout. All Carbo could do in answer to that was to apply himself mercilessly to his training, and pray to the gods. Despite his frustrations, he found the martial life rewarding—more so, he was sure, than he'd have found training to be a lawyer. If he couldn't be a soldier, then he'd be a gladiator. And a damn good one.

†

Late one night, a messenger came to see Batiatus. Albinus, one of the most senior politicians in Capua, was playing host to no less than Marcus Licinius Crassus, a praetor who was reportedly the richest man in Rome. Apparently, Crassus had expressed an interest in visiting Batiatus' ludus. Keen to impress, Albinus had offered the lanista a huge sum of money to stage a special fight in the school during Crassus' visit. The gossip went that it was to be a combat to the death. Naturally, both gladiators were to be picked from within their number. The next morning, every part of the yard was filled with huddles of anxious, muttering fighters. The same question fell from everyone's lips. Who would the two men be?

Batiatus, Phortis and the senior trainers strolled through the yard as the gladiators ate their breakfast. Most men picked morosely at their porridge, while they cast furtive glances at the group. Spartacus, refusing to be intimidated, made it his business to eat every last scrap in his bowl, while conducting a loud conversation with Getas, Seuthes and Carbo. In between the casual glances he was taking over his shoulder, Spartacus eyed the young Roman sidelong. Under his protection, Carbo's zest for life had returned. He was becoming a skilled fighter. He seemed to be loyal too. *How strange to have a Roman following me.*

"Do you really think Crassus is coming here?" asked Carbo.

"Sounds like it," replied Spartacus.

Carbo swore. "I'd love to have a few moments alone with him."

"What do you care about the prick? Have you met him?"

"No." Quickly, Carbo told his story.

"I'm not surprised you'd want to give him a good seeing-to." Spartacus thought of Kotys. *What I'd do to you, you whoreson . . .*

Carbo sighed. "Not that I'll ever get a chance for revenge."

"You won't," Spartacus growled. *And nor shall I.* "Get used to it."

Catching the sharp tone in the Thracian's voice, Carbo fell silent. *I'd still love to thrash Crassus within a whisker of his life.*

Phortis began to call out names. He did not pick any rookies,

Spartacus noted. This clash had to impress, and therefore experienced gladiators would fit the bill better. It wasn't long before the Capuan had picked out five men—two Germans, a pair of Thracians and a Gaul. Spartacus also saw that the most successful fighters, individuals such as Oenomaus and Crixus, had not been selected. Batiatus wanted to put on a good show, but he wasn't going to lose one of his best gladiators. Do I qualify as one of those yet? Spartacus wondered. He had nowhere near the stature of someone like Crixus, who had more than thirty victories to his name.

Those chosen stood miserably near Batiatus and Phortis.

"Are these sufficient, master?"

Batiatus rubbed his jaw. "No. I want one more."

Spartacus tensed. He could feel Phortis' eyes boring into the side of his head.

"Spartacus!"

He locked eyes with Getas, and then Seuthes. Both their mouths opened and closed, like fishes out of water. Carbo also looked stricken.

"Spartacus! Get out here!"

He strode out to stand with the five other fighters. He looked at none of them.

Batiatus approached, Phortis at his right shoulder, and the trainers a few steps behind.

"Tell me about each one."

The trainers filled the lanista in. Phortis threw in a comment here and there. The rest of the fighters watched from their benches, Crixus prominent among them.

"This one won't fight well. He's not confident enough," said Batiatus, dismissing the Gaul.

Looking relieved, the man hurried back to the safety of his comrades.

Two others were also allowed to go, leaving a strapping German, a black-haired Thracian and Spartacus, the last candidate. The tension raised several notches, and the three gave one another wary looks. The muscles in Spartacus' jaw bunched. The man was a tough proposition.

Spartacus had seen him training, and heard about his last fight, when he'd defeated a far more experienced Gaul from another ludus.

Batiatus paced up and down, studying the trio. "Give me their details again," he ordered.

The trainers obeyed.

Spartacus stared rigidly in front of him. Is this what my dream is about? he wondered. Breathe. Keep breathing.

"One Gaul, but two Thracians," mused Batiatus. "Why am I not surprised by that?"

Phortis chuckled. "Because they're quarrelsome whoresons, master?"

"Probably," replied Batiatus with a smile. He stared at the black-haired warrior. "Should I pick you?"

"No, master," muttered the Thracian in heavily accented Latin. "I . . . new recruit. Not good enough . . . fighter."

"That's not what I've heard," said Batiatus, turning to one of the trainers, who gave a vigorous nod. "Apparently, you're one of the best *tirones* that we've had in years. Plus I hear that your tribe is on poor terms with the Maedi, his people." He jerked his head at Spartacus. "I think that you'd make an excellent candidate for this fight." The Thracian said nothing, and Batiatus smirked. "Cat got your tongue?"

There was still no reply, and Batiatus glanced at Spartacus. "What about you? Should you take part?"

"No," replied Spartacus firmly.

"Why not?"

"Because it would be a complete waste of my abilities, master."

Batiatus' eyebrows rose. "How so?"

"If I kill the other man quickly—and there's a very good likelihood of that—you'll have lost in either of these an excellent gladiator. If by some small chance, however, I am slain, you will never have the opportunity to see what kind of fighter I can be."

"Proud words. Confident words," Batiatus proclaimed. "Yet how can you expect me to believe that you can defeat either of these two men? They're both courageous, skilled fighters."

"What you believe is up to you, master," Spartacus answered, steely-eyed. "But in my previous fights for the ludus, I've barely even been tested." Behind Batiatus, he caught Phortis scoffing. Spartacus stared at him with complete hatred. *Gods willing, I'll nail you one day, you bastard.*

Batiatus heard the Capuan's snigger. "What's so funny?"

"The dog's lying, master! He's a capable enough gladiator, but nowhere near Crixus' class, for example."

"How can you be sure?"

"Because of the way he fights," Phortis exclaimed. "He's won all his bouts, but not in a champion's manner."

"It's easy to be economical. I've just done what it took to get by," said Spartacus truthfully. He gave the Capuan a scornful glance. *Why would I bother stretching myself for a miserable cocksucker like you?*

The veins in Phortis' neck bulged. "You fucking—"

"Enough," said Batiatus. His gaze grew calculating. "He could be lying, but then again he might not be. Why be surprised that a man in his situation only did the bare minimum? It's probably what a lot of them do."

Phortis lapsed into a spluttering silence, giving Spartacus the briefest twinge of satisfaction. The feeling vanished when Batiatus looked from him to the Gaul to the black-haired Thracian—and back again. Spartacus didn't drop his gaze. Despite the gods' apparent capriciousness, he would face his fate like a man. At the same time, it was hard not to feel that this was what his dream about the snake had portended.

Batiatus walked to stand in front of the German, who, perhaps unsurprisingly, wouldn't meet his gaze. That was enough for the lanista. "Piss off," he barked. "Coward." As the German obeyed, Batiatus' attention shot back to the black-haired Thracian. "You'll do," he pronounced. "In fact, I think you will be a worthy adversary for Spartacus."

The man nodded jerkily.

Spartacus waited to be dismissed. *Just because the snake was around my neck doesn't mean that I couldn't kill it,* he told himself. *Yes, I would need the Rider's help, but it wouldn't be impossible.*

"Go on, then! Get yourself ready," snarled Phortis at the black-haired Thracian. "The fight starts at midday."

As the warrior sloped away, Batiatus' cold eyes returned to Sparta-cus. "If you survive this bout, you had best impress me from now on. If I'm not happy, I'll set up a fight with Crixus. To the death. I don't give a damn about how much money you've made me so far. Understood?"

"Yes." Somehow, Spartacus knew that the mocking laugh he could hear was that of Crixus.

"Insolent arse wipe! Yes, *master*," growled Phortis.

Spartacus gritted his teeth. "Yes, master."

"Good. Now piss off, before you test Batiatus' goodwill even more."

His goodwill? thought Spartacus sourly. He kept his mouth shut, however. Backchat could earn him a flogging, and that was the last thing he needed. He'd have to be in top form to defeat the black-haired war-rior.

†

Shortly before Albinus was to arrive with his prestigious guest, the fighters were forced to return to their quarters. While it didn't come as a surprise to Carbo—why give nearly two hundred dangerous men access to nobility?—the order infuriated him. Once he was in his cell, there was no possible way he could harm Crassus. The gladiators were also angered by the move, but Phortis had been expecting their re-sponse. Deploying all the guards, armed with bows, he ordered every-one into their quarters. The more reluctant individuals were encouraged with strokes of his whip. A torrent of abuse rained down on the Capuan as he locked door after door. Objects—coins, cups and oil lamps—were hurled from the cell windows. The insults and missile-throwing made no difference. Within a quarter of an hour, the court-yard had been emptied.

The semicircular seating area that filled one end of the yard now looked immense. It could comfortably hold five hundred people. Be-ing the only people to occupy it would reinforce the extravagance of Albinus' gesture to his guest, thought Carbo. Batiatus knew how to throw a grand spectacle. Yet Capua's arena was even more impressive. The huge circular edifice was constructed from great slabs of stone, decorated with statues of the gods and towered over the neighboring residential buildings. Carbo didn't know how many citizens packed in to see the gladiator contests, but it must be several thousand. During the frequent visits he'd made there, Carbo had never imagined that one day he would actually fight on the circle of sand within. But that day was fast approaching. His training was nearly over. Carbo was looking forward to it. His time as a wet-behind-the-ears tiro was nearly over.

Soon Spartacus and the black-haired Thracian appeared. Carbo studied them both closely. Nervously. Spartacus had only a single greave against the other's two, but that was of little consequence, for his mail shirt and scutum offered a great deal more protection than his opponent's helmet, *manica* and small, square shield. The pair threw each other wary glances while their trainers muttered in their ears. Phortis stood in the background, observing. There was no sign of Batiatus. He wouldn't emerge until the important visitors arrived.

Carbo's stomach twisted with tension. Since Spartacus had taken him under his wing, he'd spent plenty of time watching him train. He was good. Damn good. But so was the other Thracian. Carbo felt guilty that his concern stemmed only partly from his regard for Spartacus. If the black-haired warrior proved victorious, Carbo stood every chance of losing the protection he'd enjoyed in the previous few months. If that happened, life would become just as dangerous as it was in the arena. Carbo had no desire to return to the life he'd endured during the dark days after he'd first entered the ludus. Spartacus had to win.

†

Batiatus appeared the moment that Albinus and his party arrived. He was dressed in his best toga, his hair pomaded. His profuse, unctuous welcome turned Spartacus' stomach. He studied Albinus, a self-satisfied, stout man with a pompous air, and his guest, Crassus, who was as broad-shouldered as his host was fat. A faintly supercilious expression was fixed on Crassus' handsome face. He took his seat in the center of the front row—the most prestigious place—with poor grace, complaining about the hard stone. Batiatus apologized and hissed a command at Phortis, who returned a moment later with a plump cushion. This seemed to mollify Crassus somewhat. With pursed lips, he sat down. Albinus, looking worried, took a place beside him. He was joined by Batiatus, while the rest of the party—low-ranking officials and bodyguards—went to sit on the top row of seats.

Carbo couldn't stop staring at Crassus. *He looks just as arrogant as I thought he would. Prick.*

Spartacus was also eyeing him. *The son of a whore looks as if he hasn't had a shit in a week.* He pulled his gaze away before the politician noticed. *Don't lose focus. Stay calm.* Spartacus recalled how the icy look had melted from Ariadne's face when she'd heard he'd been picked for this fight. He remembered what she'd said. Hung on to it. "This is *not* what your dream is about. It *can't* be."

Not being an organized *munus*, there was none of the usual pomp of the public spectacle. No group of trumpeters to march around the arena, playing for all they were worth. No slave-carried platforms with painted statues of the gods being honored that day. No procession of the prizes on offer to the victors: palm branches and leather purses full of cash borne aloft on silver platters. When Spartacus and his opponent made their way, fully armed, to stand before Batiatus and the others, a solitary trumpet sounded.

In Carbo's mind, this made the contest more ordinary, but far more chilling.

It was now that Batiatus came into his own. He waxed lyrical, describing the black-haired Thracian in glowing terms. He paid particular attention to his victories thus far. At a sign from Phortis, the Thracian raised his arms and turned a circle, so that Albinus and Crassus could admire his muscular physique. The lanista did the same for Spartacus.

The gladiators whistled and cheered for both men at the tops of their voices. The noise mingled in an ear-shredding crescendo that filled the ludus.

Watching from their cell, Ariadne's breath caught in her chest. Despite herself, she admired Spartacus' body, but this was the last situation she'd have chosen to see it exhibited. *Would you prefer him in your bed then?* She shoved away the disquieting thought.

With the preliminaries over, Phortis moved out on to the sand. He would act as the *summa rudis*, the referee for the bout. He ordered the two fighters to stand fifteen paces apart before looking to Batiatus. The lanista nodded and Phortis signaled to the trumpeter. A short series of notes rang out, and the Capuan stepped out of the way.

Spartacus didn't barrel forward as he had in his fight against Carbo. Instead, he shuffled toward the warrior, his bare feet silent upon the sand. Moving with the grace of a dancer, his opponent did the same. Spartacus wasn't prepared at all for the warrior's speed and skill. When he was no more than half a dozen steps away, he suddenly broke into a sprint. Darting forward like a wolf closing in on a deer, he thrust his sica straight at Spartacus' face. Spartacus had no time to raise his scutum. Desperately, he wrenched his head to the side. The warrior's blade whistled past, missing his left cheek by a whisker length.

Spartacus roared with anger, but his opponent was already gone, using his momentum to deftly spin off, out of harm's way. The movement brought the warrior around behind him. Spartacus turned to meet the next attack, another wicked stab at his face, which he managed to parry with his scutum. His riposte, a lunge that would have spitted the warrior through and through, met only thin air. Panting, they separated from each other.

Crassus leaned over and whispered in Albinus's ear. When he'd finished, the portly politician gave Batiatus a pleased nod. "An impressive start."

"Thank you, sir," gushed the lanista.

Out on the sand, and oblivious to their audience, Spartacus and the warrior circled warily around each other.

Without warning, Spartacus launched a savage attack on his opponent. Using a one-two technique of punching forward with his shield boss followed by a brutal thrust of his gladius, he drove the

BEN KANE

warrior backward across the arena. His opponent had no option but
to retreat. No one could stand against such an overwhelming assault.
Spartacus' tactic worked. Before long, one of the warrior's feet slipped,
and he stumbled backward, falling on his backside.

Spartacus yelled in triumph. Drawing back his gladius, he prepared to run the defenseless warrior through. He gave no thought to
Batiatus or Crassus, and whether they wanted him to kill the other so
fast. He'd gone into battle mode, when all that mattered was finishing
one's opponent as quickly as possible.

But the fight wasn't over.

In desperation, the warrior raised his left arm. Swinging his shield
around like a discus, he smashed its metal-rimmed edge into Spartacus' right knee.

The impact made Spartacus stagger. Roaring in pain, he dropped
the point of his sword, giving his opponent a chance. The warrior
rolled away and scrambled to his feet, swiftly launching a counterattack of his own, a relentless flurry of slashes aimed at Spartacus'
unprotected face. It was all Spartacus could do to lift his scutum and
deflect the other's blows. And then the warrior changed his tactic. Spinning with the grace of a maenad in ecstatic frenzy, he swung around to
Spartacus' rear again. With consummate skill, he brought his sica
down in a flashing arc, across the back of Spartacus' shield arm. Blood
sprayed into the air. Spartacus' answering bellow was a combination
of shock, pain and rage.

Albinus and Crassus called out in appreciation.

"*Iugula! Iugula!*" shouted many of the gladiators.

Ariadne closed her eyes, but the bloodthirsty cry still echoed in her
ears. Steeling herself, she stared out at the arena again. *Dionysus, do not
give up on him.*

Gods above, it can't end like this, Carbo thought, offering up desperate prayers.

A feral smile twisted the black-haired warrior's face as he closed in
again. Spartacus snarled back, letting him know that he was far from
finished. His opponent began a new attack, probing forward with his

sica as a child might poke a stick at a crab. He met Spartacus' weakened ripostes easily with his shield.

Clever bastard, thought Spartacus. He's seeing how much strength I have left in my bad arm. Twisting it so he could see, he assessed the long, shallow wound. It didn't look to have severed any muscles or tendons, but he was already struggling against the weight of his scutum.

Even as Spartacus looked up, the warrior's blade hissed in. He jerked away, but still received a nasty cut on his right cheek. An involuntary hiss of pain left his lips. *Rider, help me! I could easily lose this.*

The warrior clearly thought so too. A little smile flickered across his lips. All he had to do was stay out of reach, and keep chipping away.

Spartacus cursed silently. His opponent was shrewd. Thanks to the wound on his arm, wearing him down wouldn't take long. But he wasn't finished yet. Not with his life at stake. Not with Ariadne to look after.

Letting out a shrieking war cry, Spartacus threw himself forward. With supreme effort, he kept his scutum high. Over and over he thrust his gladius at the warrior, who desperately defended himself with his small shield. It was a risky plan, but Spartacus didn't have long before his strength really began to fail.

As his sword struck the warrior's shield for the seventh or eighth time, the blade drove through the leather covering. It splintered the wood beneath to emerge on the other side. The warrior goggled, amazed that he hadn't been gutted. He fell back a step, and Spartacus saw a golden opportunity. Ripping his weapon free, he shoved it into the other's shield again. And again. Within a few heartbeats, it had cracked apart, and the warrior was forced to discard it. Looking scared now, he retreated further.

Spartacus had to pause to catch his breath. The pain from his arm was coming in waves, lancing up into his shoulder and beyond. He was no longer able to keep his scutum high enough to protect his throat. Nonetheless, he couldn't let up his assault. Clenching his jaw, he went at the warrior like a wild beast. His gladius' thrusts were so savage that his opponent had no chance to strike at his neck. It took every scrap of skill that the warrior possessed just to avoid Spartacus' long iron blade.

Fortunately, the warrior's good fortune ran out before Spartacus' own strength failed. His sword sliced into the side of the black-haired fighter's belly, through the taut muscles there, to emerge red-tipped on the other side. There was a wet, soughing sound as Spartacus ripped the gladius free, and the warrior shrieked with the agony of it. With blood pouring from his wound, he staggered away, his sica dangling from his slack fingers. When Spartacus followed, there was little resistance. Two massive overhand blows, and the warrior had dropped his weapon. Spartacus plowed on, pushing the other away from the curved sword, and any chance of redemption.

The warrior was unarmed now, and the manica on his right arm was his only defense. Of the two, his wound was far more serious. He was therefore desperate to retrieve his sica. Spartacus met every attempt with unbridled fury, however, and with each moment that passed, the warrior grew weaker. Spartacus didn't delay. Toying with an opponent might please some, but it was not in his nature. The fight had gone on long enough. He needed to get his arm seen to. It was time to end it.

Shoving his shield boss at the other's chest, Spartacus stabbed him in the left thigh. As the blade slid free, the moaning warrior collapsed to the sand. He made no attempt to get up.

A loud roar rose from most of the cells as the gladiators showed their approval.

Ariadne closed her eyes, and sagged with relief against the bars of the window.

Thank all the gods, thought Carbo.

Looking down at his opponent, defenseless and bleeding, Spartacus felt cold to the marrow of his bones. The warrior was one of his own, and he was about to kill him—at the behest of those he hated. Romans. At this moment, this is the way it has to be, he told himself fiercely. He glanced at Batiatus, who turned with a questioning look to Albinus and Crassus. "Do you still wish this to be a mortal bout?"

"Have I said otherwise?" asked Crassus in an acid tone.

Batiatus colored. "No."

"Then the loser must die."

"It is as my revered guest says," said Albinus pompously. "It's also what I paid you a fortune for," he added in an undertone.

"Of course, sir." Batiatus swiftly regained his poise. "It would be my honor to ask Crassus if he wishes to make the gesture."

Crassus' tongue flickered over his lips, like that of a snake. "Very well." Looking at Spartacus, he jabbed the thumb of his right hand at his own throat. "*Iugula!*" he ordered.

At once the cry was repeated by the incarcerated gladiators. Feet hammered on the floor of the cells. Spoons clattered off the window bars. The din was incredible. Spartacus wasn't surprised that the ludus' inmates approved of his victory. Their bloodlust had been roused by the fight's intensity and now the black-haired warrior had to pay the price. As he would have if the situation had been reversed. "Get up," he ordered.

Groaning, the black-haired fighter managed to sit up. Fiddling with the knot, he undid his chinstrap and tugged off his helmet. It fell unnoticed to the ground. Another effort brought him on to his knees. Spartacus inclined his head in respect. "You fought well. It was a close contest. But the Rider chose to help me, not you."

"He did," replied the warrior, grunting with pain. He lifted his head up, exposing his throat. "Make it swift."

"I will," Spartacus promised. He looked up at the sky. "I offer this man's life to you, Great Rider."

Without delay, he took aim and thrust his gladius down into the hollow at the base of the warrior's neck. The man's eyes opened wide with shock as the sharp iron slid through his skin and the soft tissues beneath. An instant later, he was dead. Driven with immense force, the blade had sliced apart the major vessels around the base of his heart. With a smooth movement, Spartacus pulled out the gladius.

A thick, graceful arc of blood sprayed through the air as the warrior's corpse fell limply to one side. It pumped out for a short time, creating a large red stain around the motionless corpse.

Crassus began to clap slowly in appreciation. Batiatus, Phortis and the rest of those watching joined in. So did the gladiators, roaring and shouting their pleasure from their cell windows.

Unmoved for once by the ovation, Spartacus stared down at the body, and the scarlet coloring the sand. That could so easily have been me, he thought. And then the Roman bastards would have been applauding him, while I lay dead before them. Fuck them all.

Feeling the weight of someone's stare, he looked up.

"Come here!" Crassus beckoned.

His mere tone made Spartacus' knuckles whiten on the hilt of his gladius. "Me?"

"I'm hardly talking to him, am I?" Crassus indicated the dead warrior. He glanced at Albinus and Batiatus, who both tittered dutifully.

Arrogant bastard. Spartacus took a step forward.

Go on, thought Carbo. Kill the whoreson!

"Archers!" bellowed Phortis.

Spartacus froze. Without even turning his head, he could see four bows levelled at him from the balcony. There'd be at least another six to ten outside his range of vision. If Phortis said the word, they'd turn him into a practice target. The Capuan wanted him to keep walking, but Spartacus did not move. His had been a tiny act of rebellion, but it was over.

"Drop the sword!" ordered Phortis.

"What, this?" Spartacus raised the weapon. He was pleased to see Batiatus flinch slightly. Neither the Capuan nor Crassus reacted. He was surprised by the politician's calm.

"Just do it," snarled Phortis. "Unless you want to choke to death on a dozen barbed arrowheads!"

Spartacus opened his fingers and let the bloodied gladius fall to the sand. "Happy now?"

Phortis' nostrils pinched. He glanced at Batiatus, who jerked his head meaningfully. The Capuan swallowed his rage. "Approach!"

Spartacus obeyed.

"That's close enough!" shouted Phortis when he was ten steps away.

Gods damn them all! I'm being treated like a wild beast. Now Spartacus couldn't stop himself from glowering at Phortis, who smirked.

"You fight well," said Crassus. "For a savage."

"Savage?" retorted Spartacus.

"Y̵o̵u̵?̵"

"Where I come from, we do not force men to slay each other for the amusement of . . ." He laid special emphasis on the last words. ". . . important visitors."

Batiatus leaped up from his seat. "How dare you?" He waved his arm in furious summons. "Guards! I want this man tied to the palus and given fifty lashes."

"Stay your hand," said Crassus.

Shocked, Batiatus glanced at his guest. "Sir?"

"You heard what I said. Let it go. The slave has a point, after all."

With a confused look, Batiatus sat down again.

"While Thracians may not stage gladiator fights, they are nonetheless barbarians. They are called brigands even by other brigands," declared Crassus smugly. "I've heard how every five years, the Getai nobility pick one of their number to serve as messenger to the gods. He's sent on his way by tossing him in the air to land on his comrade's spears." As Batiatus and Albinus tutted in horror, Crassus smiled. "And the Triballi regard it as normal for sons to sacrifice their fathers to the gods. Scarcely the acts of civilized people, eh?"

Spartacus scowled.

"Am I not right?"

"You are," Spartacus admitted reluctantly.

"You're surprised by how much I know of your race."

He nodded.

"You are a proud man," observed Crassus.

Spartacus did not answer.

"It galls you to be a slave? A gladiator?"

"Yes." He'd said it before he could stop himself. "Of course it does." Spartacus threw Phortis a filthy stare. The Capuan's lip curled in response. "I shouldn't be here."

"That's what every man says," interjected Batiatus.

Albinus and Phortis laughed.

Whoresons, thought Spartacus.

Crassus smiled politely at the joke, but his attention remained on Spartacus. "How did it happen?"

Spartacus blinked in surprise that the other should ask. "I returned to my village after fighting with the legions—"

"You fought for Rome?"

"Yes. For eight years. Upon reaching home, I discovered that the rightful heir to the throne had been murdered by the man who now calls himself King of the Maedi. So had my father. I immediately made plans to overthrow the usurper, but I was betrayed."

"By whom?"

"A friend."

"It's no surprise that you are bitter. And what would you have done if you had achieved your aim?"

Spartacus hesitated, holding Crassus' gaze, and wondering if he should keep silent. But he was too angry to stop. "After putting Kotys and his henchmen to death, I would have made plans to lead my tribe against Rome again."

Crassus arched an eyebrow. "And what would have been your aim?"

"To drive the legions off our lands. Forever."

"Forever?"

"Yes."

"You must know little of Rome and its history," said Crassus with an amused look. "Even if you had succeeded, our armies would have returned in vengeance. They always do."

"You have led legionaries into war?" demanded Spartacus.

For the first time, Crassus' self-assurance faltered. "Not abroad."

"Where then?"

"Against my own people, in a civil war."

It's no surprise you did that, thought Carbo savagely. You have no mercy.

"And I thought that I was the savage?" asked Spartacus.

"This is too much," protested Batiatus.

"Be silent! I am still talking to this . . ." Crassus hesitated. ". . . gladiator." He added in a hiss, "At least he doesn't see the need to lick my arse."

Batiatus flushed and looked away. Beside him, Albinus harrumphed in quiet indignation.

Encouraged by this tiny victory, Spartacus quickly continued, "I would have unified the tribes. What would Rome have made of that?" He was pleased by the trace of fear in Albinus' and Batiatus' eyes. Phortis bristled, but did not dare speak while Crassus, his better, held the floor. A man who showed no apprehension at Spartacus' words at all. *No career soldier then, but he's not short of courage. I wonder if he could lead an army, as I could.*

"You risk much by revealing this. A single word from me, and you'll be a dead man," said Crassus, ignoring Batiatus' alarm.

Spartacus cursed himself silently for having let his anger speak first. He looked down at the sand. *Great Rider, I ask for your help once more.*

"I won't give the order, however." Crassus inclined his head at the lanista, who beamed in gratitude. "Why? Because there's more chance of the heavens falling than you leading an army against Rome. Look at you! Reduced to fighting for our amusement." He smiled maliciously. "You're little more than a performing animal, damned to perform the same primitive dance whenever we demand it."

Spartacus dropped his gaze even lower, as if in subservience. Inside, however, he was incandescent with rage. "That's all I am, yes," he said. *Or so you think. Give me half a chance, and I'd show you different.*

Crassus turned away, satisfied. "After all that bloodshed, I feel the need for some wine." At once Batiatus jumped in, promising fine vintages in the humble luxury of his quarters. "Good." Crassus added in an undertone, "If you have other fighters of similar quality, we can do business. I'll want that Thracian, but I will need at least twenty more for my upcoming munus."

Spartacus' ears pricked, but Phortis had noticed him. "Piss off. Get that wound seen to."

The last he heard was Batiatus asking, "All mortal bouts?" and Crassus barking in reply, "Naturally. I need to impress."

From his cell, Carbo hawked and spat in Crassus' direction. *Great Jupiter, bring me face to face with him one day, please.*

Spartacus shuffled off toward the infirmary. His mind was racing. Crassus' contempt had driven home further than ever before the triviality of his existence. If he was soon to be forced into another fight to the death, what was the point in carving out a following and a position of respect among the gladiators in the ludus? He was nothing but a child's toy. A Roman plaything.

A seething fury took hold of him. Spartacus recognized and welcomed the volcanic emotion. It was how he'd felt when he was riding to war with the Maedi against Rome, a lifetime ago. How he'd felt when plotting to overthrow Kotys. This time, he only had thirty or so men who'd follow him, but that no longer mattered.

He saw the snake wrapped around his neck, but shoved the disturbing image away.

Something had to be done.

Somehow he had to be free.

VIII

As soon as the cell doors had been unlocked, Ariadne hurried in search of Spartacus. Like faithful shadows, Getas and Seuthes followed her. They were as concerned as she. Ariadne found her husband in the sick bay, which was positioned beside the mortuary. She tried not to dwell on the significance of that proximity. *He won. He's alive.* How long will his luck hold out, though? she wondered in the next heartbeat. What if his dream means that his death is imminent?

Ariadne managed to pull a smile on to her face as she entered the whitewashed room, which was furnished with several cots and an operating table covered in old bloodstains. Shelves lined one wall, stacked with a frightening variety of probes, hooks, spatulas and scalpels. Dark blue bottles of medicine stood in careful rows alongside the metal instruments.

The surgeon, a stoop-shouldered Greek of indeterminate age, was crouched over Spartacus, obscuring the view of the door. "Hold still," he ordered, pouring the contents of a little vial over the cut. *"Acetum,"* he said with satisfaction as Spartacus hissed with pain. "It stings like a dozen wasps."

"More like twenty, I'd say," replied Spartacus sarcastically.

"It's excellent at preventing gangrene and blood poisoning, though," said the surgeon. "So the pain is well worth it."

"The pain is nothing," snapped Spartacus. "How bad is the wound?"

Ariadne stopped herself from calling out. A pulse hammered at the base of her throat. Dionysus, stay with him, she pleaded.

"Let me see." Picking a probe from the tray beside him, the surgeon began to examine the gash. He poked and prodded, and Ariadne saw Spartacus' free hand clenching into a fist. Her heart bled for him, but she said nothing. She was too worried.

"It's not deep," pronounced the surgeon a moment later. "The blade sliced through the skin and the subcutaneous tissue, but the muscle below hasn't been damaged. You're lucky. I'll place a line of metal clamps along the wound. It should be healed within two weeks. You'll be able to fight again in a month."

"Wonderful," said Spartacus dryly. "Batiatus *will* be pleased."

The surgeon reached over to the nearest shelf and in doing so, noticed Ariadne. "Ah! You have a visitor."

Ariadne hurried forward. Close up, the blood from the shallow cut on his cheek looked horrifying. Without even realizing, she reached out to touch his face. "You're all right?"

He smiled. "I will be, yes."

They stared at each other, and then Spartacus reached up to enclose her hand in his.

Ariadne bit her lip, but she didn't move. She could feel a strange but pleasant warmth in the pit of her stomach. He was going to be fine. *Thank you, Dionysus.*

The surgeon came fussing in with a bowl of metal staples and the magic vanished, like a feather carried away on the wind. "There'll be plenty of time for that later. What he needs now is for that wound to be closed, before any foul airs get into it. Leave us in peace."

Spartacus' lips twitched. "You heard the man. I'll see you in our cell in a short while."

"Yes." Reluctant to let Spartacus out of her sight, Ariadne backed away. She lingered by the door until the surgeon gestured irritably at her to get out. Feeling happier than she had in an age, Ariadne walked toward the baths. This was a good time of the day to have a wash. The gladiators mostly washed in the evening, when their day's work was done. Getas and Seuthes would check that the area was empty, and then she could relax in peace. And think about Spartacus, she thought with a guilty stab of pleasure.

She smiled at the two Thracians as they disappeared inside. For once, life was very sweet.

"Going to clean yourself up and give him a victory fuck, are you?"

Ariadne turned in horror to find Phortis three steps away, with half a dozen guards at his back. Several were carrying lengths of rope. The Capuan clicked his fingers. "You know what to do." Grinning, the men shoved past, into the baths.

Too late, Ariadne cursed her decision not to carry her snake. She'd thought only to be gone from her cell for a few moments. "W-what are you doing?" Her eyes flickered around the yard, desperately looking for Carbo, or any of the Thracians allied to Spartacus. She couldn't see a single one.

Knowing what she was doing, Phortis moved fast. He stepped in close, and shoved his face into hers. His breath stank, and Ariadne recoiled. "Why, nothing. I just wanted us to have a little time together without your shitbag of a husband."

She tried to step away, but Phortis pinned her against the wall. One hand immediately dropped to her groin. Letting out a sigh of lust, he cupped her crotch with his palm. "Sweet," he breathed into her ear. "Very sweet."

Ariadne sank her teeth into his neck.

With an animal squeal of pain, Phortis pulled free. Ariadne had a brief impression of the blood oozing from her teeth marks before he backhanded her across the cheek with all his might. Half stunned, she felt her knees give way beneath her, but then Phortis threw an arm around her shoulders and hauled her body inside the door, shoving it closed with his foot.

Through eyes that were barely able to focus, Ariadne saw Getas and Seuthes lying tied up side by side. Both their faces were cut and bruised from the attack that had rendered them helpless. The leering guards stood over them. This was all planned, she thought dully. With that, Phortis threw her to the floor. Ariadne's head cracked off the mosaic, and another sheet of pain slashed through her brain. She was barely conscious as the Capuan ripped off her clothes and pulled down his own undergarment. Old, terrible memories of her father were woken, however, when he knelt and she saw his throbbing erection spring free. "No!" Ariadne mumbled. "Please, no."

"That means you really want it, you whore," Phortis snarled. "You're all the same!"

"No," she said, pitching her voice as loudly she could. *Dionysus, help me!*

"Leave her alone, you bastard!" shouted Getas.

One of the guards kicked him in the belly, and Phortis delivered another mighty slap to Ariadne's face.

She slumped back on to the floor, unable to stop him from forcing her legs apart. He moved up to crouch over her, and she felt his stiffness pressing against her groin. "I've been waiting for this moment since I clapped eyes on you." With that, he leaned down to kiss her on the lips. Ariadne closed her eyes as the Capuan forced his tongue into her mouth. She tried with all her willpower to bite off the probing piece of flesh, but there was no power in her jaws. A heartbeat later, the magnitude of her ordeal was amplified a thousandfold when Phortis shoved his pelvis forward and tried to enter her.

Nausea and revulsion washed over Ariadne in a great tide—as it had so many times in her childhood. All at once, she felt an overwhelming need to vomit. She gagged; Phortis recoiled, and then she was sick all over her front. Little spatters of puke flew up to cover his face.

I wish you'd drown in it, you cocksucker.

Phortis used the arm of his tunic to wipe off the worst of the gobbets before leering down at her. "You dirty bitch! That's only whetted my appetite." With a deep grunt, he pushed himself inside her and began to thrust to and fro.

Ariadne gasped with the shock and pain of it. She wasn't surprised, when she looked up again, to see her father's face instead of Phortis'. She saw the same lust twisting his features. The same glitter in his cold, dead eyes. Heard the same animal noises of pleasure leaving his lips. "I hate you," she hissed. "I always did, and I always will."

"Huh?"

She blinked. Phortis had reappeared. "I call down a curse on your miserable head," she breathed. "May Dionysus' maenads stalk your every footstep. The moment that you stumble, they will swarm all over you, and rend your flesh to shreds. Nothing will be left of you but a grinning skull and a jumble of gnawed bones." Ariadne saw the fear mushroom in Phortis' eyes, felt him shrivel inside her, and somehow she dragged a manic laugh from the bottom of her lungs. "Call yourself a man? You're nothing but a limp-pricked pig!"

This time, it was Phortis' turn to recoil. Ariadne's reprieve lasted no more than a heartbeat, however. He drew back his right arm to strike her again. She closed her eyes, and steeled herself against the pain that would follow.

"Phortis!"

Ariadne felt the Capuan tense. His blow did not fall.

"Phortis, where are you, damn it? Crassus is about to leave. We still have much to discuss." Batiatus sounded irritated.

Phortis grabbed Ariadne's chin and forced her to look at him. "You're in luck, you whore. Next time, you won't be so fortunate. And don't think that there won't be a next time! I'll be watching you, from dawn till dusk. Spartacus and his pathetic rabble can't watch over you every moment of every day. A gag in your mouth will stop you from spewing your poison. If you should choke to death on your vomit while I fuck you, no one would be better pleased than I."

"Phortis!" yelled Batiatus.

"I'm coming, master!" Adjusting his clothing, the Capuan got to his feet. He glared at the guards. "Untie those two. Follow me out when you hear me move off with Batiatus." With a final, malevolent look at Ariadne, he was gone.

Overcome by her pain, her shame and her terror, Ariadne lapsed into the oblivion that had been threatening to overcome her.

✝

When Ariadne awoke, her head felt as if someone was pounding a pair of lump hammers off it. A thin, thready pulse beat off the back of her eyelids. She opened her eyes, and a wave of nausea swept through her. She retched, and at once someone—the surgeon?—rolled her on to her side, placing the cold lip of a vessel to her lips. "Let it out. Let it all out."

After a moment, it was clear that there was little left in Ariadne's stomach to come up. The bowl was taken away, and she was moved on to her back again. "Spartacus," she croaked.

"I'm here," he said gently.

Her eyes swiveled, finding him only a step away, right behind the surgeon. "Thank the gods," she whispered.

His smile was supposed to be reassuring, but the worry was etched clearly on his face as he turned to the Greek. "Well?"

"I couldn't feel any breaks in her skull, but it's far too early to say if there's been any lasting damage," muttered the surgeon. "She needs to stay in bed for at least a day and a night."

Lasting damage? thought Ariadne in amazement. There was a fuzzy edge to her vision, and her headache was excruciating, but she could feel her strength beginning to return. "How long was I unconscious?"

"Long enough. Phortis is an animal!" replied the surgeon savagely. He handed Spartacus a glass vial. "She must take a sip of this every hour. Call for me if there's any deterioration in her condition. I'll check on her later." He disappeared from view.

"Gods." Ariadne finally recognized the interior of their cell. "You carried me in here?"

"Yes, after Getas came screaming for me like a madman. He told me what had happened." Shame coated Spartacus' every feature, and he hung his head. "I'm sorry. I failed you. I should have been there."

"You were having your arm seen to," she chided. "How were you to know that Phortis would attack me then? Getas or Seuthes aren't to blame either." Panic seized her. "You haven't done something to them, have you?"

Spartacus' sheer fury twisted his good looks into something bestial. Something primeval. It was truly terrifying. "Not yet," he grated. "But they will pay, have no fear of that."

"No." Forcing away her weakness, Ariadne took his arm. "You must not. They were only following your orders, to check the baths before I went in. Phortis sent in six men to tie them up while he attacked me."

"So what?" he spat. "They should still have protected you."

"Getas and Seuthes are not gods, they're men. Just like you. They're also your most loyal followers. And they are your friends." Seeing him flinch, Ariadne gentled her voice. "Knowing they failed will make them both twice as determined not to make the same mistake again."

He nodded slowly. "They've sworn to die rather than let anything happen to you ever again."

"Forgive them then," she urged.

"I have to forgive myself for what happened." Spartacus let out a heavy sigh. "So I suppose I can give the fools a second chance." His brows lowered. "As for that bastard Phortis! He will die screaming for his mother. Soon."

"Good. I want to watch him suffer too. But—"

"I know." Regret replaced the fury. "There can be no quick revenge. He'll be waiting for that. Just like he'll be looking for another opportunity to—" Spartacus' jaw clenched. "Did he actually . . . ?" he asked without looking at her. "Getas and Seuthes couldn't see, but they heard . . ."

Emotion closed Ariadne's throat, but she wrenched it open. Spartacus deserved to know. "He did, briefly."

"The goat-fucking, yellow-livered, spineless son of a whore!" The veins in Spartacus' neck bulged dangerously. "I'll cut off his prick and feed it to him!"

"I'm alive. I'll recover," she murmured, forgetting for a moment her own pain. "It's not as if it hasn't happened to me before."

His jaw dropped. "Who? When? How?"

She couldn't look at him. "My father. All through my childhood. It only stopped when I went to train in Kabyle."

"I'm sorry," he said, stroking her hand. "I didn't know."

"No one does. You're the first person I've ever told." She managed a tiny glance at him before her shame dragged her eyes away again.

"What kind of monster was he?" Spartacus raised his right fist and clenched it until the flesh went white. "If the bastard was here, I'd make him pay!" His gaze flickered back to Ariadne. He took in some of the suffering in her eyes. "Let's not talk about him, or Phortis."

"No," she whispered. "Just hold my hand, please."

"Of course." He squeezed her fingers.

Reassured, she closed her eyes.

Spartacus watched over her as she slipped into a deep sleep. Alone with his thoughts again, he fantasized about killing Phortis and Ariadne's father. Despite his overwhelming desire for revenge, he knew that murdering the Capuan would prove far more difficult than it would have previously. He'd take great care from now on never to be without protection. Yet Spartacus was more concerned about Phortis making further attempts to rape Ariadne. He made a silent oath to the Rider. That couldn't happen. Wouldn't happen.

Even as he swore, Spartacus felt doubt gnawing away in his gut. Although many men were now loyal to him, he wasn't omnipotent. No matter how hard he tried to ensure that Ariadne was guarded, Spartacus couldn't guarantee that a week or a month or a year down the line, an opportunity wouldn't arise for the Capuan to strike. And strike he would. Getas had mentioned his threat to Ariadne.

It's not just me that's a piece of meat, to be observed fighting and dying, he realized with bitterness. Ariadne is one too. To abuse. To rape. To discard.

Rage consumed Spartacus again. He wanted to jump up and punch the wall, but Ariadne still had a grasp on his fingers. He looked down at her tenderly. I cannot let that fate befall her, he promised himself. I *will* not let it. Other than killing her, or jointly committing suicide, which were not options Spartacus would entertain, there was only one other avenue to take. The one that had come to him in the aftermath of his fight before Crassus.

I will escape this shithole, he decided. And I'll take Ariadne and every damn gladiator that will follow me! The Thracians who are sworn to me will definitely come, and with the Rider's blessing, more will too. Phortis will be the first to die before we leave. Batiatus too, if I can manage it. It's a pity that Crassus won't be here. I'd gut that bastard as well.

Finally, a smile traced its way across Spartacus' lips.

It was good to have a real plan at last.

In the same instant, an image of the snake wrapped around his throat flashed in Spartacus' mind. Suddenly, he felt very cold. Would he be slain in the escape? The frustration he'd been battling over Ariadne's failure to explain the dream's meaning flared up. The lapse in his resolve was momentary. He shoved out his chest. Death was a better end, and more appealing than waiting for Phortis to make his move. If it came, he would make it a warrior's death. Ariadne would fight too.

They would have an end fitting for any Thracian, man or woman.

†

Ariadne did not wake again fully until the next morning. Spartacus was immensely relieved that she seemed much better. Even the surgeon was satisfied with her improvement, agreeing to let her sit outside in the warm sunshine rather than stay in bed.

"I'm not going to hide away," asserted Ariadne. "I want that animal Phortis to see that he can't crush my spirit . . . or own my flesh."

"If you're sure," said Spartacus, impressed by her courage and determination.

"I am."

Gently, he helped her out of the door. Getas and Seuthes were already waiting. So was Carbo. They ushered Ariadne to a stool, and the Thracians stood on either side of her, bristling like a pair of guard dogs. Carbo smiled at her, trying not to think about how he'd feel if the same had happened to Chloris.

Spartacus gave his friends a questioning look.

"We will both die before anyone lays a hand on her," swore Getas.

"You'll also hear us bellowing your name," Seuthes muttered.

"No one will harm her," promised Carbo. "I swear it."

"Good," said Spartacus, satisfied. "And the other matter we discussed?" Now that he was about to act on his decision, he wanted a final reassurance.

Carbo hadn't ever thought of escaping the ludus—why would he, when things were going well? But if Spartacus was going to lead, he would have to follow. He was one of the Thracian's men now, for good or ill. If he didn't remain loyal, he'd never be able to hold his head up in pride again. Carbo hated to admit it, but there was also another reason. With Spartacus gone, he would again become easy prey to the predatory fighters who remained in the ludus. "We're all with you, and so are the others. Thirty-two of us."

"To the death," added Getas.

Spartacus' eyes glinted dangerously. *That's what I want to hear.* He wasn't totally sure of Carbo yet, but he didn't think that the young Roman was a snitch.

"What are you talking about?" asked Ariadne.

Spartacus squatted down by her side, and the others moved away so they could talk in private. In a whisper, he explained what he'd decided the night before. "I'm going to approach the other leaders today." He was pleased by her fierce nod of approval.

"We've got to do something," she agreed. "I will ask Dionysus to watch over you."

"Thank you." As Spartacus stood, he saw again the snake coiling itself around his neck. *I have to do this. Regardless of the cost.*

"What's wrong?"

"Nothing." He was surprised that she'd noticed.

Liar. "Who will you ask first?"

"Oenomaus," replied Spartacus instantly. "He has the most followers."

"If he throws in his lot with you, others will follow," she said, probing.

"That's my hope, yes."

"How will you persuade him?"

"I'll find a way."

Ariadne honed in on the slight uncertainty in his voice. She stared into his eyes long and hard. "Did you dream of the snake again?"

He nodded unwillingly. *She sees much.*

For the briefest instant, Ariadne considered lying, telling him that Dionysus had shown her an explanation for his vision. No, she decided. That might anger the god. Might make things worse than they already were. "And you think that this could mean your death?"

"Our deaths," he answered quietly.

Ariadne looked at him. The loud sounds of activity in the yard died away as the world closed in around them. Even Getas and Seuthes, who were only a few steps away, seemed less real.

"If things go wrong, I can't leave you behind for that fucking jackal. I, or one of us, will end it for you first."

She gripped his hand. "I wouldn't want it any other way. We will stay together—in life or death."

He smiled grimly. "So be it."

Ariadne watched as Spartacus walked off alone. She nodded a welcome as Getas, Seuthes and Carbo resumed their positions, but inside, doubts plagued her. After what had happened the previous day, it was all too easy to presume the worst possible outcome from his dream. *Dionysus, help him,* she prayed. *I have ever been your faithful servant. Do not forsake me or my husband now.*

†

Spartacus headed straight for Oenomaus, who was sitting at a table, eating with his men. The certainty he'd felt the night before was still there, but he had no idea if the German—or anyone else for that matter—would agree with him. He'd never spoken to Oenomaus, and his plan did border on the lunatic. *Great Rider, stay by my side. I ask you to guide my path.* Spartacus was a dozen steps from Oenomaus when a barrel-chested man with long hair and a bushy beard stood up and blocked his way. Several others moved to join him, their hands reaching into their tunics for hidden weapons. "Stop right there," growled the first man in poor Latin. "What do you want?"

Spartacus raised his hands in peaceful greeting. "Nothing much. Just a word with Oenomaus."

"Fuck off. He doesn't want to speak to you."

Spartacus peered around the other's bulk. "Oenomaus!"

The German turned his head. "Who called my name?"

"I did," answered Spartacus. He glanced at the bearded man blocking his way. "Your polite friend here says that you wouldn't want to talk to me."

"Polite? Him?" The corners of Oenomaus' lips lifted a fraction. "He's right, though. Why would I bother with the likes of you?"

"What I've got to say might interest you."

"You're the one who fought before Crassus?"

"Yes."

"Most men would have succumbed to the wound you took. You did well to win."

"Thank you."

Oenomaus indicated the bench across the table from him. "Take a seat." The men opposite hastily shuffled out of the way.

Stepping around the glowering German, Spartacus walked forward. He glanced around as he sat down, checking that none of the guards appeared interested. To his relief, none were even looking in their direction. Phortis was nowhere to be seen either. All the more reason to move fast.

"So, what do you want?" asked Oenomaus bluntly.

He's direct. That's good. Spartacus glanced at the fighters to either side. "What I've got to say is private."

"These are my most trusted men," growled Oenomaus. "Speak your piece or piss off."

"Fair enough." Spartacus leaned closer. "I'm going to escape from the ludus with my followers. I wondered if you wanted to join me."

Shock filled every face around him. Oenomaus was the first to recover. "Say that again."

Spartacus took a quick look around. Still no sign of Phortis. Calmly, he repeated himself.

"You don't know me or what I'm capable of. How can you be sure that I won't just turn around and tell Batiatus what you're planning?" demanded the German.

"I can't," replied Spartacus with a careless shrug. "But in my experience, a man who leads more than fifty others is not usually a rat."

Oenomaus looked pleased. "You're right about that. Go on."

Spartacus seized his chance. "There are two hundred of us in the ludus. Batiatus has, what, thirty, thirty-five guards?" He thumped one hand into the other, quietly, so that no one would see. "If enough of us took part, there is no way that they could stop us from seizing the armory."

Oenomaus' gaze flickered to the balcony above. "The guards are well armed. Many men would die before we laid our hands on the weapons."

"Probably," retorted Spartacus. "Isn't that better than dying in the arena to the roars of a Roman crowd?"

"Some would say not, especially if they have survived a year or two within these walls." Oenomaus' eyes were shrewd. "If their woman was under threat from Phortis, of course, they might feel differently."

"That's not the only reason I want to escape."

"No?"

"When I killed that warrior yesterday, I saw Batiatus' and Crassus' reactions. To them, I was no more than a circus act. Crassus said as much too."

"Do you not think I know that? We fight. Sometimes we are wounded. Sometimes we die. A little prize money comes our way from time to time. The best of us have a woman. It's not much different to being a warrior in a war band."

Have you no spine? Spartacus wanted to shout. He had the wits not to. That would be the surest way of turning the German against him. He pitched his voice low. Assertively. "By escaping, we would recover not only our independence and the right to determine our own fate, but our pride. Our pride!"

Oenomaus rubbed a finger along his lips, thinking.

Spartacus waited. He mustn't push too hard.

"It's risky. Very risky," pronounced Oenomaus a moment later. "Who else is with you?"

The stakes were too high to lie, thought Spartacus. "I came to you first."

"No one else has said 'yes' then?"

"I have thirty-one men who will follow me to their deaths."

"That's certainly what they will do if there are no more of you," replied Oenomaus acerbically.

"So you won't join me?"

"If you manage to persuade some others, we can talk again." Oenomaus made a gesture of dismissal.

Spartacus raised his eyes to the heavens. Is that it? he screamed silently.

The bearded brute who'd tried to stop him talking to Oenomaus was already at his back. "Time to go."

Furious, Spartacus stood. There was no point creating a scene. That would burn the foundations of any bridges he might have just built.

Oenomaus turned away to confer with one of his cronies.

"Come on," growled the bearded German. He laid a hand on Spartacus' arm.

"Don't touch me," hissed Spartacus. He was gratified when his order was actually obeyed.

He'd taken perhaps half a dozen steps when a finger of memory tickled his brain. Why hadn't he thought of it before? He spun around, alarming the bearded man. "Wait. I must speak with Oenomaus again."

"No fucking way. You had your chance." Ham-like fists reached out to grab Spartacus' tunic.

Spartacus ducked back, out of the way, and then darted forward to plant a fist in the other's solar plexus. He used all his strength. The bearded man's mouth opened in a great "O" of surprise as the air left his lungs, and he sank to his knees like a stunned ox.

There was instant uproar. Benches clattered to the ground. A dozen Germans jumped up. Weapons glinted as they were whipped out, and Spartacus knew he had the briefest instant to speak before they were buried in his flesh. "Oenomaus! I regret downing your man, but he wouldn't listen to me. There is something else."

To his surprise and relief, Oenomaus raised a hand. His glowering supporters held back. He raised an eyebrow. "This had better be good."

"It is," promised Spartacus. "As Crassus went upstairs yesterday, I heard him say that he needed twenty skilled fighters for a munus. He seemed keen to buy them from here."

"Nothing remarkable about that," snapped Oenomaus. His men took a step toward Spartacus and this time, he didn't stop them.

"They are all to fight in contests to the death." Again he had all of their attention. What Spartacus didn't say—didn't need to say—was that at least half of the men would be German.

"You're lying!"

Spartacus stared straight at Oenomaus. "I swear on the grave of my mother, and by Dionysus and the Great Rider, that I am not."

Oenomaus frowned.

Spartacus threw up another prayer, asking the gods for their help.

"Who would lead this enterprise?"

Another loaded question, thought Spartacus. Thank the Rider he'd come up with the answer beforehand. "No one man. Both of us will look after our own followers. The same will apply to Gavius and the Gauls' leaders, if they want to be part of it."

Oenomaus grunted. "Where would we go?"

"I don't know yet. But one of my men is the new auctoratus. He knows the area, and can give us some ideas." *That's it. I've done my best.*

There was a long pause.

Then Oenomaus leered. His expression was all teeth, like a wolf's.

"Count us in." He winked at those around him, and like a pack who have spotted an easier prey to take down, they growled in agreement.

Spartacus' heart leaped. He gave a tiny nod, as if he'd expected nothing else. "Good."

"Can you persuade the others to join too?"

He offered the German a confident smile. "Leave them to me."

"Keep me informed."

"I will. Not a word to anyone." Movement flickered at the edge of Spartacus' vision. A quick look told him it was Phortis. *Shit!* He framed the Capuan's name with his lips.

Oenomaus winked to show he'd understood.

Spartacus kicked the bearded German. "Tell this idiot to watch his step."

"Go fuck yourself," yelled Oenomaus.

Spartacus backed away slowly, as if wary of being attacked. The Germans showered him with insults as he went. When Spartacus looked again, Phortis was smirking at the apparent enmity between him and Oenomaus. *He's taken the bait. Good.*

†

Encouraged by his early success, Spartacus spent the rest of the day approaching other leaders in the ludus. When Gavius, the stocky fighter who led more than forty Samnites, heard of Oenomaus' involvement, he was quick to promise his support. So too were the majority of the Thracians. Spartacus had no such luck with Castus and Gannicus, who led two separate groups of Gauls. Neither seemed as if they'd inform on him, but the pair couldn't put aside their suspicion of the other factions, let alone of each other. He made no effort to talk to the remaining fighters. They were made up of too many nationalities. Spartacus didn't bother trying to win over Crixus either. The big man's glare followed him around the yard and told him his likely response.

Troubled by his failures, he took counsel with Getas and Seuthes. Carbo lingered in the background, feeling honored to be included.

"Maybe we should just forget about the Gauls," said Getas, scowling. "They're troublesome bastards at the best of times."

Seuthes chuckled. "He's not wrong there."

"Yes, but they're fearsome bloody fighters," added Spartacus. "Once we're on the outside, we'll be completely alone, with no friends. Every man's hand will be turned against us. Think of that." *If we succeed, where will we go?* He felt a thrill of hope. *I could go back to Thrace. Find Kotys.*

"It's true," said Getas gloomily.

"Fifty Gauls would make a huge difference to our capabilities," admitted Seuthes. "But you've already failed to persuade Castus and Gannicus, and Crixus is unapproachable. What else can we do?"

Spartacus frowned. "There has to be some way around this obstacle."

"Would they follow you if you beat them individually in combat?" asked Carbo suddenly.

"Eh?" Seuthes rounded on him. "You want Spartacus to take on three champion fighters, one after another? Why don't you do it instead, fool?"

Flushing, Carbo buttoned his lip.

"I think you're on to something."

Spartacus ignored Getas and Seuthes' shocked expressions, and Carbo's confused one. "Obviously, I don't want to fight all three of them. Even if I succeeded, I'd probably end up in the infirmary for a month. Neither Castus nor Gannicus would necessarily join if the other did."

"Of course not. They hate each other's guts," said Getas.

"But if I were to beat Crixus and he joined us, they might change their minds."

"Have you taken leave of your senses?" whispered Seuthes. "Your arm isn't healed. And the man's a beast."

"Just leave it," advised Getas. "We can do it without the Gauls."

"Can we?" Spartacus inclined his head at the patrolling guards. "Think of the casualties that those whoresons could cause in the first few moments. We've all seen attacks broken by a volley of arrows before. The same could happen here."

A grim silence descended, and Carbo wished he'd kept his mouth shut. They had all seen the guards practicing in the yard. Most could feather a target with half a dozen shafts inside sixty heartbeats.

If there was ever a time to fight Crixus, it was now, thought Spartacus.

Up till now, he'd avoided confrontation because it would have been pointless. Now, there was so much to gain. If virtually every man in the ludus was taking part, they had a much greater chance of success. His gut feeling was that he should do it, and if he admitted it, Spartacus knew it was also because he wanted to be seen as the man who had unified the gladiators. Regardless of what happened once they'd escaped, *that* would not be forgotten. "What's the worst that can happen? Crixus might break a few of my ribs," he joked.

Getas' mouth opened in protest, and shut again. "When?"

"In the morning," replied Spartacus. "After a good night's sleep."

"But—" said Carbo, worried now.

"Leave it," warned Seuthes. "I've seen that look in his eyes many times before."

"You're risking your life."

"And that's my choice," grated Spartacus.

Carbo looked down. What if he fails? he thought in anguish. What if Crixus kills him? I'll have no one to protect me. Guilt suffused him for being so selfish, but he couldn't help it.

IX

The following day, Spartacus did not bother with breakfast. Having an empty stomach might give him an advantage over Crixus. Even a tiny detail such as that could tip the balance between failure and success. Before leaving his cell, he'd warmed up and oiled his muscles. He sat with Getas, Seuthes, Carbo and six other Thracians, watching the Gaul and his cronies shoveling down porridge. *Eat as much as your belly will hold, you pig.*

Spartacus had been slightly surprised by Ariadne's lack of protest at his decision. Whether it was because of her ordeal at Phortis' hands, he did not know. Whatever the reason, it had been a relief. With thoughts of the escape occupying his every moment, Spartacus had been pleased not to have one more thing to consider. It was bad enough that his dream about the snake had recurred overnight. Unsettled, Spartacus shoved away an image of him being choked to death by Crixus, not the serpent.

"Wish me good fortune," he said. The shock etched on all their faces rammed home to Spartacus that they all thought he might fail. His determination redoubled. "Come on," he said, leading the way.

There was a rush to join him. Everyone knew his job. They'd already discussed making sure that Crixus' men did not intervene. Feeling the rush of adrenaline and the sweaty palms that accompanied an entrance into battle, Spartacus nodded grimly at Getas and Seuthes, who were to guard Ariadne. Then he swaggered over to where Crixus sat.

His followers jumped to their feet but Crixus did not budge from his seat. He glowered at Spartacus. "What the fuck do you want?"

Guide my way, Great Rider. "I've got a proposition for you."

Crixus' lip curled. "What makes you think I'd be interested?"

"Because you only have to agree to it if I beat you in single combat, with no weapons."

Crixus' grin stretched from ear to ear. "Spit it out."

Raising his hands peacefully, Spartacus moved closer. "Many of us are planning to escape from the ludus," he said in a low voice. "I want you to join us."

A mixture of emotions flitted Crixus' face. Disbelief. Shock. Jealousy. Anger. "What, with you as leader?"

"No. Each fighter follows the man he's loyal to."

"Who else is taking part?"

"Oenomaus, Gavius and nearly all the Thracians. About a hundred and twenty men."

"Castus? Gannicus?"

Spartacus shook his head.

"Understandable really," sneered Crixus. "Who'd want to join with a pack of savages?"

His men snickered with amusement.

"That's what I thought you'd say," replied Spartacus equably. "Would your answer change if I best you in a fight?"

"If that happens, I'd follow you into a sewer." Crixus' laugh came from deep in his belly.

"I won't ask you to do that. We fight until one man submits, eh?"

"Sounds good to me. I've been looking forward to this for an age," snarled Crixus, standing. He waved his arms. "Get out of the damn way!"

As the nearby Gauls scrambled to obey, Spartacus ran straight at at Crixus. He'd covered the distance between them in two heartbeats. Before Crixus could even react, Spartacus' head smashed into his belly. There was an audible whoosh as all the air left Crixus' lungs. They fell to the sand in a tangle of limbs, with Spartacus on top. He scrabbled to get up. Winded or not, Crixus was very dangerous. He was already trying to enfold him in the circle of his great arms. If that happened, the fight would be over.

Shoving away Crixus' forearms, Spartacus began to roll away. He had the time to plant a fist in the Gaul's groin before he stood. A loud groan told him that he'd hit the spot. He crouched, wondering if he could get in a kick to the head, but Crixus was already sitting up. Utter fury twisted his handsome face. "You dirty Thracian bastard! The fight hadn't started!"

"There's no summa rudis here. No rules either," taunted Spartacus. He wanted to really rile Crixus. An angry man was more likely to make mistakes.

Getas and Seuthes whooped in encouragement.

"That's how it is, eh? I'll gouge your fucking eyes out," shouted Crixus. "You'll submit quick enough then."

His men roared their approval.

"You think? Come and try!"

Furious, Crixus charged forward like a rampaging wild boar and they clinched together like two lovers. At once Spartacus was grateful for the wrestling holds taught to him by a Greek mercenary with whom he'd served in Bithynia. Crixus was far stronger than he. Spartacus' skill—and the slippery oil that coated his skin—was all that saved him from defeat in the moments that followed. They grappled to and fro, arms locked, with their faces locked in savage grimaces. Bent on revenge, Crixus aimed a knee at Spartacus' crotch, but Spartacus was able to block it with a hastily raised thigh.

"Your balls hurting still?" jibed Spartacus.

"Not half as much as yours will when I get to them!" With a great heave, Crixus threw Spartacus to one side. Caught off balance, he stumbled and went down. Crixus was on him like a raging beast, throwing body punches that sent waves of searing agony through Spartacus' every fiber. Trying to ignore the pain, he swiftly planted a leg against Crixus' muscular belly. Gripping the Gaul by the shoulders of his tunic, Spartacus threw him to one side.

Incredibly, Crixus got up quicker than Spartacus could. Spartacus was on his knees still when the Gaul came barrelling in and struck him in the face with one of his enormous fists. Spartacus felt his nose split like an overripe plum, heard the crunch as the tissue within broke. Driven back on to the sand by the force of the blow, he bellowed with the pain of it. Pausing only to kick Spartacus a few times, Crixus leaped on top of him again. His fingers clawed toward Spartacus' face. "I'm going to tear your fucking eyes out of your head!"

Spartacus was half blinded by blood and in complete agony. He also knew that if Crixus locked his thumbs into his eye sockets, the game was up. There had been occasions when he'd used the tactic himself, and it was brutally effective. Spartacus wondered if Crixus would stop once he'd ripped out his eyeballs? Probably not. The thought of living out his life as a blinded cripple, or dying right now, filled him with utter desperation.

Drawing up his arms inside those of Crixus, Spartacus whipped them sideways with all the strength in his body. Unprepared for such a move, Crixus toppled down on top of him. Spartacus sank his teeth into the first part of the Gaul's flesh that met his lips. It happened to be his nose. Spartacus bit down as hard as he could, worrying it as a dog does a rat. He was dimly aware of Crixus screaming and raining weakened punches on his unprotected abdomen, but he did not release his grip. *Take that, you bastard!*

Somehow, cold reason penetrated the red mist that coated Spartacus' consciousness. *If I bite off half his nose, the prick will never join us.* He unclamped his jaws, and Crixus reared back, showering him in gore. Spartacus heaved over on to his side, and struggled free from the other's grip. There was no resistance. Scrambling up, he wiped the blood from his eyes. Three steps away, Crixus was climbing to his feet, clutching his ruined nose with one hand. "I'll kill you!" he snarled.

This was his best chance. For all his noise, Crixus was hurting badly. Spartacus twisted and danced, aiming punches at the Gaul's belly. Crixus blocked them and threw a couple of immense blows with his free hand. Spartacus let one land, grunting with the shock of it. Another one quickly followed, striking his wounded arm. The pain was overwhelming, and Spartacus' vision blurred for a moment. *Come on!* Shaking his head, he stayed where he was. The punishment had to be endured. Managing to stoop under Crixus' swinging fists a moment later, he enveloped the Gaul with both his arms. Taking all of the other's weight on his right hip, and ignoring the agony radiating from his wound, Spartacus flung him bodily to the sand.

Crixus landed face first, and it was Spartacus' turn to jump on top. Sitting on the Gaul's back, he shoved his right arm around the other's neck. Grasping his right hand with his left, he took Crixus in a choke-hold. As his grip tightened, his arm formed a "V" shape around the Gaul's windpipe, blocking it entirely. A horrible rattling sound left Crixus' lips, and his arms flailed about, trying to reach Spartacus. His attempts were futile, and it didn't take more than a dozen heartbeats before his great strength began to leave him. The flesh on the back of his neck turned dark red.

Spartacus could only imagine what Crixus' face looked like.

Still the Gaul didn't give in.

You stupid, stupid bastard, thought Spartacus. He glanced quickly to either side. The faces of the watching Gauls were aghast, stricken with horror, while those of his men were filled with triumph. *Killing the big ox won't help our cause!* Gods above, but he hadn't considered this option. *I can't let him live, though. He'll try to kill me the first moment he can.* Expertly, Spartacus tightened his hold even further. *Choose your own death then. I'll have to convince Castus and Gannicus some other way.*

Then Crixus' left hand rose weakly into the air. The forefinger extended upward, in the appeal for mercy. Spartacus didn't quite believe his eyes, didn't trust Crixus even now. "Do you yield?" he roared.

The finger rose a fraction higher, before the whole arm flopped back on to the sand.

"Let him go!" roared a Gaul.

"You've killed him!" yelled another.

With great care, Spartacus released his grip around Crixus' neck. The Gaul slumped down and did not move. *Great Rider, keep him alive!* Climbing off, Spartacus rolled his opponent over on to his back. He was shocked by Crixus' appearance. The Gaul's face was a shocking purple color. A steady stream of blood ran from the dreadful wound on his nose, which was covered in sand. His eyes were glassy and the whites had turned scarlet. His engorged tongue protruded from fat, sausage-like lips, and there was a reddened ring around his neck, marking where Spartacus' hold had been.

"Get some water!" shouted Spartacus. He slapped Crixus across the cheeks.

There was no initial response, but a moment later, the Gaul coughed weakly.

Spartacus could have cheered.

Someone—Spartacus was vaguely surprised that it was Restio, the betmaker, because he hadn't been present initially—handed him a leather water bag, and he emptied it over Crixus' head.

The Gaul's eyes came back into focus. He coughed again and rubbed at his neck.

"Damn sore, I'd say," said Spartacus, noticing for the first time that the wound on the back of his right arm was bleeding. "You should have given in sooner. You're as stubborn as a mule."

"I've never lost a fight," said Crixus in wonderment. His voice had a new, gravelly timbre to it.

"There's always a first time," replied Spartacus, still trying to gauge what the Gaul's response would be. "I'm not quite sure how I did it."

"By being the dirtiest bastard in Italy," retorted Crixus, gingerly touching his nose.

"That was the hardest fight I've ever had," said Spartacus. He wasn't sure if it was true, but that wasn't what was important. Getting Crixus to honor his word was. "You're like Hercules himself."

"Hercules didn't lose," Crixus grunted irritably.

Spartacus' heart beat a little faster, and he leaned closer. "About my proposition," he said in a low voice.

Restio nudged the Gaul beside him. "What's he talking about?"

He was ignored.

"I'm a man of honor. I lost the fight, so me and my lot will join you," growled Crixus.

"Good." I can't trust him one iota, thought Spartacus. But at least the bastard has agreed to come on board. Sensing the silence, he scanned the yard. Unsurprisingly, all eyes—even those of the guards—were on them. Phortis was only twenty steps or so away. "We're being watched. Act as I do," Spartacus whispered. "That will teach you to insult my people!" he yelled. "Watch your mouth in future. D'you hear me?"

"I hear you," muttered Crixus furiously. He appeared entirely convincing, and Spartacus jerked his head at his men. "Let's go."

He was pleased to notice Phortis, looking furious, turn away and resume his conversation with one of the trainers. With luck, the Capuan would regard the fight as nothing more than a brawl between two of the best gladiators.

Now all he had to do was persuade the other Gauls to take part.

Preoccupied, Spartacus did not notice Restio scurry away from the crowd.

†

Rather than go to the surgeon to have his injury tended, Spartacus headed straight for the baths. He'd seen Castus and Gannicus heading in there with a bunch of their men. "Carbo, come with me," he ordered when they'd reached the door. "The rest of you, stay here."

Carbo was thrilled to be picked, but his stomach twisted with tension. *This could get very nasty.*

"Once we're out, where's the best place for us to head?" Spartacus' attention was already focused on the men within the changing room. They moved out of his way, and he smiled, aware that with the blood covering much of his face, he must look outlandish. There was no sign of the Gaulish leaders, which meant that they'd already progressed into the tiled bathing area.

I can be useful to him! I know the whole region. "What are you looking for?"

"Somewhere secure. Hard to reach. Easily defendable. A mountain, or perhaps a forest." *Once we're there we can decide what to do.*

"Vesuvius."

Spartacus looked at him blankly.

"The flat-topped peak that's visible to the south of here. The lower slopes are farmed, but not many people visit the summit. It's supposed to be one of Vulcan's resting places."

A memory tugged at Spartacus, but, feeling impatient, he took no notice. "It sounds perfect. What about the surrounding countryside?"

"It's mostly full of latifundia." He saw Spartacus' interest. "They'd be easy pickings."

"Good." Spartacus beckoned him closer. "Castus and Gannicus need to be persuaded that joining us would be a good idea. It's your job to sell Vesuvius to them. Think you can do it?"

"Yes," said Carbo confidently. This was no time to appear indecisive.

Spartacus clapped him on the arm. "Follow me."

Ignoring the curious looks of the others present, the pair went into the *frigidarium.* The cold room was empty, so they moved on to the *caldarium,* which was packed. Ribald banter and gossip filled the muggy air. Men lounged about on the tiles or in the warm water, luxuriating in the heat. This was one of the few indulgences in the gladiators' lives. Castus, a short man with bright red hair, was at one end of the pool with a number of his followers while Gannicus, moon-faced and jovial, occupied the opposite end with a gaggle of his. Both were studiously ignoring the other.

Spartacus strode to the midpoint of the pool so that the two leaders could see him.

All conversation ceased.

Spartacus leered. Blood had run from his nose down into his mouth, staining his teeth red. He's like some kind of crazed demon, thought Carbo with a thrill of fear.

"You think I look bad?" Spartacus' gaze moved from Castus to Gannicus and back again. "Ha! Take a peek at Crixus next time you see the prick."

"Why in Hades' name did you pick a fight with him?" asked Castus.

"To make the fool see sense."

"Sense? Crixus?" Gannicus tapped the side of his head. "Not much chance of that." He laughed, but there was no humor in his eyes.

"My tactic worked."

In the silence that followed, Carbo saw the two leaders lean forward with interest. He glanced at Spartacus, realizing that his delay in continuing was deliberate.

"Crixus has agreed to join me and Oenomaus," he said at last.

"And you want us to take part too," said Gannicus softly. "That's why you're here."

"Yes."

"What will you do if we refuse?" asked Castus.

"Kill you both."

Carbo shot a look at Spartacus. *What's he playing at? There are at least twenty Gauls present.*

Castus' nostrils pinched white. "You dare to threaten us in front of our men?"

"We could have you slain on the spot," threatened Gannicus. His eyes flickered, and several Gauls took a step toward them.

Spartacus didn't even turn his head, and Carbo marveled at his cool. He was fighting an overwhelming urge to piss.

"Killing us would be easy. I knew that when I walked in the door," revealed Spartacus. "But I came in with only Carbo because I *know* that you won't want to miss out on our opportunity." He paused. "Did you know that Crassus is going to buy twenty gladiators from Batiatus? To fight in mortal combats?"

"What?" cried Castus. Despite his diminutive size, he was one of the top fighters in the ludus. Gannicus was also clearly unhappy. His expression was mirrored by many of the men around the pool.

"Ask any of the guards."

"Supposing it's true," said Castus. "Why would that make us join you? We have no weapons, and all Batiatus' men have bows. It'd be a slaughter."

"No, it wouldn't!" Spartacus replied contemptuously. "What can thirty guards do if nearly two hundred gladiators set upon them? Fuck all! We *will* succeed."

Castus and Gannicus stared at each other. Carbo could tell that neither wanted to make the first move. Yet the eager muttering that had broken out among their men had to be answered. He felt Spartacus nudge him. "Now's your chance." Loudly, Spartacus said, "Listen to the new auctoratus. He's a local."

Carbo cleared his throat. "There's a huge mountain not far from here. Vesuvius, it's called. It's flat-topped, and hard to climb. It would be a good place to hide out. The land around it is given over to large farms, which would provide us with plenty of food and equipment."

"And women!" cried a Gaul.

Carbo gaped. He hadn't considered that option, and didn't know how to answer.

Spartacus did. This hadn't been his game plan, but it was imperative that Castus and Gannicus gave him their support. "There'll be lots of women to be had. Plump ones. Skinny ones. Field slaves. Domestic slaves. More than any of you can fuck!"

A vociferous growl of approval met these words.

"Well, when you put it like that," said Gannicus, leering, "it's hard to refuse."

His men began to cheer.

Yes! Spartacus' gaze swiveled to Castus, who shrugged. "I'm sure my lot wouldn't want to miss out. Would you, lads?"

The walls resounded with the din of a score or more of men bellowing in unison.

Spartacus raised his hands and, to Carbo's surprise, the noise diminished at once.

"If Batiatus or Phortis hear a word of this, we'll be royally fucked."

"My boys can keep their mouths shut," said Gannicus.

"Mine too." Castus' eyes reminded Carbo of a snake's. "Anyone who doesn't will end up with his throat cut."

"Excellent. We'll talk later, before we're locked in for the night."

"When do we make our move?" asked Castus.

The room went deathly silent.

"There's no point hanging about," Spartacus replied. "Tomorrow or the next day."

"You move fast," said Castus.

"It's too dangerous to delay. There's always at least one rat in the grain store."

"I know what you mean," growled Castus. "I vote for tomorrow."

"Me too," added Gannicus keenly.

"I'm not going to argue with that. The moment that they hand out the practice weapons then," answered Spartacus with a tight smile. *Thank you, Great Rider!*

Carbo waited until they were safely outside before he said anything. "You promised them indiscriminate rape!"

"Of course I did."

"That's barbaric!"

Spartacus stopped dead in his tracks. "You don't have to come along if you don't want to, boy."

Carbo's heart pounded. He didn't want to be left behind. "No. I'm coming," he muttered.

"Fine. Next time I want advice on tactics, I'll ask you."

Carbo colored, and said nothing.

"If it's any consolation, I don't like the idea of it either. But it's going to happen anyway, no matter what. I won't encourage it, but that's how war is. All I did was to use the idea to turn the tide in my favor. If I hadn't, Castus and Gannicus could well have refused to join me." Spartacus clapped him on the shoulder. "Us."

"I understand," said Carbo, feeling better.

Spartacus grinned. "Good."

†

The hours that followed were the longest of Spartacus' life. He did not want to be training, or running around the yard. Instead, he burned to be outside the high walls that surrounded him. Breathing the free air. Clapping his eyes on Vesuvius. He even pictured himself returning to Thrace. He had to make do with imagining it all, however. And trying not to dwell on his dream about the snake.

Spartacus waited until training was over for the day before talking to the Scythians who'd traveled with him from Illyria. While he wasn't exactly friendly with them, Spartacus didn't want the quartet to be completely in the dark about what would happen the next day. He approached them at the evening meal. To his surprise, the tattooed warriors greeted him with welcoming gestures. Spartacus didn't know if they had learned sufficient Latin to understand his words, but their eager grunts of agreement soon proved different.

After dinner, it was as much as Spartacus could do to briefly talk with Oenomaus and Crixus before Phortis began ordering the gladiators back into their cells, much earlier than normal. Protests and curses filled the air. The Capuan's reason, as he screamed repeatedly, was the three bodies that had been found in the toilets. Clearly, some men had given Castus and Gannicus cause for concern.

The best that Spartacus could manage was a meaningful look in Oenomaus', Gavius' and Crixus' direction. He was reassured somewhat by the fierce grins that they flashed at him in return, but there had been no time to discuss who would do what when it all started. They'll just have to follow my orders, he thought, praying that the five other leaders would comply. If one or more disagreed, it could prove disastrous.

Ariadne rushed to his side as he entered. "What's been happening?"

"A lot. Almost everyone is in. There should be around a hundred and eighty of us, all told." He threw her a smile. "More than enough."

"And the rest?"

"We didn't involve them. The stakes are too high. They don't have standout leaders; they speak different languages. The room for misunderstanding is huge."

"That's wise. When is it to be?"

"In the morning, the moment that they distribute the practice weapons. There's no point in waiting."

"That's true. Seize the day," Ariadne said, yet inside, she was terrified. *Protect us all, O Great Dionysus. Let us escape safely.*

"When it starts, you are to stay in here until I call you outside," Spartacus ordered. "Is that clear?"

"I—"

"No, Ariadne! It will be far too dangerous."

Seeing the steel in his eyes, she nodded meekly. "Very well."

"By tomorrow evening, we'll be sitting around a fire, enjoying our first night of freedom," Spartacus said confidently, refusing to imagine any other outcome.

Ariadne thought she was going to be sick. *What if it all goes wrong?*

"Aren't you pleased?" Have you seen something? he wanted to ask.

"I can't wait," she managed. *The gods grant that it will be so.*

Spartacus did not ask why she was ill at ease. *If I am to die tomorrow, I don't want to know.*

†

The next morning, the cock's familiar crowing was most welcome. *The waiting is almost over.* Rolling over, Spartacus found Ariadne looking at him.

"Ready?"

"Yes." He scanned her face for clues. "Did anything come to you?"

"No, nothing," she said lightly. *My worries kept me tossing and turning instead. Yet, on this of all days, I have to show you the most confident face I have.* "And you?"

"No dreams that I can remember, thank the Rider." His lips quirked. "I was awake for much of the night. I fell asleep just before that damn bird started to call. I was glad to hear it, though. I couldn't have taken much more in the way of killing time."

"I feel the same." *Not until we are actually outside the ludus' walls will I believe the gods are still with us.*

"If I am killed—"

"Don't talk like that." Her eyes brimmed with instant tears.

"It's stupid not to consider the possibility of my dying. If Getas and Seuthes aren't also slain, they will look after you. Failing that, use the money in my purse to get to the east coast. Take a ship to Illyria, and make your way home to Thrace."

"To Kotys and the welcome he'll give me?" Ariadne replied, more harshly than she'd intended. "No thanks. I'll use my snake on myself."

"You're a true Thracian," he said respectfully. "I'm proud to have you as my wife."

Ariadne blushed to the roots of her hair.

Clack, clack, clack. Phortis' sword rattled off the bars of the cells on the far side of the yard. "Wake up, you whoresons! It's another beautiful day."

Spartacus sprang up off the bed. Throwing on his tunic, he waited patiently until the Capuan reached their barred window.

"Pull your prick out of your woman, latro! It's time to get up."

Ariadne shuddered. The man was vile—less cold-blooded than her snake but, in his own way, as venomous.

Spartacus didn't give Phortis the satisfaction of a reply. "Have you got my breakfast ready?" he shouted.

A chorus of laughs rose up from the fighters within earshot.

"Count yourself lucky that there's any food at all!" snapped Phortis. Unlocking the door, he moved on.

"May the gods watch over you," whispered Ariadne.

"Thank you." Spartacus gave her a broad smile, which belied his churning stomach. *Stay by my side, Great Rider.* Pushing wide the portal, he stepped into the yard. All around him, dozens of other gladiators were emerging from their cells. It was a crisp spring morning. The area of sky framed by the ludus' high walls was entirely clear of cloud. Spartacus admired it. He had a good feeling in his guts.

"Hungry?"

Turning, Spartacus saw Restio leaning against the wall. The Iberian's face was an unhealthy gray color, and he had big rings under his eyes. "You look awful. Didn't sleep?"

"Not a wink," Restio muttered. "Did you?"

"Not bad," lied Spartacus. Restio was one of the few men who hadn't been told about the escape attempt. *Why would you care how I slept?* A memory tickled at Spartacus, but Carbo, Getas and Seuthes joined him, and he put it to one side. "Come on," he said to Restio. "Some porridge in your belly will make you feel better."

Stepping out into the yard proper, Spartacus felt a prickle of unease. The balcony above was lined with guards. He glanced sidelong at Restio, who appeared unconcerned. He wasn't surprised that Carbo hadn't noticed, but Getas and Seuthes were already scowling.

"Practically every shitbag Batiatus employs is up there," hissed Getas in his ear. "And there are far more men on the gate than normal."

Spartacus grunted. *Someone's told Batiatus, or Phortis.*

They joined the queue for the porridge. Oenomaus was at the end of the line with his closest henchmen. One of them immediately engaged Restio in a conversation about money. Spartacus moved closer to Oenomaus, relieved that the Iberian could no longer hear what he said.

"Seen the extra company we've got?" growled the German.

"Yes."

"What do you think?"

"I'm not sure. There's nothing that we can do right now anyway. Let's eat and see what happens."

With a noncommittal look, Oenomaus turned his back on them.

Spartacus frowned. Were the Germans still with him? Oenomaus' men crowded around him, preventing any further chat. "Seen Crixus?"

"He's over there," said Getas, jerking his head at the furthest benches.

Spartacus was about to leave the queue when something made him look around. Phortis was staring at him with naked aggression. *Something's definitely not right.* Rather than make his way over to Crixus, he shuffled forward with the rest.

"Look, it's the latro! Come for some porridge?" cried Phortis.

Silently, Spartacus picked up a bowl and held it out.

Phortis leaned over and grabbed it before the kitchen slave had even lifted his ladle from the pot. "I'll take that," he said. Clearing his throat, he spat a large gob of phlegm into the dish. "Fill it up," he ordered. A moment later, he handed the steaming bowl to Spartacus. "With my compliments."

Spartacus' blood pounded in his ears, and all sound died away. He was so incensed that his entire world shrank to a narrow tunnel before him. At its end was the smirking Phortis, his lips moving in more insults. Spartacus felt his mouth twist into a snarl. *It would be so easy. Just dash the bowl in his face, leap over the table and smash the whoreson to a pulp.*

He forced his eyelids into a blink, and came crashing back to reality. "Thank you." Without meeting the Capuan's gaze, Spartacus reached out and took the bowl. He didn't see the two guards on the balcony behind him lowering their bows, nor the fleeting look of disappointment on Restio's face.

"Fucking coward," Phortis snarled.

We'll see about that. Externally, Spartacus didn't even register the insult. He walked off and sat down beside the four Scythians, who threw him eager grins. Carbo, Getas and Seuthes plonked themselves alongside. Their table was nowhere near those of Crixus or Oenomaus, but he didn't dare approach them. From the corner of his eye, he could see

Phortis still glaring at him. Spartacus dipped his spoon into the top layer of porridge and took a mouthful, swallowing the thick liquid without even tasting it.

"Why did he do that?" Oddly, Restio had joined him again.

"The fucker enjoys goading me." *What do you care, anyway?*

"Why?"

"He's tried to rape Ariadne once already," said Spartacus. "If I were beaten unconscious by the guards, I wouldn't be able to stop him when he tries again." *More likely, it would foil the escape attempt before it even started. If the Thracians were no longer part of the equation, would the other leaders risk their men's lives? I doubt it.*

"Dirty bastard," said Restio sympathetically.

Spartacus ate some more porridge from the top of the bowl. When Phortis was finally distracted, he emptied the rest on to the sand by his feet. Spartacus' nerves were wire-taut, killing any appetite he might have had. Ignoring Restio's attempts at conversation, he sat in silence until breakfast had stopped being served.

Time for the trainers to appear, and the room containing the practice weapons to be unlocked. Long moments dragged by, and nothing happened. Carrying the empty porridge pot, the slave had vanished into the depths of the kitchen. Phortis was nowhere to be seen. *It's just a short delay.* Yet Spartacus could see his unease mirrored on many of the gladiators' faces.

He hadn't sneaked a look at the guards for a short time. Seated under the walkway, he could only see the ones at the far end of the balcony. Glancing upward, Spartacus' heart stopped. Why did they have arrows notched to their bowstrings? They surely weren't alone acting in such a manner. He could taste bile in the back of his throat now. *We've definitely been betrayed.*

All at once, things began to happen very fast.

Batiatus appeared on the balcony, Phortis by his side. Both men's faces were hard. Cold.

Spartacus clenched his fists. He wasn't going to back out now. *Even if the Germans and Gauls don't join in.* He tensed, preparing to leap up and roar at the Thracians to run for the stairs.

There was a flicker of movement at the edge of his vision. Spartacus glanced to his left, and was startled to see one of the Scythians hurtling over the table at him. There was no time to move. The bearded warrior crashed into him, driving them both backward, to the sand. In the same instant, Spartacus felt something strike the Scythian in the back. The man grunted in pain, and went limp. *Is he dead?* Angry voices shouted and Spartacus could sense a struggle going on overhead.

Abruptly, the body was hauled off him. Getas and another of the Scythians filled his vision. The warrior offered his hand. "Quick! We go now. Quick!"

Spartacus scrambled up. "What the hell happened?" he cried. The warrior who'd leaped on top of him lay at his feet. There was a filed-down length of iron protruding from the middle of his back. Restio lay beside him, with a similar weapon jutting from his chest. His mouth worked loosely, letting a thin stream of bloody bubbles fall. His face bore a faintly surprised look.

"Iberian want...kill you," growled the second Scythian. "My friend stop him. Took...blade meant for you. When the others see... they attack the guards. We must go!"

"Eh?" *Why would Restio try to kill me?* But Spartacus couldn't deny what his eyes were telling him. He knelt by Restio's side. "Did you sell us out?" The Iberian made no response. Fury consumed Spartacus, and he jiggled the base of the iron spike back and forth.

An animal squeal of pain ripped free of Restio's throat.

"You went to Batiatus?"

There was a faint nod.

"In the name of all the gods, why?"

"No one asked me to join," whispered Restio. "But Batiatus promised me freedom. I was to become one of the official betmakers at the arena."

"For that, you were willing to murder me?" demanded Spartacus harshly.

A shadow crossed Restio's face.

"We must move!" Seuthes' voice was full of alarm.

"Spartacus!" cried Carbo. Any doubts that he'd had about joining the escape attempt had vanished. The guards were indiscriminately shooting down men he knew and liked. *Bastards!*

"There's no one worse than a man who betrays a comrade," snarled Spartacus, thinking of Medokos. "And there's only one penalty for such scum." Placing both his hands on the piece of iron, he shoved it home.

Restio's eyes went wide with shock and his mouth gaped open. A last, sawing breath left his lungs, and he sagged down on the sand, dead.

Spartacus jumped up, praying that he hadn't left it too late. Getas, Seuthes and the three Scythians were bunched protectively around him, but the entire courtyard was in chaos. Gladiators ran hither and thither, shouting at each other, and without purpose. Waves of arrows were scudding down from above, striking down men at random. From the cells came the screams of the watching women. *Ariadne!*

"Chloris," said Carbo, looking alarmed.

"Amatokos will take care of her," barked Spartacus. "Look at the two sets of stairs." He was delighted to see Gavius and the three Gaulish leaders at the base of one, shoving their warriors upward to the first floor and the all-important armory. The other was deserted, however. *No surprise. My countrymen aren't going to act unless there's someone to lead them.* Spartacus' gaze shot to the gate, and horror filled him. There was already a large pile of arrow-riddled bodies heaped before it. The eight guards there were giving a good account of themselves. With six men around him, Oenomaus was standing in the open, screaming encouragement at the rest of his followers. Many of the guards on the balcony were also concentrating their aim on the critical area, so few were prepared to obey. *It's a fucking slaughter. We have to smash open the armory, or there's no hope.* "Follow me!" he bellowed at the men around him. Then, repeating his cry in Thracian, Spartacus darted out from the walkway's protection. He sprinted across the yard toward the second staircase, sensing fighters running to join him. Strangled cries rang out as some fell prey to the guards' arrows.

"There he is!" screeched Phortis. "Bring him down!"

Gritting his teeth, Spartacus increased his pace. Reaching cover, he felt a heartbeat's relief. He was also encouraged by the set, determined faces that surrounded him. As well as Carbo, Getas, Seuthes and the three Scythians, there were about thirty Thracians. "We need to go up, hard and fast. There are enough of us to rush the guards. Once some of us are armed, we'll have more of a chance. Know that I ask no man to do what I will not do myself. I will lead the way," Spartacus shouted. *Watch over me, Great Rider.* "Who will follow?" Pride filled him as every man present roared back his support.

"You're not to go first," declared Getas.

"You're too important," added Carbo fervently.

"He . . . right," added one of the Scythians. "If you killed . . . we . . . fucked."

To Spartacus' amazement, the rest of the warriors shouted in agreement.

Shoving him to one side, the Scythian and his comrades swarmed up the steps. They were followed by Carbo, Getas, Seuthes and a tide of Thracians.

Spartacus had another chance to assess the greater situation. What he saw filled him with dread. Oenomaus was standing by the gate yet he was alone. Huddles of his Germans were visible under the walkway; occasionally, one or two of them made a break for their leader, but they didn't get more than a dozen steps before being cut down. Crixus and Gavius appeared to have charged up the other staircase, but Castus and Gannicus remained at the bottom. Their wild eyes and desperate expressions told Spartacus that they had met with little success on the balcony above. *I have to talk to them. There must be something else we can do.* Ducking down as low as he could, Spartacus ran over to where the pair stood.

"My men are being butchered up there!" roared Castus.

"The same will happen to yours," added Gannicus. "There are extra quivers of arrows stacked up behind the bastard guards. They knew exactly what was going to happen."

"It was Restio."

"The Iberian?" cried Castus.

"Yes. He's dead. Forget about him," urged Spartacus. "We need another plan."

"You don't fucking say!"

"Without any shields and swords our men can do little—except die where they stand," said Gannicus. "What's your plan now?"

Spartacus' eyes flickered around the yard. The sand was littered with the injured and dying. Some men screamed for help that wasn't coming. Others cursed, or cried for their mothers. Most lay completely still. Fewer arrows were falling, but the ones that did were better aimed. A Nubian went down, bellowing his innocence, with a shaft in his belly. Two more Germans tried to join Oenomaus, who had somehow obtained a shield and a sword and was now heroically attacking the guards at the gate. He remained alone—his men were struck down long before they got near.

We're finished. Spartacus' hope had all but disappeared when he saw the terrified-looking slave who'd served breakfast peering out from the depths of the kitchen. Insight struck him like a hammer blow. "There are weapons in there!"

Castus goggled at him. "Where?"

"In the kitchen! Knives. Meat spits."

"By Belenus, you're right!" cried Gannicus.

Time to take control. "The attempt on the armory is futile. We stop it at once," said Spartacus crisply.

"Someone will have to hold the bottom of both sets of steps," Castus butted in. "The instant that he realizes what's going on, Batiatus will send the guards down to stop us."

"True. I'll take a group into the kitchen to gather what we can. The rest can carry tables over to block up the staircases. The wood will give them some protection too."

"We'll do that," snarled Gannicus.

"As soon as my lot are armed, we'll attack the gate." Spartacus' lips peeled back into a snarl. "You will hear when we've opened
it."

Looking more heartened, Castus grinned. "Until then!"

"Until then!" Spartacus pounded back to his men. By this stage,
the base of the steps was clogged with injured fighters. He shoved past
and began to climb, his feet slipping on the slick, bloody treads.
Reaching the first floor, Spartacus could see little but a mass of yelling
Thracians heaving to and fro at the guards. Bodies—feathered with
arrows or sporting savage sword wounds—lay everywhere. "Pull back!"
he screamed in Thracian and Latin. "Pull back!"

Carbo's head turned, and Spartacus gestured urgently. "Come on!
I have another plan!"

To his relief, Carbo heard him. Understood him. Began telling his
comrades.

Within moments, Carbo and the rest were in full retreat. Triumphant screams followed them as the guards pressed home their advantage. Spartacus tumbled down the stairs at the fighters' head, and was
pleased at the bottom to find six Gauls carrying tables. As the last
men—two of the Scythians—spilled out of the staircase, Spartacus
grinned. Following his instruction, four of the tables were heaved on
to their ends against the opening, blocking it entirely.

"Hold them there!" bellowed Spartacus. "The rest of you, follow
me to the kitchen."

Without explaining, he wove his way across the yard. Even without
the arrows being loosed from above, it was lethal going. Thanks to the
number of dead and injured, there was barely room to place one's feet
on the sand. A quick glance over either shoulder, however, told Spartacus that he had plenty of support. Carbo, Getas and Seuthes were right
behind him. *The guards can't bring them all down.*

"Find anything that will do as a weapon," yelled Spartacus as they
clattered into the kitchen, wild-eyed, chests heaving. Gasping with
terror, the porridge boy retreated into a corner. Like wild animals descending on their prey, the gladiators seized whatever they could find:

large-bladed cleavers, slender filleting knives and thick iron spits. A few even grabbed the heavy wooden pestles that were used to grind their barley.

"To the gate!" Spartacus spun on his heel and charged outside. "Quickly!"

He glimpsed Oenomaus under the walkway nearby. It was no surprise that he'd pulled back. *He's god-gifted still to be alive.* The German's face lit up as he took in Spartacus and his men charging forward. Roaring a battle cry, he ran out to join them. A mob of his countrymen followed.

Spartacus focused on the guards protecting the gate. They looked petrified. *Finally, the tables have been turned.* "Prepare for Hades, you cocksuckers! The ferryman awaits you," he shouted.

Two of them made a run for it at once. Led by Carbo, Getas and Seuthes, half a dozen of the men behind Spartacus split off and went for them like rabid dogs. The pair vanished, screaming, beneath a frenzy of blows. The rest of the guards by the entrance were made of sterner stuff than those who had fled. Four of them shuffled in close, holding their shields together while their companions stood to the rear, loosing arrows in low arcs overhead. Spartacus felt, rather than saw, several shafts as they hissed past him to sink into fighters behind him. His heart thumped madly in his chest, but he didn't falter. Ten paces from the guards, he raised his cleaver high. His other hand gripped a large, heavy pan. "For Thrace!" he shouted at the top of his voice. "For Thrace!"

He couldn't have chosen better words.

A threatening, primeval roar—the *titanismos*—filled the air around Spartacus as the warriors answered his battle cry. With faces distorted by fury, they smashed en masse into the guards' shield wall. A pair of fighters each took a sword in the belly, but the impact drove their enemies several steps backward; two of the guards stumbled and fell. They were trampled into the sand and hacked apart like slabs of beef.

Spartacus was facing one of those who'd kept his feet, a piggy-eyed individual whom he knew and disliked. Panicked, the man made the elementary mistake of swinging his gladius overhand at Spartacus' head.

Sparks flew as Spartacus met the blow with his metal pan. "Eat this," he hissed, slicing the cleaver sideways into the guard's face. The razor-sharp blade opened his flesh with ease. Powered by Spartacus' rage, it smashed his teeth apart, cut off half his tongue and ripped out of his other cheek. A sheet of blood followed the cleaver, misting the air with tiny red droplets. Uttering an indescribable shriek of pain, the maimed guard collapsed to the ground. *He's finished.*

Dropping his pan, Spartacus swept up the man's sword. Leaping over the screaming heap, he threw himself at one of the guards with a bow. The terrified archer was desperately trying to notch an arrow to his bowstring. It was the last thing he did. With a smashing blow of his cleaver, Spartacus swept the weapon out of the way. He followed through, stabbing the man in the chest so hard that the gladius pinned him to the gate timbers.

Panting, Spartacus looked to either side. He could see no living guards, just a mass of grinning, bloodied gladiators. Getas was two steps away. *Where's Seuthes?* he wondered. There was no time to look. "Open the gate! Go out on to the street, beyond arrow range. Wait for us there," Spartacus roared. "Castus! Gannicus! Gavius! Oenomaus! The entrance is secured." Through the din, he heard his call being answered. *Good. Some of them will get away at least. Whether I—or Ariadne—will remains to be seen.* "Getas, come with me." Spartacus grabbed one of the Scythians by the arm. "I must fetch my wife. Will you come?" He was gratified by the man's instant nod.

"My friend come too. We protect you," growled the Scythian. A fierce grunt of agreement from the second man proved the point.

Spartacus spun and ripped his gladius free. The guard's lifeless body slid down the gate, smearing a wide, red trail on the wood. "Follow me!" Pushing his way through the throng, he sprinted for his cell. He had never felt such a pressing need for speed. The moment that the men holding the tables at the base of the stairs abandoned their posts, the guards would swarm into the yard. If he, Getas and the Scythians didn't rescue Ariadne very fast, they'd all be killed.

What made his heart stop was not a tide of guards, however, but the sight of Phortis making his way, sword in hand, toward his cell. *He's going to kill her.* "No!" Spartacus screamed. But he was too far away. Too far to do anything but watch.

Phortis reached the door. Gripping the handle with his left hand, he flipped it open. "Where's your man now, you whore?"

There was a heartbeat's delay, and then something thin and black was tossed from within the cell, into Phortis' shocked face. A cracked scream left the Capuan's mouth, and he staggered backward, clutching at his throat. His sword clattered to the ground, unnoticed.

Her snake! She threw her damn snake at him! Spartacus exulted as he reached Phortis, who had fallen to his knees. His face had already turned purple and his swollen tongue poked out of his black, bloated lips. Spartacus hawked and spat on the Capuan. *Good enough for you.* "Guard the door," he ordered Getas. He neatly sidestepped the snake, which had raised itself up into a threatening posture, and bounded into the cell. "Ariadne?"

"Spartacus!" She threw herself into his arms, sobbing.

"It's all right. I'm here. Phortis is dying."

"What happened? It all went wrong."

"Not now," he muttered. "We've got to get out of here."

"Of course." Quickly, she grabbed up a fabric-wrapped bundle and a wicker basket from the bed. "I'm ready."

Gods, but she's brave. Taking her by the hand, he led her outside. He was relieved to find that although the guards had emerged into the yard, they were making little headway. Holding tables, Crixus and the last of his men were mounting a ferocious rearguard action, allowing more gladiators to escape. *Time is still of the essence.*

"Wait."

"Ariadne!"

Pulling free, Ariadne began talking to her snake in a low, calm voice. When she had approached to within a few steps, she threw a cloth over it and swiftly grabbed it behind the head. Shoving it into the basket, she gave Spartacus a pleased look. "I can't leave it behind. It saved my life."

"Let's go!"

Together with Getas and the Scythians, they raced past Phortis' corpse, following the walkway around to the gate rather than crossing the yard. Spartacus was about to shout at Crixus to pull back when the Gaul turned and saw him.

"Where's Gavius?" asked Spartacus.

"Dead. The remainder of his men have broken."

Spartacus hid his disappointment. "Time to go then." Quickly, he led Ariadne out on to the street, which was filled with gladiators. Among them were Castus and Gannicus. He saw Carbo's face there, and those of Amatokos and Chloris too. *Considerably less than a hundred. So few.* "All men with weapons, to the front! When Crixus and his lads come out, I want a false charge at the guards. Show them that we mean fucking business. It'll remind them that Batiatus wields no power beyond the ludus. Clear?"

They roared their agreement back at him. Barely armed or not, the gladiators' bloodlust was up. Spartacus felt the same, but he calmed himself.

They waited on either side of the gate as the Gauls withdrew in good order toward them.

"Crixus! Tell your men to split in the middle as you come out," Spartacus shouted. "We'll drive the bastards back."

Crixus bellowed something in Gaulish.

With eager faces, the gladiators around Spartacus moved forward a step.

"Hold!" He lifted his gladius high. "Hold!"

They did as he said.

Crixus and his men shuffled backward out of the ludus.

The guards' instinct kicked in, and their advance slowed.

The Gauls split apart, opening a central corridor.

"Let's show them that we'll rip their hearts out!" roared Spartacus.

"Now!" He charged forward, and was followed by a heaving mass of gladiators.

The guards took one look at them and came to a dead halt. Then, as one, they began retreating into the ludus.

Spartacus burned to pursue them. Instead, he slowed down and stopped. "Halt," he cried. "They're scared enough. Back to the street!" Keeping his face to the front, Spartacus began reversing. On the balcony, he could see Batiatus screaming abuse at his men. *Shout all you like, cocksucker. They have more sense than to die needlessly.* In forlorn twos and threes, the fighters who had been left behind stood and watched as the escaping gladiators withdrew. They had their chance, thought Spartacus harshly. "Pull the gates to. The dogs won't dare open them again for a while."

The four other leaders were waiting for him. They exchanged a brief, wary look.

"Which way?" demanded Oenomaus.

"Carbo?" cried Spartacus.

"Vesuvius is that way." Carbo pointed confidently down the street. "If we skirt around the walls, we can join the main road to the south of the town."

"Good," said Spartacus.

Oenomaus was already issuing orders to his men. The three Gauls were doing the same.

Spartacus glanced at Ariadne, who nodded her readiness. About twenty men were waiting for his command. The majority were Thracian, but Carbo was there too. He also spotted at least one Greek, and a pair of Nubians. Another woman in addition to Chloris. And, of course, the two remaining Scythians. *I don't even know their names.*

His eyes darted around. "Where's Seuthes?"

Getas' face darkened. "He didn't make it."

"What happened?"

"One of the guards at the gate was playing dead. He stabbed Seuthes from below." Getas' fingers touched his groin. "Seuthes didn't have a chance. He bled out as I watched." His face twitched with grief.

Spartacus' gaze flickered back to the gate. *Sleep well, brother.* Then, out loud, "Time to move."

He loped off. Ariadne ran beside him. Behind them came Getas, Carbo and his men. In a swarming tide, the remainder followed.

From the vegetable garden, the cock crowed again.

Spartacus forgot his sorrow for a moment. At least he'd never have to listen to the damn bird again.

X

Marcus Licinius Crassus exited the great bronze doors that framed the entrance to the Curia, the building where the Senate met, and where he had just spent the morning listening to debates. Scores upon scores of toga-clad senators were also leaving. When they saw Crassus, the vast majority were careful to move deferentially out of his way. Many smiled; most murmured a respectful greeting as well. Keeping his expression genial, Crassus returned every salutation, no matter how lowly the politician who had made it. *A friendly word of recognition today can become a new friend tomorrow.* As always, his efforts bore rich fruit. In the time it took Crassus to reach the Curia's front steps, he'd received the promise of two votes in his favor in the upcoming bill on slave ownership, been offered first refusal on the purchase of a newly discovered silver mine in Iberia and had a groveling request for more time from someone whose debt to him was due the following week. Catching sight of Pompey Magnus nearby, accompanied only by his immediate coterie of followers, Crassus permitted himself a tiny, internal gloat. *You might have come back to Rome on a flying visit to bask in the Senate's adulation over your so-called victories in Iberia, but you're still an arrogant young pup. Watch and learn, Pompey. This is how political success is achieved.*

Crassus had been irritated by Pompey from the very time that his star had begun its meteoric rise to prominence. His initial reason was simple. Crassus had had a much harder climb to the top. His ancestors might have included those who had served as censor, consul, and *pontifex maximus*, the highest-ranking priest in Rome, but that hadn't stopped Crassus' family fortunes from plummeting during the reign of first Marius, and then Cinna. Times for those who had supported Sulla were bitterly hard for several years. *Not for you to lose your father and a brother in the proscriptions,* thought Crassus, eyeing Pompey sourly. *Not for you to flee Italy with a handful of followers and slaves, there to live in a cave for eight months, like skulking beasts. No, you somehow escaped the Marian bastards' attentions. Yet for all the way you raised three legions when Sulla returned, and your victories in Africa since, you weren't the man whose forces won the battle at the Colline Gate; who, with one masterstroke, restored Sulla to power. I was!*

Crassus flashed a practiced, false smile at Pompey, who responded similarly. Like the misery of autumn rain, both of them had to accept the other's presence on center stage. That didn't mean they had to like each other but it was important to remain decorous. To appear friendly, even when the direct opposite was the truth. *Such is the way of politics,* thought Crassus. *It's a way of life that I was born into, Pompey* Magnus, *while you're nothing but an upstart provincial.* He cast a jaundiced eye at the handful of army veterans who'd been waiting for Pompey to emerge. Raucous cheering broke out when they noticed him. It stung Crassus to see it. Few ex-soldiers of his sought him out to praise him to the skies, yet it happened for Pompey all the time.

"Look at the scumbag! For all his vaunted military credentials, Pompey has made a dog's dinner of sorting out Sertorius in Iberia. Three damn years it's taken him so far," said a high-pitched voice in his ear.

Startled, Crassus looked around. Recognizing Saenius, his major domo, he relaxed. Not many people knew his mind as Saenius did. Twenty years of faithful service meant Crassus trusted the thin, effeminate Latin as no other. "Yes, it's been an overly long campaign," he replied acidly.

"It only looks like ending now because Perperna recently assassinated Sertorius and assumed control of the Marian forces. Everyone knows that Perperna couldn't organize a hunting party, let alone an army. If it hadn't been for that piece of good luck, the fool Pompey would have been in Iberia for the rest of his life," Saenius hissed. "You would've finished it long since."

"I'd like to think so," said Crassus modestly, before adding, "I should have been given the command in the first place."

"Of course you should."

The discreet major domo didn't mention the reason that the Senate had passed his master over, but Crassus brooded over it anyway. *I didn't have the standing army that Pompey had back then. The Senate could hardly deny the prick his demand to be sent to Iberia.* Crassus wouldn't admit it to a soul, not even Saenius, but when the next opportunity for serious military advancement presented itself, he needed to seize it. To be utterly ruthless.

Romans liked smooth politicians, who were friends to all. They honored those who kept an open house, who feasted the people, and who donated a tenth of all they had to Hercules. Crassus knew that he fitted the bill well for all of those qualities, but he had not yet been the recipient, as Pompey had, of the greatest accolade that Rome could award to one of its citizens.

A triumph.

And the public adoration that, like the spring after winter, inevitably followed.

Crassus couldn't help but feel jealous as he watched the veterans proudly salute Pompey, who responded with gracious nods. Ordering Saenius to follow, he prepared to stalk off into the Forum.

It was then that a man on a lathered horse came clattering across the cobblestones. Indignant cries rose into the air as people scattered to avoid being trampled. Crassus' gaze fixed on the new arrival like that of a hawk. *What in Hades' name is going on?* Dragging on the reins, the rider halted on the Graecostasis, the waiting area reserved for dignitaries who wished to address the Senate. Abandoning his mount, he darted forward toward the Curia. "Where are the consuls?" he shouted. "Are they still within?"

The crowd of senators recoiled from the man, who was unshaven and wearing a sweat-soaked tunic. A corridor opened before the messenger and, with a curse, he sprinted up the steps. He looked exhausted, thought Crassus. And frightened. He must be carrying urgent news. Crassus stepped into the man's path, forcing him to come to a juddering halt. "They are still inside, I believe," he said smoothly.

It took a heartbeat for his words to register. Then the other's faded blue eyes took him in. "My thanks, sir," he said, and made to move past.

Turning nimbly, Crassus fell in with him. "Where are you from?"

"Capua."

"And you bring important news from there?"

"Yes, sir," came the terse reply.

"What is it?"

The faded blue eyes regarded him again. "I don't suppose it matters if you hear it first. A band of gladiators has broken out of the ludus in Capua."

Crassus' interest soared. "The ludus? I know it well. Did many escape?"

"Only about seventy."

"That's of little consequence," declared Crassus in a bluff voice. "Hardly a matter to trouble the consuls of Rome with, is it?"

The man gave him a nervous glance, but then his chin firmed. "I'd argue the opposite, sir. Within the day, we, the townspeople of Capua, sent a force of more than two hundred men after the bastards. A simple matter to deal with, you'd think. Yet our lads were virtually annihilated. Less than a quarter of them made it home."

Crassus sucked in his surprise. "That's remarkable," he said casually.

Looking vindicated, the messenger made to go.

A finger of recognition tickled at Crassus' memory. "Wait. Do you by any chance know any of the renegades' names?"

The man turned. He made the sign against evil. "Apparently, the leader is called Spartacus."

"Spartacus?" echoed Crassus in real shock.

"Yes, sir. He's from Thrace."

"Who cares what the whoreson is called?" growled a senator who'd overheard. "Get in there and tell the consuls. They'll soon organize enough troops to go down there and butcher the lot of them."

"They will," purred Crassus. "Capua need not worry. Rome will seek vengeance for its troubles."

With a grateful nod, the man hurried off.

The gladiator whom I saw fight has even more balls than I thought. A pity I did not order his death when I had the chance. Crassus put the matter from his mind. A few hundred legionaries under the command of one of the other praetors would sort it out. He had far bigger fish to fry.

†

Standing on the very lip of the cliff, Spartacus looked over the edge. He squinted into the brightness of the abyss, spotting a number of eagles and vultures hanging in the air at roughly the same dizzying height. Above was a turquoise sky, filled by a warm spring sun. Below, the view was stupendous. A dense carpet of holm oak, turpentine, beech and strawberry trees spilled down Vesuvius' slopes from Spartacus' fastness on the summit. He let out a long breath. *No one lives up here but birds of prey, wild beasts—and us. I am truly a latro now, Phortis.*

Spartacus' gaze followed the gradient as it flattened far below. There the land changed. An intricate network of farms, resembling a crazy mosaic pattern, extended out on to the Campanian plain as far as the eye could see. The vineyards were innumerable. Between them were vast fields of young wheat. Beyond, twenty miles away, lay Capua and the ludus. To the west and southwest were the towns of Neapolis and Pompeii, and the sea. The Via Annia, a minor road linking Rome with the south, was situated east of Vesuvius, along with the town of Nuceria. Beyond those lay the Picentini Mountains, a tall range of peaks which could serve as a refuge if needs be.

Memories of the events three days prior filled Spartacus' mind. It hadn't surprised him, or any of the gladiators, that a strong force had immediately been dispatched from Capua to crush them. Arrogant and sure of success, the ten-score veterans and townspeople had been easy to ambush. The gladiators had fallen upon them like howling wraiths. Only a fraction of the ragtag militia had escaped to tell the tale. Despite this, Spartacus' sour mood deepened. The matter wouldn't end there. *Rome doesn't work like that. Ever.* Already the message would have reached the Senate in Rome. Already the plans for reprisal would be in train.

He glanced around at the massive crater that formed the top of the mountain. Its enclosing walls were covered in wild grapevines, and the green space was filled with vegetation: twisted juniper trees towered over spurge olive bushes, myrtle and sage plants. A number of large pools provided ample rainwater to drink. The gladiators' camp was spread out over a wide area. It comprised a dozen or so tents—seized the previous day—and the same number of makeshift wooden lean-tos. Spartacus scowled. *Seventy-three of us escaped the ludus. When the four women are taken into account, that's sixty-nine fighters. Just over a third of Batiatus' men. Hardly even a decent-sized war band.* His gut instinct replied at once. *The Senate won't look at us in that light. Not only did we arm ourselves with the gladiator weapons from that wagon train heading for Nola, but we've smashed a superior military force.* If there was ever a time to strike out for Thrace, it was now. Ariadne had mentioned this possibility, but so far Spartacus had resisted it. He hadn't admitted it to Ariadne, but he liked having men follow him. He liked being a leader. If he left for Thrace, only a few loyal supporters would go with him.

A man by one of the lean-tos lifted his hand in greeting, and Spartacus returned the gesture. *At least new recruits are starting to trickle in.* So far it was only a handful of agricultural slaves. That number had to grow, and fast. If it didn't, any troops sent against them would crush them as a man swats a fly. Spartacus' fists bunched. Even if their numbers did increase, what real difference would it make? It took weeks—*no, months*—of training to turn men who were used to pushing a plow into soldiers who could stand against Roman legionaries. They'd be lucky if even a fraction of that time was granted to them. Seeing Crixus wrestling with one of his comrades, Spartacus' frustration grew.

Any semblance of unity among the gladiators had dissolved the moment that they'd reached Vesuvius. Like oil separating from vinegar, the different groups had re-formed under their original leaders. They camped apart too: three parties of Gauls; the Germans under Oenomaus, and the Thracians and other nationalities with Spartacus. The physical separation had increased their differences even further. From the word go, Spartacus had struggled to get enough sentries. Unsurprisingly, his men weren't too happy standing watch while the others relaxed in the crater. But at least they followed their orders, he reflected.

Intoxicated by their newfound freedom, Crixus, Castus and Gannicus had laughed in his face when he'd confronted them over it the previous evening. "We're free now! Relax and enjoy it, why don't you?" Gannicus had said. Castus had simply shrugged and pointed to his men, who were guzzling down the wine they'd taken from the dead after the ambush. "What need have we of sentries?" Crixus had roared. "Look what we did to those whoresons from Capua! No one is going to come near us in a hurry. Unless they want to commit suicide, of course." He grinned at his supporters, who guffawed in approval.

It had taken all of Spartacus' self-control not to leap on top of Crixus again, fists pounding. But he'd done nothing. While the Gaulish leaders were infuriating, ill-disciplined and prone to drunkenness, they and their men represented a sizeable—and vital—chunk of their forces. There were twenty-five Gauls, of whom one was a woman. Spartacus could not alienate them totally. With the recent addition of some runaway agricultural slaves, he had twenty-nine men and two women, including Ariadne and himself. If it came to a real fight, however, he could only rely on the seventeen of his followers who were gladiators. Oenomaus had a few more followers than the total number of Gauls: twenty-six men and two women, but the Germans' unity gave him the most powerful grouping by far.

Fortunately, Oenomaus also had more sense than the others. He'd listened to Spartacus' complaints about the sentries, and immediately agreed that his men should share the duty. His goodwill had not extended further, however. When Spartacus had mentioned weapons drill, Oenomaus had frowned. "We had enough of that in the damn ludus." Spartacus' argument about facing legionaries had met with simple indifference. "We'll cross that bridge if we come to it," the German had said.

When we come to it. A grim sense of foreboding filled Spartacus and he turned his eyes back to the Campanian plain. The roads he could see were as small as the ribbons on a doll's dress, but he could still make out the tiny shapes of wagons and oxen. For now. As sure as the wheat ripened at summer's end, one day he'd see the distinctive column of a Roman army, marching toward Vesuvius. Even if it only comprised a thousand men, it would look the same as the ones Spartacus had grown used to during the conquest of Thrace. Scouts and skirmishers to the front. Cavalry, and then the main body of infantry. The camp surveyors and their equipment, followed by the commander and his bodyguards. More cavalry. The senior officers with their escort. The rearguard. And after them, the raggle-taggle that trailed in the wake of every army since the dawn of time. Whores, traders of every description, soothsayers, shysters, entertainers and slave traders. Perhaps even the man appointed in Phortis' place, sent by Batiatus to bring back those unfortunate enough to be captured alive.

I won't be among them. Nor will Ariadne, Spartacus thought grimly. Death was far more attractive than returning to captivity, especially when it was achieved by hacking apart as many legionaries as he could. While that end appealed, it was impossible to deny that it was futile. *Why not just leave?*

"Was this the mountain you dreamed of?"

Ariadne's voice by his ear made Spartacus jump. "You crept up on me!" he muttered, a trifle embarrassed. He studied his surroundings more closely. In the adrenaline rush of events since their escape, he hadn't had the leisure to reconsider his dream. "Possibly. It's certainly remote enough."

"And you have a sica." She tapped the sheathed weapon hanging from his baldric.

"True." He'd been delighted to find a Thracian sword in the consignment that they'd chanced upon on the road from Capua.

"You're at altitude."

"Yes, but I'm not alone." He gestured at the camp below.

"Not everything about a dream has to be accurate."

Spartacus' stomach tightened, and he scanned her face for clues. She spent much of her time praying to Dionysus. Maybe her prayers had been answered at last. "Have you gained an understanding of what I saw?" He saw the regret flare in Ariadne's eyes, and once again, he felt the snake wrapped around his throat. *Does it represent the soldiers sent by Rome? Or the fate that awaits me if I try to return to Thrace?* He lifted his eyes balefully to the heavens. *What end have you planned for us, Great Rider?*

"It might not mean what you think."

"It's hard to see how it doesn't." Patting his flat belly, Spartacus changed the subject. "I've a mind to fill this with meat. Any meat will do. Beef. Pork. Lamb. Even goat. We need supplies too—particularly blankets and leather for making sandals. I'll round up the men and search out an easy farm to raid. I'll take everyone except Getas. He will stay here with you."

Ariadne knew better than to ask if she could come. As a priestess, her value to the gladiators was incalculable. Besides, she didn't want to see the casual slaughter and rape that would be an integral part of the expedition.

†

Spartacus slipped to Carbo's side as they followed the game trail downward through the forest. Atheas and Taxacis, the two Scythians, followed him silently, barely moving the thick bushes as they passed. Atheas was the one with the bushy black beard, while Taxacis had a broken nose like a squashed sausage. Since escaping the ludus, the pair had become his shadows. They even slept outside his tent, like faithful hunting dogs. Spartacus didn't know why the skilled warriors had chosen to become his bodyguards, but he rested easier because of them. Getas couldn't do it all on his own. Having to contend first with the fearsome Scythians would make any disgruntled gladiators think twice before trying to kill him.

He eyed Carbo sidelong. With all that had been going on since their escape, he hadn't had a chance to talk to the young Roman. This was a chance to gauge Carbo's loyalty once more. Inside the ludus, it hadn't truly been tested, but things were about to change. "With luck, this little jaunt will bring us some sheep, or even cattle. Nothing like fresh meat roasted over a fire, eh?"

"My belly's rumbling already," admitted Carbo. His face clouded. "Will anyone be killed?"

"I hope not. We'll only be facing farm slaves and whatever asshole owns them."

"I didn't mean any of us."

Spartacus shot him a sharp look. "I expect there'll be a few casualties, yes. Don't be surprised when escaped gladiators take their vengeance on some of the people that treated them like animals."

"I thought you were looking for food."

"We are," replied Spartacus innocently. "And if we happen to kill a Roman or two, it will be an added bonus."

"That's not right!" The words had escaped Carbo's lips before he could stop them.

"Is it not?" Spartacus jabbed a finger into Carbo's chest. "Your fucking legions have done far worse to my people. I've watched innumerable settlements being razed to the ground. Lost count of the old and infirm who were butchered because they were no use as slaves. Have you ever seen a baby that's been gutted? Or a woman who's been raped so many times that she's lost her mind?"

Carbo flushed, and had the wits not to reply. *He's probably right.*

"If you don't want to be part of it, you can piss off."

Carbo's feet stayed on the path.

There was a long pause.

"Well?" demanded Spartacus.

"I'm staying."

"And when the time comes to fight?" demanded Spartacus in a grating tone. "It'll be legionaries who come against us next. Will you run rather than kill your own countrymen?"

"No." *Where would I go? To Rome, to become a lawyer? I'd rather be a latro.*

"How can I be sure?" Spartacus' gray eyes were threatening. "I have no need of a man I can't rely on."

"You looked out for me in the ludus. No one else did, so I'm loyal to you," said Carbo passionately. "Even if it means fighting my own kind."

Spartacus' anger subsided a fraction. "I'll be watching you," he warned.

Carbo nodded in grim acceptance. *It's no different to the arena. Kill or be killed. That's my only choice.*

†

An hour later, Spartacus genuinely felt like a latro. The estate they'd found had seemed perfect. It was typical of the large latifundia in the area. Sprawling fields full of crops and livestock surrounded a yard, farm buildings and an enormous villa. The gladiators had headed for the latter before bothering with the sheep and cattle. It was unlikely that anyone would come to the owner's aid but it paid to be cautious. They'd rounded up all visible slaves too. Spartacus didn't understand it but some slaves felt an allegiance to their owners. He didn't want anyone running off to spread the news until they were gone.

The killing had started soon after they reached the buildings. Hearing the commotion, the owner had emerged from his front door. A stocky man in early middle age with close-cut hair, he'd looked like an army veteran. Taking in the yelling gladiators and his wailing, terrified slaves, he'd plunged back into the villa. A few heartbeats later, he'd emerged at the head of a group of armed retainers. Waving an old but serviceable gladius, the Roman had charged straight at Crixus. Whooping with delight, the Gauls had closed around their attackers like a pack of hungry wolves.

Now, covered in stab wounds, and with his head almost severed, the man lay in a huge pool of blood. Similarly treated, the corpses of his domestic slaves lay all around him. His wife and two teenage daughters were on their backs nearby, screaming at the top of their lungs. On top of each was a bare-arsed gladiator, shoving away between their open legs. Laughing and joking with one another, a dozen others waited their turn. Spartacus, who was sitting on the edge of a fountain by the entrance to the yard, kept his gaze averted. He was waiting for the most disciplined of his men—the Scythians and two of the Thracians—to return and report what they'd found in the way of weapons, grain and other supplies.

"Can't you stop this?" Carbo waved at the baying mob of fighters. "It's disgusting."

"It is," agreed Spartacus wearily. "But it's also inevitable. Moreover, if I tried to stop what was going on, those men would kill me without batting an eyelid. So I let them get on with it."

"They're animals!" spat Carbo.

"No. They're warriors who haven't had a woman in months, or even years. Do your precious legionaries act any differently when they sack a town? I doubt it very much."

"Legionaries would never carry on in such a sickening manner." Carbo knew the words weren't true as they left his lips.

"Believe that if you will."

Carbo flushed and fell silent.

"Why don't you make yourself useful? Go into the house and search for weapons."

With a relieved look, Carbo disappeared.

A new set of high-pitched screams reached Spartacus. It was coming from the slave quarters. That's where the other warriors are. Stupid fools, he thought. Carbo had a point. We need more recruits, not enemies. Who'll want to join us if our men have raped their womenfolk? Calling for Atheas and Taxacis, he marched toward the wailing sounds.

Some discipline had to be maintained.

†

Two weeks passed without any sign of Roman soldiers. With every day that went by, however, Spartacus' tension grew. It was inevitable that the Senate would send a force to crush them. The only unknown was when it would arrive. The sands of time were slipping away, and while they did, the other gladiators did nothing to prepare. Together with their leaders, they watched and jeered as Spartacus mercilessly trained his men and a number of the slaves who'd joined them. Most of his followers were now better armed than their erstwhile comrades. They had Carbo to thank for it. He was the one who had found a large stash of weapons—swords, javelins, spears and daggers—at the villa. The weapons were a major addition to the Thracians' cause, but they still lacked shields and helmets. It would make little difference to the outcome, but it galled Spartacus. His men deserved more.

Spartacus also poured energy into instructing Carbo. It was a pleasure to have a pupil so eager to learn. The young Roman appeared to have learned his lesson at the *latifundium*, and had not mentioned the episode again. It's as well, thought Spartacus, because rapes will happen anyway. Ugly as it is, it's an integral part of war. Carbo's keen attitude also helped to take Spartacus' mind from his concerns. During this time, he did not ask Ariadne about his dream either. There was little point. He'd come to the conclusion that the snake symbolized Rome and its legions, and that it was his fate to die in battle against them. Spartacus brooded about it each day as he sat on the lip of the crater, studying the countryside far below. It wasn't the worst fate a man could have. It was better than dying in the arena while thousands of Romans bayed for his blood. His decision to stay had been the right one. He was returning the loyalty of his followers by leading, not abandoning them. His men were also the reason it had been better not to head for Thrace. *I cannot desert them. What of Ariadne, though?* Troublingly, to this he had no answer.

Spartacus was in this spot one morning when, from the corner of his eye, he saw Atheas quietly approaching. He didn't turn his head. "What is it?"

"Important . . . visitor."

Spartacus' focus drifted away from the panorama below. "Spit it out, then."

"A farm slave has come . . . to join us."

"And?"

"He has seen soldiers . . . marching toward . . . mountain."

Spartacus spun around. "How far from here?"

"A day away, he says."

So near. "Bring him to me at once!"

Atheas hurried off, returning soon after with a strapping figure in tow. Curious, Spartacus eyed the unarmed newcomer, who was clad in a coarse tunic that was little more than rags. He was young, broad-shouldered, and his skin was burned dark brown from a lifetime working outdoors. His round, pleasant face was marred by an ugly purple scar that ran across his left cheek.

"Stop," Atheas ordered when they were ten steps from Spartacus.

Gazing at Spartacus with open curiosity, the slave obeyed.

"What's your name?"

"Aventianus, master."

"There are no masters in this camp, Aventianus. Here we are all equal. Free men."

"They said that you treated everyone in this way, but I put it down to rumor. Until now."

"It is no rumor. You bring news, I believe?"

"Yes. Yesterday, a large force of soldiers—"

"How many?" interrupted Spartacus.

"About three thousand."

Spartacus mouthed a curse. *What was I thinking? Eighty of us do against that many? The figure might as well be a hundred thousand.* "Go on."

"They reached the edge of my master's land by mid-afternoon. The commander, a praetor, asked permission to camp for the night; my master was happy to oblige. He invited the detachment's senior officers to dine with him. During the evening, it was revealed that the troops had been sent by the Senate itself. Their mission is to come to Vesuvius . . . and crush your uprising."

Spartacus lifted a hand, stopping Aventianus again. "There are men who need to hear this." He glanced at Atheas. "Fetch the other leaders. Tell them it's urgent."

Spartacus was surprised that his dominant emotion was one of relief. *The waiting is over.*

It wasn't long before Atheas returned with Oenomaus and the three Gauls. All four men's faces were concerned and angry.

The word is already out.

"What in Toutatis' name is going on?" demanded Crixus.

"Fill them in on what you've told me so far," Spartacus ordered.

As Aventianus obeyed, Crixus began to swear violently under his breath. Oenomaus, his face impassive, listened in silence. Castus and Gannicus gave each other sour glances.

"Three thousand fucking legionaries!" spat Oenomaus. "Any cavalry?"

"No."

"They'd be useless up here anyway," said Crixus.

"Do we know their commander's name?" asked Spartacus.

"Caius Claudius Glaber," replied Aventianus. "He's a praetor."

"Never heard of the prick," Castus growled.

His name's irrelevant. Spartacus rubbed a finger along his lips, thinking. "Has he any military experience?"

"No. He seemed confident, though."

"Of course he did, the cocksucker," snarled Castus. "He has almost forty men to every one of ours."

Aventianus cleared his throat. "They're not regular legionaries."

The Gauls were so angry that they didn't take in Aventianus' words, but Spartacus did. So did Oenomaus. "Say that again," ordered Spartacus.

"Glaber said that the Senate refused to classify this as an uprising, merely naming it an emergency. It didn't warrant a levy of troops on the Campus Martius. Glaber protested, but was overruled, so he had to recruit his soldiers on the march south from Rome. There are some veterans, but most are citizen farmers or townspeople without much military experience."

"Some good news!" said Spartacus. *Will it make any difference, though?*

Castus made a contemptuous noise. "I imagine that there will be plenty of them to do the job."

"At least we can make a glorious end for ourselves." Crixus mimed a savage sword thrust, and then another. "One that the gods will have to notice."

Castus and Gannicus glowered in silence.

"I'm sorry," said Aventianus.

"You have nothing to apologize for," responded Oenomaus at once. "You have come here to warn us, risking your life of your own accord. It is we who are in your debt."

"I tried to get others on the farm to join me, but no one would. They said there were too many soldiers." Aventianus hung his head.

"You are a brave man." Spartacus stepped over and gripped his shoulder. "How long did it take you to get here?"

"I ran for about three hours."

"So they will get here by this afternoon," said Spartacus, approximating.

Aventianus nodded. "It's what Glaber was counting on."

"That's useful to know." Spartacus pointed north. "Leave now, and you could reach your master's property by nightfall. They might not have even noticed your absence."

"No," protested Aventianus. "I came here to join you!"

"We're all going to be killed," advised Spartacus softly.

"I don't care!" Aventianus pointed at the irregular scar on his face. "See this? That was made by a hot poker. My punishment for a minor offense two years ago. Dying here with you—as a free man—is far more appealing than returning to that."

Spartacus threw a meaningful look at the three Gauls. *Why can't you pricks be like him?* "In that case, we'd be proud to have you join us."

"Thank you."

"You must be tired and hungry," said Spartacus. He glanced at Atheas again. "Take Aventianus to the cooking area. See that he is fed and watered. Afterward, he'll need a weapon and somewhere to sleep."

As the pair disappeared, he turned to the others. The news had made his determination resurge with a vengeance. "What do you think?"

"I think that we're fucked," snapped Castus.

Spartacus bit down on his anger. *If you and your men had bothered to do some training, you might not be so damn pessimistic.* "Oenomaus?"

"It's hard to disagree with Castus. Unless we want to find ourselves alone, however, we should keep it to ourselves. I'm not running away and I'm not about to surrender. I'm here to fight."

Crixus bristled. "So am I!"

"And me," added Gannicus quickly.

"I'm glad to hear it," Oenomaus replied. "The first thing to do then is to come up with a plan of action. Decide on the best way to cause maximum casualties among the whoresons before they overrun us."

A cruel smile spread across Castus' face. "Sounds appealing."

"And to me," said Spartacus. *Well handled, Oenomaus.* "I've been giving it some thought. With only one decent path to the summit, it's obvious which way they'll come. I've earmarked a good position at the steepest point. If we stockpile large stones and boulders there, they can be easily rolled down on any attackers."

"The track is very narrow," added Crixus. "By my reckoning, three men with shields standing abreast could hold it against all comers."

"Shields?" asked Spartacus.

"I know, I know. We don't have any. But once we've killed a few of the dogs, that will change." Crixus glared at them, daring them to challenge his idea.

"I was thinking along the same lines," said Spartacus. He didn't say what else was on his mind. *How many men will we lose in the process?* "The two Nubians have slings. They can rain down stones on the Romans the moment that they come within range; smaller rocks can be gathered for the rest of us to throw. Their shields will give the bastards some protection, but we'll injure plenty of them. They won't be able to do a thing about it." *Don't fool yourself. It will be like trying to halt a column of ants. Easy to stamp on a few hundred, but impossible to stop them all.*

But his words had the desired effect. Castus in particular looked much happier. "I'll get my men to start searching out boulders. The more we have, the better," he said, stamping off. Gannicus walked away with Crixus, already arguing over who would stand in the front line.

Oenomaus waited until the Gauls were out of earshot. "What if they don't attack?"

Spartacus had half thought of this option, but dismissed it. After all, the Romans were fond of confrontation—open battle. *But not always.* "You think they'd do that?"

"Unless Glaber wants to lose scores of soldiers before they've even reached our lines, it's the sensible choice. I would set a couple of hundred men to watch the path and then just sit and wait."

"Starve us out of here, you mean," growled Spartacus.

"Yes. It's slow, but effective, and far less costly in human lives."

"If we charge down to attack them, we lose our only advantage. That of height."

They stared at each other without speaking. The good feeling that had been present a few moments before had vanished. Their cause seemed hopeless once more.

Spartacus set his jaw. *This is no time to give up. I chose to be here.* "Let's prepare everything as we discussed. There's no point worrying about things we can do nothing to prevent."

"Agreed."

"I'll talk to Ariadne. Maybe her god will give us some guidance at last."

Oenomaus grinned. "That'd be most welcome."

If it doesn't come soon, it will be too late.

XI

It was mid-afternoon when Glaber and his soldiers were spotted. Hearing the lookout's yell, everyone in the camp stopped what they were doing and climbed up to the crater's lip. In the middle distance, a long, winding black line could be seen on the road that led from Capua. It was too far away to make out the individual figures of men or beasts, but after Aventianus' news, the column could be but one thing. The instrument of their doom. For a long time, none of those watching spoke to, or even looked at, another. All eyes were locked on the approaching troops. The ominous silence was broken only by the faint whistle of the wind.

Eventually, Spartacus stirred. It wasn't just pointless staring at the Romans, it was dangerous. He could feel the gladiators' morale diminishing with every moment that passed. "Back to work! There is still plenty to do," he shouted. "I want hundreds of large rocks ready to roll down at the enemy. Thousands of stones to throw, and for the slingers to use. Every sword and dagger needs an edge on it that will shave the hairs off your arm. Those whoresons are going to regret that they ever came here!"

All the men did as they were told, but few smiled. Even fewer laughed.

Spartacus threw Ariadne a questioning look. The tiny, dismissive shake of her head that he received in return felt like a punch to his solar plexus. *Is this it, Great Rider?* He shook his head, pushing away his worry. "Atheas, Taxacis. Follow the path down the mountain. Get as close as you can to the Romans without being seen. I want to know their every move. How their camp is laid out. The number of sentries. Be sure to return before sunset."

Grinning fiercely at their new duty, the Scythians trotted off.

Spartacus went to pray to the Great Rider.

And to sharpen his sica.

†

Thanks to the trees blanketing Vesuvius' upper slopes, the Roman column was lost to sight as it reached the base of the mountain late that afternoon. If anything, its disappearance increased the tension. Tempers grew short, and men snapped irritably at one another. Some distance from the camp, a German gladiator who was collecting rocks ran away when his comrades' backs were turned. Angry shouts went up when he was spotted, but Oenomaus ordered that the fugitive should not be pursued. "Who wants a man like that by his side when the fighting starts?" he bellowed.

The sun was low in the sky when Atheas and Taxacis reappeared. Spartacus was conferring with Oenomaus and the three Gauls, but their conversation stopped the instant the warriors approached. "Well?" demanded Spartacus.

"They have made . . . camp. Typical type," Atheas began.

Spartacus saw the others' confusion. Born into slavery, they would never have seen the temporary fortifications thrown up every night by Romans on the march. "It will be rectangular, with an entrance on each side," he explained. "The whole thing will be surrounded by an earthen rampart the height of a man, topped with stakes. Outside that, they'll have dug a waist-deep protective ditch."

Atheas nodded in agreement. "We count . . . one picket in front . . . each wall. Hundred paces out."

"Is that all? Arrogant bastards," sneered Crixus.

"Any activity on the path to the peak?" asked Spartacus, his stomach clenching.

"Yes. Three hundred legionaries . . . stationed across it. And several small groups marched . . . good distance up . . . mountain. They hid . . . both sides of track. No tents."

"Sentries then," grated Gannicus.

Spartacus cursed savagely. *Oenomaus was right.*

"Those men are just to prevent us escaping tonight! The sons of whores will attack in the morning, surely?" demanded Crixus. He looked at each man. Something in Spartacus and Oenomaus' expressions made his face harden. "Neither of you think so."

"It makes more sense to lay siege," admitted Spartacus. "They can wait down there in relative comfort until we simply run out of food."

"The chicken-shit, toga-wearing, motherless goat-fuckers!" raged Crixus. He stamped up and down, filling the air with more colorful expletives. When he had regained some control, he fixed the others with his stare. "Like I said, let's choose a hero's death. We'll go down there in the morning and charge their lines. Make an end that will be remembered by slaves forever."

Scowling, Castus and Gannicus stared at the ground.

"We can do better than that," said Oenomaus.

"How?" demanded Crixus.

Oenomaus had no immediate answer.

Spartacus racked his brains. They had no armor and no shields. They were totally outnumbered. Their supplies would be finished within three days at most. Maybe their only option was a suicidal attack? He glared at the heavens. *Very well. I submit to your will, Great Rider.*

"Gannicus, are you with me?" asked Crixus.

"I've nothing better to be doing."

"Good. And you, Castus?"

"Damn it, why not?" came the snarled response.

"Count me in too," said Oenomaus harshly.

"Spartacus?"

He didn't reply. *What a useless way to die.*

"Spartacus?" Impatience mixed with anger in Crixus' tone.

His eyes dropped from the skies above, and caught on the vines that covered the steep slopes of the crater. Suddenly, the bones of an idea began to form in his mind.

"Are you going to answer my damn question?"

"Not right now." Spartacus walked off, leaving the others open-mouthed behind him.

"He's fucking lost it," Crixus declared. "I knew it would happen."

"What the hell is he doing?" demanded Castus. "This is no time for a stroll!"

Spartacus was pleased to hear Oenomaus growl, "He'll be back."

†

Returning to the other leaders a short time later, Spartacus held out his hands. "It was in front of us all along."

"That's a length of wild grapevine," said Gannicus in an incredulous voice.

Crixus' scorn was clear. "What shall we do with it? Strangle Roman soldiers?"

Castus laughed.

"Can you explain what's going on?" asked Oenomaus, looking bewildered. "The place is overrun with vines. So what?"

"It's clear as the sun in the sky."

Crixus' lip curled. "Put us out of our misery."

"These vines are excellent for weaving baskets, are they not?"

"Yes," replied Oenomaus, visibly controlling his irritation.

"Instead of baskets, we can make ropes. Ropes strong enough to take the weight of a man. Once it's dark, we can lower ourselves down one of the cliff faces on to the slopes below. I don't imagine that the Romans expect to be attacked from anywhere other than the path." Spartacus' confident smile belied his churning stomach. *The odds against us are still terrible, but this will be a damn sight better than committing suicide in the morning.*

"That's a fantastic idea!" Oenomaus clapped him on the arm.

"It would give us a fighting chance," admitted Gannicus.

Spartacus glanced at Castus. His sour expression had weakened. "I thought you had gone mad. But you haven't," he admitted. "It's a good plan."

"It might work," said Crixus with a dubious shake of his head. "Or then again, we could all break our damn necks."

"It's worth a try," said Oenomaus.

To Spartacus' delight, Castus and Gannicus rumbled in agreement. Crixus scowled. "Very well."

Thank you, Great Rider. It'll be easier with him on board. Spartacus made a quick calculation. "It's at least a hundred paces from the lowest part of the cliffs to the ground below. We'll need a minimum of two ropes. More if they can be woven in time."

"And then?" asked Oenomaus.

Spartacus was pleased to see that this time, all four waited to hear his response. He offered up more silent thanks. "Wait until it's nearly midnight. Pray for cloud cover. We'll blacken our faces and limbs with ashes from the fires. Climb down to their camp. Kill the sentries at their pickets. Fall upon their tents in silence."

"The bastards won't know what hit them!" interrupted Gannicus.

"They won't. We'll slay as many as we can before the alarm is raised," said Spartacus.

Oenomaus frowned. "What will happen after that?"

"Who knows? Perhaps we'll escape!" He didn't voice the other, more likely outcome. No one looked disheartened, however, which satisfied Spartacus. "An offering of thanks to Dionysus is imperative now. These are his vines."

No one argued with that.

†

By the time darkness had fallen, the gladiators had three ropes, each 120 paces in length. Every man and woman present had labored to complete the cords. Some had stripped vines from the crater walls while others had trimmed them down to a central stalk. Plaited in threes and securely knotted into four sections, the ropes were tested by having a pair of the heaviest men haul with all their might on each end. To Spartacus' delight, none broke. He ordered the fighters to prepare themselves, but they were to wait until he gave the word before making a move.

While the other leaders drank wine with their followers, Spartacus sat by the fire with Ariadne. They did not talk much, yet there was a new, intimate air between them. *This might be the last time I ever see her,* he thought regretfully. Across the fire from him, Ariadne's mind was racing. *Those vines belong to Dionysus. Did he make Spartacus aware of them? It seems too much of a coincidence to be anything else.*

Despite the blanket around his shoulders, Spartacus eventually began to feel chilled through. He glanced upward. The sliver of moon in the sky had been covered by a bank of cloud. There was little wind. "Time to move."

"I have asked Dionysus to lay a cloak of sleep over their camp."

"Thank you." He rubbed a final bit of ash on to his arms and stood. "By dawn, it will be over. I will see you then." He shoved away a pang of uncertainty. *Great Rider, let it be so.*

"Yes." Ariadne was unwilling to trust her voice further. *Come back to me safely.*

Without another word, he walked off into the darkness.

†

"There's the picket," whispered Spartacus, pointing at a huddle of shapes no more than a long javelin throw away. Fierce satisfaction filled him at what they'd achieved thus far. They'd scrambled down the cliff face with little problem. One man had broken his ankle, and had been left behind, but the others had moved like eager, silent wraiths, scrambling through the darkness to their present position. A hundred paces beyond the Roman sentries lay the southern rampart of Glaber's camp. Spartacus was lying on his belly in the scrub grass, the Scythians to his right, and Getas and another Thracian to his left.

The remainder, including the new recruits, were waiting some distance to their rear. Given their small numbers, Spartacus had decided not to bother assaulting the other sides. Their best hope lay in a savage, frontal attack using all of their force. The other leaders had seemed happy with that idea too.

"We go," muttered Atheas, lifting his dagger.

Taxacis grunted in agreement.

"Make it quick. Keep quiet," warned Spartacus. "The slightest sound could screw it up."

"Have you forgotten?" hissed Getas. "I've been doing this since I was old enough to wield a knife. The Scythians are no different."

"I know." Spartacus tried to relax. He couldn't stop his throat from constricting, however, as the four crept forward and disappeared into the pitch black. He waited, counting his heartbeats and trying to calculate how long it would take to reach the Roman sentries. He had nearly reached five hundred when a rush of movement reached his ears. Spartacus froze. The sound of fierce struggling rapidly ended with a couple of short, choking cries. *They've done it. Did anyone hear?* A cold sweat bathed Spartacus' forehead, but the silence that followed remained unbroken.

His men returned not long after, grinning fiercely. They were soon joined by the three Gaulish leaders and Oenomaus. "It's time to move," said Spartacus.

"Let us thank Dionysus again," whispered Oenomaus. "May he continue to watch over us. What lies ahead may cost us all our lives."

Eighty of us are about to attack a camp containing three thousand legionaries. It's complete madness. "I wouldn't be anywhere else," hissed Spartacus. "Not for all of Crassus' gold. Whatever the outcome, this will show the bastards that we are no ordinary latrones."

Rather than argue, Crixus made a low, growling sound in his throat. Castus' teeth flashed in the darkness, signaling his agreement. "It'll show them we're not just fodder for their games," added Gannicus.

With that, they shuffled back to fetch the gladiators.

✝

Spartacus had the men trail him in a long line as they padded toward the Roman camp. None of the others protested at this. Grim satisfaction filled him that they were prepared to let him take the lead. He paused by the dead sentries, allowing some of the more poorly armed fighters to strip the corpses of their weapons. Then he carefully walked on, pleased that those following him were making almost no sound. They reached the ditch without being challenged, and Spartacus' heart began thumping in his chest so hard that he wondered if it was audible. *Breathe.*

He eyed the ramparts. Without doubt, there would be sentries patrolling. How many, Spartacus did not know, but it would be no less than two per side. The nearest ones would have to be neutralized as the pickets had been. Scrambling out of the other side of the trench, he lay down. "Stay where you are," he hissed at the men behind him. As his order spread, the gladiators' advance stopped.

It wasn't far to the earthen fortifications, which were little more than a long, raised mound running from left to right in front of them. Spartacus scanned the top of the wall, finally picking out the shapes of two helmets off to his left. Straining his ears, he could just make out the murmur of voices. "See them?"

"Yes," hissed Atheas.

"I want them silenced in the same way as the pickets. Think you can do that?"

"Of course."

"Make a noise like an owl when you've finished." As the warriors crept away, Spartacus inhaled deeply and slowly let the air out again. The tension was as great as the final moments before any of the battles he had fought. *Calm, stay calm.* Focusing on his breathing, he closed his eyes.

When the eerie sound reached him, Spartacus felt a surge of relief. The Romans might think of an owl's call as bad luck, but he certainly didn't. Another obstacle had been removed.

They stole up to the entrance——little more than a gap between two overlapping portions of the rampart——without difficulty. Spartacus immediately conferred with the other leaders. "The men should file out on to the open space that lies behind the rampart when they get inside. They must maintain complete silence. Wait until my signal. The more tents that are attacked simultaneously, the better, eh?"

"Fine," replied Oenomaus. "I'll take the left flank."

"You three to the right," said Spartacus. "And I'll take the center." The Gauls nodded.

"Try not to let your men spread out. If we attack in groups, it will make us seem like a bigger force." He waited, but no one argued. *Excellent.* "Wait for my signal: a raised sword, and an owl call."

Spartacus watched as the four vanished to advise their men. Sudden doubt reared up in his mind. *What are we doing? This is fucking crazy.* Then his fingers tightened on the hilt of his sica. *Far better to die like this than to be overrun by thousands of legionaries in the morning.* He began to walk toward the tents.

The regular lines which came into view felt weirdly familiar to him. During his service with the legions, Spartacus had slept in many such camps. He had sat around campfires, singing and drinking wine with men such as those they were about to attack. *That is all in the past. I am here to kill. We are here to kill.* Spartacus muttered instructions to the Thracians following. Silently, they spread out on either side of him. Behind, he spotted the dim figures of men—Gauls and Germans—trotting to the left and right.

And then they were ready.

Spartacus raised his sica and glanced to either side. Seeing swords lifted in acknowledgment, he cupped a hand to his mouth and let out the owl call he'd practiced as a boy. The distant figures began to move, and Spartacus gestured to the men behind him, whom he'd ordered to work in pairs, staying along the same line of tents. He noticed Aventianus nearby, a club gripped tightly in his fist. Carbo was beside him, his face tense. Seeing Spartacus' look, the lad gave a resolute nod. *He'll do all right.*

Closer and closer they went. Still there was no alarm, no noise unless a legionary coughed in his sleep, or grunted in the midst of a dream. Ten steps from the nearest tent, Spartacus could take the waiting no more. He quickened his pace to a trot. Getas was right on his heels. As soon as he was close enough, Spartacus slashed down with his weapon, cutting through the leather paneling with ease. The blade's trajectory came to an abrupt end when it sank deep in human flesh. A heartbeat later, the silence was shattered by a terrible scream. Getas chopped down several paces away with similar success. "Quickly!" hissed Spartacus, pulling back his arm and swinging down in a different direction. There was a meaty thump as the sica sliced into another man. Another bawl of pain. *Take that, you Roman bastard!*

†

Ariadne sat alone by the fire, staring into the glowing embers and brooding. Did Spartacus' dream signal his death at the hands of Roman soldiers? Would it happen tonight? She was unsurprised but dissatisfied to find nothing to inspire her in the red-orange flames. The occasional shower of sparks that rose lazily into the night sky were no different. Dionysus had never revealed anything to her through the medium of fire before. He wasn't about to start now, she thought. Ariadne tried, and failed, not to feel bitter. Only once could she recall needing guidance this much—in Thrace, when Kotys had been threatening her.

Do not lose faith. The god had come through in the end, bringing Spartacus into her life. She pictured him in her mind's eye. It was easy to do so—did she not gaze at him secretly whenever she got the chance? Especially when he was undressing. Ariadne was glad that there was no one present to witness the sudden flush that colored her cheeks. Yet she had long ago stopped denying to herself that Spartacus was damnably attractive. Gods, she was only human! He was handsome, with a powerful physique. He was slow to anger, quick to laugh, and deadly with a sword or his bare hands. He was a natural leader of men. Most importantly of all, he had consistently looked out for her when there was no gain in it for him. He had not argued on the occasion when she had rebuffed him. Moreover, he had not tried it on with her again.

Now I want him to. Shocked by her own daring, Ariadne started forward from her seat. She sat down again, her heart pounding in her breast. *Why in hell's name not? With Dionysus' blessing, it will expunge the only other memories I have of sex. My father. Phortis.* Dread overtook her excitement at once. *For anything ever to happen between us, Spartacus has to survive tonight. And if his dream—*

"Stop it!" Ariadne said out loud. She saw the other women's heads turn from their fires, and quickly regained control. *He will survive,* she thought fiercely. But without a sign from the gods to the contrary, it was entirely possible that the snake Spartacus had seen foretold a terrible doom for him.

Ariadne resolved to make her best effort yet to seek guidance from Dionysus. The deity had already shown his goodwill in prompting Spartacus to use the wild vines. Perhaps he could be persuaded to extend some more aid? With new determination, Ariadne went to fetch her two statues of Dionysus. Spartacus, her husband, was fighting for his life on the plain below. The least that she could do was to spend the rest of the night on her knees in search of divine inspiration.

†

Spartacus delivered no more than four huge blows with his sword before he realized the effect of what he and Getas had done. The surviving men within—some of whom were wounded—were yelling and thrashing about, trying to free themselves from the collapsed tent. *Even if the whoresons get out, they won't want to fight. They're absolutely terrified!* "We can't kill them all. There's no need," he whispered to Getas. "Tell the others: 'Attack and move on. Attack and move on.'"

Moving between the gladiators was already hellishly difficult. The only things visible in the darkness were the outlines of tents, and the shadows in between that were his men. The screaming and shouting that now filled the air added to the confusion. Spartacus gave up all pretense of being quiet. "It is I, Spartacus," he bellowed. "Hack at every tent a dozen times and move on. Speed is of the essence!"

Spartacus turned. "Getas?"

"I'm here."

"Remember the Maedi war cry?"

"Of course!"

"Make it now! Let's do it for Seuthes!" Throwing back his head, Spartacus let a primeval roar rip free of his throat. Getas echoed his cry. Theirs was the same ululating sound that all Thracian warriors used when going to war. Named the "titanismos" by the Greeks, it curdled the blood in the veins of a coward. Three thousand of the whoresons are waking up to it, thought Spartacus grimly. I can think of no better way to die than like this. He cut down at a fresh tent with a blur of blows. One, two, three, four. Each strike hit a target, caused a fresh victim to scream at the top of his lungs. Spartacus sensed rather than saw Getas alongside him, his sword flashing up and down in imitation of his own.

They moved on to the next silhouetted structure. And the next.

It wasn't until Spartacus had reached his fifth tent that he saw his first legionary. The man stumbled into the night air. Clad only in his undergarment, he was unarmed. "What's going on?" he shouted in Latin.

"Hades is come, that's what!" Spartacus swung his sword across in a scything blow that took the Roman's head clean off his shoulders. A dark jet of blood spurted into the air from the stump of his neck. The man's right leg actually took another step forward, and then, like a puppet whose strings have been cut, the headless corpse toppled to the ground.

"Gaius?" called a voice. Another figure stepped out of the tent. This one was carrying a sword. Before Spartacus could react, Getas swept in and plunged his blade deep into the man's chest. The soldier was dead before Getas had shoved him off the iron back into the tent. Inspiration struck Spartacus and he slashed at the guy ropes. The front of the tent collapsed, trapping those within. Standing over the heaving leather mound, they chopped down again and again. The Romans' confused shouts soon turned to wails of pain and agony.

"Enough!" ordered Spartacus. He spotted Atheas and Taxacis nearby. "On! On!"

Like maniacs, they plunged deeper into the Roman camp, slicing into tents and hacking down any legionaries who got in their way. This can't go on, thought Spartacus eventually. All it needs is for an experienced officer to rally twenty or thirty men together. They'll make a stand against us, and our attack will stall at once.

It was as if the gods had heard him.

Spartacus heard the characteristic cry, "To me! To me!" Bile pooled at the back of his throat. "Where is he?"

"Over there!" Getas pointed to their left.

Spartacus made out a knot of figures about twenty paces away in the gloom. *Five, six men?* In the middle was a gesticulating outline wearing a transverse-crested helmet. "It's a fucking centurion!" He was off like a hound after a hare.

"It's just you and me," shouted Getas.

"So what! If we don't silence the bastard, it'll all be over for us!" Spartacus wasn't surprised that Getas' pace did not slacken. *If I have to die, I'm glad that he's the one by my side.*

"Great Rider, protect us with your sword and shield," Getas intoned.

They did not know it, but Carbo was charging along behind them. *I can't let Spartacus be killed. Not after all he's done for me.*

The odds against them were long indeed, thought Spartacus. Two more soldiers had joined the centurion. There were seven, or even eight, of them now. Most had shields too. Spartacus pictured his men, the gladiators who'd had the faith to follow him out of the ludus. He imagined Ariadne in the camp high above. If he and Getas failed, his men would be butchered. Their women would suffer a degrading fate. A cold, calculating fury descended upon him. *I will succeed here or fall in the attempt.* "Come on, boys!" he roared at his invented comrades. "Ready to send these Roman scumbags to Hades?" He whooped and yelled in response to his own cry, and understanding, Getas did the same.

Spartacus imagined that he heard a third voice joining in, but he wasn't sure. In the madness of that moment, he didn't care. All he wanted was to hack a great hole in the centurion's throat and leave him in a bleeding heap. Silence him forever.

They closed in on the group of legionaries. *Why the hell aren't they forming a shield wall?* Spartacus wondered. *If they did that, we'd be fucked.* Blind hope struck him. *Maybe they're panicking?* "For Thrace!" he roared. "For Thrace!"

He reached the first soldier, who lunged at him with his gladius. Spartacus dodged inside the clumsy thrust, ripped down the man's scutum with one hand and skewered him through the neck. A horrible, bubbling sound left the other's lips as his airways filled with blood. Spartacus pulled free his blade and ripped the shield from the dying soldier's grasp. He let it fall forward and stooped over it to grab the horizontal grip. Pulling it up to protect his body, he advanced toward the next legionary, who had already missed the chance to cut him down.

"Kill the bastard!" shouted the centurion. "Just fucking kill him!"

A second soldier joined the first, but Spartacus didn't hesitate. He could hear Getas shouting a war cry behind him. And a third voice? Spartacus still had no time to consider. He rushed at the pair of legionaries like a mad bull, and they took a step backward. His spirits rose. Dropping his shoulder behind the scutum, he thumped into the first man, knocking him off balance. Spartacus didn't bother to finish him off. He simply trampled over the screaming soldier and launched himself at the centurion.

"Goddamn latrones!" The centurion lifted his shield high and took a step forward. "Sneaking in on us like the animals that you are!"

Spartacus didn't bother answering. He banged his scutum off the other's, but there was to be no easy barge over as he'd done with the legionary. The centurion's sword came probing over the side of his shield like the tongue of a snake. Spartacus lifted his scutum as hard as he could, smashing the blade up and out of the way. He followed through with a brutal thrust at the other's face, but the centurion dodged to one side, and the sharp iron gouged a line in the cheekpiece of his helmet instead.

"You'll have to do better than that!" He slashed downward at Spartacus' feet.

Spartacus had to move backward to avoid losing several toes.

"Scum!" Snarling with delight, the centurion advanced. His blade skimmed over the top of Spartacus' shield. Spartacus ducked down so that his face wasn't sliced into ribbons. Coming up, he braced himself against the charge that would follow.

The centurion slammed into him, but Spartacus stood firm. With their faces two handsbreadths apart, they stared at each other with utter hatred. In unison, they raised their swords. This is it, thought Spartacus. I'll kill him, but he'll do the same to me. It was all happening so fast. He had to thrust first, and hope that the centurion's blow would not land, or at least that it would only injure him.

"For Thrace!" Getas came barging in from the side, his weapon lunging wildly.

Spartacus could nothing but watch in horror as the centurion smoothly moved his arm, letting Getas run on to his blade. It sank to the hilt in his belly, a death blow if there ever was one. Getas gasped in pain, and dropped his sword.

Hot tears of grief and rage half blinded Spartacus, but he savagely blinked them away. Before the centurion could react, or pull his gladius from the ruin of Getas' stomach, Spartacus had reached around to hack deep into his left knee. Keening with agony, the centurion fell to the ground like a bar of lead. Spartacus leaped on him, spittle spraying from his lips. "Animal? Who's the fucking animal?" He drew his sica across the base of the centurion's neck, laughing as the severed jugular veins pumped out gouts of dark blood. He didn't stop there. With a series of powerful chops, Spartacus beheaded the officer. Discarding his shield, he pulled off the transverse crested helmet and lifted the head by its hair. There was still a startled expression on the centurion's features.

When he straightened, Spartacus saw the demeanor of the three legionaries before him change. Their fear morphed into complete terror, and then panic. "Catch this, you miserable bastards!" he shouted in Latin, and tossed the still bleeding head straight at them. "You're next!"

As one, they turned and ran.

Wild-eyed, Spartacus glanced to either side. The bodies of legionaries lay everywhere. He registered Carbo standing nearby, his sword at the ready. *The third voice.* Beyond, bright orange-red flames lit up the night sky. The silhouettes of men ran hither and thither, accompanied by screams and the clash of arms. "Someone's fired a tent. Good idea. Better light to kill by," he muttered. There was a moan nearby, and Spartacus' attention came crashing back.

Getas lay several steps away, both hands clutching a fearful wound at the top of his belly. Spartacus dropped to his knees. Even in the poor light, he could see the blood oozing thickly between Getas' fingers. "What kind of fool are you?" he chided.

"He was going to kill you." Getas coughed weakly, and the flow of blood from his injury became a tide. "Better me than you."

Spartacus' throat tightened with grief. "Oh, my brother," he whispered. "You shouldn't have done it."

"Yes, I should. You're the leader. I'm only a warrior."

"The finest warrior ever to come out of Thrace."

The trace of a smile flickered across Getas' lips. "Don't talk shit."

"I'm not," protested Spartacus. "The Great Rider himself will welcome you into paradise."

"The Great—" Getas stopped. His eyes went wide and he took in a rattling breath.

Spartacus gripped him by the shoulder. "He's waiting for you. Go well, my friend."

Getas' mouth went slack, allowing the last gasp to go free. His body sagged back, going as limp as a discarded toy.

Accept this brave man into your presence, Great Rider. If ever a warrior was worthy to serve you, it is Getas. Spartacus reached out and slid down Getas' eyelids. With a heavy heart, he stood. As he registered what was going on, his grief was sublimated into a dark, brooding joy. Everywhere he could see, the legionaries were running. Running! "The fuckers have broken!"

"Yes," said Carbo in an awed voice. "It happened after you killed that centurion. All the men who saw it turned and fled. They were screaming that there were maniacs and demons on the loose. That there was no hope."

"Maniacs and demons, eh?" Spartacus laughed. "Well, I wouldn't want to disappoint them. Let's gather the men and terrify them some more. Hound the bastards completely out of the camp!"

Is he scared of nothing? wondered Carbo as he followed Spartacus. It seemed not.

†

It was soon apparent that the gladiators' success was complete. Routed like an unruly mob charged by disciplined cavalry, the legionaries had fled into the night. They left behind everything: their clothes, weapons, food and supplies. The mules that had carried their heavy equipment from Rome were still tethered in lines by one entrance. To cap it all, the various units' gilded standards and the very fasces of the lictores were found in a tent beside Glaber's quarters. The magnificent armor found within proved that Glaber had also left in a hurry. Seeing the Romans' most precious items abandoned hammered home to Spartacus the enormity of what they'd done. While the victorious gladiators engaged in looting, he stood in Glaber's luxurious pavilion alone, marveling. *If it doesn't signal my death, what in the Rider's name does my dream mean?*

"Spartacus! Where is Spartacus?"

Outside, he found Carbo confronting a black-bearded German. It was the same man who'd refused him an audience with Oenomaus. "I'm here. What is it?"

The German pushed past Carbo. "You must come."

The first needles of suspicion pricked Spartacus. "Why?"

"It's Oenomaus." The German's blood-spattered face twisted with an unreadable emotion. "He's hurt."

"How badly?"

"He's dying. He asked for you."

"Take me to him." Spartacus glanced at Carbo. "You come too."

Without another word, they ran along one of the straight avenues that bisected the camp. The German led them to a group of silent figures standing in a rough circle by the irregular outline of a collapsed tent. The corpses of at least a dozen legionaries littered the area. Cursing, the bearded man pushed through the throng. Spartacus and Carbo followed.

Oenomaus lay on his back within the ring. He was pale-faced, and his eyes were closed. Someone had laid a cloak over him, but the massive red stain in the fabric over his chest told its own grim story. No one can lose that much blood and live, thought Carbo.

Spartacus looked at the black-bearded German, who gestured that he should approach. He knelt and took Oenomaus' hand. It was cold to the touch. *Is he dead already?* "It is I, Spartacus."

Oenomaus did not respond.

"Spartacus is here," said the black-bearded man loudly.

Oenomaus' eyelids fluttered for a moment, and then opened. Dimly, he focused on Spartacus, who leaned in close. "You wanted to see me?"

"Your plan . . . worked."

Spartacus squeezed Oenomaus' hand. "It did, thanks to you and your brave men."

Oenomaus' lips gave the tiniest twitch upward.

Spartacus knew that the German's life was ebbing out fast. "What did you want to say?"

Oenomaus' mouth opened, but instead of words, a torrent of blood gushed out. It covered Spartacus' hand, and dripped to the ground as Oenomaus relaxed for the last time. Spartacus looked at his reddened fist before clenching it and lifting it in the air. "Oenomaus shed his blood for us! He was a good man and a strong leader. Let us honor his passing!"

A great roar went up from the German gladiators. Carbo joined in, oddly feeling more at ease with these hairy barbarians than he'd ever done with his peers in Capua.

Spartacus felt weary to the marrow of his bones. *Getas is gone. Oenomaus, my only ally among the other leaders, is dead. That is a heavy price to pay for victory.* A meaty paw was thrust in his face, and Spartacus stared at it, surprised. Then he accepted the grip, letting the black-bearded man haul him upright.

"My name is Alaric."

"You have lost a great man here tonight."

Alaric nodded. "The thread of his weave came to a fine end. I saw him kill at least six Romans before he took the mortal wound."

Spartacus cut to the chase. "Who will lead you now?"

With a frown, Alaric turned to the assembled men and barked out a few sentences in his guttural tongue.

Spartacus clenched his jaw. *It's probably Alaric. Soon none of the other leaders will listen to me.*

There was a rumble of agreement from the Germans. Alaric smiled.

Spartacus steeled himself for the inevitable.

"We all agree. You must lead us."

Spartacus blinked. "Me?"

"That's right. We are fighters, not tacticians or generals. None of us would have thought of using the vines, not even Oenomaus. That was pure genius."

Spartacus looked from face to grim face. He saw the same certainty in each. "Very well. I would be honored to lead you." *Thank you, Great Rider! Now I have the largest faction. Crixus and the others are more likely to continue following where I lead.*

In that moment, the loss of Getas and Oenomaus seemed a fraction less heavy.

†

The gladiators' losses were light, all things considered—eight men had died, and a dozen had been injured. Of those, four would never fight again. The dead were buried where they'd fallen. It was as good a place as any, thought Spartacus somberly, as he stood over Getas' grave. Lying in Thracian soil would have been better, but that was impossible. *Sleep well, my brother.*

With his respects paid, he turned his attention to more practical matters. Every last weapon and scrap of food had to be taken from the camp. Crixus and his men had found the stores of wine, and were already making deep inroads into it. Spartacus didn't even try talking to him. It took all of his powers of persuasion to get Castus and Gannicus to stop their followers joining in. Moving the provisions in the darkness was hard enough without everyone being paralytic. Waiting until sunrise meant risking the return of the legionaries, but Spartacus considered that unlikely. He placed men on watch in any case. After their stunning victory, it would be stupid to have the tables turned upon them.

Those gladiators who weren't drunk were organized. Using a stock of torches that had been found to illuminate the scene, systematic checks were made of every Roman body. Unsurprisingly, many legionaries were still alive—injured, unconscious or simply playing dead in the hope of escape later. On Spartacus' orders, every single man was to be executed. Universal whooping broke out at this announcement. "It's better treatment than the bastards would give us," he snapped, catching the burst of anguish in Carbo's eyes. "All we would get is a cross. The women too. Have you ever seen someone die on one of those?"

"Yes. My father took me when I was a boy to witness a local criminal being crucified." If he concentrated, Carbo could still hear the man's piercing screams as his ankles were nailed to the wooden upright. Within a short time, his noises had died away to a bubbling, animal whimper. It only increased in volume when he attempted to take the pressure off his roped arms by standing up on his ruined, pinioned feet. The criminal had lasted until the next afternoon, but his body wasn't taken down for weeks. Walking past the stinking, blackened thing, seeing all the stages of decay before it ended up as a grinning skeleton, had almost been worse than seeing the crucifixion, Carbo thought. Almost. "It was horrific."

"Exactly. It's far better to have a sword slide between your ribs and end it in the blink of an eye."

"I suppose," admitted Carbo. He'd slain at least two legionaries that night. He had no desire to kill more of them in cold blood. He surprised himself with his next thought: *I would if I had to.*

It must be hard for him, reflected Spartacus. But he fought well during the attack. That is sufficient evidence of his loyalty.

†

Ariadne tried tossing her knucklebones over and over, but she saw nothing of any relevance in the patterns in which they fell. She was relieved, therefore, when her meditation carried her far beyond the levels she'd achieved in recent weeks. Although she was used to long periods when Dionysus would give absolutely no indication of his intentions, it had never been more frustrating. Spartacus' dream about the snake was of great importance. Was it a good omen or a bad one, however? Like Spartacus, Ariadne burned to know. Her concerns over it ate her up, yet she knew they paled in comparison to the unease Spartacus must feel. He hid it well, but she saw it all the same. As far as she was concerned, matters had reached the stage where it would be better to know—even if the indications were bad. An enemy named was an enemy that could be fought. Unnamed, it was like a disease, eating the flesh from within.

All the same, it was horrifying when an image of Spartacus, with the snake around his neck, flashed into her mind. *No wonder he was frightened.* Ariadne could feel her own heartbeating faster. She waited. The serpent uncoiled and reared up in Spartacus' face and, terrified, Ariadne prepared for the worst. The characteristic pattern on its skin was the same as that on her own lethally poisonous snake. If Spartacus was bitten, he would die as fast as Phortis had.

Ariadne could not quite believe her eyes when Spartacus lifted his left arm. The serpent did not attack. Instead, it smoothly uncoiled from his neck and slithered over, coiling itself around his arm, as Ariadne's did. Spartacus raised his right arm and, with a thrill, Ariadne saw the sica in his hand. Armed thus with sword and snake, he turned to the east, the direction in which Thrace lay. He called out in a great voice, but she could not make out the words. With that, he was gone.

This can mean only one thing. He has been marked by Dionysus.

A great and fearful power surrounds him.

Ariadne's vision wasn't over, however. The mountaintop he'd occupied was none other than Vesuvius. And the crater was filled with tents. Hundreds of them.

Do they belong to his followers?

Ariadne waited for a long time, but nothing more was forthcoming. She offered a last heartfelt prayer for Spartacus' safety, and then she covered herself with her blanket and lay down. If the god wished to send her more insight, he could do it as she dreamed. Falling asleep was not as easy as Ariadne might have wished, however. Her mind raced endlessly. What was going on in the Roman camp? Had Spartacus' plan worked, or had the gladiators all been massacred? Ariadne batted the various outcomes around until she was exhausted. Just because Dionysus had marked him out didn't mean that a stray sword couldn't find its home in his flesh, ending the dream before it even started. *Do not let it be so.* When sleep finally claimed her, the first pink-red fingers of light were tingeing the eastern horizon.

XII

An hour after the sun had risen, Spartacus came trotting up the path to the crater. There had been no sign of any Romans on the plain and he was content leaving the gladiators to gather the weapons and equipment together and pack it on to the mules. They could follow him up later. Crixus had mentioned taking the Roman camp as their own, but Spartacus had advised against it. "We're far too few to defend the damn thing. Better to stay on the peak. It's easier to hold, and the lookouts can spot anyone coming for miles." Bleary-eyed and weaving where he stood, Crixus had grumbled but protested no further. Castus and Gannicus seemed happy enough with the decision, so Spartacus waited no longer. Carrying the news to Ariadne was now the most important thing on his mind.

He found her asleep by the fire they'd shared. Seeing the knuckle-bones, he bit back the "Hello" rising in his throat. *She could have been up half the night, praying.* Treading quietly to where she lay, he squatted down on his haunches. Strands of her dark hair lay across her cheek. She looked very peaceful. *Beautiful too.* Pride filled Spartacus that she was his wife. She was strong and fierce. And brave. Ariadne wouldn't sleep with him, but he could bear the sexual frustration for the moment because she was such a good catch.

He shifted position, scuffing some gravel with one of his heels.

Ariadne's eyelids fluttered and opened. A fleeting look of incomprehension flashed across her face, and then she was leaping up. Throwing her arms around him. "You're alive! Oh, thank the gods!"

"Yes, I'm here." He crushed her to him. Awkwardly, because they'd never been so close. "I'm covered in blood."

"I don't care." Deliberately, she buried her face in his neck. "You're here. You're not dead."

Spartacus was doubly glad that Getas had saved his life.

They stayed like that for a long time before Ariadne pulled away. "Tell me everything," she ordered.

Taking a deep breath, Spartacus began. Ariadne did not take her eyes off his face as he spoke. "Getas died that I might live," he concluded. "It was a great gift, and I must honor him for that."

"He was a fine warrior," said Ariadne sadly. Inside, she was rejoicing. *Thank you, Dionysus, for taking Getas instead.*

"Oenomaus is gone too."

Her hand rose to her mouth. "No!"

"Yes. But he did not die in vain. The Germans have made me their leader." He threw her a fierce smile. "I now have more men than any of the Gauls. That is a strong position to be in."

Jubilation filled Ariadne. Elements of her vision were making more sense. "The god visited me last night," she said.

He pinned her with his gaze. "What did you see?"

"I saw you here, on the top of the mountain. A snake was wrapped around your neck. In your right hand you held a sica."

"Go on." *I will accept whatever she has to say. Whatever the gods have sent for me.*

"The snake reared up in your face, but it did not bite you," she revealed, smiling. "Instead, it wound itself around your left arm. You turned to the east and raised your sword. You cried out, as if you were honoring someone. Then you vanished."

"What—"

She touched a finger to his lips, silencing him. "I'm not finished."

"When I looked back at the crater, it was filled with tents." She gestured around her. "There were hundreds of men here. They were your followers."

"What are you telling me?"

"I am saying that Dionysus has favored you. It was his snake around your neck. You are surrounded by a great and fearful power. Men will see that. They will come to offer you their loyalty."

"You are sure of all this?" he asked softly.

"Yes." Ariadne's voice rang with confidence. "As I am a priestess of Dionysus."

"I thought that perhaps this would happen to me in Thrace, if I succeeded in overthrowing Kotys," Spartacus said wonderingly. "But my path did not unfold in that way. Instead I am in Italy, in the heartland of our people's worst enemy. So be it. It is Dionysus' will that I should lead men against the Romans. Who am I to argue with a god?"

"I will stand at your side."

He smiled, and her stomach fluttered.

"Good. That is where I would have you."

"It is where a wife should stand." Before she could stop herself, Ariadne forced her feet to move. She stepped up to Spartacus. Leaning in, she kissed him on the lips.

He responded with fierce enthusiasm.

For the first time in her life, Ariadne felt a rush of sexual desire. She did not fight it.

At length, Spartacus pulled away.

Panic immediately flared in Ariadne's lower belly. *He doesn't like me.* "What's wrong?"

"Nothing at all. Much as I'd love to stay here, there is too much to be done." He grinned. "We can take up things right where they left off later."

Reassured, she gave him a last, shy kiss. "Good." Ariadne's stomach twisted at the thought of lying with him, but she ignored it. "What are your plans?"

"To get all the equipment we've seized up here. To arm every man properly. Then I'm going to explain to the other leaders that our victory last night was a one-off. The Romans won't ever make that mistake again. If we're not to be crushed by the next force sent against us, the gladiators have to start training. Like soldiers. The Thracians will do what I tell them. So will the Germans, but I need the Gauls too."

"They'll listen to you now."

"They'd fucking well better. Fighting as a disciplined unit is our only hope," replied Spartacus grimly. "Can you take charge of the women? An inventory of the food and wine would be useful."

"Of course."

"My thanks." Despite his concerns over their future, Spartacus walked off with a spring in his step. *Gods, but I can't wait until tonight.*

†

Conscious that most gladiators wanted to do nothing more than drink the Roman wine—copious amounts of which remained—Spartacus placed Atheas, Taxacis and half a dozen Thracians on guard over the majority of the amphorae. Chaffing the fighters about how much they could knock back that night, he made a big show of helping to load a train of mules with bundles of weapons and then slogging all the way up to the crater with it. When he got back, Spartacus did the same thing again. His tactic worked. While the men continued to grumble, they followed his orders. That was good enough. *A certain amount of complaining is healthy anyway. It shows that they're throwing off the slave mentality.* He'd made the decision to say nothing about training until the following day. That issue was potentially far more contentious than denying the fighters wine, and it would be easier to propose when everyone had a hangover.

It took the whole day for the military paraphernalia and supplies to be transported to the camp. The respite between the departure of one column of mules and the arrival of another provided ample time for the freshly arrived cargo to be counted and arranged in piles. Arming a delighted Carbo with a stylus and parchment, Spartacus had him draw up the records. The stacks of *pila*—javelins – gladii and shields were soon taller than a man and more than twice his height in length and breadth. They had arms enough for thousands of men. This realization darkened Spartacus' good mood again. *There are still less than one hundred of us.*

He didn't feel bad for long. *Yes, and look what we managed to achieve.*

Spartacus intentionally had the amphorae brought up last of all. Raucous cheering broke out as the mules and their precious load arrived at the lip of the crater. Without waiting until the column reached the tents, the most eager fighters ran over and unloaded one of the large clay vessels. Everyone watched as it was opened and then hoisted up on to a man's shoulder. He held it in place while his comrades took it in turns to stand, mouths open, beneath the stream of ruby liquid that poured out. Applause and laughter filled the evening air as the soaked fighters raised their arms in triumph.

"There it is, boys!" shouted Spartacus. "More wine than you can drink!"

"Do you want to make a wager on that?" roared a broad-chested Gaul. "If I have anything to do with it, there won't be a drop left by dawn."

His comment was met by hoots and cackles of amusement.

Spartacus smiled. "It's all yours. After last night, you've earned it."

The gladiators bellowed their delight at him.

Spartacus waited until the drinking had been going on for a while before he approached Castus and Gannicus. United perhaps by their achievement, the two were sitting by a fire over which chunks of wild boar were cooking. There was no sign of Crixus and his men.

"Look, the smell draws him in," teased Gannicus.

"It's good enough to wake the dead," said Spartacus.

"Aye. There are few things more appealing than the aroma of roast pork." Castus waved genially at a stone beside him. "Take a seat. Wine?"

Spartacus accepted the silver cup with a grateful nod. "A fine vessel."

"They're from Glaber's own table," gloated Castus, raising his own. "He didn't mind me taking them."

Spartacus chuckled. "To a fine night's work. To Getas, Oenomaus and the others who fell." He raised his wine high.

The two Gauls saluted him with their cups, and they all drank deeply.

They made small talk about what had happened during their attack. Although they must have known, neither Gaul mentioned Spartacus' accession to power over the Germans. He wasn't surprised. No doubt they were resentful of it. He tried to judge when would be the best moment to mention training the men. Too soon, and the pair might take offense, thinking that had been his only intention in talking to them. He wanted to leave it until the wine had dulled their senses, but not so late that they became argumentative or too drunk to understand his proposal.

A familiar, mocking voice cut across their conversation.

"Well, well. What have we here? A gathering of the leaders that I wasn't invited to?"

"It's nothing like that." Spartacus took in Crixus' flushed cheeks. He must have sobered up somewhat to climb the mountain, but it didn't look like much. *Damn it. Why did he have to appear?* He patted the ground beside him. "Join us."

"I will." With a sneer, Crixus threw himself down. "What've you been doing? Claiming how you each won the battle last night?"

"No, we leave that to you," responded Castus sharply.

Crixus glowered as Gannicus roared with laughter. "Funny man, aren't you?"

"So some say." Castus' words danced, but his eyes were as flat and cold as a snake's.

"A man knows when he's not welcome. I'll drink elsewhere," growled Crixus. He made to get up.

"Wait," said Spartacus. *I might as well tackle them all now. Maybe their antagonism against each other will stop them from unifying against me.* "I have something to say."

"Why does that not surprise me?" needled Crixus.

Castus' face took on its usual suspicious expression.

"Spit it out then!" said Gannicus.

At least one of them sounds genial, thought Spartacus. "What we achieved last night was astounding."

"Damn right!" cried Crixus belligerently, as if it had been his idea all along.

He mentioned Ariadne's interpretation of his dream, and the trio of Gauls roared with approval. "But we can't just rely on that. The luck we had against Glaber won't come our way so easily again."

All three men's eyes focused on him as hovering hawks do on a mouse.

"Why not?" demanded Castus.

"Because plenty of legionaries escaped. They'll tell of our surprise attack. The next commander that we face will have so many sentries on duty each night that they'll be falling over themselves."

"And you're sure that they will send another force?" Gannicus registered his companions' incredulous reactions and sighed. "All right. That's wishful thinking."

"That's right. It is," said Spartacus harshly. "And there will be more than three thousand of the bastards too. Count on it."

"This wine is sour," Castus snapped, pouring the contents of his cup on the ground. He poured himself a generous measure from the jug and tasted it again. His face screwed up.

Spartacus raised an eyebrow. "Doesn't taste so sweet now, eh?"

Castus grunted irritably.

Gannicus leaned forward. "What are your thoughts?"

"If we are to have any chance of surviving"—Spartacus let the words hang for a moment—"then we have to learn to fight as the Romans do. As disciplined infantry."

"Oh, it's back to this, is it?" mocked Crixus. "You want the men to train."

The fool. Can't he see it? Spartacus' temper began to rise, but he forced himself to remain calm. "Yes, I do. Every day, with shield and sword, until they can stand in a line like legionaries and respond to orders instead of charging in like maniacs." Like Gauls, he wanted to add.

Crixus' eyes glittered in the firelight. "I can tell you now that mine won't do it."

"My lads won't be too keen either," added Castus, sounding regretful to be agreeing with Crixus.

Spartacus turned his head.

"I don't know . . ." said Gannicus.

"By the Rider, can you not see what will happen otherwise? On an open field of battle, the legions are invincible! Without proper training, we will be crushed like beetles underfoot." He glared at each of them.

"What's the point? We'll be annihilated sometime no matter what," muttered Crixus. "We may as well live like lords until that day."

"Who's to say that we'll be wiped out?" challenged Spartacus. "We're far more mobile than the Romans. Ambush and move on, that's what I have in mind. Stay in the mountains when at all possible. If we do that, it will take far more than a force of mere infantry to even find us." He wasn't happy with the skulking image that conjured up, but their position was a damn sight better than it had been just a short time before. It would do for the moment. Spartacus stared around at them, waiting.

Crixus curled his lip.

You'd cut off your nose to spite your face. Shame I didn't do it for you. "Castus?"

Castus' eyes flickered uneasily, but he did not answer.

Gannicus cleared his throat, and then spoke. "There's nothing wrong with the idea of training, I suppose. Some routine might stop the lads from doing nothing. Keep them fit."

"Good." Encouraged, Spartacus turned back to Castus.

"Don't listen to him, Castus!" Crixus advised. "The fucker is power mad. Can't you see it?"

"That's not what it's about," snapped Spartacus.

"Isn't it?" Crixus threw back.

"Would you like to lead us all?" asked Castus.

"Spartacus."

Recognizing Aventianus' voice, he turned his head. "What is it?"

"There's something you should see." Aventianus pointed to the point where the path from below met the lip of the crater.

Spartacus stood up. Spotlit by the rays of the setting sun, he made out the figures of men emerging into view. Dozens of others were already milling about the edge of the camp. "Who the hell are they?"

"Slaves," said Aventianus simply. "Herdsmen, shepherds and agricultural laborers for the most part. They heard what you did to Glaber and his men, and they've come to join you."

What I did. Fierce pride coursed through Spartacus' veins. "How many are there?"

"The sentries have lost count."

"Excellent!" Spartacus turned to the Gauls. "We've got the food and the weapons to equip an army. All those men need is training, and we can give them that. Can't we?"

"That sounds good," declared Gannicus.

Castus hesitated for a heartbeat and then he nodded. "So be it."

"Will you join us, Crixus?" asked Spartacus in a friendly way.

"I suppose." It was said grudgingly. "Someone will need to take charge of those fools or they'll run the first time they even see a legionary."

"You'd be excellent at knocking them into shape."

For the first time, Crixus grinned. "Fine."

"We can start tomorrow. I'll begin the gladiators' instruction." Now their glances were more inquiring than rebellious. *Thank you, Great Rider.* "I spent years fighting with the Romans, so I have a good idea of how they're trained to fight."

No one argued, and again Spartacus gave silent thanks. For the moment at least, the others would follow his lead.

"Thank you for the wine." Draining his cup, he set it down beside Castus. "I'll see you in the morning."

"Where are you going?" demanded Castus. "There's a whole night of drinking to come."

"For you, maybe. I'm going to talk to the new arrivals." *And Ariadne is waiting for me.* Ignoring their protests, Spartacus walked away. He was glad that none of the Gauls followed him. If they were more interested in getting drunk than making a good first impression on the slaves who'd fled their masters to come here, that was their loss.

The four sentries were relieved to see him. Although they'd been trying to keep the slaves from spreading out, theirs was an impossible task. It was like trying to stem the tide, thought Spartacus, looking at the ill-dressed, nervous-looking rabble before him. Even a rough head-count took him to a hundred, and more men were spilling over the crater's lip with every heartbeat. Here and there, he spotted a woman too.

"Welcome!" he shouted in Latin.

At once he became the focus of attention. "Who are you?" The question came from a strapping man with old, healed burns all over his arms.

A blacksmith. Just the type we need. "I am Spartacus."

"You're Spartacus?" The man's face was incredulous.

"That's right."

"But—"

"What?"

"I thought . . ."

"That I'd be seven feet tall and breathe fire? Is that it?"

There was a burst of laughter and the blacksmith colored beneath his tan.

Moving closer, Spartacus fixed the man with his piercing gaze. "I am Spartacus the Thracian, who fought as a gladiator in the ludus at Capua. Last night, I led eighty men into a camp where more than three thousand legionaries were sleeping. We killed hundreds of the whoresons, and sent the rest screaming for their mothers. If you think I'm lying, perhaps you'd like to take me on. Bare hands or with weapons. It's your choice."

The blacksmith looked into Spartacus' eyes and saw his death there. His confidence vanished like morning mist. "I meant no offense."

"None taken," Spartacus replied amiably. "Why are you here?"

"I've come to join you. If you'll have me," the blacksmith added quickly.

"You're a smith?"

"Yes. Been doing it since I was a lad."

"Do you want to fight the Romans? Kill them?"

"Yes!"

"And the rest of you?" asked Spartacus. "Is that what you've come for? To become fighters?"

The baying roar that answered him filled the crater with a wall of sound.

Spartacus waited until it had died down. "Good. I will feed you and give you tents to sleep in. I will arm you and train you. And I will lead you against the Romans." He drew his sica and stabbed it into the air. "Is that what you want?"

"YES!" they roared.

Spartacus smiled. Ariadne's words were already coming true.

From the smallest seed, a great oak can grow.

It was a start.

†

Ariadne had kept herself busy all day, but that hadn't stopped her mind from racing. As she counted bags of wheat, slabs of dried pork, containers of salt, spices and other foodstuffs, all she could think of was the kiss that she had shared with Spartacus. And what would inevitably happen when they went to bed that night. The thought of *that* filled her with anticipation, and terror. *I could still say "No."* Ariadne dismissed the idea at once. She hadn't come through all that she had with Spartacus, helped him, developed feelings for him, just to give up at the final hour. Deep down, Ariadne knew that if she didn't have sex with Spartacus soon, she would never do so with anyone. Willingly, at least.

Having made her mind up, Ariadne was annoyed to feel nervous still. She was a grown woman, was she not? Without meaning to, she visited some of her irritation on Chloris and the other women, snapping unnecessarily when they miscounted something, or didn't move fast enough to the next job. They were already wary of her—a priestess of Dionysus—and so rather than answer her back, they scuttled about, trying to avoid her gaze and making even more mistakes.

I'm acting like a bully. This realization made Ariadne gentle her tone. Instead of criticizing the women when each task was completed, she started praising them. The atmosphere lightened, and their work rate improved. By the time the sun had dropped to the crater's edge, virtually all the food had been checked over and had its details recorded.

"It looks as if you've been busy."

Ariadne jumped at the sound of Spartacus' voice. Suddenly conscious of the sweat marks on her dress and her straggly hair, she turned. "We've hardly stopped all day."

"Neither have I. It didn't stop me thinking about you, however."

She blushed. "I've been doing the same."

He gestured over his shoulder. "Hundreds of slaves have been coming in, wanting to join us."

"As in my dream?"

Giving her a pleased look, he nodded.

"Dionysus be praised. That's great news!"

"It is. And don't ask me how, but I got the Gauls to agree to training for the men. It's to start in the morning."

She was already moving. "The new arrivals will need food and drink."

Bemused, Spartacus watched her as she ordered the other women to ready themselves for an influx of hungry men.

She reappeared by his side. "That will do for now."

"I suspect that they'll be happy enough with all the wine that's on offer."

"It will help," she agreed. "But I'm forgetting myself. Are you hungry?"

"Not for food. Are you?"

"N-no," Ariadne said, aware that her voice had gone husky.

"Shall we go back to the tent?"

In answer, she took Spartacus' hand and led him away.

†

Ariadne lay on her side, gazing at Spartacus' sleeping form. In the gray light of predawn, it was hard to make out his features in detail. Taking great care to move slowly, she shifted position on the blanket until she was lying right next to him. Here she was, in bed with a man she had chosen to couple with. It felt good, just as last night had. Ariadne had been surprised by that. She'd been willing, even eager, to engage in the physical act with Spartacus, certain that it would bring them closer, cement the bond between them. But she hadn't expected to enjoy it.

Spartacus had been gentle yet sure, and so attentive. Several times, feeling her tense, he had paused. He'd looked at her inquiringly, and on each occasion, Ariadne had nodded fiercely to indicate that he should continue. Gradually, her lust had risen, if not to match his, then to lift her for the first time above the hurt that had blighted her for so long. The whole experience had felt, in no small way, healing. A tiny, self-conscious smile twitched across Ariadne's lips. By the end, she'd felt quite wanton.

"You're watching me. Eyeing me up, in fact."

Ariadne was startled from her reverie. "Maybe I am," she flashed back. "A woman is allowed to admire her man, isn't she?"

"Of course. As long as I'm allowed to do the same to you," he murmured, reaching out for her.

She wriggled into the circle of his arms. "I expect nothing less." Surprising herself again by her own daring, Ariadne moved her right hand to his waist—and below.

"I need to get up," he protested weakly.

"I need you more," Ariadne retorted. "I've waited so long for moments like this. Half an hour won't make any difference to the men's training."

He smiled and pulled her to him. "True."

TWO DAYS LATER, IN ROME...

When Saenius had ushered the last bowing client from his simple yet elegant courtyard, Crassus clicked his fingers at the body slave standing behind his chair. "Take away that mule piss," he ordered, indicating the wine on the sturdy table before him. "Bring me a decent vintage. Remember to water it down."

"Yes, master." The slave was used to Crassus' routine. Those who came seeking his favor were given plenty of refreshment, but not of the expensive kind. Once the morning's business was dispensed with, his master liked to relax with a glass of quality wine.

"Bread and cheese too."

"Yes, master." The slave was careful to hide his half-smile. He would have brought those items anyway. In many respects, Crassus was as predictable as the tide. In order that his slaves knew his likes and dislikes, he trained them all himself.

Saenius came padding back through the tablinum, past the death masks of Crassus' ancestors, and the *lararium*, the shrine to the house gods. He found Crassus trailing a hand in the brick channel that carried water to the lemon trees and vines filling the courtyard. "That last one was quaking with fear as he left," he observed.

"All I did was remind him that his debt was due in a month," said Crassus mildly.

"That's enough." Saenius' smile was acid. "He knows that you're a bull with hay on his horns."

Crassus gave a pleased nod. He never tired of hearing the popular expression being used about him. Every Roman worth his salt knew that only dangerous bulls had their horns covered in this way. Such a beast was to be avoided if at all possible. It was a good—no, an excellent—reputation to have, he reflected.

The domestic slave returned with a bronze tray upon which sat a jug, two blue glasses and a platter of bread and cheese. He set it down carefully, before pouring wine for his master.

"Care to join me, Saenius?" asked Crassus.

"Yes, thank you."

As was their custom, master and servant drank together in companionable silence. Above them, the sun beat down from a cloudless sky. Despite the shade offered by the plants and trees, the temperature in the courtyard was climbing steadily. Crassus felt the first beads of sweat trickling down his forehead. "Thank the gods that there's no session in the Senate today. I don't want to go out, even in a litter."

Saenius murmured in agreement. Walking through Rome at midday in the height of summer was akin to sitting in a caldarium for too long: hot, sweaty and uncomfortable.

Crassus closed his eyes, luxuriating as a light breeze trickled across his face. An instant later, his nose wrinkled. The rising heat exacerbated the omnipresent reek of human waste. While he—naturally—had the comforts of piped sanitation, most of Rome's residents did not. The public toilets weren't nearly numerous enough to cope either. The maze of alleyways lacing the city were therefore home to vast, steaming dungheaps, the ammonia-laden odor of which now filled Crassus' nostrils. He frowned. He could order that some *olibanum* be burned, but it would only mask the stench and leave a cloying, unpleasant taste at the back of his throat. "Maybe it's time for a break," he mused. "A month at the coast would be very pleasant."

"Your villa there is always ready," said Saenius, clearly pleased at the idea of quitting the capital. "And the sea breezes make the heat easier to bear."

Crassus was about to agree when a totally different scent reached him. *Smoke.* His head turned, seeking the direction from which it came. "Do you smell that?"

Saenius leaned forward, sniffing. "Ah yes." He concealed his disappointment well, thought Crassus with amusement. "Something's burning," he said.

"It's certainly the right weather for it," replied Saenius. "The city hasn't had a drop of rain for weeks, and some fools will always leave a brazier untended."

Crassus threw back the last of his wine and stood. "The coast can wait. Let's go and have a look around."

Saenius knew better than to argue. "I'll gather the slaves." Calling for those who made up Crassus' entourage, he vanished into the depths of the house.

Crassus took a deep breath, filling his lungs with the harsh tang of burning wood. It was most effective at concealing the stink of shit, he thought wryly.

Anticipation filled him next. The powerful odor meant that somewhere not too far away, there was money to be made.

†

The source of the fire wasn't hard to track down. Crassus' large but plain house was situated on the lower slopes of the Palatine Hill. By simply walking to the nearest crossroads, he could gain a partial view over the center of Rome. That told him that the conflagration was on the Aventine Hill. The score of slaves trailing Crassus—a mixture of bodyguards, laborers and architects—spied the billowing smoke at once too. Faint cries were also audible above the hum of ordinary life. Debate broke out among the men about the size of the blaze, what had started it and how many people would die before it was put out.

Crassus ignored their chatter. All would become clear when they got there. He strode down the street, indicating that his slaves should follow. "It's bad luck to live on the Aventine," he said softly, repeating the old saying.

His bodyguards quickly moved in front of him. Armed with cudgels and knives, they bellowed and used their fists to clear a path through the teeming, narrow streets. "Make way for Marcus Licinius Crassus, praetor and the most generous man in Rome!" they shouted. "Scion of one of the Republic's oldest families, son and grandson of a consul, he regularly donates a tenth of all he owns to Hercules."

Crassus smiled benevolently.

"So fucking what? Crassus is so damn rich that he could afford five times that amount and still not notice the loss!" a voice suddenly yelled from the throng.

The bodyguards' heads spun angrily, looking for the culprit.

"Leave it. There's no time to waste," ordered Crassus. *Besides, it's true enough.* Similar comments were made everywhere he went. Like the lewd political and sexual graffiti that decorated the walls of houses throughout the city, it was a nuisance that had to be borne, as a dog suffered its fleas. He pulled a heavy purse from inside his tunic and handed it to Saenius. "Offer that to the crowd," he said loudly.

· 247 ·

A wave of excitement rippled through those within earshot. Scores of hungry, dirty faces turned toward them.

"All of it?" cried Saenius, acting out the ritual they'd played countless times before.

"Why not? The worthy citizens of Rome deserve no less," replied Crassus. He added in an undertone, "I'll recoup it a thousand times over where we're heading."

Saenius' answering grin was wolf-like. Filling his fist with coins, he fell out of step long enough to fill the air with showers of bronze *asses*, silver *sestertii* and *denarii*. Crassus glanced back at the mob, which had gone wild. *Excellent.* To add to the spice, he'd added an occasional gold *aureus* to the change in his purse. One of those was but a drop in the ocean to him, but to the average impoverished resident of Rome, the rare piece of currency represented food for weeks, if not months.

It took perhaps a quarter of an hour to work their way to the Aventine. The multi-story buildings pressed in on either side, creating a gloomy, claustrophobic world and preventing a view of the fire's exact location. The problem was easily solved, however. Hordes of frantic, wild-eyed people were fleeing the quarter. All Crassus had to do was order his bodyguards to drive against the crowd's flow. Drawing their cudgels from their belts, three of them formed a wedge and shoved forward. From then on, anyone who got in their way was simply smashed over the head. Magically, the center of the street opened up. Set on a new course, the rabble streamed by on either side of Crassus.

Some citizens carried their belongings, wrapped in sheets, on their backs. Others had nothing but the clothes they wore. Children who had been separated from their parents screamed. Husbands cursed under the weight of what their wives had made them carry. Upset by the din, babies added their mewling cries to the general mayhem. Crassus ignored the fear-stricken masses, focusing instead on the shopkeepers' faces framed in the entrances of the establishments that lined both sides of the street. Their precious stock, whether it be meat, pottery, metalwork or amphorae of wine, meant that each of them stood to lose far more than the average person if the fire spread. It also meant that the traders did not panic unnecessarily. The expressions of the men he saw here were not that concerned. Yet. "Press on," Crassus ordered his bodyguards. "The blaze is a good way off still."

They found it a dozen streets farther up the hill.

Thick brown smoke filled the air all around them now, and the temperature rose sharply. The area was already almost empty of people, and the only ones visible were scuttling in the opposite direction. Crassus wasn't surprised. Other than the owners of affected buildings, there was no one to fight fires in Rome. The ground floors of most structures were constructed using bricks, but above many towered the dizzying wooden heights of the *insulae*, three, four and even five stories of tiny, miserable flats. This was where most people lived. Existed would be a more accurate description, thought Crassus, feeling grateful for his station in life. Built with little regard to safety or architectural design, the insulae were death-traps waiting to collapse or burn down. Fire was the more common of the two disasters. And once a blaze had a foothold in a building, it was virtually impossible to put out. Thanks to the fact that everything was constructed either directly adjoining or actually touching the structures around it, it was the norm for the flames to spread lethally fast. Anyone who stayed in the vicinity risked being incinerated. Conflagrations in which entire neighborhoods were destroyed, killing hundreds, were commonplace during the summer months.

He caught sight of two anguished figures ahead: a middle-aged man wearing a grubby shopkeeper's apron and an attractive woman of similar age. Crassus smiled. This would be the owner and his wife. Those whose livelihoods were in peril could never bring themselves to leave until the very last moment.

Now the crackling of flames could be heard. Looking up through the swirling eddies of smoke, Crassus saw bright orange-yellow tongues licking hungrily at the third floor of a wood-faced block of flats. "It started in a *cenacula*. It's out of control already."

"Is it ever any other way?" asked Saenius.

"Rarely," admitted Crassus dryly. He pushed aside the bodyguards. "Greetings, friend!"

The man he'd spied didn't hear his salutation. Ignoring his wife's warnings, he darted into the open-fronted shop that formed the structure's base. He emerged a moment later, carrying a large ceramic pot. Setting it down beside half a dozen others, he prepared to run inside again.

"You risk much, friend," said Crassus loudly. "Many's the man who's been buried alive when a building collapsed."

The shopkeeper regarded him with a dazed expression. "I have no choice," he said in a monotone. "My life savings went into constructing this block of flats. I'm ruined, I know, but without any stock, we'll starve." He turned away, distracted by his wife's sobs.

"That need not happen," declared Crassus. "Believe it or not, the gods are looking down on you today."

"Are you mad?" cried the man. "If they are, they're laughing."

"I'll buy your building and everything in it from you, friend."

"Eh?"

"You heard me."

The shopkeeper's face twisted as the bitter truth struck him. "You must be Marcus Licinius Crassus," he said in a cracked voice.

"That's correct." He glanced at Saenius. "My fame goes before me."

"As it always does."

"I don't want your money," snarled the trader. "You come skulking here with your henchmen, to watch as my whole life goes up in flames!" He made a dash for his shop just as a deafening, cracking sound shredded the air. Cursing, he skidded to a halt by the entrance.

Crassus watched with some satisfaction as the shop's ceiling collapsed, burying everything within in a mass of burning timbers. "You'll have to make do with those few pieces," he said mildly, pointing at the pathetic pile of crockery. "They won't sell for much, I don't think."

The shopkeeper's fists bunched with rage. He took an impulsive step toward Crassus, whose bodyguards grinned evilly at one another.

"No!" screamed the man's wife. "I can't lose you as well."

The man's shoulders slumped in defeat. "How much?" His voice was barely audible above the crackle and snap of burning wood.

"I was going to be generous," said Crassus coolly, "but your aggression has changed my mind. Five hundred denarii for the lot."

"It cost twenty times that to build," said the shopkeeper in disbelief. "And my stock, it—"

"That's my first and last offer," snapped Crassus. "Take it—or leave it."

The man stared at his wife, who gave a tiny, helpless shrug.

"I won't wait around," warned Crassus. He turned as if to go.

"I accept! I accept . . ." The man's voice trailed off, and a choked sob left his mouth.

"A wise decision. You'll sign over ownership by nightfall, and be paid tomorrow. Now, if you'll excuse me, there's work to be done," and Crassus turned to his men. "Get to it! You'd better move fast, or the blaze might spread to the buildings on either side."

"That wouldn't be such a bad thing, would it?" asked Saenius.

Crassus' wagging finger was belied by his smile of agreement.

"Best get out of the way," Saenius advised, ushering the shopkeeper and his wife some way up the street. "Once the structure begins to fall, it can become very dangerous."

Crassus followed at a leisurely pace. "Is anyone inside still?"

"I don't think so, sir," replied the shopkeeper.

"Good." Crassus made a chopping gesture with his arm. His slaves had been waiting for his command. Moving with the ease granted by long experience, they began tearing at the first story of the burning building with specially designed, long iron hooks. The structure was flimsy, and it didn't take long for gaping holes to appear in the wood. Crassus' men redoubled their efforts, eventually ripping the entire front off the first story and pulling the debris down to the street. At once the building's timbers began to emit loud, groaning noises.

It was then that the screaming began. "Help me! Please!"

Crassus looked up into the billowing smoke. For a few moments he saw nothing, but his eyes finally settled on a pale, terrified face peering from a window opening on the top floor. "Gods above!" wailed the shopkeeper's wife. "I think it's Octavia's daughter. She's only eight. Her mother works in another part of the city; she often leaves the child at home. The poor mite must have been asleep."

Saenius made a poor show of looking sympathetic.

Crassus didn't overly care either, but it paid to keep up appearances. "Check the staircase!" he ordered.

Saenius sprinted to the wooden stairs that ran up the side of the building. On each floor, a door gave access to the cenaculae within. He returned, shaking his head in false sorrow. "It's burning."

"What can we do?" cried the woman, tears streaming down her face.

He'd made a token gesture. Anything more would be hazardous in the extreme. Crassus wasn't prepared to risk any of his men's lives for an eight-year-old gutter rat. He shrugged. "Pray that she has an easy passage to the other side."

The woman began to scream, and her husband pulled her close. "Shhh. There's nothing we can do."

Crassus didn't want to listen to the screeching of either the doomed child or the distraught woman, so he walked farther up the street. He scanned the shops on either side with a practiced eye. Surprise, and then pleasure, filled him. They were not the usual shabby run-of-the-mill enterprises, selling offcuts of meat, shoddy tools or badly woven clothing. Instead there was a silversmith's, a moneylender's and a Greek surgeon's premises. This was a quarter with a good future, he reflected. It would be a profitable place to rebuild.

His smile grew broader. Despite the heat, this had been a good day.

†

Crassus' good mood did not last. When he arrived home, tired and reeking of smoke, he was looking forward to a cold, refreshing bath and a change of clothes. He was greatly put out, therefore, to discover a messenger from the Senate waiting for him in the courtyard. One who would not wait to be seen.

Crassus glared at the man down his long nose. "What in Jupiter's name do you want?"

"An emergency meeting of the Senate is to be convened this afternoon, sir."

"For what bloody reason?"

The messenger twisted beneath his gaze. "Caius Claudius Glaber has returned."

Crassus' mind was still on his new acquisition on the Aventine, and a bath. "Who?"

"The praetor who was sent to Capua."

"Oh yes. His job was to seek out and kill the runaway gladiators. He had three thousand men, if I recall. It was but a simple matter. March down there, mop things up, come back to Rome." Crassus took in the other's scared look. His eyebrows made a neat arch. "Clearly that's not what you have come to tell me."

"No, sir. The gladiators attacked Glaber's camp at night. They killed the sentries and fell upon the legionaries as they slept . . ." The messenger hesitated.

"Go on," ordered Crassus in disbelief.

"According to Glaber, all was confusion and chaos. His men panicked, and fled."

"Three thousand men ran from seventy-odd scumbag gladiators?"

"Y-yes, sir."

"Were many of Glaber's soldiers killed?"

"Four or five hundred, sir. The rest escaped safely."

"Escaped? It's not as if they were even defeated in a battle! Fucking cowards," thundered Crassus. "And this fiasco is what Glaber has come back to tell us about?"

"Yes, sir," whispered the messenger. Terror filled his eyes. It wasn't uncommon for those who bore bad news to be punished, or even killed.

Crassus chewed his lip in concentration. *Spartacus is not just a skillful fighter. He is clearly a man of some ability. A tactician.* His Roman pride lashed out at once. "So what if he can marshal a few men together to make a craven attack at night?" he said to himself. "This humiliation cannot be tolerated. Will not be tolerated! The next force that is sent will be twice the size." Even that prospect did not ease Crassus' anger, and he paced up and down, musing about how he would deal with such a situation.

The messenger waited, trembling, for his sentence to fall.

After a moment, Crassus finally noticed him again. "What are you still doing here? Piss off. Tell whoever sent you that I will attend the debate in the Senate."

"Yes, sir, t-thank you, sir," stammered the messenger, backing away.

Crassus headed for the bathing complex, which lay off the courtyard. He could think about this as he relaxed in the cool of the frigidarium.

One thing was certain, however.

Glaber had to pay for his mistake.

†

Later, Ariadne would look back on the days and weeks that followed as a halcyon time. Spring moved into summer, and she allowed herself to forget her troubled childhood, Kotys, their journey to Italy and the ludus. She even expelled Phortis from her mind. She did not consider the future or the idea of traveling back to Thrace. What was the point? She was happier than she'd ever been. And it was all down to one man. Spartacus. She couldn't get enough of his company. She wanted to know everything about him, and he seemed to feel the same way about her. Truly, the gods must have united them, Ariadne thought. Here she was, free as a bird, living at the top of Vesuvius with her man, and his ever-growing band of followers.

Within a month, it had become clear that there would be no immediate reprisal for the humiliation inflicted upon Glaber and his soldiers. Firstly, there were no troops in the area. Secondly, as Spartacus said, choosing a new commander and the best plan of attack would take the Senate time. So would raising a new force of legionaries. Unless there was great need, Rome kept no legions on its home territory. Thirdly, there could be no surprise assault on the gladiators. Their camp's lofty position granted stupendous views on all sides, and on every estate for fifty miles there were now slaves who would burst their lungs to carry to Spartacus the news of a Roman column.

Spartacus drove himself hard. This period of respite had to be used wisely. It was a time to train the gladiators mercilessly, honing them into infantry. To forge the many hundreds of raw recruits—most of who had never even held a weapon before—into soldiers. To organize hunting parties, and bands that could range far from Vesuvius, raiding for newly harvested grain and stocks of iron and bronze. Often led by Crixus or Castus, who used the opportunities to avoid training, the marauders spread the word that any man used to working in the fields or tending livestock would be welcome at Vesuvius. Domestic slaves were not wanted. They needed men who were used to rough, outdoor lives. Men who could fight.

But for Ariadne, it was a time of pure, unadulterated joy. Although the threat of reprisal was ever present, it was easy enough in the warm days to forget all about Rome and its legions. To exult in the fact that, for the first time in her life, she was in love.

Unsurprisingly, her daylight hours were filled with toil. Organizing the womenfolk, of whom there were now more than two hundred, came naturally to her. So did acting as the camp's quartermaster. She also revelled in being the rebels' talisman. From the start, Ariadne had made sure that Spartacus spoke about his dream often, and of her interpretation of it. The gladiators and slaves lapped it up. They had found not just freedom by running away from their masters, and a charismatic leader, but a mouthpiece of their most revered deity, one unsuccessfully banned by Rome more than a century before. In their eyes, Ariadne was a priestess of Dionysus, and Spartacus was his appointed one. They regarded both with awe, and news of the couple spread far and wide.

Spartacus' time was also taken up with drilling the gladiators and new recruits, or consulting with Pulcher, the blacksmith who had challenged him. Pulcher was now one of his trusted men, and the rebels' de facto armorer. Along with several other smiths, it was his job to melt down slave chains and fashion arrowheads and swords. To bake sharpened stakes until their fire-hardened tips would skewer a man with ease. To hammer out sheets of bronze into plain, serviceable helmets. A motley group of slaves worked alongside Pulcher, making shields.

Periodically, Spartacus would lead a raiding party out to gather information, but for the most part, he stayed at the camp. Every dusk, sunburned and covered in sweat, he would saunter toward their tent. His smile lit up Ariadne's heart. So did the words he murmured in her ear as they sat side by side looking out over the Campanian plain, and the way he made her feel when they retired to their blankets. Falling to sleep in his arms under a canopy of glittering stars felt like all she'd ever wanted.

It was no surprise that Ariadne looked forward to each evening with a fierce hunger. She clutched the hours to her as if they were the last she'd ever see. The dawn became her enemy, because its arrival meant the end of her time with Spartacus. Until the next sunset.

She wished that the summer—the fantasy—would last forever. But of course it didn't.

XIII

One morning, not long after the grain had been harvested, Ariadne woke feeling chilled to the bone. During the hot months, she'd grown accustomed to sleeping outdoors, with little in the way of blankets. That would have to change, she thought, shivering. The blades of grass around her were coated in a fine layer of dew, and there was a damp cool in the air that hadn't been there the previous dawn. An inexplicable sadness stole over her. Somehow the drop in temperature felt like the cooling of a body after death. She could almost taste the sweet decay.

"Autumn is around the corner," said Spartacus from his pile of covers.

"It is." She gave him a bright, false smile.

He saw through it at once. "What is it?"

"I don't know. Something's changed. The air feels different."

His face hardened. "It will be the Romans, then. They had to come sooner or later."

"You're sure?" Ariadne could feel the cold truth of it in her belly, but she didn't want to be the one to say it.

He shrugged. "If it isn't today, it will be tomorrow or the next day. Maybe we'll even have a week's grace. It doesn't matter."

"Why not?" *I wanted our time never to end!*

"We have to face our fate eventually, Ariadne," he said gently, sitting up. "You know that as well as I do."

"Too much waiting around, and the men will go stale."

"More than that. They'll start refusing to train. Become proper latrones. They might turn against me."

She shot him a horrified look. "They wouldn't dare!"

"You say that. Crixus is only happy because he's been roaming the area like a Cilician pirate on the Adriatic, attacking whatever he chooses. Castus is the same, and there are a couple of Germans who've started giving me the eye when I order them to do something. Those who were slaves are learning to love their freedom, which is good, but . . ." Spartacus smacked one fist into the other. "It's time to lead them into battle. That will settle things down. Thin their blood a little."

She couldn't stop herself. "You could be killed!"

"That's right, my love."

It was the first time he'd ever used those words, and Ariadne's heart skipped a beat.

"But I'm not going to run away from this fight. That's not the type of man I am. Don't forget that Dionysus has honored me with his blessing."

"I know," she said, trying to make her pride more evident than her worries.

He reached over and kissed her. "I'm not going to throw away my life like a fool either. The men have been training hard, but they're still not up to standing toe-to-toe with thousands of legionaries. And while they might think so, neither are Crixus' and Castus' followers. We're not going to fight the bastards in open battle."

The ache in Ariadne's belly eased. "What will you do?"

"Ambush them. Come at the column in woods or forest if we can. Break up their lines. Cause panic, as we did in Glaber's camp. That's the way to take the fight to them."

"The fight," she repeated slowly.

"Yes," cried Spartacus. "That's what it is. Except it's in Italy, not Thrace."

Ariadne's fear resurged. *Is this what you meant, Dionysus?* Seeing the passion burning in his eyes, she took a deep breath and let it out again. "This is your path."

"For the moment, it is." He tapped his chest. "I can feel it here."

"Therefore it is mine too." *To whatever end.*

"That gladdens my heart." He squeezed her tight. "I have to go. Men must be sent out to find this new Roman force."

†

When the scouts returned, they reported nothing but the usual traffic on the local roads. They'd seen traders and their mules, farmers with heavily laden carts and small bands of travelers. A messenger had been spotted; so too had an itinerant soothsayer and a group of lepers. There had even been a rich man in his litter, accompanied by a retinue of bodyguards and slaves.

But no soldiers.

Unperturbed, Spartacus called Carbo, Aventianus and two other slaves to him. The four gave each other curious looks as they gathered before him. They didn't know each other particularly.

"Wondering why you're here?" asked Spartacus.

They all murmured in assent. Carbo hadn't seen much of Spartacus in the previous months. That was fine. He felt privileged just to have been instructed by him. If the truth be known, he had been fitting in extra training. Running up and down the mountain's slopes twice a day. Carrying weights and sparring with whoever would take him on. He still wasn't up to taking on Amatokos, but he fancied that the looks Chloris had thrown in his direction were approving. At least he hoped so. Carbo's efforts had paid off in other ways, however, because Spartacus had nodded in approval a day before when he'd knocked a German twice his size on his arse. The small gesture had made Carbo's spirits soar. Whatever duty he was offered now, he would accept. How his life had changed, he reflected. He now lived among, and fought with, slaves. He truly was an outcast—but he didn't care. Carbo was proud of what he'd become. What he'd made of himself.

"Ariadne—the priestess who revealed that I have Dionysus' favor," Spartacus added for effect, "had a strange feeling this morning when she awoke. I've learned to pay attention when she tells me such things. As you know, the scouts have found sod all in the surrounding countryside, but we've seen neither hide nor hair of the Romans for months now. Just because there's no sign of the dogs doesn't mean that nothing's happening. I want you to head singly for the nearby towns and see what information you can glean. A man can find out a lot by hanging around a marketplace for a day or two." He saw Carbo's questioning look. "You're all native speakers. You'll fit in far better than me, with my Thracian accent, or Atheas and Taxacis, who can barely order a cup of wine in Latin. No one will give you a second glance."

"And if anyone demands to know our business?" asked Aventianus.

Spartacus reached down and picked up four little purses that lay by his feet. He tossed one to each man. "You're a contract laborer who has finished his summer's work, and is on his way home to his wife or his family. That's your pay."

Aventianus smiled. It was an entirely plausible story.

"Where shall we go?" inquired Carbo. *Please don't ask me to travel to Capua.*

It was almost as if Spartacus sensed his reluctance. "You head for Neapolis, on the coast. The rest of you can decide where you want to go: north to Nola and Capua, on the Via Appia, and Nuceria, to the south. If there's any gossip to be had, you'll hear it in those towns." He held up a warning finger. "I don't care if you spend all the money before you return, but be careful! Don't get too drunk. Wine loosens men's tongues. If you get found out, you'll end your days nailed to a cross."

They nodded grimly at him.

"One more thing. Leave your swords behind. Take only a knife and a staff with you." He grinned at Carbo's scowl. "I know you've grown used to being armed, but nothing will attract more attention than a peasant with a gladius." Spartacus waved a hand in dismissal. "Come back as fast as you can. May Dionysus and the Great Rider watch over you."

Carbo went to fetch his sleeping roll and a water carrier. By leaving immediately, he could reach Neapolis before dark. *How I've changed.* Once, he'd have been insulted at being called a peasant and having the blessings of strange gods called down on him. Now he was more upset at not being allowed to carry a weapon.

Carbo knew which person he preferred.

†

Dusk was falling as Carbo neared Neapolis. He'd run some of the ten miles from Vesuvius to make sure that he arrived in time. Yet he'd cut it very close indeed. The three guards had already pushed one massive door to, and were moving toward the second. He broke into a sprint. "Wait!"

The sentries' heads turned. They were typical city watchmen: two were middle-aged, with sagging paunches, and the other was a stripling youth with cheeks as smooth as a newborn's bottom. "What have we here?" cried one. The solitary silver *phalera* pinned to his tunic told Carbo that he'd once been a legionary. *He's the leader.* Only brave men earned such decorations. "To be in that much of a rush, a man can only be searching for one of two things. Is it wine or a whore?"

"Or both?" added the second graybeard with a toothy leer.

"You're exactly right, friends. Both," lied Carbo, coming to a grateful halt. "I've been working on a latifundium for the last six weeks, existing on little more than acetum and stale bread. Not so much as a woman in sight. At least not one that it was safe to go near."

"The *vilicus* kept a close eye on you, eh? That's often the way. You must have a hard-on like Priapus!" The veteran gave him a wink. "I was the same when I was your age. Neleus here wishes he was like that too, but he's so shy that he won't even approach the whores by the market.

And they'd straddle a corpse if it had a coin to spare!" He chortled as the embarrassed youth hung his head.

Gods, thought Carbo with delight. They didn't even look at my scars. And they took me at face value. Pride filled him. *I'm a man now.*

"Pass, friend." With an expansive gesture, the veteran indicated that Carbo could enter. "Whoever you choose, give her one from me."

"I will." Carbo grinned. "Is there an inn where I could find a corner to sleep in?"

"Several. The Bull is the one where you're least likely to be eaten alive by fleas and bedbugs. You're less likely to be robbed there too. It's off the street that leads from this gate. Third alley on the right. Don't pay any more than an *as* for a bed in the stable."

"My thanks."

With that, he'd passed under the great stone arch and into the city. Carbo had never been to Neapolis before. He glanced curiously at the fine buildings as they faded into the rapidly falling darkness. Most were newly built. After centuries of loyalty to Rome, Neapolis had been elevated to a *municipium* nearly two decades previously, but its fortunes had taken a real tumble during the brutal civil war just a few years later. Carbo could remember as a boy his father telling his mother in hushed tones about the city's sacking. Under Sulla "the butcher," an army had burned its large fleet at anchor, and killed many hundreds of civilians. Finally, they had set Neapolis ablaze. The residents' crime had been to have opposed Sulla. *And they call Spartacus a latro?*

Carbo hurried to find the Bull. The narrow thoroughfare was emptying before his eyes; he had no desire to linger outside longer than necessary either. There was no street lighting. Lamps hung outside an occasional large house, but their glow did not extend far. The shadows were growing longer with every heartbeat. As he came alongside an alleyway, a shape moved in the gloom within. Carbo's grip on the hilt of his dagger tightened. If Neapolis was anything like Capua, only a fool went abroad after dark. A fool, or a cutthroat.

He was relieved to find the inn soon after. The hum of loud conversation, shouts and out-of-tune singing led him in. The stench of manure, stale urine and human sweat filled his nostrils as he approached the open-fronted establishment. A wooden staircase ran up the side of the building to the flats above. Oil lamps decorated the graffiti-covered walls, inside and out. Their yellow-orange glare illuminated a jumble of rough tables and benches that spilled from the grimy interior on to the alley. Straw had been scattered everywhere; from its soggy appearance, it looked to have absorbed more than its fair share of wine. Or blood.

The place was thronged. *I'm not the only one with a dry throat.* It wasn't a surprise. The harvest had recently been taken in, and although the Vinalia Rustica was over, the temperatures were still pleasantly warm. A man could do worse than drink a few cups of wine with his friends at night. Carbo took in the customers, a selection of merchants, travelers and locals. There were whores aplenty too, sitting on men's laps, flashing their breasts at anyone showing interest, or working the tables for custom. Lowlifes were also numerous: shifty, poorly dressed men in ones and twos whose gaze flickered constantly over the gathering like hungry wolves eyeing a flock of sheep. *Friends? I don't have any. Not here anyway.*

Pushing his way to the bar, Carbo spoke to the proprietor, a wall-eyed man with heavy stubble coating his long jaw. As promised by the guard at the gate, a bronze coin secured him a corner in one of the stables. Throwing down his sleeping roll, he returned to purchase a jug of wine and some bread and cheese. With his hands full, Carbo headed for an unoccupied table against one wall. The best—and safest—place to observe the goings on was one where he could sit with his back against cool brickwork. His belly grumbled noisily as he sat down, reminding him that he hadn't eaten since midday. Carbo forgot all about the other customers and set upon his food with purpose.

It didn't take him long to clear his plate and throw back two cups of the watered-down wine. Feeling much better, Carbo belched. He filled his cup again and cast his gaze casually around the room. A couple of tables over, four traders were loudly playing dice. Ignoring the demands of those around him to shut up, a man with wine stains all down his tunic bawled an out-of-tune ditty about Odysseus' journey. A pair of graybeards argued over the pieces on a "Robbers" board. Beside them, a florid-faced merchant pawed greedily at a whore's crotch. Three watching veterans sniggered and made lewd suggestions about what the pair might get up to.

Carbo thought of Chloris and his groin throbbed. He felt the little purse, which hung from a thong around his neck, and considered taking one of the whores upstairs. It was commonplace for such women to use a room over taverns. He studied them all one by one, and decided against it. *They're cheap and nasty. I'll catch some disease.* A higher-class establishment would be far better. There at least they might wash between customers. *Get a grip. That's not what I'm here for.* Carbo decided to finish the jug of wine and go to bed. Markets began trading at dawn, and he wanted to be there from the start.

"Come far?"

To the right, a man was sitting with his back to the wall, as Carbo was. He had brown hair, cut in the military style, two differently colored eyes, and high, wide cheekbones. He was perhaps a decade older than Carbo.

"Are you talking to me?"

"Yes. I saw you come in. It looked as if you'd been on the road. You must have barely made it before they closed the gate." His accent was well educated, at odds with the other clientele.

He's only being friendly. "You have the right of it. Another few moments and I would have been left outside for the night. I'm damn glad that didn't happen."

The other pointed to his jug. "You'd get none of this piss for a start!"

Carbo chuckled. "No."

"Tempted to try one of the whores as well?"

"Not the ones in here. They're pox-ridden for sure."

"You're not wrong there. I'm Navio." He leaned over and clinked his cup off Carbo's. The movement revealed his waist, which was encircled by a gilded belt. Navio saw Carbo's eyes take it in. "Yes, I'm a soldier." His expression soured. "Or I was."

"My name's Carbo." He waited, but no more information was offered.

"You must be a farmer's son, eh? Come to seek out the city's fleshpots?"

Carbo shot Navio a wary look.

Navio smiled. "Come on. Your tunic might be homespun and your knife cheaply made, but your accent is not that of a laborer. You're from a good family, like me."

Alarm filled Carbo. *Gods, I hadn't thought of the way I sound.* He scanned Navio's tanned face, but could see no suspicion in it. *One story's as good as another.* "Is it that obvious?"

"Yes." Navio took a mouthful of wine.

Wanting to fit into his new role better, Carbo adopted a sullen tone. "I've been working on the farm all summer without a break. No thanks from my father, of course. I decided to have a few days off. It's been well earned."

"Is that all you have to complain of? Do you know how lucky you are?" asked Navio sourly.

"I've got plenty more to worry about," replied Carbo sharply, thinking of his mission. "As no doubt you have."

"I'm sorry," said Navio, with an embarrassed look. "Things haven't gone well for me recently."

"Were you discharged?"

Navio's lips twisted with bitterness. "It was a bit more permanent than that." Noticing Carbo's interest, a shutter came down across his face. "It's none of your business, though."

"No," said Carbo stiffly. *He must have been thrown out of the army.* "As you please."

"Forgive my rudeness. Have some of my wine." Navio filled Carbo's cup to the brim before raising his own. "To new friends and good company!"

Relenting, Carbo repeated the toast.

"The landlord told me about a whorehouse one street over," confided Navio with a wink. "The women there are veritable Venuses compared to the ones here, he said. Clean too. Fancy trying it in a bit?"

Carbo suddenly pictured a woman different to Chloris, with her Greek looks. A large-breasted, creamy-skinned beauty, lying on her back, urging him to fuck her. *Where's the harm in that?* "Sounds like a good idea."

"Let's drink to that!"

They both drained their cups. Carbo poured more wine for both of them, and they fell into a more neutral conversation, bantering with each other about the inn's other customers. Which of the four merchants would win the next dice game. Whether someone would eventually silence the caterwauling singer. Which prostitute would snare a customer first. Whether an argument between a pair of men would turn into a fight. It passed the time admirably.

Two jugs of wine later, Carbo was viewing the world with much more benevolence. A warm, fuzzy feeling filled his head. The whores had even become appealing. Navio caught him ogling the youngest one, and laughed. "It's time to find that brothel. Come on!"

They threaded their way unsteadily between the tables. Carbo took the opportunity to squeeze a prostitute's buttocks as he passed, grinning as she squealed in mock horror. She immediately turned and lifted her skirt, revealing the dark triangle of hair in her groin. "Fancy a bit of this? Two sestertii and it's yours for an hour."

"An hour? He'd only need two or three thrusts to finish!" Navio cried. He was nearly in the alley. "Come on, Carbo. Let's go."

Reluctantly, Carbo tore his eyes from the whore's crotch and headed for the entrance.

Satisfied, Navio strode off.

"Hold on, I need a piss." But Navio didn't hear his mumble. By the time Carbo had emerged, the soldier was already twenty paces away. "Screw him, I can't wait." Carbo fumbled his way to the nearest wall and pulled up his tunic. After some difficulty with his licium, he freed himself. With a sigh of relief, he watched his stream of urine splashing off the bricks.

When he turned back, the alleyway that led back to the main street was empty. Cursing under his breath, Carbo hurried after Navio. He was about to call out, telling his new friend to wait, when he heard a soft *thud*, as a body makes when it hits the ground. Carbo's words dried in his throat. *That was how I was attacked after leaving the tavern in Capua.* He reached for his dagger, and was reassured by the cool bone of its hilt. Pausing for a few moments to let his eyes adjust to the Stygian gloom, Carbo slid his feet along the dusty ground as quietly as he could.

Two score paces on, against the faint light of a lamp on a house's wall, he made out a man's shape crouching over a motionless form. *Navio!* White-hot rage washed away the fuzziness in Carbo's head. He didn't even consider returning to the safety of the inn. Instead, he drew his knife, gripping it in his fist with the blade pointed toward the ground. It was the method taught to him by Spartacus. "This way, no bastard can knock the weapon out of your hand, and you can still stick it wherever you like."

Navio's assailant rolled him over and began pawing through his clothes. "Where's the fucking purse?"

Navio groaned and Carbo's heart leaped. *He's not dead then.* Squinting, he judged that the distance between them had closed to perhaps fifteen steps. There was no sign that the lowlife had any companions, but Carbo still wasn't near enough.

Coins clinked, and the thief made a pleased sound. "Anything else?" he muttered, stooping over Navio again.

Thanking the gods for the lowlife's greed, Carbo hurried forward.

Ten paces. Eight. Six. Four.

Undoing Navio's gilded belt, the thief tugged it from around his waist. "This'll fetch a tidy sum." His hand reached out and picked up a club, and then he straightened.

There was a *click* as one of Carbo's sandals scuffed a stone.

The thief half turned in surprise. "What—"

It was the last thing he said. Carbo hammered his knife down into the side of the thief's neck. He drove it so hard that it went in right to the hilt. Carbo ripped it out savagely, setting free a gout of blood that splattered his face. Uncaring, he stabbed the thief once, twice, three times in the chest. The blade grated off ribs and into the chest cavity, shearing the vital tissues into pieces. Carbo twisted it for good measure each time. It was when the thief slumped into him, unmoving, and the club dropped from his nerveless fingers, that Carbo realized that he was dead, or dying. *Just what you deserve, you bastard.* With a satisfied grunt, he heaved the thief to one side.

He crouched in the darkness, his knife ready, listening for anyone else.

The only sound was Navio's labored breathing.

Carbo dropped to his knees. "Navio! Can you hear me?"

There was no answer. *How hard did the whoreson hit him?* Carbo reached out, feeling Navio's face and scalp for signs of damage. Finding a sticky mat of hair, he lifted his hand, peering at it in the dim twilight. The fluid on his fingers was dark. *Blood.* Carbo returned to the spot, pressing down gently as he'd seen the surgeon in the ludus doing.

"Hades, that fucking hurts!" Navio growled. "Are you trying to kill me?"

Carbo let out a long breath of relief. "Sorry."

"As if that sewer rat didn't hit me hard enough," complained Navio.

"Can you sit up?"

"I think so. Help me."

Carbo put a hand around Navio's shoulders and lifted. "Why the hell didn't you wait for me? I was only having a piss."

"I thought you were going to waste your money on that mule-faced whore."

"No, I wasn't."

"I'll know better next time." Navio locked eyes with him. "I owe you. Thank you."

"You're welcome," replied Carbo, mollified.

"Now, where's the brothel? It can't be far." Navio twisted his head to see, and then he groaned.

"I don't think that's such a good idea," warned Carbo. "Can you even stand, never mind ask your prick to do so?"

Navio chuckled throatily. "Maybe you're right."

"Let's go back to the inn."

"My belt. Where is it?"

Carbo fumbled around until his fingers closed on the gilded metal and leather. "Here. I'll carry it for you." With his help, Navio stood. He kicked feebly at the thief's body. "You made short work of that scumbag. Have you been trained to use weapons?"

Carbo thought fast. "We had a slave, a Samnite who'd fought in the Social War. He taught me a lot."

"The Social War, eh?" There was a bitter edge to Navio's weak laugh.

"What?" Carbo moved forward, supporting Navio.

"Nothing."

Carbo didn't push it. Instead, he supported Navio back to the inn. Few people paid them any heed as they re-entered, for which Carbo was grateful. Although no one would care that he'd killed a thief, he didn't want to have to explain himself to the city watch. "Let's get you to bed," he muttered to Navio. "You need to sleep your injury off."

"No damn way. I owe you a drink. It's the least I can do."

"But the blood on your head—"

"Fuck that. I've had far worse. I want wine. Lots of it, in fact."

The determination in Navio's voice was clear. "All right." Carbo guided them back to the table he'd sat at. They ordered another jug. When it arrived, Navio poured them both a cup with a shaking arm. "To friendship!" he said, lifting his wine. Carbo echoed the toast with a grin, and they downed the first cup in one swallow. Navio did the honors again, spilling some on the tabletop. "That the whoreson who tried to rob me gets a warm welcome from Hades!" Carbo nodded and threw back the second cup. It would settle his nerves. *The thief would have killed me in the blink of an eye. He's no damn loss.*

Without hesitation, Navio filled their cups again. "To courage and loyalty!"

"I'll drink to that," said Carbo fervently.

"I'd say you would," said Navio with a shrewd look. "You're a good man."

Feeling self-conscious, Carbo studied the tabletop.

"Most men wouldn't have risked their skins to save me as you just did."

"Maybe not." Carbo began to feel quite proud.

"I can guarantee it." Navio leaned over the table, breathing wine fumes all over him. "I'd wager that you can keep a secret too."

"If I have to," replied Carbo cagily.

"I've recently returned from Iberia."

"And . . ." said Carbo, not understanding.

"I was a soldier there."

"What, fighting against Sertorius and his men?"

"Not exactly, no." Navio hesitated.

The wine was coursing through Carbo's veins now, filling him with confidence. "Spit it out, man."

Navio let out a great sigh. He glanced casually to either side, and dropped his voice to a whisper. "It was the opposite, really. I was one of Sertorius' officers."

Carbo hadn't expected that. He nearly dropped his cup. "Eh?"

"It's not that surprising," said Navio defensively. "I'm from Neapolis, and it was natural for my father to support Marius against Sulla. After Marius' death, Sertorius, his right-hand man, fled to Iberia. My father went too, taking our whole family. Mother died soon after our arrival, and I grew up in a world where everything was about fighting what Rome had become. All I knew was war." Navio hawked and spat. "We did well for a long time too."

Like anyone, Carbo knew the broad strokes of what had happened in Iberia over the previous seven years. How Sertorius had won over many of the peninsula's fierce tribes, and how he'd proved himself a master at guerrilla warfare, defeating all comers sent against him from

Rome. He had had the temerity to make contact with another enemy of Rome, Mithridates of Pontus. In return for money and ships, Sertorius had sent military officers who would train Mithridates' army. Yet things had gone awry eventually. In the previous year or so, Carbo knew that things had soured for Sertorius, as Pompey Magnus and his generals had finally turned the tide against him. "Has the situation got worse?" he asked vaguely.

Navio frowned. "You haven't heard?"

"Our farm is out in the sticks," lied Carbo.

"Yes, I'd forgotten. Well, Sertorius is dead."

"Slain in battle?"

"I wish," replied Navio bitterly. "No, he was stabbed and killed by Perperna three months back. The traitorous fucking dog."

"Perperna?"

"Do you remember Aemilius Lepidus' failed rebellion four years ago?"

"Yes. He tried to take Rome, but the proconsul Catulus defeated him at the Milvian Bridge. Fled to Sardinia, didn't he?"

"That's right. When Lepidus died soon after, his principal followers—of whom Perperna was one—sailed to Iberia with the remnants of their army. Sertorius welcomed them with open arms. He even set up an opposition Senate with them."

"I remember my father wondering why the Senate in Rome didn't offer Sertorius a pardon when Sulla died," said Carbo. "There was no real reason to continue the war in Iberia, and Sertorius was such a talented general. Why didn't they welcome him back into the fold?"

"It was nothing but their damn arrogance and pride," cried Navio. He winced in pain.

"Take it easy."

"I can do that when I'm dead." Anger throbbed in Navio's voice. "Sertorius was a better man than any of Marius' followers. He always stood up to the extremists in the party, and he took no part in the massacres sanctioned by Marius. They should have given him a chance to return with his honor. Instead, he bled out his life at a banquet in some Iberian shithole."

"Did Perperna take command of Sertorius' forces?"

"Yes."

"And you stayed with him?"

Navio glowered. "I was a complete fool, all right? My father said that we should wait until Perperna defeated Pompey before taking any action against him. I followed his lead." He swallowed audibly. "I will regret that to my dying day."

"What happened?"

"It was simple. Perperna wasn't half the leader Sertorius had been, so Pompey made mincemeat of us. He finished us off in less than two months. My father and younger brother were killed in the final battle. I managed to escape, but most of the survivors were taken prisoner. I suppose I should be grateful for one thing. Pompey offered every man who would swear his loyalty to Rome a pardon. Except for Perperna. He executed him."

"Sounds as if he got what was coming to him," said Carbo with feeling. "So you took up Pompey's offer, and then came home?"

"Eh?" retorted Navio in disgust. "Accept a pardon after the way the Senate treated Sertorius? I'd rather be tied in a bag with a dog, a cock, an ape and a viper and thrown in the Tiber."

"Why didn't you try to fight on in Spain?"

"Pompey gave such generous terms to the Iberian tribes that they have no desire to go on fighting. Sertorius was an orator, and he might have changed their minds, but I'm just a simple soldier. I didn't know what to do, so I took passage back to Neapolis. *Home.*" Navio spat out the last word. "Where everyone now rushes to kiss the arses of men like Pompey and Crassus."

"What do you plan to do?"

"I'm going to wage war on the Senate. On Rome. I want vengeance for Sertorius. For my family."

"You're going to do that on your own?"

Navio gave a cracked laugh. "You think I'm mad, don't you?"

"Not mad, no." *Crazed with grief and guilt, maybe?* "Your cause is hopeless, you know. No one can take on the Republic in open battle and win."

"So what? I'd rather keep my pride than bend my knee to the likes of fucking Pompey. He was supposedly the Republic's best general, yet Sertorius defeated him—not once, but twice!" Navio reached over to grip Carbo's shoulder. "There you have it. I bet you didn't think you'd hear a story like that when you entered the inn. And if you fancy a nice lump sum of cash, all you have to do is report me to the authorities in the morning. I think the current reward for rebel officers who haven't surrendered is two hundred denarii. Not bad, eh?"

"I'm not going to do that."

"Why not?"

"I don't need the money!" joked Carbo. "No, it's far more than that."

"Do you also hate Rome?" asked Navio joyfully. "Are there still some who support Marius?"

"It's not that either." Carbo scanned Navio's face, seeing his earnestness. *He placed his trust, and his life, in my hands. And we could use him.* He took a deep breath. "But I follow a man who does."

"You're making fun of me."

"I'm not." Carbo looked Navio in the eyes. "I give you my word."

"He must be loyal to Marius."

"He's not a Marian supporter."

"I don't understand."

"Swear that you'll tell no one."

"On my life."

"He's a gladiator," said Carbo.

"A gladiator?"

"Yes. He's from Thrace. About six months ago, he led a breakout from the ludus in Capua. There were only seventy-three of us at the start, but thousands of slaves have joined since then. Spartacus is training them to fight."

"You're as mad as I am!" Noticing the pride in Carbo's eyes, Navio's expression changed. "No, you're fucking serious."

"Never more so."

"How in all the gods' name did you come to be serving a runaway gladiator?"

"It's a long story," said Carbo. "I joined the ludus as an auctoratus. Inside, it's a different world. There's no difference between a man who's a citizen and one who's been enslaved. Being young and inexperienced, life was hard for me. Spartacus offered me his protection, so I became his man. I escaped when he did."

"A fine story, but gladiators aren't the same as trained soldiers. You'll be wiped out in the first battle."

Quietly, Carbo told Navio the story of their attack on Glaber's camp.

"Eighty of you beat three thousand legionaries? That is an incredible feat." Navio whistled in respect. Then his brow furrowed. "It's not the first time, come to think of it. The slaves who rebelled on Sicily won quite a few victories before they were defeated."

Carbo threw the dice again. "Why don't you join us? Spartacus is the only one among us with experience of Roman army training. But there are too many slaves for him to instruct properly."

"Are you offering me a job?"

"I can't do that. But I'll take you to Spartacus. You can ask him yourself."

"Are you meant to be recruiting men?"

"No." Carbo explained his mission. "Obviously, I'm supposed to tell no one."

Navio's lips quirked. "In that case, will he not crucify us both?"

"I don't think so."

"You don't *think* so?" Navio laughed softly. "Hmmm. Would I risk my life just to ask a runaway slave if I can fight for him?"

Carbo's heart thudded in his chest. If Navio said no, he was possibly going to have to kill him. Otherwise, his story might be spread all over Capua by the next day.

"Why the hell not?" Navio exclaimed. "It sounds more appealing than fighting a war on my own."

Relief flooded through Carbo. "Good. Let's go and drink to that," he declared. His relief lasted no more than a few heartbeats. Through the alcoholic haze that enveloped him, he had one crystal-clear thought. *Gods, what if I've made the biggest mistake of my life?* Despite his bravado, there was every chance that Spartacus would kill them both. He downed another mouthful.

Instead of doing the sensible thing and retiring to bed, Carbo and Navio continued drinking. In the process they cemented their friendship, swearing undying loyalty to each other over cup after cup of wine. By the time they collapsed on to their bedding in the stable, the first fingers of light were tingeing the eastern sky. All too soon they were woken by the sharp end of the ostler's pitchfork. The moment that they were awake, he hounded them out into the stable yard. Red-eyed and with pounding heads, the pair stared blearily at each other. "I feel like shit," Carbo groaned.

"There's only one cure for this," announced Navio. Stripping off his tunic, he wove over to the trough for the mules, which had just been filled by a slave. Grabbing a bucket, he dragged it through the water and then emptied it over his head. "Gods, but that's cold!" He repeated the procedure several times before shoving the pail at Carbo. "Now you."

Shivering in anticipation, Carbo put himself through the same process.

"Feel better?" asked Navio, flicking water from his skin.

"A little."

"Dionysus' revenge, my father used to call it."

"I'd best head to the market to see what I can find out." Trying to ignore his pounding head, Carbo dried himself with a clump of straw and pulled on his tunic.

Navio's face brightened. "We can get bread and cheese there. Nothing like some food to settle the stomach, eh?"

"Maybe." In the cold light of day, Carbo's plan to bring Navio back to Spartacus' camp seemed rather less appealing. But he couldn't back out of it now. He'd given Navio his word. Several times.

†

Neapolis' marketplace was situated in the main forum, a large open area in the very center of the city. The mass of stalls, tents and mobile pens was surrounded on all sides by temples, government buildings and the mansions of the rich. Despite the early hour, it was already packed with people. Every foodstuff under the sun was on sale.

There were stands groaning under the weight of cabbages, onions, carrots, chicory and cucumbers. Huge bunches of sage, coriander, fennel and parsley were laid carefully out on low tables. Scores of wasps hung over the arrangements of ripe pears, apples and plums. There were even some peaches on offer. The insects were attracted to these nearly as much as the sealed pots of honey nearby. Rounds of cheese, covered in cloth to keep them fresh, were piled one on top of the other. Bakers hawked flat loaves of bread that were still warm from the oven. Small children greedily eyed the sweet pastries on offer. Butchers stood by their massive wooden blocks, wielding cleavers and extolling the quality of their freshly killed meat. Cattle, sheep and pigs roared their unhappiness from the pens close by.

Attracted by the smell, Carbo and Navio descended on a stall where a stout woman was frying sausages. They bought two each. Carbo lingered, chatting to the woman as he ate. Mention of Spartacus' men raiding a neighbor's farm elicited a tirade of cursing, but no mention of soldiers.

It was the same story all over the market. Buying a selection of bread and fruit, Carbo chatted idly to the vendors, mentioning Spartacus to all and sundry. Unsurprisingly, none had a good word to say about his leader, but, to Carbo's pleasure, none mentioned any punitive force from Rome either.

Within an hour, he was happy enough to leave. He'd drunk several cups of fruit juice, and his head was feeling much better. Navio looked brighter too. "Still prepared to come with me?" Carbo asked.

"Of course," said Navio with a lopsided grin. "As I said, I'm only a simple soldier. On my own, I'll get nowhere. So if your leader will lead me against Rome, I'll follow him to Hades."

Carbo smiled confidently. Falsely. He had no doubt that if Spartacus was unhappy with what he had done, they'd both be on crosses by the day's end. *Let's hope he sees the same thing in Navio that I did.*

XIV

Half turning so the senators opposite would not notice, Crassus tugged at his toga, ensuring that it hung over his bent left arm just so. When the time came to speak, he had to look the part, and in the Senate having one's toga correctly in place was imperative. Here everyone had to be the embodiment of Roman *virtus*. Crassus was sitting with six hundred-odd other senators in the Curia, the hallowed oblong building that had housed the Republic's government for half a millenium. Perhaps sixty paces wide by four score long, it was simply built of brick-faced concrete with a stucco frontage. High on the walls, glass windows—a rare commodity—let in plenty of light. A triangular façade over the entrance featured a centerpiece of skillfully painted carvings of the triad of Jupiter, Minerva and Juno. On either side were depictions of Romulus and Remus, Rome's founders, and Mars, the god of war.

Inside, the Curia's sole furnishings were the three low marble benches that ran the length of the room on each side, and the two rosewood chairs that sat on a low dais at the end. There, protected by their lictores, sat the two consuls—the men elected to rule Rome every twelve months. Crassus studied Marcus Terentius Varro and Gaius Cassius Longinus sidelong. Despite the grandeur of their positions, it was hard not to regard them with contempt. Both were "yes" men, figures who were easy to manipulate and who had been chosen by a more powerful politician. Pompey Magnus had put Varro forward and Marcus Tullius Cicero was Longinus' main backer. Crassus' lips twitched. *It could just as easily have been me. And to be fair, the pair are only a sign of the times.*

The Republic was a weakened beast now compared to its heyday centuries before. The ancient law that no man should hold the consulship more than once in ten years had been discarded by leaders such as Marius, Cinna and Sulla. It wasn't about to return any time soon. The wishes that Sulla had expressed when he'd relinquished power had been utterly ignored. *His plan would never have worked anyway,* thought Crassus. *Not when senatorial juries are so often guilty of flagrant corruption. Not when upstarts like Pompey refuse to disband their armies, and use them to browbeat the Senate. Rome needs men like me, who are strong enough to stand up to fraudsters and bullies.*

The hammering of fasces on the mosaic floor ended the host of muted conversations and attracted Crassus' attention. *So to the matter in hand. Spartacus and his band of cutthroats, and the praetors who are being sent to annihilate them. In the process they will erase from the record books the humiliation suffered by Glaber.* Of course, the fool Glaber was long dead, ordered to fall on his sword in penance for his abject failure. His property had been seized by the state and his family exiled. The senior officers who had served under him had been demoted to the ranks. But that did not mean that the matter could be forgotten. Far from it.

"Silence!" thundered the senior lictor, an imposing figure with a dozen *phalerae* decorating his chest. "All stand for the consul of the day, Marcus Terentius Varro."

Six hundred senators rose to their feet.

Varro, a squat individual with an unfashionable square beard, nodded at Longinus, his co-consul, before glancing down the room at the massed ranks of senators. "Honorable friends, you all know why we are here today. I do not need to remind you of the disgraceful events at Vesuvius some months ago. They have been discussed in detail, and those responsible have been punished."

An angry rumble of agreement rose to the vaulted ceiling.

"Two of the Senate's most worthy praetors have been appointed to wipe the renegade Spartacus and his followers from the face of the earth. Publius Varinius is to command the mission. He will be ably assisted by his colleague Lucius Cossinius, and the legate Lucius Furius." Varro paused long enough for the senators to nod approvingly at the three men in full uniform who stood together near the consuls' chairs. "Sacrifices have been made, and the omens declared favorable. The force is to set out tomorrow. Varinius will take with him six thousand legionaries—"

"Veterans?" interjected Crassus.

As Varro's eyes bulged with surprise, shocked whispers rippled through the senators.

To Hades with etiquette, thought Crassus impatiently. Everyone knows the answer, but the question needs to be asked. To be placed on the record. "Are they veterans, consul?" he repeated.

"N-no. I don't know what that has to do with it, praetor," replied Varro in an irritated tone. "Even the newest recruit to the legions is worth ten escaped gladiators."

"Damn right!" shouted a voice.

"The lowlifes will shit themselves when they see our soldiers coming," cried another.

Varro looked pleased. "Just so."

"According to those figures, Spartacus must have attacked Glaber's camp with, let me see, thirty thousand men," said Crassus loudly.

An awkward silence fell.

"Yet we are told that he had not six legions of followers, but a paltry one hundred."

"Come now, Crassus," said Varro, boldly trying to take control. "Glaber was attacked in a cowardly manner, in the middle of the night. That won't happen again, you can be sure of it." He eyed Varinius, who nodded his head vigorously. "This time, we are sending six thousand men. What slave rabble will stand against more than a legion, eh? It will be a massacre!"

Spontaneous cheering broke out among the senators, and Varro's face relaxed.

Crassus waited carefully until the noise had died down. "What you say is in all likelihood correct. Let me be clear: I am not doubting the quality of the soldiers who are to be sent to Vesuvius, nor the skill of Varinius and his colleagues."

"What in Jupiter's name are you getting at then?" demanded Varro.

"All I am saying is that this Spartacus is not a mindless slave, with no idea how to fight. He should not be underestimated. I have seen him in action."

A shocked silence fell.

"Where?" demanded Varro.

"At the ludus in Capua. I paid for a mortal bout there. Spartacus was one of the two men selected by the lanista. He won, obviously. I spoke with him afterward. The man's a savage, but he's intelligent."

"Thank you for your advice," snapped Varro. "But Publius Varinius is no callow youth. He is more than capable of dealing with a rogue gladiator. His task is simple, and straightforward. I imagine that we'll see him back here within the month, his mission successfully completed."

Varinius winked at his colleagues, who grinned like happy children. Lucius Cossinius, a broad-shouldered man, puffed out his chest. "If I get the chance, I'll fight and kill Spartacus myself."

Laughter and roars of approval met this comment.

"I look forward to hearing all about it," said Crassus, stepping back into the crowd. "Don't say I didn't warn you," he added.

Cossinius chuckled.

Cocksure fool, Crassus thought. You'd best hope that your men cut Spartacus down, because you wouldn't have a hope against him.

†

Carbo was glad not to encounter any rebel patrols until they'd reached Vesuvius and begun making their way through the fields of wheat stubble that covered its lower slopes. When they finally did run into a section of ten men, Carbo was recognized. The patrol leader accepted his word that Navio was another slave who'd come to join Spartacus, and they continued their climb to the crater.

"Now do you see why I made you take off your belt?"

"Otherwise they'd have known me for a soldier."

"Precisely. And you'd already be food for those." Carbo pointed at a pair of vultures that were circling overhead.

"Fair enough. It would be stupid to be killed before I've even had a chance to plead my case," admitted Navio. He squinted at the peak above them. "It's a good place to choose for a camp. Hard to approach. Easy to defend."

"We can't stay there forever, though. The next commander to arrive will be wise to the trick we played on Glaber. He'd just starve us out."

"Where's Spartacus going to go next?"

"South, I'd say. Away from Rome."

"That makes sense. Has he mentioned Sicily?"

"What, because of the slave uprisings there?" He hadn't thought of Sicily before, but then he wasn't a soldier, like Navio.

"Yes. I'd say that two large-scale rebellions within thirty years of each other makes for fertile recruiting ground, wouldn't you?"

Carbo flushed. "Where would we get the ships to transport thousands of men?"

"The Cilician pirates sail in these waters. I'm sure some of their captains would be open to offers."

"Pirates would sell their own mothers into whoredom if they fetched a good enough price."

"Beggars can't be choosers. There won't be too many other candidates willing to carry a slave army."

Annoyed and impressed at the same time, Carbo did not reply. They were nearing the crater, and his nerves began to jangle. *Stop it! Navio would be an asset to any leader.*

†

They found Spartacus drilling a large group of slaves. He had them in pairs, armed with *scuta* and swords, sparring against each other, and was stalking among them, barking orders and reprimands in equal measure. Atheas and Taxacis lounged nearby, in the shade of a tree. They eyed Navio with naked suspicion. Seeing this, Carbo's skin snaked with dread. He stopped in his tracks.

Navio shot him a concerned look.

Carbo rallied his courage. "Spartacus!"

Spartacus turned. His eyes flickered to Navio, and returned to Carbo. "You're back." Pausing to correct the way a dark-skinned slave held his shield, he strolled over. Like shadows, so too did the Scythians. "What news?" he demanded.

"There's not a word of any troops in Neapolis."

"That's to be expected, I suppose. They probably don't see the need to come from more than one direction." Spartacus saw Carbo's surprise. "You weren't the first to return. Aventianus got back last night. Apparently, there's a large force about to set out from Rome. Two praetors, a legate and six thousand legionaries. The praetor in charge is called Publius Varinius. They'll be here in less than a week."

"Shit." *What use is Navio now?*

"You could say that." Spartacus smiled, but his eyes were like two chips of flint. He jerked his head at Navio. "Is this someone you picked up on the way back?"

"I thought he'd be useful to us."

"Of course he will. Every sword will count—even if the men using them are more used to handling a hoe or a spade." Spartacus studied Navio. His gaze lingered on his hair, and Carbo's worries increased tenfold. "Ever held a gladius in your hand?" demanded Spartacus.

"Plenty of times," answered Navio stolidly.

"Really?" Spartacus glanced at the Scythians.

Without a word, Atheas and Taxacis glided to stand on either side of him.

Spartacus' stare returned to Carbo. "Care to explain?"

Carbo could think of nothing to say apart from the simple truth. "He's a Roman soldier."

He didn't have time to add that Navio wanted to join them. Atheas and Taxacis leaped forward in unison, drawing their swords as they moved. A heartbeat later, Navio had a blade pricking the skin on each side of his neck. He was careful not to move a muscle, but his eyes flickered to Carbo's. "Tell my story!"

The Scythians looked at Spartacus. "Kill him?" asked Atheas hopefully.

"In a moment," said Spartacus. His face grew fiercer than Carbo had ever seen. "You'll be joining this prick in Hades, Carbo, unless you can persuade me otherwise. I don't take kindly to Roman soldiers strolling into my camp, especially when they've been invited by one of my own men."

"It's not how it seems," said Carbo desperately. "Navio's no friend to the Senate! He's been fighting Rome for years. He was one of Sertorius' men."

"Sertorius?"

"You've heard of Marius?"

"Of course."

"Sertorius was one of his men."

Spartacus' nostrils pinched white with anger. "You'd best do better than that. I can remember when Sulla passed through Thrace on his way to Pontus. The bastard left a swathe of destruction in his wake that was several miles wide. I can't believe that Marius would have been any different if he'd ever got that far."

"Sertorius wasn't like that," protested Carbo. Spartacus' expression did not change, so he hurried on. "After Marius' death, things went against his supporters in Italy, so Sertorius fled to Iberia. So too did Navio and his family. Sertorius quickly raised an army from the Iberian tribes. He carved out a large territory for himself, and defeated the legions sent against him by the Senate on numerous occasions. He held out for the best part of a decade, but he was murdered by a traitor a few months ago. The general Pompey Magnus had little difficulty mopping up his supporters after that. Navio survived the final battle and made his way back to Neapolis, his home town."

"Why didn't you fall on your sword?" snarled Spartacus at Navio. "I thought that was the Roman way after defeat."

"It is," said Navio, before adding fiercely, "but that would end the fight. I still want vengeance on Rome! The deaths of my father, brother and Sertorius have not been paid for in blood."

"Even if what you say is true, you're only one man. One sword. Why would I even risk taking you in?" Spartacus drew a finger across his throat. "If my men kill you, they can just toss you off the cliff. That'd be one less thing for me to think about."

"Because he can help you to train our men!" cried Carbo, acutely aware that if sentence of death fell on Navio, it would fall on them both. Atheas and Taxacis would kill him without even blinking. *Jupiter, watch over me now.* "Navio's an officer and a veteran soldier. He has years of experience instructing men to fight as legionaries."

Spartacus rounded on Navio like a snake about to strike. "Is that true?"

"It is. Virtually all of our soldiers were Iberian tribesmen. They were warriors, and brave too, but hadn't the first idea about discipline, or fighting as a unit. Sertorius' orders were that every new recruit had to be taught to fight in the Roman manner. I've done it with hundreds of men."

Spartacus' expression became calculating, and Carbo held his breath. "What would you do with this lot here?" He indicated the slaves behind him.

"How much training have they had?" Navio's voice was crisp.

"It depends. Some have been here for weeks, so they've had quite a lot, but they've been coming in every day. Most have had a week or two's instruction with gladius and shield. A few have had as little as a couple of days."

"How many men are there?"

"A little over three thousand in total. About a hundred of them are gladiators or proven fighters."

Navio firmly pushed away first Atheas' blade, and then Taxacis' one. The Scythians glanced at Spartacus, but he said nothing. "Shall I tell you what I'd do?" asked Navio.

There was a terse nod.

"Assign your troops into Roman cohorts. Half a dozen units of around five hundred men, divided into six centuries. They'll need officers, at least two for each century."

"Go on," said Spartacus slowly.

Warming to his subject, Navio spoke for some time, describing how he'd instruct the slaves to fight as one, holding their shields together. To use their swords purely as thrusting weapons. To respond to basic commands relayed by instruments such as the trumpet or whistle. To advance only when told to. To retreat in good order. At length, he paused. "If there was more time, I'd run them up and down the mountain in full kit every day, and train them against the palus too. The basics can come later, though, if we win."

They could be made into an army yet. Spartacus smiled. "We?"

Navio colored. "I meant 'you.'"

"Hmmm." Spartacus eyed Carbo coldly. "I had thought you loyal."

"I am!"

"Yet you saw fit to disobey my orders."

"I—"

"You told someone else who you were, and what you were doing in Neapolis," snapped Spartacus. "As if that wasn't stupid enough, you then had the temerity to bring a Roman soldier into my camp!"

"Because I imagined he could help us," retorted Carbo, his temper flaring at the injustice of it. "Clearly, he can't. Neither can I." He glared at Taxacis and Atheas. "Why don't you get on with it? Just fucking kill us and have it done."

Raising their weapons, the Scythians looked expectantly at Spartacus.

Carbo's heart thudded in his chest as he readied himself for the worst.

Navio stuck out his chin.

"So you will vouch for this Roman . . . Navio?" asked Spartacus.

"I will," replied Carbo, shooting a look at Navio. *Do not betray me.*

"With your life?"

"Yes."

"Fine. In that case, Navio can start training the men with me. You can help too. For the moment, Atheas and Taxacis will act as your understudies. At the slightest sign of treachery, they have my full permission to kill you both. However they choose." At this, the Scythians leered evilly, and nausea washed over Carbo again. "Is that clear?"

They both shook their heads in agreement.

"If you prove to be faithful, I will reward you well."

Carbo's tongue felt thick in his dry mouth. "I thank you," he croaked.

"You won't regret this, sir," said Navio.

"I'm glad to hear it." Spartacus stepped up and patted his cheek. "There's no need to call me 'sir' either. We're not in the damn legions!"

"What should I call you?"

"What everyone else calls me. Spartacus." With that he was off, waving at them to follow. "Come on. Every hour counts!"

"I judged you correctly, didn't I?" muttered Carbo to Navio.

"You did," said Navio solemnly. "I swear before all the gods that I am no spy. I hate Rome with all my heart, and I will do my utmost to help Spartacus. Is that enough?"

"Yes. Thank you."

"It's I who should be thanking you. Not only did you save my life, but you've given me new purpose." Navio punched him on the chest. "Let's get a move on. Spartacus is waiting."

As they walked off, neither could help but notice the two Scythians dogging their footsteps.

It mattered less to Carbo than he'd have thought possible a few moments previously.

SIX DAYS LATER...

Alerted by the hissed warning, Spartacus shinnied up the holm oak tree, climbing from black-barked branch to branch. Halfway up, he found the sentry, a young shepherd who'd recently joined them. "Firmus? Is that your name?"

Firmus beamed at being remembered. "Yes, sir."

Spartacus had given up telling his men not to call him "sir." It made no difference. "What have you seen?"

"A Roman column, sir."

Spartacus peered through the gap in the leathery, dark green leaves. The tree they were sitting in was situated at the edge of a large, thicketed area about four miles from the base of Vesuvius. The road that led from the Via Appia to the latifundia in the surrounding area ran right through it, making the spot perfect for an ambush. If it was worth doing, thought Spartacus, spotting the column's dust cloud about half a mile away. They might be completely outnumbered.

When word had come the previous afternoon that the enemy was approaching, he had convened with the three Gaulish leaders. In just five days, Navio's input had made a noticeable difference to their new recruits' resolve, but that didn't mean most wouldn't cut and run the minute they faced a wall of Roman scuta. Spartacus had argued that using their better-trained recruits—including the gladiators, about thirteen hundred men—in another surprise attack was their best chance of success. The rest would be more risk than they were currently worth. Of course Crixus had argued against his plan, wanting more of a full-scale attack. Thankfully, the others had agreed with Spartacus. It seemed that his idea of using vine ropes and their success in attacking Glaber's camp still carried some weight.

Newly arrived slaves had reported that the Roman commander had divided his force into three. If this information was incorrect, and Varinius' entire force of six thousand legionaries was approaching, they'd simply melt away into the bush. Abandon Vesuvius that night, and make for the mountains to the east. From the safety of broken terrain, Spartacus knew that they could serve as a thorn in the Romans' side for months, if not years. Just as he'd wanted to do in Thrace. Fierce excitement—and pride—gripped him at what he'd achieved thus far. Even when Crixus' and Castus' foot-dragging over training were taken into account, the gladiators were in a far stronger position now than they had been when Glaber arrived. Let the slaves' reports be true, Spartacus asked silently. We face no more than two thousand soldiers under the legate Lucius Furius.

They'd been in place since well before dawn. It had been a long wait. Now Spartacus was relieved that one way or another, something would happen soon. He watched intently as the first troops tramped into sight. They were infantry. The legionaries marched six abreast, with their scuta slung from their backs, and a yoke carrying their spare equipment balanced on one shoulder. They carried two pila each in their other hands, which served as staffs when on the march.

"They've got no horse. In the name of all the gods, why?" Spartacus saw Firmus' confused look. "Glaber had none either. It's the most basic mistake that a commander can make. Few foot soldiers will stand against cavalry, not least men like ours, who have hardly any military experience. The presence of horsemen would increase the Romans' chances of success enormously, but the whoresons are so damn arrogant that they haven't bothered."

Firmus shrugged. "We're only slaves, sir."

"Eh?"

"We're only slaves. Why would they need cavalry?"

"You're right, lad." Spartacus chuckled at the simplicity of it. "That's exactly what they must think." *Long may they hold that opinion!* He looked out at the marching soldiers again. Still no sign of any cavalry. He could see the end of the dust cloud too. A gut feeling told him that there were fewer men than the five thousand in a legion marching toward them. Far fewer, in fact. *Thank you, Great Rider.* "Leave it as late as you can before you come down. Whatever you do, make sure you're not seen. Return to our position."

"Yes, sir."

Spartacus scrambled down to the road, which was little more than a wide dirt track through the dense mixture of trees and shrubs. With a backward glance in the direction of the Romans, he trotted toward Vesuvius, which was just visible over the treetops. A thousand paces or so farther on, Spartacus saw the first eager faces appearing between the gaps in the buckthorn and juniper bushes. "Get down, you fools!" he barked. "This isn't a fucking game!"

The heads popped out of sight.

Spartacus came to a halt by a twisted evergreen myrtle tree. White star-like flowers covered its surface. His lips twisted at the irony. The blooms had medicinal uses; so too did the dark green leaves. Perhaps later there would be time to use them on the wounded. *If we survive.* He had hidden his and Gannicus' men—half the force—to his left, and the rest to the right. They had been allocated into centuries. Once Navio had started his training, it had seemed logical to do so. The Gaulish leaders had grumbled, but having their followers all appointed as officers had appeased them. Every gladiator who could fight was here. They were mixed among the new recruits, roughly half a dozen to a century. Gaps had been cut in the thick vegetation, wide enough for four men to charge out at a time. The spaces had been filled with cut branches, which could be hauled out of the way in the blink of an eye.

"Gannicus! Castus! Crixus!"

The Gauls were with him in a heartbeat. All three were clad in mail shirts and bronze-bowl helmets with white or red horsehair crests, and were carrying Roman scuta and gladii. Spartacus grinned fiercely. But for their long hair and mustaches, they looked like legionaries.

"Are they coming?" demanded Crixus.

"Yes."

"How many?" Gannicus' expression was wary.

"It's not the full six thousand men, or even five; I know that. Half that number, or even less. There is no cavalry visible either."

Gannicus clenched his fists. "Do we attack?"

"Eh?" Crixus shot him a hostile look. "Of course we do!"

Castus said nothing.

"I asked Spartacus, not you, Crixus," Gannicus snapped.

"You lapdog—" accused Crixus.

"What did you say?" Gannicus' face went puce with rage, and he laid a hand to his sword.

Crixus' eyebrows rose. "You want to pick a fight with me? Come on then!"

"Let's not quarrel now," said Spartacus firmly. "We have more important business at hand."

Like children who have been rebuked by a parent, the Gauls subsided, glowering at each other with obvious dislike.

"We'll fight if I say so. I won't make that decision until the last moment. If I think that our attack will fail, I won't use this." Spartacus lifted up the centurion's bone whistle that hung from a thong around his neck. At Navio's request, he'd had Glaber's abandoned camp ransacked for examples like it. The Gauls now had one each too. "You all know what it sounds like. Unless you hear me blow one long blast, tell your men to stay down. We'll just lie hidden until they're gone. It's imperative that they understand that! If any of those Roman bastards catch as much as a glimpse of us, we're fucked. Clear?"

They all nodded, although Castus' face bore a dubious expression.

"If you hear the whistle, however, blow your own, and then immediately launch your pila."

"When will you sound it?" asked Gannicus.

Spartacus pointed at the bend in the road, some three hundred paces toward Vesuvius. "Once the vanguard has disappeared around that." He glanced at Crixus. "Your position is closest to the curve. Are you happy not to let any escape?"

Crixus' lips peeled back into a feral snarl of agreement.

Good. He thinks that he's got the most important job. Fool.

Spartacus' assumption couldn't have been more wrong.

"Make sure you whistle at the first opportunity. I might not be able to hold my men in otherwise," said Crixus offhandedly.

Spartacus ground his teeth with rage. "If they break cover too soon, it could entirely screw up the ambush."

"That would be down to you not sounding your whistle quickly enough," said Crixus, his eyes glittering with malice.

Utter fury took hold of Spartacus. A cunning time to pick an argument, he thought. He could think of nothing else but calling Crixus' bluff. "What is it?" he demanded, pulling the leather thong from around his neck and shoving it at the Gaul. "Is this what you want? If it is, we'd better move the men around quickly."

Immediately, the others looked dismayed. "It's too late for that," said Gannicus. "The damn Romans will be on us any moment. Leave it, Crixus," he advised. "It doesn't matter that much who blows the bloody whistle. And Spartacus will pick the right moment. Eh, Castus?"

Spartacus held his breath.

"He will," growled Castus.

Crixus' jaw bunched with anger. "You do it then," he snarled at Spartacus. "What do I care?"

Spartacus nodded curtly. "Launch one volley of javelins only. Aim short and low." Most of the men had never thrown pila before, but he'd insisted that everyone armed themselves with some of the hundreds of missiles that had been left in Glaber's camp. Even thrown by novices, they would cause confusion at such close range, as well as plenty of casualties. So too would the Nubians with their slings. "At my second whistle, charge."

Castus still wasn't completely happy. "What if they make formation and hold it? Our men will never break through a Roman shield wall."

"True enough," said Spartacus with an accepting shrug. "We'll pull back, disappear into the scrubland. But only do that if you hear three short blasts on my whistle, repeated. Otherwise, press home the assault."

"It still seems like complete madness," protested Castus.

"What?" exclaimed Crixus.

"We're outnumbered. Most of our men are slaves, with little training, yet we're about to attack thousands of legionaries. In broad daylight."

Great Rider, don't let him back out now. "It feels fucking great, doesn't it?" Spartacus grinned savagely. Confidently. "Far better than fighting in some shitty arena for the amusement of a Roman mob."

Castus held his gaze for a moment before he too smiled. "That's true."

"We'll teach the whoresons a lesson they'll never forget," promised Crixus, his bullishness returned.

Spartacus caught the uncertainty in Gannicus' eyes. *Even if Crixus is too pigheaded to see it and Castus has been won over, he knows that our fate hangs on a thread. Gods, how I wish that Getas and Seuthes were here with two hundred warriors of our tribe.* But they weren't. "Remember: Ariadne said this morning that the omens were good."

Gannicus looked happier. "And she should know."

"That's right!" Spartacus gave silent thanks to Dionysus as well. Since he had revealed what Ariadne had said about his dream, her status had grown even further. He gripped Gannicus' shoulder, "Ready to repeat what we did to Glaber?"

"Yes!"

"Into position, then. Remember, wait for my whistle."

He waited until the others had disappeared from view before checking the road for a final time. Nothing. Unsheathing his sica, Spartacus made his way to the rear of the myrtle tree. There he found an edgy-looking Carbo. Navio was beside him, jiggling with excitement. Atheas and Taxacis hovered in the background. They won't be necessary, thought Spartacus. *If Navio is a traitor, I'm no judge of men. Carbo too.* "All set?"

"Yes," replied Carbo. "Are they coming?"

"They'll be here soon."

Carbo squared his shoulders. "I'm ready."

"May Mars watch over us with his spear and shield," said Navio with fierce enthusiasm.

"And the Great Rider," added Spartacus. *Stay with me, as you have done until now.*

†

Spartacus trotted up and down his lines, pausing regularly to mutter encouragement in men's ears, and slap them on the back. He told them what brave soldiers they were, and of how their deeds that day would be sung about for a hundred years. Lying through his teeth, he said that the legionaries who were approaching were cowards to a man, who would run at the sight of slaves with swords. That raised a laugh from most, but it was a nervous laugh, and Spartacus knew that his words would be forgotten the instant that the battle began. Then, as always, it would come down to each man's resolve, and the resolve of his comrades. To the impact of the volley of javelins. To the level of surprise and fear their attack generated in the Romans. To the number of legionaries that they could kill in the first few moments. If all those factors went in their favor, perhaps they had a chance.

Spartacus' grip on his sica tightened. *If things go against us* . . .

He'd been on the victorious side in combat enough times to know what happened to the enemy. It would be a rout. Soldiers who broke were the easiest prey of all to kill. As fear overcame them completely, they entirely lost reason and discipline. Their shields were the first things they discarded. Then it was their swords. Comrades who stumbled or fell were ignored or even trampled into the dust. Few, if any, tried to defend themselves. They simply ran. And legionaries were masters at hunting down such men. It was common for ten enemy combatants to be killed for every Roman casualty. If the slaves fled, the figure would probably be even higher.

Stop it. This is what I've prayed for over the years. The chance to lead an army against Rome once more. An opportunity to gain vengeance for my tribe's defeat, and Maron's death.

Hearing the sound of running feet, Spartacus straightened.

Firmus came hammering into the gap a moment later. "They're coming!"

"How far away are they?"

"I kept pace with them through the bush. No more than a quarter of a mile, sir."

Spartacus pricked his ears. He could just make out the *tramp* of thousands of hobnailed sandals striking the ground in unison. "Seen any horsemen?"

"No, sir."

"How many do you think there are?" Spartacus barked.

Firmus quailed before him. "I'm not sure, sir. More than I can count."

Spartacus bit back his angry and instinctive rebuke. *He's only a shepherd, same as the other scouts. They're not used to estimating enemy numbers.* "Well done. Cross the road and tell Castus and Crixus that their men are to prepare for a volley of javelins. But they must not launch until my whistle!"

Firmus nodded and was gone. At once the gap was filled with branches.

"Javelins at the ready!" ordered Spartacus. "Spread the word."

Muttering broke out as his order passed through the waiting ranks. "Are we going to fight?" asked Carbo. He was grateful that his churning guts weren't audible.

"I don't know yet," admitted Spartacus with a wink. "It depends on how many of the mangy dogs there are."

"I see." Carbo smiled as confidently as he could.

"It's all right to feel nervous," said Spartacus in a quiet voice. "This will be your first pitched battle. Most men are shaking like leaves, or praying like lunatics to every god under the sun. It's common for soldiers to vomit or even piss themselves. You're doing none of that. Instead, you're standing firm, ready to fight."

Grateful, Carbo felt his resolve strengthen.

"Good lad. I know you'll do well." Spartacus turned away to peer through the branches at the track.

"He knows just what to say," whispered Navio in Carbo's ear.

Carbo spun round, and was relieved to see no judgment in Navio's eyes.

"It's one of the signs of a great leader."

"I'd follow him anywhere," said Carbo passionately.

"Silence!" hissed Spartacus.

They crouched down and waited.

Soon all that could be heard was the heavy tread of the approaching legionaries.

Despite Spartacus' reassurance, Carbo's stomach was twisting itself in knots. *We could easily be slaughtered.* He felt saliva pooling around his tongue, and it took a supreme effort not to be sick. A piercing alarm call distracted him and he looked up, catching sight of a blackbird in the myrtle tree. It cocked its head, its beady eye regarding the lines of hidden men with clear suspicion. It trilled again. And again.

We must be on its territory. The damn thing will give away our position.

Spartacus reached up and waved his arm. To Carbo's relief, the blackbird flew off, still chattering angrily. If any of the legionaries noticed, they would think it was their presence that had disturbed the bird. He dried his palms one by one on the bottom edge of his tunic, and cocked his right arm again. The weight of the javelin was still unfamiliar, but Carbo had been practicing with it every day. He could now hit a target most times he threw. He tried not to think about the fact that it would be sinking into Roman flesh.

This is the road I've chosen. The legions wouldn't have me.

I'm with Spartacus now.

XV

Time dragged on. Carbo's heart was thudding like that of a trapped beast. *Where are they?* A flash of movement caught his eye, and he looked to his right. Through the gaps in the branches, he saw the red tunics and silver mail of rank upon rank of legionaries marching past. His nausea returned with a vengeance. Carbo bit his bottom lip until he tasted blood. To his relief, the pain pushed the nausea into the background. He refocused his attention on the enemy. *The enemy, because that's what they are.* Ten rows went by, then fifteen and twenty. Thirty. Fifty. Still they kept coming, none so much as glancing to either side. They were so near that their banter was discernible. Some were singing ribald tunes; others complained about the distance they'd marched; still more cursed Spartacus and his cowardly slaves, whom they'd butcher to a man. Cheers rose up at that prospect.

The tension was growing unbearable. Carbo glanced at Spartacus, whose whistle was clenched between his lips. Then at Navio, whose face was strained too. Even Atheas and Taxacis were leaning forward like hounds eager to slip the huntsman's leash. Beyond them the slaves were looking ever more nervous. Carbo wanted to scream at Spartacus. *Are you going to give us the damn signal?*

Spartacus was oblivious to his men's anxiety. He still had not decided what to do. The wrong decision would see his men massacred. What he most wanted to know—how many Romans there were—would not be clear until they'd all passed by. By then, it would be too late. Another line of legionaries came into view. Not one of them was more than twenty-one or -two years of age. *However many there are, they don't look like seasoned veterans.* With that realization, Spartacus' uncertainty vanished. He took a in a deep breath and blew with all his might.

Peeeeeeep!

The shrill sound rose to the very heavens. No one in any proximity could fail to hear it.

Spartacus' right arm went back, and he threw his javelin, low and short.

Peeeeeeep! Peeeeeeep! Peeeeeeep! went the Gauls' whistles.

Carbo's instincts took over and he threw his *pilum*. Beside him, he sensed Navio and the two Scythians also hurling theirs. Hundreds of other javelins joined them from either side, and, for the briefest moment, the tops of the bushes were topped by a bizarre layer of wood and metal. Then the missiles were gone, dropping down among the unsuspecting legionaries in a deadly, barbed rain.

Peeeeeeep!

Spartacus began hauling branches out of the way. Carbo and Navio rushed to join him.

The screams and shouts of confusion hit their ears in a cacophony of sound.

"Move! Move!" bellowed Spartacus. "Speed is everything!"

Two heartbeats later, the gap had been cleared. Carbo stared wide-eyed at the mayhem their javelins had caused. The column's neat formation had fallen apart. Instead of precise ranks of legionaries, all he could see was a heaving mass of yelling, confused men. Fallen soldiers lay everywhere. Many were dead but the majority were wounded, roaring in agony and clutching at the javelins that had pierced them through. Carbo couldn't see an officer anywhere.

Spartacus clattered his sica off his scutum, once, twice, thrice. "CHARGE!" With that, he was gone, bounding up like an Olympic sprinter of old.

Roaring like madmen, Atheas and Taxacis were next.

I can't let Navio get out there before me, thought Carbo. He felt his feet begin to move of their own volition. *Jupiter, Greatest and Best, watch over me.* He'd already drawn his gladius, holding it close to his right side. With only his eyes visible over the metal rim of his shield, he charged forward. Other men were scrambling out with him. The legionaries were ten to fifteen paces away. What surprised Carbo was the shocked expression on their faces. *They don't know what's hit them!*

Awestruck, he watched Spartacus.

"For Thrace!" shouted Spartacus, smashing his shield boss into that of a soldier who looked even younger than Carbo. The impact drove his opponent back several steps and off his feet. Spartacus was on him in a flash. His sica flickered in the sunlight; a stream of blood spouted into the air. The young legionary's legs kicked spasmodically and relaxed.

"Watch out!" Navio cried.

Too late, Carbo's head spun away from Spartacus, to his front. He had barely enough time to take in the snarling face of an unshaven legionary not three steps away, his gladius lunging at Carbo's eyes. He ducked down behind the curve of his shield and heard the blade whistle overhead. There was a *thump* as the legionary's scutum connected with his, and Carbo staggered. Frantically, he shifted one foot back and managed to brace himself as the legionary drove into him again. The man's sword came sliding around Carbo's scutum and grated off his mail shirt. Carbo lifted his head, aware that if he didn't get a blow in quickly, the show was over. He was just in time to see Navio's sword thrusting through the legionary's armor and deep into his side. The man crumpled untidily to the ground. With a snarl, Navio ripped his blade out. Rage replaced Carbo's panic and he stepped in and rammed his gladius into the legionary's open, screaming mouth. His arm came to a juddering halt when the hilt of his weapon chinked off the man's few remaining teeth.

With a grunt, Carbo tugged it free. He had the briefest impression of a red, ruined maw and two dead, staring eyes before Navio thumped his helmet. "Keep moving! Stay close to Spartacus!"

Everything then became a blur, a succession of disjointed tableaux that Carbo struggled to remember afterward. Shoving his way with Navio to stand by Spartacus. Seeing Atheas and Taxacis on their leader's other side. The clash of arms and men's shouts being so loud that he could barely hear himself think. Having to tread on bodies, some of which were moving. Or screaming. Forming a shield wall with several others. Driving forward. Seeing the fear blossom on the legionaries' faces. The *crash* as they hit home. Spartacus' deep voice, urging them on. Atheas and Taxacis' ululating cries, which to Carbo sounded like those of demons in Hades. Repeatedly thrusting with his gladius. Seeing legionaries go down, one after another, with blades buried in their faces, chests, bellies and groins. Laughing manically. Advancing. Killing again. Noticing that the blood of the men he'd slain coated not just his entire blade, but his right arm too. He had totally forgotten that the men he was fighting were his own countrymen.

"There! There!" shouted Spartacus.

Carbo peered, seeing the scarlet crest on a centurion's helmet bobbing up and down behind the nearest legionaries. Beside the officer was a man with a lion-skin headdress carrying a gilded standard. He heard the centurion's frantic cries to rally around the standard-bearer. Spartacus pointed at the silver hand surrounded by a wreath. "Take that and they'll break!" He threw himself at the Roman ranks, not looking to see if anyone followed.

Spartacus had no idea how the battle was going elsewhere, but in his section, his men were more than holding their own. It would take but one great effort to turn the tide of battle in their favor. He'd seen before the effect when a Roman standard was taken. Courage leached from the legionaries' veins as quickly as if their throats had been cut. Their legs turned to jelly, and they ran like cowards. It wasn't that simple, of course. To retain a standard, they would commit suicidal acts of bravery. But in the immediacy of battle, Spartacus knew that this was his next task. He could only hope that the Gauls were doing well too.

Right on cue, a legionary carrying the jagged stump of a gladius threw himself at Spartacus. The Thracian parried the broken weapon easily with his shield and hooked his sica around to take the soldier in the groin, below his mail shirt. It slid in like a hot knife through cheese. Spartacus didn't bother with a second stroke. He'd severed a major artery in the Roman's groin.

Atheas' scutum clinked off the left side of his. Stained teeth shone from his laughing, open mouth. "We take . . . standard?"

"Yes!"

Working together, they dispatched a pair of legionaries, and another lone one. And then there was nothing between them and the standard-bearer but the centurion, a squat man with a beaked nose. A leather harness over his mail was covered with phalerae, and a gold ring encircled his upper right arm.

"I'll fight you one-to-one!" the centurion shouted.

Spartacus sensed Atheas' eyes on him, felt the Scythian begin to draw back. A deep, coursing anger took hold of him. "What do you think this is—the damn ludus?" he shouted at the centurion. "You're just another fucking Roman. With me, Atheas."

They split left and right, sliding their feet carefully across the gore-spattered ground.

The centurion was a brave man. He didn't back away. He couldn't advance without endangering the standard-bearer, so he raised his scutum and grimly prepared to meet their attack. "Come on, you bastards," he growled. "I've killed better men than you before!"

Spartacus was in no mood for skillful sword play. "Ready?"

The Scythian bellowed his assent.

"Now!" shouted Spartacus. *He'll try to kill me first. He knows I'm the leader.*

Sure enough, the centurion went for him. He used the classic one-two of punching with his scutum and following through with a huge thrust of his gladius. Except Spartacus was ready for the move, twisting to meet the Roman's shield side on, missing the other's deadly iron blade, and letting the centurion's momentum carry him to the left. Where Atheas was waiting. Unbalanced, the officer had no time to react, to defend himself properly. The Scythian's weapon hacked in, shearing off the cheekpiece of his helmet and rupturing one of his eyeballs before coming to rest deep in his skull. Gobbets of gray brain matter came showering out as Atheas heaved his gladius free, and the centurion dropped like a stone down a well.

Spartacus swarmed forward at the standard-bearer, who had only a small round shield to defend himself. The man knew that death was facing him in the eyes, but he did not run. He backed away carefully, roaring for his comrades. From the corner of his eye, Spartacus saw several legionaries' heads turn in their direction. Adrenaline surged through him. If he didn't win the standard now, he never would. He'd be dead too. With a savage grimace, Spartacus feinted with his shield. Then he swung his sword arm around and brought it back in the opposite direction a man would expect—from left to right. The soldier saw it coming, and despite himself, he couldn't help but raise his standard. If he hadn't, he would have lost his head. As it was, Spartacus' sica carved clean through the standard's wooden staff and cut a deep flesh wound in his neck.

A thin, keening cry left the standard-bearer's throat, but Spartacus wasn't interested in that. He exulted as the gilded hand, severed from the rest of the staff, angled to one side and crashed to the ground. There were instant wails of dismay from all around him. Snatching up the stump with the hand attached, Spartacus shoved it at Atheas. "Guard that as you would me!"

Taxacis, Carbo and Navio reached him an instant later.

"Form a ring around the standard!" shouted Spartacus.

Quickly, the four surrounded Atheas and readied themselves to defend him at all costs.

At least ten legionaries were already closing in on them, and Carbo prepared to sell his life dearly.

It was then that a bloodcurdling roar shredded the air.

Carbo gasped; Castus had arrived on the scene. He had four Gauls with him, all screaming war cries at the tops of their voices. The five men were spattered from head to toe in scarlet gore. Their helmets, their faces, their arms and their mail were covered in it. It was impossible to tell whether the blood was Roman or their own, but the effect was the same. Their appearance was shocking, turning them into very devils of the underworld. The legionaries' advance stopped dead in its tracks. Laughing, Castus and his men threw themselves at the Romans, whose faces crumpled in complete terror. Without hesitation, they turned and ran.

"After them!" yelled Spartacus. "Don't give the fuckers time to think!"

Howling like a pack of wolves, Carbo and the others followed him.

†

An hour or so later, it was all over. Spartacus paced up and down, staring at the figures of hundreds of legionaries fleeing to the north. There was scarcely room to move on the road. Mangled bodies lay everywhere: ringed by crimson stains, missing limbs, with pila jutting from their bellies. Discarded Roman equipment littered the ground as far as the eye could see.

"We did it." Carbo's three words conveyed all kinds of disbelief and awe.

"That's right," replied Spartacus with grim satisfaction. "It often takes just one little thing to create panic. But when it starts, it's like the plague. Unstoppable."

"The tipping point was your seizure of the standard."

"And Castus' manic charge. It's a pity we didn't kill more of them. Still, it's to be expected." Spartacus jerked a thumb at the nearest slaves. Whoops of delight rose up as they stalked among the Roman injured, killing whomever they found alive and looting choice pieces of equipment. "They're not soldiers yet. In the circumstances, we did well."

Well? thought Carbo. It was incredible! "How many got away, do you think?"

"It's hard to say. Half of them; maybe more. It doesn't really matter. What counts is that we won!" Spartacus' teeth shone white amid the blood on his face. "We won, Carbo, and that's what the men will remember. It's what the slaves in a hundred-mile radius will hear. Mark my words: our numbers will double again in the next week."

Spartacus' enthusiasm was infectious, and Carbo's spirits rose even further. "What will you do next?"

"Keep training the men." Spartacus paused, before fixing Carbo with his steely gray eyes. "I haven't forgotten when you brought Navio to the camp, you know. There was a time when I'd have had a man executed on the spot for such a transgression."

Carbo's brow went slick with sweat.

Spartacus' face softened a fraction. "I'm glad that I didn't. I watched him fight today. Navio's no friend of Rome. He's also excellent at military instruction."

"I—"

Spartacus held up his hand. "I'm convinced that the men fought better today because of what Navio has taught them. You have my thanks. And so does he."

Carbo grinned like a fool.

"We can't remain complacent. On the scale of things, today was but a minor victory. The rest of the six thousand legionaries have to be tracked down. I want to know what they're up to."

"Are you going to fight them?"

"In open battle? Not if I can help it. We'll try and surprise the dogs as we did here." *As I would have done in Thrace, if I'd ever got the chance.*

The idea of ambushing more of his own countrymen filled Carbo with excitement. Why don't I feel like a traitor? he wondered. His heart gave him an instant answer. Spartacus believed in him. Trusted him.

Apart from Paccius, no one else ever had.

†

Upon returning to their camp, Carbo fell into conversation with Egbeo, a hulking Thracian gladiator who was one of Spartacus' most loyal followers. He was stunned to hear from Egbeo that Amatokos, Chloris' lover, had been slain during the fight with Furius' soldiers. "Apparently, he killed more than half a dozen legionaries when his sword snapped," said Egbeo sourly. "That was it. The poor bastard had no chance after that." A dark joy suffused Carbo at the news, but he quickly faked a sorrowful expression. "He'll go straight to Elysium."

Egbeo's frown eased a little. "The warrior's paradise? Aye, there's no doubt about that. I'll warrant that the Rider himself will welcome Amatokos inside."

Carbo murmured in agreement, but he was already wondering when to approach Chloris. If he didn't move fast, another fighter might muscle in on her. At the same time, he didn't want to appear ghoulish. Amatokos' corpse hadn't even been placed in the ground. In the event, he decided to wait. In all likelihood, the funeral would take place that evening, and the chances of anyone staking a claim to Chloris before the following day were slim indeed.

Carbo was afforded no chance to talk to her the next morning. Many of the Roman dead had been stripped of their weapons and armor but plenty of equipment still littered the field. Spartacus ordered that every able-bodied man was to do his bit, whether that was standing on guard, on the lookout for Varinius, or collecting discarded gladii, shields and pila. Carbo sweated alongside his troops, loading up the mules that they'd taken from Glaber's camp, and which had proved immeasurably useful. He was glad when the job was done, not least because of the flies that coated the entire area in black, humming clouds and the stench of death that filled his nostrils: a potent, decaying mixture of blood, shit, vomit and piss.

The first thing Carbo did upon his return to the crater was to strip naked and wash the encrusted grime from his body. Then, wearing his only clean tunic, he headed in the direction of the tent that Chloris had shared with Amatokos. Hearing the sound of raised tones as he neared it, Carbo's pace quickened.

He made out Chloris first. "Leave me alone!"

"I just thought you might like some company." Carbo didn't recognize the gravelly voice.

"Well, I don't. Piss off and leave me alone."

Instantly, the man's manner changed. "Be like that if you want to, gorgeous. I like a bit of rough."

Chloris screamed, and Carbo broke into a sprint. *Thank the gods I'm wearing my sword.* A heartbeat later, he burst on to the scene. Chloris was backed up against the entrance to her tent, her hands raised defensively against a wiry figure in a mail shirt. "Aren't you going to put up a fight? I'd prefer it that way."

"Hey! Cocksucker!" Carbo's blade was in his hand before he even knew it. "I'll fight you."

Slowly, the man turned. He had a narrow, weasel-like face, and Carbo recognized him as one of the few Samnites who had escaped from the ludus. His lip curled, and his hand strayed toward the hilt of his own weapon. "Will you now?"

"Step away from her!" Carbo ordered. "She wants nothing to do with shitbags like you."

There was a leer. "She wasn't protesting too much."

"You piece of maggot-blown filth! Raping a woman is what it takes to excite you, is it?" Carbo's fury boiled over, and he lunged forward, thrusting his gladius at the Samnite's belly. Alarmed, the man scrambled off to the side.

"You're fucking crazy! Going to kill me over a whore like this?"

"She's no whore," snarled Carbo, stabbing at the other again and again, giving him no chance to draw his sword.

"All right, all right, I get the idea. I'm not going to argue with one of Spartacus' cronies." Raising his hands in the air, the glowering Samnite withdrew.

Carbo spat after him. Only when the man was out of sight did he relax. Chloris was eyeing him when he turned, her dark eyes full of unshed tears. "Sorry I didn't get here sooner."

She took a step toward him. "You came in good time. Thank you."

"It was nothing."

"Far from it. He would have raped me."

"The prick won't come back if he values his balls."

She smiled. "Why won't he?"

Carbo colored, realizing that by driving the Samnite off, he had made a very public statement. Weirdly, he felt more scared by that than he had before the ambush. Chloris came closer, gazing at him with her deep, dark eyes. *Damn it, say something!* "Would you like . . . ?" he faltered.

"To be your woman? Yes, I would." She stepped in, and laid her head against his chest.

"Right." Awkwardly, because of the sword in his right hand, he put his arms around her. His fingers traced the flesh of her back, and she folded herself against him. They stayed like that for a few moments. Carbo didn't know what to do next. He felt as bashful as a virgin. When Chloris lifted her face to his and kissed him, he felt a surge of relief. The electric sensation rocked him back on his heels. He had never imagined kissing could be so pleasurable. Opening his mouth, Carbo felt her tongue dart lightly against his. He responded awkwardly, terribly aware that he had never done this before. Chloris didn't appear to notice, and he slowly grew more confident. He brought a hand around to her chest, and cupped a breast. It was deliciously pliable beneath his touch. Finding the nipple, he squeezed it gently. Chloris made a throaty little sound of pleasure, so Carbo did it again. His left hand wandered lower, toward her groin, and she pulled away.

"Come with me." She took his hand and led him to her tent.

Inside, with the leather flap closed, words failed Carbo as Chloris reached down and took hold of the hem of her dress with both hands. Lifting the garment up and over her head, she dropped it to the floor. Beneath, she was naked apart from a ragged piece of cloth around her hips.

His eyes focused instantly on her pert breasts, which were tipped with brown nipples. His gaze dropped appreciatively, but then his mouth opened in horror. A meshwork of scars extended around from Chloris' back, under her arms, their long, livid tails marring the smooth skin of her chest and belly. "Gods above."

As if he'd ordered her to, Chloris turned, revealing the full extent of her injuries. Her back was a ruin. Carbo's eyes were drawn to the worst cicatrice, a long, purple mark that looked like a burn. "Who did that to you?"

"The pirate captain who abducted me from Greece," she whispered.

"He must have been a complete savage," spat Carbo. "Why did he do it?"

"It gave him pleasure. He could only get hard by beating me. Then he would . . ." she stopped.

Carbo felt sick. *The Samnite was no different. And here I am, wanting sex as well.*

She picked up her dress and covered herself. "You think I'm disgusting. Everyone does."

"No! I don't," protested Carbo. "I think you're beautiful. You look like a statue of Diana or Juno come to life."

"Really?"

"Yes," said Carbo passionately.

Chloris' dress fell to the ground again. She reached out to stroke his arm, sending a jolt of energy through his flesh. She laughed deep in her throat at his reaction. "You are romantic as well as courageous. I like that."

"Do you?"

"Of course. I've liked you since the first time we met in the ludus. I was with Amatokos then, so—"

"It was a shame that he was killed," lied Carbo.

"The gods have their own purpose. And now you've come into my life." She was so close now that Carbo could feel her breath against his lips. No girl had ever willingly been this close to him, and he trembled with nervousness and desire.

"So you find me attractive?"

His tongue felt thick and useless, like a plank of wood in his dry mouth. "Yes."

"You're sure?"

He dragged his eyes up to hers. "Gods, yes!"

"Then kiss me."

Carbo obeyed. The fact that Chloris wanted him to protect her from other fighters, that she might well have approached other men and been rebuffed because of her scars, was immaterial. She seemed to like him, and that was what mattered. He wasn't going to say a word of protest, for that risked breaking the exquisite magic of the moment. *This* was what he had dreamed about for so long. Her hand dropped to his groin and within a few heartbeats, Carbo had lost all ability to think.

†

Lucius Cossinius sighed with pleasure and lay back, his eyes closed, luxuriating in the warm water. After the heat and dust of the march from Rome, this was pure bliss. Seeing the large outdoor pool in the grounds of a fine villa as his men searched for a place to camp had been too much temptation to avoid. Naturally enough, the property's owner had been delighted to welcome one of the officers sent by the Senate to deliver the locals from Spartacus' menace. I deserve no less, thought Cossinius righteously. He was sunburned, his back ached, and he had saddle sores on the insides of his thighs. Of course he'd ridden rather than marched as his two thousand legionaries had, but Pompeii was still more than a hundred miles from the capital. It was considerably more exercise than Cossinius was used to. Going on an occasional hunt with his friends was a different prospect to sitting on a horse's back from sunrise to sunset for five consecutive days. And although this was his first year of office as a praetor, he'd been living in Rome for far longer, traveling everywhere by litter. *As is my right.*

Aware of the need to show one's willingness to lead troops into battle, Cossinius had leaped at the chance to join Publius Varinius, his friend, as an adviser. Their mission was to seek out and destroy the rabble that, months before, had somehow put Caius Claudius Glaber's troops to flight. Cossinius' top lip curled. He'd heard Glaber's account with his own ears, but it was still hard to believe. It was laughable. Three thousand legionaries had been defeated by a tiny number of runaway gladiators and slaves! Another surprise defeat had transpired just a week previously, but Cossinius dismissed the matter out of hand. Lucius Furius, the legate who'd commanded one-third of Varinius' force, was also a fool. To have been ambushed near Vesuvius, losing hundreds of men, could only mean that he was an incompetent of the highest order. After hearing his report, and absorbing the remnants of Furius' men into his own force, Varinius had sent the man to Rome in disgrace. *Good riddance. The remaining five thousand legionaries are more than enough to sort out a few hundred slaves. There'll be all the more glory for me and Varinius.*

Cossinius opened his eyes. Excellent. The slave, an attractive black-haired girl in a revealing shift, was still there. He'd made her take off his cloak and dusty armor, which had been very titillating. He lifted his arm. "More."

Carrying a small amphora, the girl moved forward to the edge of the pool and carefully filled his proffered glass.

Cossinius slurped the wine down in two swallows. The villa's owner—what was his name again?—had said it was his best vintage, and by all the gods, he wasn't lying. It tasted like ambrosia, the wine of the gods. Cossinius shoved his glass at her again. "More." Turning in the water, he was afforded an excellent view of the slave's breasts through the top of her shift as she stooped over him. It was most rewarding. On impulse, he caught her by the wrist. "Perhaps you'd like to join me?"

"Yes, master."

Her voice was a monotone, but Cossinius didn't care. It had been a long day. He was feeling horny. She was a slave. Her master wouldn't care if he fucked her. Even if he did, the fat fool wouldn't dare say a thing. Once they realized, the soldiers who were on guard twenty paces away would know better than to look in his direction. He, Lucius Cossinius, was a praetor, second in rank only to the consuls, and one of just eight men chosen to fill that position. He could do as he damn well pleased. Putting down his glass, Cossinius pushed back from the edge of the pool to get a better view. "Take off your clothes. Slowly."

Placing the amphora on the tiles, the girl stood up. Her face wore a resigned look. Oblivious to this, Cossinius squinted appreciatively at her. He wasn't one for the typical pale-skinned Roman matron. Thanks to the late afternoon sunlight, the slave's skin was a delightful olive tone. He could see her nipples through the thin fabric of her dress too. His groin tightened. The hell he'd endured on his horse for the last five days was beginning to seem worth it, even before they'd crushed Spartacus and his band of outcasts.

She pulled up the hem of her shift slowly, as he'd ordered her, stopping just below her groin. Cossinius held his breath as she lifted it further, revealing a linen undergarment. *Wonderful.* He didn't like it when they were naked underneath. Having to wait a little longer increased his desire to no end.

Her belly came into view next. It was flat, and its smooth skin was only a little paler than her arms or legs. The bones of her hips sat high on either side, enticing him to grip them from behind. Cossinius licked his lips as the bottom of her breasts peeked from under the edge of the fabric. "Wait. Stand like that."

Mutely, the slave obeyed.

Cossinius drank in her beauty for a few more moments. "Take it off."

She pulled the shift up and over her head. Dropping it to the ground, she stared off into the distance.

"Look at me." Unwillingly, her eyes crept back to his. They were bright blue, he noticed with surprise. They made her even more desirable. "Now the undergarment."

Her fine-boned fingers reached down and began sliding the fabric downward.

Cossinius could feel his excitement growing.

Her gaze moved upward again, taking in the ground behind him. Her hands stopped.

He frowned. "Well, get on with it!"

A trace of fear crossed her face.

Cossinius began to grow impatient. "For Jupiter's sake, I'm not going to beat you. Take it off and get into the water."

Instead of obeying, the slave opened her mouth and screamed.

At last, Cossinius took in her degree of terror, and he realized that she wasn't screaming at him. His head spun around, to the magnificent lawns that rolled away on either side of the pool. What he saw was surreal. Perhaps twenty men—armed men—were running across the grass toward him. More were emerging from the trees at the edge of the villa's garden. The leaders were no more than thirty paces away. Many of the intruders wore crested bronze helmets and carried scuta, but they were clearly not legionaries. No Roman soldiers had mustaches or wore their hair long. No Roman soldier ran into battle barechested or yelled such unearthly battle cries. Cossinius' blood turned to ice in his veins. *Spartacus' men.*

Still shrieking, the slave turned and ran away, back toward the villa.

His erection vanished, Cossinius scrambled frantically out of the pool. It was all he could do to grab his scarlet cloak from the bench where he'd left his clothes and sprint for safety. Everything else, from his polished muscled cuirass to his ivory-handled gladius, his magnificent crested helmet, his finely woven tunic and his padded *subarmalis*, was left behind. There was certainly no time to pull on and lace up his open-toed boots.

Cossinius could see his own shock mirrored on the faces of the ten soldiers he'd brought here to guard him as he bathed. Their commander, a weak-chinned optio, gaped at the sight of his superior sprinting in his direction, prick and balls bouncing up and down. Cossinius didn't care. "Form the men up!" he yelped. "Prepare to fight a rearguard action while I raise the alarm!"

The order was a death sentence, and the optio knew it. He blinked, and then regained control of himself. "Yes, sir!" He glared at the ten legionaries, some of whom had begun shuffling backward. "You heard the praetor! Form a line! At the double!"

Cossinius slowed his flight long enough to see that the legionaries were doing as they were told. Breathing a tiny sigh of relief, he ran for the stables, where his horse had been stabled. Gods willing, the savages hadn't had the wits to attack from more than one side of the villa. All he needed was a moment's grace and he'd be up and away. The camp was literally five hundred paces away. Cossinius prayed with all his might that Spartacus hadn't attacked it at the same time.

The short ride to his camp was the longest of Cossinius' life. Frantic glances over his shoulder soon told him that he was being pursued. Dozens of armed men had spilled on to the road, and more were still emerging from the villa's grounds. Acutely aware of the fact that he was wearing nothing but his cloak, Cossinius urged his already tired horse on with desperate thumps of his heels. Before long, he saw off to one side, the shapes of hundreds of legionaries standing in a loose semicircle around a large rectangular mound of earth—the rampart for the temporary camp. He had never been more glad of army routine. Fully half of his command—one thousand soldiers—were standing guard as the remainder built an enclosure for the night. There would be more than enough to defeat the slaves. "Sound the alarm!" he squawked. "Sound the alarm!"

No one heard him. Cossinius spat a savage curse and saved his breath. He was too far away, and the lazy bastards were probably gossiping rather than looking out for signs of danger. The fact that they were in safe territory, just a few miles from Pompeii, was irrelevant, he thought furiously. After the slaves had been annihilated, he would have the duty officer flogged within a whisker of his life. Perhaps he'd even have him tortured.

"Enemy in sight! Sound the alarm!" he bellowed again.

Finally, heads began to turn. Cossinius saw the legionaries' faces crease in recognition, shock and then hilarity. Laughter broke out in the ranks. Even the officers were struggling not to smile. Cossinius flushed crimson. He could only imagine what he looked like, a bollock-naked praetor astride a horse, with his red cloak billowing behind him. There was nothing for it, however, but to keep riding, straight up to his men. "Are you fucking deaf?" he yelled as he drew nearer. "Sound the alarm!"

The nearest centurion's mirth suddenly vanished. "The alarm, sir?"

"Yes, you fool! The villa has been overrun. My guards are dead, and the road behind me is full of Spartacus' men. Stand the troops to arms!"

The centurion was a veteran, even if his soldiers weren't. "You heard the praetor!" he roared at the trumpeter. "Sound the fucking alarm!

NOW! The rest of you, form up. Twenty men wide, four ranks deep. Double quick!" He turned back to Cossinius. "Get yourself inside the rampart, sir. Your baggage is already in there. We'll contain the bastards until you return."

Giving the centurion a tight nod, Cossinius rode on. As the trumpet blared a series of short, staccato sounds, he was pleased to see all the legionaries in sight being hurried into formation by their officers. No one was laughing at his nakedness now. *It won't take me long to get dressed. Then we can sort the scumbags out.* He permitted himself a small smile. *I'll have that slave brought to my quarters tonight. Might as well fuck her in comfort.*

†

A short time later, all thoughts of sex had left Cossinius' mind. Hastily donning one of his spare uniforms and a pair of sandals, he'd slung a baldric suspending his second-best sword over his right shoulder and shoved a helmet on his head. When he was fully dressed, the terror he'd felt in the pool vanished to be replaced by red-blooded fury. *How dare they?* he raged silently. *Filthy slaves. I'll make them pay.* Accompanied by a couple of confused-looking staff officers who'd been milling around by his tent, Cossinius headed straight for the front entrance. Thanks to the rampart, which was already higher than a man, he couldn't see the ground before the camp. However, the sounds of battle, unfamiliar to his ears, formed a deafening crescendo as they trotted along. Sword clattered off sword; trumpets shrilled over and over; incomprehensible shouts echoed to and fro. Intermingled with this cacophony was the unmistakable sound of men screaming.

Cossinius didn't like it. "What's happening?"

"I'm not sure, sir," muttered the younger of the two staff officers, an arrogant youth who had been appointed to his position thanks only to his father's wealth. Although Cossinius' background was similar, he loathed him.

"Why in Hades' name don't you know? It's your bloody job to inform me of what's going on!"

"I'm sorry, sir," said the second officer. "Last we saw, our lads were holding their own."

"Holding their own?" Cossinius spluttered indignantly.

"Yes, sir. I'm sure that when you appear, we'll soon drive them off."

"Damn right!" Cossinius drew his sword and made for the entrance, which was a narrow passageway ten paces long, formed in the specially constructed gap between two overlapping parts of the earthen rampart. He stumbled back in surprise as a wild-eyed legionary came storming inside. Cossinius glared at the soldier, who had no shield or sword. "What is the meaning of this?" he snapped.

The legionary's eyes came back into focus, registering Cossinius' ornate armor and the two staff officers by his side. "I . . . we . . . they're all over us, sir. There are hundreds of them . . . hundreds."

"So, what, you ran away?" accused Cossinius.

The legionary's eyes flickered from side to side, like a cornered rat. "I—"

Grimacing, Cossinius rammed his sword into the soldier's groin, below the edge of his mail shirt. Letting the screaming man fall off his blade, he stared down the staff officers, whose faces were the picture of horror. "That's more than the piece of filth deserves! Now follow me."

He stalked outside, determined to end the farce once and for all. Like chastened pups, they clung to his heels.

Cossinius could not have imagined the scene of utter chaos that met his eyes. Instead of serried ranks of legionaries pressing home the attack under the calm direction of their officers, he saw isolated pockets of men fighting desperately against encircling groups of yelling slaves. In the time it took him to scan the field from left to right, Cossinius saw at least six soldiers hacked to pieces. Slowly but inevitably, his troops were being driven backward or, more often, wiped out. Scores of the attackers were already pressing forward into the gaps in the Roman lines, toward the camp. There was no one to halt their progress.

The ground was littered with the injured and dying, the maimed

and the blind. In threes and fours, legionaries were retreating, or even
running from the fight. Here and there, a centurion valiantly tried to
regain control, but there was no order, no design to the bitter struggle.
Of the troops who'd been laying out the camp, Cossinius could see
no sign. He looked to the defensive ditch, where he'd last seen them
working. It was full of discarded tools. Alongside the trench stood
neat stacks of shields and pyramids of javelins. The cold realization of
what had happened clutched at his vitals. *The shitbags have left their weapons
and run already.* Suddenly, Cossinius' mouth was as dry as the bed of a
desert stream. This kind of misfortune did not happen to him. Half
the men under his command did not just run away. Slaves did not
overwhelm regular legionaries. *The world's gone mad.*

"Sir?"

Cossinius was dimly aware of someone tugging at his arm.

"What are your orders, sir?"

He looked stupidly at the more senior staff officer. "Eh?"

The officer gestured at the carnage with a trembling arm. "What
shall we do, sir?"

An image of Glaber falling on his sword filled Cossinius' mind.
Not for him the ignominy of that end. He would not leave such a
shameful stain on his family's good name. Far better to die in battle,
facing the enemy with a sword in his hand. He felt a passing twinge of
regret. He'd never get to screw the attractive slave now. "We advance,"
Cossinius said calmly.

"A-advance, sir?"

"You heard me. Roman senators and noblemen do not run from
slaves!" He reached down and picked up a discarded scutum, the back
of which was spattered with blood. Its owner's blood, thought Cossinius vaguely. "Find shields, both of you. We'll show these whoresons
how Romans can die."

"Yes, sir!" The officer grabbed a scutum. Shamefaced, his companion did the same. They drew their gladii.

"Form up either side of me," ordered Cossinius. "Stay close."

As the officers obeyed, a group of nearby slaves saw their pathetic shield wall. Without hesitation, they charged in a heaving, screaming mass. Swords and javelins waved, promising death in all kinds of ways.

"Prepare to meet an enemy attack," ordered Cossinius. Crassus was right, he thought wryly. Spartacus is a man to be respected.

XVI

The sun was dropping in the sky as Spartacus worked his way through the camp, which now sprawled over a huge area, far beyond the earthen ramparts erected by Glaber's men. Greetings rang out from everyone who noticed him, and he made sure to smile in return or engage in a few words of encouragement before moving on. Inside, Spartacus was troubled by the number of gaunt faces on view.

After Cossinius' defeat and death, the tide of new recruits seeking to join him—men, women and children—had turned into a veritable flood. The camp at the top of Vesuvius had rapidly swelled to bursting point. With more severe weather imminent, he had taken the decision to move everyone down to the remnants of Glaber's encampment at the bottom of the mountain. While this meant that his fifteen thousand followers were shielded from the worst extremes of the elements, it did not provide them with any food.

It also left them open to attack from Varinius, who had regrouped his forces and camped about five miles away. Despite the swelling of his forces' strength, Spartacus still did not want to fight the Romans in open battle. Perhaps five thousand men were trained to the standards he'd want, but the rest weren't nearly ready for face-to-face combat; nor did they have enough equipment. Slave chains gave Pulcher and the other smiths limited amounts of iron to forge swords and spears, and fire-hardened sharp-ended stakes would only go so far when fighting fully armored legionaries. Sometimes Spartacus wished that he were in Thrace, with as many battle-hardened warriors as he had followers here. He didn't dwell on the pleasing thought, because having that many Thracians under one banner—his—was little more than a fantasy. His quest to unify the tribes against Rome might have succeeded, but it was as likely that he'd have been slain during his attempt. His men here were real. He just needed to train them, and keep the army from splitting up. *Damn Crixus for a fool!*

Brooding, he approached the fire by his tent, where Ariadne stood. She was tending a blackened pot that hung over the flames. Spartacus' breath plumed in the chill air. He rubbed his hands together and extended them toward the heat. "That smells good. What is it?"

Ariadne looked up. "It's what's left of last night's stew, with more water added."

He shrugged. "The men are raiding every farm, and killing whatever game they can. But the Romans are everywhere now. It's difficult to hunt when you're keeping one eye out all the time for an enemy patrol. At least we've something to eat. There are others in the camp going hungry."

She sighed. "I'm sorry. You have enough to worry about without me complaining."

"It's all right." He put an arm around her waist. "But we need to move from here. Soon, too."

She cocked her head at him. "Why now?"

"We might have defeated Varinius and his men twice now, and raided their camps as well, but he has learned from his mistakes—and those of his officers. The fortifications around his new encampment are taller than I've ever seen, and the defensive ditch is deep enough to float a damn ship in. We'd have more chance of storming Hades than it." He scowled. "Winter is coming too. It's going to get harder to find supplies. The best way to avoid people starving is to find a safer place to camp."

"Surely that's simple enough?" She looked at his face and used her intuition. The same thought had troubled her since they'd broken out of the ludus. "Let me guess. Crixus won't go along with your idea."

"Of course not. He wants to fight Varinius. He says only cowards run from an enemy. Castus agrees with him."

"But we wouldn't be running! Merely moving to a more secure base." There was another option, thought Ariadne guiltily. She and Spartacus and a few others—the Scythians, the Thracians and maybe Carbo—could leave. Make their way out of Italy. It seemed cowardly even to think it, so she did her best to bury the idea.

"I told him that," said Spartacus. "It's not as if we won't have to fight the Romans again! The prick wasn't having any of it, though. He's talking about leaving, taking his men with him. Castus might go too."

The Gaulish leaders had quickly realized that the recruits flooding in were a source of recruits to their own factions. All three had won great popularity among countless hundreds of the slaves. If Crixus and Castus departed, it would considerably reduce Spartacus' strength. Worried now, Ariadne stared at him. "What are you going to do?"

"I'm going to enjoy my stew, and then I'm taking my wife to bed. Maybe she can warm the chill from my bones." He squeezed her hip.

Ariadne wanted the same thing too, but she forced a frown. "I'm being serious."

His grin faded. "I know you are. I've called a council of war for the morning."

"And?"

"With the Great Rider's blessing, I will persuade them both to stay with us." The muscles in his jaw worked. "If they have any sense at all, they'll have come to that conclusion anyway."

She pulled away from his embrace. "Feed yourself," she said crisply, reaching for her cloak. "I'll be back in a while."

Spartacus' eyebrows rose. "Where are you going?"

"To ask for Dionysus' support. We need all the help we can get."

Spartacus' thoughts of sex faded. He stared grimly after Ariadne as she vanished into the gloom. *She's right.*

†

Reluctant to turn in before he heard whether Ariadne had any news, Spartacus stayed by the fire. Wrapping a pair of blankets around himself to ward off the cold, he poured out a bowl of stew and sat down to eat. The food was gone all too soon, but his still grumbling belly was the least of his concerns. Crixus. It always came down to the arrogant and argumentative Crixus. *I could fight him again.* Spartacus dismissed the idea at once. After their previous clash, the Gaul would insist on fighting with weapons. Even if he beat Crixus, he'd probably have to kill him, which would be counter-productive. There was no guarantee that Castus would stay in that instance either. *Take him on too? No. I can't fight everyone in the damn army. There must be a way of convincing them not to leave.*

More than two hours passed. Full night had fallen, and the moon was climbing from the distant horizon. It was growing steadily colder, and the camp had gone quiet. Apart from the sentries, everyone had sought the comfort of their shelters. Thanks to the equipment seized after their victories over Furius and Cossinius, a sizeable number had leather tents. Hunching his shoulders, Spartacus moved his feet closer to the edge of the fire. *There could be a frost tonight.*

"You're still up," said Ariadne, emerging from the darkness.

"Of course." He studied her face for clues, but her expression was closed.

"Is there any stew left?"

"Yes, I left you half."

She tutted at him. "You need food far more than I do."

"I've had plenty," Spartacus lied, knowing that she usually gave him the lion's share. He watched in silence as Ariadne scraped out the pot and sat down to eat.

· 321 ·

"Aren't you going to ask me if I saw something?"

"Did you?"

"Yes."

As ever, his belly tightened. "What was it?"

She countered with a question. "What are your long-term plans?"

"I haven't got any," he replied frankly. "In my game, it's best not to. A warrior never knows when his life might end."

"You must have had some thoughts about it."

He considered her words. "I'd like to forge an army, a proper army. Beat the Romans in open battle."

"To what end? That wouldn't be enough," she retorted. "The bastards never give up." *That's been my plan since I first left my village all those years ago.*

"I know. Even after Hannibal wiped out their army at Cannae, they didn't despair. It took them nearly twenty years but they beat him in the end. And Hannibal had a proper army. What have I got? A few thousand slaves!"

Ariadne hadn't heard him talk like this before. "Don't give up," she urged.

"You mistake me," he retorted. His eyes glittered fiercely in the firelight. "I have more men here than the warriors of several tribes in Thrace. I haven't had to fight to unify them either. While that number follows me, I will never give up! Nor will I ever be a slave again. But I also know the realities that we face. The Republic did not become the power that it is for no reason. Its people are proud, warlike and brave, but most of all, they are stubborn. The majority of races eventually accept defeat—Thracians included," he added bitterly. "Not the Romans, however. They would rather be wiped out than give in. That simple fact is what someone like Crixus will never understand. Varinius is but one commander of a score that the Senate could call upon. His troops are a tiny fraction of Rome's manpower. Each time we defeat them, we make it more inevitable that ever greater numbers of soldiers will be sent against us. That's why it is so important not to run off and offer battle to Varinius like a wild beast defending its territory, but to make every encounter take place at a time and a place of our choosing. Another truth that Crixus does not see."

"There is a different option," said Ariadne softly.

He gave her a sharp glance. "What—to leave Italy?"

"Yes. It would be easy enough to do. A small band, traveling fast, could easily avoid the troops looking for us. Carbo says that it's only three hundred miles or so to the Alps."

"Winter is just around the corner. The mountains are no place to be when snow is falling."

"Hannibal crossed them at this time of year," she challenged.

"But he was coming *into* Italy, to fight the bastard Romans. Not to run away from them."

"That's not what you would be doing," Ariadne protested.

"Is it not? Supposing we made it back to Thrace and I overthrew Kotys. Would I just forget all about what we're doing here?"

Ariadne felt her cheeks flame.

"Is that what you saw?"

"No."

"Good. I can hear the whispers in my village even now. 'Spartacus raised an army of slaves, and just when they needed him most, he abandoned them to their fate.'" He scowled. "Because that's what I'd be doing. If I left, what do you think would happen to the people in the camp here?"

"They'd splinter into small groups. Get picked off by the Romans, probably."

"That's right. The lucky ones would be enslaved again. The rest would starve to death or get killed by wolves." He stared at her. "I can't leave them. I won't."

Ariadne wasn't surprised by his response. "My conscience wouldn't let me do that either." *Liar. If the other event I saw comes to pass, I'd try to get away in a heartbeat. I can't tell him that, however.*

"I'm a warrior who stands and fights, not a yellow-livered coward who skulks off when times get hard, leaving the weak to fend for themselves."

"I know," she said gently. "And if you could take the whole army over the Alps?"

His eyes narrowed. "That is an entirely different proposition. However, there's more chance of the Great Rider appearing before me right now than of persuading the Gauls to go along with that idea. They were born into slavery. So were most of the Germans. They hate Rome and what it stands for, but Italy is their entire world. It's a rich land, with easy pickings for men like us. Why would they even consider leaving it?" He looked at her thoughtfully. "That's what came to you? The army crossing the Alps?"

"It was one thing that I saw, yes."

"Were there others?"

She nodded.

"Tell me."

"You'll believe that I'm making it up. Trying to make you leave Italy."

"I won't think that. Whatever you see is sacred, sent to you by Dionysus."

She studied his face for a moment. "Very well. I am to bear you a son."

"A son?" Spartacus' face creased into a huge smile. "That's wonderful!"

"It might not happen," she said quickly. "Nothing about visions is certain."

"I know, I know. But a son!" He reached over and squeezed her knee. "You'll make a fine mother."

"And you a strong father." *Maybe this will change his mind?*

"If what you saw is true, it's even more reason to stay with the men," Spartacus declared. "Let's say that we left now and traveled to Thrace, and our son grew up safely there. Imagine his opinion of me when he found out what I'd done. He'd think I was a damn coward, and he'd be right too."

Ariadne was surprised to feel little disappointment. There was a trace of shame that she could even contemplate leaving, but the dominant emotion was pride. Pride in Spartacus. Yes, his ego was surely fed by his exalted position, but that was not his primary reason for staying. Ensuring the care of his men was. A tiny part of her still longed to escape their existence, however. "He wouldn't think that if you'd beaten the Romans and left them to rot while you took the whole army out of Italy."

"Now there's an idea!" he said with a smile. "All I need to do is win over Crixus and Castus. First things first, however. For you to bear me a son, we have to make one." He took Ariadne by the hand and pulled her upright. "Let's go to bed, eh?"

This time, Ariadne did not resist.

†

Carbo went looking for Spartacus at dawn. Over the previous few weeks, he had barely seen his leader. He'd been too busy himself. When he wasn't helping Navio train the men, or in his tent coupling with Chloris, he had been out on foraging missions for food. On his most recent expedition, from which he only returned late the previous evening, Carbo and his comrades had spied out the town of Nola, which lay some eight miles to the northeast of Vesuvius. Thus far, it had escaped the slaves' attentions. The wealth of the estates around Nola, and the visible lack of Roman troops, had been apparent to everyone in Carbo's party. Here, in a neatly circumscribed area, were warehouses full of grain, stores of wine, dried meat and other foodstuffs, all ripe for the plucking. This was bounty that could not be left untouched. It had fallen to Carbo to bring the matter to Spartacus' attention.

He met Spartacus heading purposefully toward Glaber's former headquarters, which had become the leaders' habitual meeting place. There was no missing his leader. Spartacus was dressed in a mail shirt that had been burnished until it shone. His sheathed sica hung from a gilded Roman military belt, and he wore a stunning Phrygian helmet. Even his leather sandals had been polished. He looked magnificent, thought Carbo admiringly.

"What do you want?" barked Spartacus.

Taken aback, Carbo began explaining about Nola.

"Tell me as I walk," ordered Spartacus. "I can't stand around to listen."

Carbo had to trot to keep up as they made their way along the camp's main avenue.

Spartacus said nothing until they arrived at the headquarters, where he stopped. "It's a good idea."

Carbo took in the waiting shapes of Crixus, Castus and Gannicus. *They don't look happy.* "Will you organize a raiding party?"

Spartacus looked at him. For the first time, Carbo noticed lines of exhaustion under his gray eyes. "We'll see. It depends on what happens here."

"All right." Carbo waited to be dismissed.

Spartacus considered him for a moment, before chuckling mirthlessly. "Stay with me. You might as well. It's your fate as well as mine that we'll be deciding."

Carbo's confusion grew.

"You'll find out soon enough what's going on. Remember to keep your mouth shut and your ears open."

He nodded.

Spartacus walked over to the Gauls, who were also clad in their finest gear.

Carbo trailed a few steps behind Spartacus. *This must be an important meeting.*

"What the hell is he doing here?" Crixus pointed a thick finger at Carbo. "You're not welcome."

Crixus had never spoken to Carbo, but he'd thrown enough glares in the lad's direction for him to know how the Gaul felt. With difficulty, he kept his face neutral. *Arrogant bastard.*

"Carbo has been giving me the good news about a town called Nola, which lies to the northeast," said Spartacus calmly. "He came across it on a foraging mission. Apparently, it's too good a prize to pass up. We'll find weeks' worth of supplies there."

At this, Gannicus smiled. Castus grunted noncommittally, but Crixus sneered. "Big fucking deal."

"Finding new sources of food is important," observed Spartacus mildly.

"That's not what we're here to talk about." Crixus glared at Carbo. "Piss off."

Although he wanted to, Carbo wasn't about to challenge Crixus. The move would cost him his life. Resentfully, he turned to leave.

"I ‌stays," said Spartacus in a sharp tone.

Delighted, Carbo froze.

"Why?" Crixus' tone was bullish.

"Some of your men are here." Spartacus indicated the half-dozen gladiators who lounged nearby.

"I can trust them," retorted Crixus. "Your lapdog, however, is a cocksucking Roman."

Carbo flushed with anger but Spartacus spoke before he could react. "Carbo has repeatedly proven his loyalty since we left the ludus. In case you've forgotten, he's also the one who brought back Navio. Don't try to deny that that man's training has made an enormous difference to our fighting capability."

"Carbo is all right," said Gannicus in a placatory voice. "Eh, Castus?"

"I suppose so," came the reluctant answer.

Crixus' face grew sullen. "Suit yourself," he growled. "It will make no difference to what I do."

"What will you do?" asked Spartacus. *As if I don't know.*

"Attack Varinius' camp again! Ambush his men at every opportunity. Wipe the bastard out as soon as possible."

"Will you join him, Castus?"

"I'm thinking of it, yes."

How times have changed. A few months ago, you wouldn't give Crixus the time of day. Spartacus eyed Gannicus, who was sucking on his mustache. "And you?"

"I'm not sure yet," Gannicus replied awkwardly.

It's as I thought. One against me, one probably against me, and one on the fence.

Spartacus considered walking away, letting them splinter their army into little pieces, but his pride wouldn't let him. *Dionysus revealed that I could forge a proper army, one that can fight Rome and its legions. The chance to do that is too good just to throw away.*

"Are you still planning to run away?" jibed Crixus.

If he'd been like this in the ludus, I never would have got the prick to agree to join us, Spartacus reflected, forcing himself to remain calm. *All he needed was the chance to prove himself in battle. Now that he's done that, men are prepared to follow him. But bravery only gets a soldier so far. Crixus has no tactical sense that I've seen.* Out loud, he said, "I want to defeat Varinius too."

Crixus' brows lowered. "Have you come to your senses then?"

"It's what I've always aimed for," said Spartacus. "Just not right now."

"You want to wait. To move to another camp."

"Yes."

"Tell me how that's not running away," cried Crixus. And he was off, ranting how he and his men would wreak havoc on the local countryside; how they would annihilate Varinius and his cowardly troops; how they didn't need Spartacus and his snake-in-the-grass Roman friends. Soon Castus added his voice to the tirade. The pair were encouraged by the vigorous noises of approval made by the watching Gaulish gladiators. Gannicus stood watching the performance, his eyes as beady as an old vulture's.

Carbo began to grow despondent. He'd known something of the rivalries between the various leaders, but he'd never guessed that it was this bad. To his surprise and disappointment, Spartacus said nothing. He just listened.

At last Crixus' outburst came to an end. "Cat got your tongue?" he asked Spartacus acidly.

Castus snickered.

That's it, thought Carbo. *It's over. They'll leave. The army will fragment. Varinius will have no problem crushing us.*

Bizarrely, Spartacus smiled. "I've got one simple question for you, Crixus."

Crixus' top lip peeled back with contempt. "What?"

"How many legionaries do you think Varinius has left?"

"Eh? What do I care?"

"How many?" demanded Spartacus.

"I don't know." Crixus gave a casual shrug. "Three thousand? Three and a half thousand?"

"A man arrived yesterday who'd been a body slave to one of Varinius' senior officers." Spartacus was pleased to see Gannicus and Castus stiffen. Even Crixus' face changed. *Didn't know that, did you?* "He has close to four and a half thousand legionaries."

"A thousand extra troops will make no difference. Nor will fifteen hundred," blustered Crixus. "They'll run just as fast as the rest."

Time to spring the trap. "If you leave, how many men will follow you?"

"Two and a half thousand, give or take," Crixus replied proudly.

"And you, Castus?"

"About the same."

"I know that approximately two thousand answer to you, Gannicus." He turned back to Crixus. "How many of your lot are ready to stand up to legionaries in open combat?"

Crixus' expression grew thunderous.

"Come on, you must have an idea. Every good general knows the disposition of his forces," cajoled Spartacus.

"Less than half," Crixus muttered.

"If that," retorted Spartacus sharply. "The same applies to your followers, Castus, or I'm no judge of a soldier."

Castus glowered but did not reply.

Carbo's spirits rose. *Spartacus is a genius!*

Spartacus caught first Crixus' eye, and then that of Castus. He ignored Gannicus. *I'll pretend he's with me, even if he isn't.* "So you're going to take on Varinius and the guts of a legion with fewer than three thousand fighting men?"

"So what if I am?" snapped Crixus, going red.

"Fair enough." Spartacus' tone was light. Carbo ducked his head to hide his grin. Crixus had been made out to be at best a braggart, and at worst a fool. "Have you thought about whether Varinius might attack the camp?" Spartacus went on.

Crixus gave a confident laugh. "After all we've done to them, they're too shit scared to try."

"Maybe so," admitted Spartacus. "I think Varinius might feel differently, however, when he hears that more than ten thousand men have left with me and Gannicus." *Great Rider, help me now. Let him have heard my words.*

"Gannicus?" Crixus' growl was furious. "You're coming with us, aren't you?"

Gannicus tugged at his mustache, but when he spoke his tone was crisp. "I'm not so sure it's a wise idea to break up the army at the moment."

Hit Crixus with it now, thought Spartacus savagely. "Imagine four and a half thousand legionaries storming the camp. They'll have catapults and bolt throwers to soften you up beforehand too. Will your men withstand that?"

Crixus' face twisted with anger. He glanced at Castus, who now looked most unhappy, and then his eyes slid back to Spartacus. "I'm not running away!"

"No one said anything about running away. Look, I know how brave you all are. Unless they're deaf, dumb and blind, so does every damn man in the camp." At this, Gannicus and Castus grinned; Crixus' mouth was still an unhappy gash, but he didn't interrupt. *Thank the Rider for that much.* "Remember, I want to defeat Varinius too. Our followers are brave, but they're *slaves*, not soldiers. Even the rawest legionary recruit is more than a match for the vast majority of our men. Our successes thus far have been thanks to the element of surprise. Varinius is no fool. He won't fall into the same traps again. That's not to say we can't beat him. But we need more time to train the men. More weapons, or iron for the smiths to work. More food. You've seen how little remains in the way of provisions," Spartacus warned. "If we're not to be crushed by Varinius, or die of starvation, we need to act."

Gannicus spoke first. "What do you suggest?"

"We give Varinius the slip. Head south, to where it's warmer. Locate a secure camp, in a place where we can find enough supplies."

"We'll need wine and women too."

"We will," agreed Spartacus, knowing that was a reality he had to live with. "Let's spend the winter training and preparing for battle. In the spring, we'll track down Varinius and his men, and put them to the sword." He glanced casually at Gannicus.

"I'm with you!"

Castus said nothing. He eyed Crixus, who was chewing a fingernail.

"You'll give me your word about killing Varinius?" Crixus rumbled.

"I will."

"Fair enough. I'll stay until then," said Crixus grudgingly.

"Castus?" asked Spartacus.

"Me too. But there'd better be plenty of women."

Can you do anything but think with your prick? Spartacus wondered. Out loud, he said, "I'm sure there will."

They gripped arms to fasten the deal. In the background, Carbo grinned from ear to ear.

Spartacus allowed himself a brittle smile. He had done better than he'd expected to. The army would remain together for the moment.

Sooner or later, however, a split was inevitable.

†

That night, in what had become their daily custom, Carbo and Chloris retired to their tent as darkness fell. The urgency of their physical union was still undimmed. Whether Chloris was faking her desire for him, Carbo could not be sure, but he was certainly not acting. He could not get enough of her. Afterward, they talked for an age. Lying under a thick layer of blankets with her, their limbs entwined, Carbo felt huge relief. Having Chloris around had removed a logjam from the dammed river of his conversation. Since the pox, he had lost all confidence in talking to anyone of the opposite sex. Now, he couldn't shut up. He wanted Chloris to know everything about him. He'd told her what had happened to his family, and of Crassus' involvement. How he'd not seen Paccius or his parents for months. Mentioning them again, he glanced into Chloris' dark eyes, seeing a pain there that he had not previously noticed. Guilt filled him. "I'm sorry.

At least I have some chance of seeing them again, whereas your father and mother . . ."

"Are dead, yes. Nothing can be done about that."

"Yet you must wish to return to Greece. To find your younger brother."

She ignored what he'd said. "I like listening to you talk. Your voice is soothing." She traced his features with a finger.

Screamingly conscious of the pockmarks pitting his cheeks, he looked away.

"You're very handsome," she murmured, lifting a hand and turning his face to hers again.

Carbo still couldn't meet her gaze.

"I thought that the first time I saw you strip off in the ludus. Good-looking, with a nice body." She reached down to his prick and chuckled in her throat. "I found that this was the best bit, though."

Her touch made him stiffen, but he wasn't entirely convinced. "And my scars?"

"They give you character." She laid a blanket of kisses on his cheeks. "They're part of you and you are a good man."

She was concealing something from him, thought Carbo. He did not know what, however, and as she rolled on top of him, all coherent thought left his head.

†

Three weeks went by, and Spartacus had put the confrontation with the Gauls from the front of his mind. Instead it lingered in the recesses of his memory like a bad smell over an open sewer. Overall, however, things had gone well. Varinius had been neatly tricked on the night that he and the army had withdrawn from Glaber's old encampment. Spartacus had insisted on meticulous planning beforehand. Patrols sent out in the late afternoon had scoured the area to make sure that there were no legionaries spying on the camp. Then, under the cover of darkness, their sentries at the front gate had been replaced by corpses dressed in mail and armed with bent or useless swords. By the light of dozens of campfires, every last tent had been taken down and packed, along with other heavy equipment such as Pulcher's anvils, on to hundreds of mules. In the hour before midnight, every man, woman and child had filed away, eastward, to the towering Picentini Mountains.

Everyone but Carbo, who was armed with a captured Roman trumpet.

It had been a dangerous duty to volunteer for, but Carbo had been most insistent. Seeing the burning desire in his eyes, Spartacus had acquiesced. The young Roman's job had been to stay awake all night, listening out for the enemy. At dawn he was to sound his instrument, in mockery of Rome's customary way of waking its soldiers, and wait to see what happened next.

Spartacus smiled at the memory of Carbo's report. It had been a real morale booster for everyone to discover that some two hours later, when Varinius had become aware that the rebels' camp was far quieter than normal, he had not dared to send a patrol to search it. Instead, one of his newly arrived cavalry units had ridden to the top of a nearby hill to look down on it from a height. Disconcerted by the slaves' disappearance, Varinius had withdrawn his forces to the northwest. Rather than having to creep away from the camp, Carbo had simply trotted after the slave host. Delighted by his report, Spartacus had called for a gathering that night. "That's how respectful the bastards are of us now," he had cried to the thousands who had assembled to hear him speak. "They are too damn scared even to come after us!" In the rousing cheer that met his words, he hadn't been surprised to be challenged by Crixus again.

"If the shitbags are that frightened, why in hell's name aren't we pursuing them?" he'd growled.

"Varinius fearing us is a good thing," Spartacus had replied robustly. "But it does not mean that we would win an open fight with him. In addition to his legionaries, he has four hundred cavalry. We have none. None! Imagine what those horsemen would do if they came hammering in to our rear in the midst of a battle. Have you ever seen a cavalry charge strike an unprepared enemy?" Crixus had glowered then, because everyone present had known that only Spartacus had witnessed such a thing. It had shut the Gaul up, though. "They smash the formation into smithereens! It's like watching a gust of wind pick up a pile of leaves and scatter it to the four ends of the earth. The fight would be lost with that one strike." No one had argued any further, which had pleased Spartacus. Of course, his approach wouldn't work forever, but his dire prediction had at least ensured that their forces had moved out of harm's way. Varinius' cavalry would be useless on steep mountainsides.

Besides, he'd withdrawn to the safety of Cumae, a city some twenty-five miles from Vesuvius. The rebels had therefore reached the Picentini Mountains without incident, and had made a temporary camp for several nights. Meanwhile, guided by Carbo, five hundred handpicked men under Gannicus had raided the town of Nola. They had returned in triumph to the accolades of their comrades, with enough grain to feed everyone for two weeks, as well as large quantities of warm clothing and footwear and close to a thousand new recruits. An attack on the town of Nuceria had yielded similar returns. Carbo had been elated by their success. It was remarkable, he realized, that his new vocation troubled him less and less. Yet the idea of becoming a lawyer now seemed positively laughable. Life with Spartacus was dangerous, but Carbo had authority, the respect of his comrades and last but not least, he had Chloris.

With enough supplies to last for a month or more, the entire army had headed south. It was guided by slaves who had worked as shepherds locally. These men kept the host at altitude because enduring the harsh weather of autumn was preferable to encountering any Roman troops. Yet, apart from the inhabitants of the small farming settlement of Abella, who had been surprised in their fields, the only company the slaves had had since was that of the creatures that lived in the forested mountains. Eagles and vultures that hung on the air overhead, surveying the long column with lofty disdain. Small birds that chattered angrily from the safety of trees at the invaders of their territory. Wolves that howled their mournful cries at dusk every night, adding to the sense of isolation and freedom. Deer and wild boar that hid from sight, leaving only their trail as evidence of their existence. Bears and lynxes lived here too, but they were only occasionally sighted by the scouts.

Spartacus had counted himself fortunate to see one lynx with his own eyes. It was a magnificent male, which had stood quite still when it had spotted him, regarding him for several moments from its slitted yellow eyes. It was the gently moving tufts on the tops of its ears that had told him it was not a statue, carved by a genius or a god. And then it had vanished, simply melting away into the undergrowth.

That is how we shall be to the Romans, thought Spartacus with some satisfaction. They will never know we're there, unless we want them to.

Two days before, they had crossed the River Silarus, using a little-known ford instead of the bridge on the Via Annia, the main road south to Rhegium. Since it lay near to the paved way with its heavy traffic, Spartacus had sent the two Scythians ahead to watch it day and night. By the time he arrived, they had been monitoring it for the guts of a week. They had seen neither hide nor hair of an enemy soldier. Spartacus had promptly convened with the other leaders. For once, they had come to a unanimous decision: to travel on the Via Annia. Moving much faster than previously, they had swept through the long, narrow plain that was the Campus Atinas, a fertile upland valley fed by the River Tanager. All travelers on the road and inhabitants of the large latifundia on either side of it had been freed, seized, or killed. No one in Forum Annii, the town they were aiming for, could be aware of their presence.

Until we walk into their houses, empty their storehouses, free their slaves. And kill them.

Spartacus had wanted to leave all this behind when he left the Roman army. But it was not to be. Fate had stepped in when Kotys had played him false, and Phortis had taken him to Italy and the ludus in Capua. Then a god had sent him a dream about a snake. Who was he to ignore such an opportunity when it was placed in his path? And yet—as in life—it was not quite that simple. Innocents always died.

Spartacus glanced around. The tree line to either side of him was packed with hundreds—no, thousands—of spectral figures. Everyone fit to bear arms was here. Even some of the women were to take part. He could sense the slaves' hunger, could reach out and touch it. The staring faces, the tightly gripped weapons, the fierce whispering reminded him of similar ambushes that he had taken part in, a lifetime ago in Thrace. The men were like starving wolves, about to fall on a flock of unsuspecting sheep in the fold. Except their prey was not animal, but human.

Spartacus stared down bleakly at the empty Via Annia, which was coated by thin tendrils of morning mist. It led through recently plowed fields for perhaps a quarter of a mile to the jumble of red-tiled roofs that was Forum Annii. He watched the trickles of smoke rising from fires that had been kept in overnight. Listened to the crowing of cocks in petulant rivalry with each other, and the fierce barking of dogs that know they will never have to back up their threats to each other. Not a figure moved in the fields below Spartacus' position, or on the streets of the town. Not a voice could be heard. It was incredibly tranquil. Peaceful, even beautiful. And so very similar to the village in Thrace that he had once called home.

His jaw clenched. *That will soon change.*

At dawn, Spartacus had spoken to the other leaders about the need for restraint. The need to limit the amount of rape and killing that would go on once their attack on Forum Annii began. His words had fallen if not on deaf ears, then on ears that would no longer listen.

"My men have been marching for more than three stinking weeks," Crixus had snarled. "It's been cold and damp and miserable. All they've had to fill their bellies is porridge and bread that's been burned over a fire. Now we've reached somewhere that is completely undefended. There isn't a legionary for fifty miles. My lads want meat and wine. They want beds and women to fuck in them. All of those things are lying down there in Forum Annii, and I'm not going to deny them the pleasure of having the lot. No one is." A tiny, challenging smile had traced its way across Crixus' lips.

Castus had whooped with excitement. Even Gannicus had looked pleased at the prospect of uncontrolled pillaging.

I had to bite my tongue, or the army would have split up then and there. Spartacus closed his eyes for a moment. *May the gods have mercy on the people down there. Let them die easily.*

He knew that his prayer was in vain.

Hell was about to be unleashed on Forum Annii.

XVII

Waking long before dawn, Carbo had risen from his blankets full of excitement. The raid on Nola had been an unparalleled success, yielding huge amounts of grain and clothing. Nuceria had been similar. No doubt Forum Annii would be the same. Carbo had drunk some water, wolfed down some of yesterday's bread smeared with honey, and looked to his weapons. By this stage, checking that his sword blade was sharp, his pilum heads securely attached and that the chinstrap of his bronze helmet was in place had become second nature. Navio, whose tent was beside Carbo's, was doing the same.

Carbo felt the first tickle of unease when he overheard a group of former farm slaves bragging about who would kill the most citizens in Forum Annii. When he'd rebuked them, they had laughed in his face. Carbo had confided in Navio, whose answer had been a simple shrug. "Some of that will go on. It always does when a town is sacked. Doesn't mean you have to be part of it, but there's nothing to be done about it. These things happen in war."

War, thought Carbo with a trace of unease. It seemed surreal, but that's what Spartacus' uprising felt like now. *It's inevitable that some innocent blood will be shed.* He was doubly glad that Chloris was staying behind in the camp.

Carbo would have preferred to go in with Spartacus, but that wasn't going to happen. During the march south, he and Navio had each been appointed to serve with one of the newly formed cohorts. Naturally enough, Navio was in charge of one, while Carbo served as second-in-command in another. His senior officer was Egbeo, a man who would obey Spartacus' order not to allow widespread killing.

Naïvely, Carbo had assumed that the same command would have been given to everyone in the army. The farm slaves' boasts had made it patently clear that this was not the case, and as he'd moved into place on the tree line above Forum Annii, he had heard plenty of similar threats being made. He struggled to accept the depth of hatred some of the slaves felt toward their former masters and all Romans in general. Had Paccius harbored such emotion? Surely not. What about the other domestic slaves that he'd grown up knowing? Carbo couldn't believe that they had also felt such loathing. For all his father's faults, he hadn't been a cruel master. Chloris seemed equable about what had happened to her.

Yet if he were honest it wasn't hard to realize why some slaves might feel bitter. Carbo thought of those who had belonged to his former friends in Capua. For them, life had been entirely different. Beatings were the daily norm. Rape was commonplace. If a slave was judged to have stolen, or committed other serious crimes, so too was torture. Carbo had seen the branded letter "F"—for *fugitivus*—on more than one man's forehead. This was the punishment meted out to those caught after they'd run away. While rare, execution was also not unknown.

If I had lived by such rules, how might I feel if the tables were turned?

Carbo's stomach twisted uncomfortably. He had only one answer, but he didn't want to admit to it. For some, life as a slave was a living torment, and any opportunity for revenge would be seized with both hands. What would inevitably happen when they descended on the town was chilling. Carbo didn't want to be part of it, but he had to be. He was Spartacus' man for good or ill. Whether they were fighting against a legion, or about to sack a town.

"Advance!" called Spartacus in a low voice. "But stay together. I want a solid line as we approach."

Carbo licked his dry lips. "You heard him," he hissed at the men to either side. "Forward, at the slow march."

As the order spread, thousands of men emerged from the trees. They were armed with spears, swords and sharpened stakes. Spartacus could see the occasional scythe and mattock. One figure was even bearing a smith's hammer. Was it Pulcher? He couldn't be sure. The tatters of mist on the fields gave the slaves some cover as their leaders forced them into line. *The discipline is holding for now. Let it continue to do so.*

It was a faint hope.

They hadn't gone more than a couple of hundred paces before a bunch of Crixus' Gauls broke free of the ranks. Raising their weapons, they charged toward Forum Annii like a pack of hunting wolves. Curse them, thought Spartacus. He lifted a hand, stalling his men. "Steady. Steady. Let the fools go."

But already Crixus was pounding after his followers, laughing like a lunatic.

What happened next was as if a logjam of winter debris blocking a river had been freed. In a seething mass, virtually the entire army swarmed forward across the plowed earth. Whoops and shrieks filled the air in a deafening and bloodcurdling cacophony. The men following Spartacus, Navio and Egbeo were the only ones to hold back.

Despite the fact that surprise was of little or no importance, Spartacus scowled at the men's indiscipline. He didn't want to miss out on the action, however. There could be large quantities of money in some houses. Perhaps even letters from Rome in the local politicians' offices. "After them," he roared. "We don't want to be last to the party."

It was all the permission the rest of the slaves needed.

With a great, inarticulate roar, they charged.

†

By the time a quarter of an hour had passed, Carbo had given up trying to control his troops. It was like trying to call off a pack of dogs after they'd caught a hare. Only when the prey was dead would they listen. He'd lost count of the number of times he had screamed at a man not to chop the limb off a screaming graybeard, or to rip the clothes from a woman's back before throwing her to the ground. When the deed was done, they finally seemed to hear his voice, turning to look at him with surprised, crazed faces. The moment he'd moved on, Carbo was sure it all began again.

Forum Annii had become how Carbo envisioned Hades. The streets were full of manically laughing, dead-eyed men with bloodied sword arms, mutilated corpses and screaming women and children. Here and there an occasional armed householder was being hacked to pieces. Some houses were on fire; the roof of one had already collapsed inward. The air was laced with the thick, choking smell of their burning, as well as the harsh tang of blood and shit. Carbo didn't know what to do. In frustration, he had even clubbed one of his men unconscious. While it had prevented the murder of a girl of no more than ten, the slave's companions had turned on him, waving their weapons threateningly. Seeing his death at their hands, Carbo had simply dropped his shield and dragged the girl away. This was no time to try and assert his authority. If he could save a child's life, that would at least be something.

By the time he'd gone fifty paces down the street, the slaves' attention had turned elsewhere. Carbo turned to the girl, a dainty, blond-haired creature in a fine tunic. "Where is it safe to hide?" he demanded.

She stared at him, her eyes black with terror.

Carbo forcibly softened his face. "I'm not going to kill you."

"M-M-Mother!" She started to sob, and Carbo glanced over his shoulder. Twenty paces away, a woman was spread-eagled on the ground. Men were standing on her arms and her legs to hold her still as she was raped by a sweating gladiator. Slurping at a cracked amphora of wine and hooting encouragement, more than a dozen slaves waited their turn. *Gods above!* "Look away," Carbo ordered. "No one is going to hurt you like that. I swear it!"

The girl started to cry.

He bent down to her level. "Try to stay calm," he said gently. "Where can I hide you? Where would be safe? Is there a temple nearby?"

She pointed down the street.

"Which god?"

"Jupiter."

No good. Jupiter is the ultimate symbol of Rome. No slave will respect that. Inspiration struck him. "What about Dionysus? Do you know of any slaves who worship him?"

She looked at him with surprise, before nodding. "Father lets our slaves worship Bacchus. He says it gives them hope. A reason to live."

"He's a wise man. Quickly, then. Take me there."

Turning away from the degrading sight that was her mother's end, the girl stumbled off up the street. With drawn sword, Carbo followed. He roared abuse at anyone who came near, threatening to cut their balls off and feed them to the pigs in the nearby sty. With so much in the way of easy pickings, those they encountered were content to snarl obscene comments about the girl and let them pass. She led him unerringly past the carcasses of two butchered horses, scatters of clothing, broken pottery and countless bodies, to a house right on the edge of town. Carbo felt a flood of relief as he scanned the area. There was no sign of any slaves or gladiators. In all likelihood, they had swept past this area and into the center of Forum Annii.

"Is this your home?"

"Yes."

Like many Roman dwellings, the building was rectangular in shape, with a high wall devoid of openings save for the occasional small glass window. The only entrance Carbo saw was a large pair of wooden doors in one side wall. These gave on to the street. Unusually, one hung wide open. Loud voices and laughter could be heard within.

Gods! The whoresons are still here. Raising a finger to his lips, he halted.

"Did it get attacked? And your mother tried to get you away?" he hissed.

Another tearful nod.

"Your father?"

"H-he stayed behind with my brother. So Mother and I could escape," she whispered without looking at him.

They're dead for sure. She knows it too. And if we enter, the same will happen to us. Blood rushed in Carbo's ears. *Have faith in the god. Ariadne is his servant, and Spartacus has been anointed by him. No one will harm us in his presence.* "Where is the shrine to Dionysus?"

"It's in the yard behind the house, which opens on to the fields."

"Can we get to it without going through the main entrance?"

"Yes. There's a little gate in the back wall of the garden. It's never locked." Her face twisted with grief. "That's how they got in."

"Don't think about that," he urged. "Just take me there."

Rubbing away her tears, she darted across the open gateway, toward the end of the street. Carbo followed her, taking the opportunity to shoot a glance within. He saw nothing but the blank walls of the entrance hall. The audible ribaldry meant that at least two slaves were inside, however. *Cross that bridge when you come to it. Get the girl out of harm's way first.*

They rounded the corner of the house, coming off the paved street and on to the freshly tilled black earth of the fields. Carbo could see right up to the tree line where they'd hidden just a short time previously. A few figures moved up there, stragglers no doubt, but they were far enough away to make it unlikely that he and the girl would be seen. All the same, he felt a surge of relief when the door came into sight. It also lay ajar. The girl turned to him, her face white with terror again.

"Don't move. I'll go in first." Carbo took a deep breath. He tiptoed to the door, and peered around its edge. There was no one in sight. What he saw instead was a large, but typical, Roman garden. Filling half the space were neat rows of vines, and lemon, fig and apple trees. The rest of the ground was given over to a combination of vegetables and herbs. A red-brick wall enclosed the space on three sides, with the back of the house taking up the fourth. Another small door in that wall provided access to the garden. Thankfully, it was closed.

Carbo's eyes flickered from side to side. There was what looked like a tool shed, and a well, but no shrine. "Where is it?"

"You can't see it. It's on this wall." The girl tapped the brickwork.

Understanding flooded through him, and he led the way inside. The area dedicated to Dionysus was immediately apparent. Two lines of pillars had been thrown out a dozen steps from the back garden wall. They supported a low wooden roof. It was nothing compared to even the most basic Roman temple, but it was undoubtedly a place of worship. The floor, which had been covered with crudely laid stone slabs, was covered with offerings. There were little oil lamps by the dozen, but also statuettes of Dionysus and his maenads, jugs of wine, piles of olives and small sheaves of wheat. Bronze coins were dotted here and there; there was even an occasional silver *denarius*.

It was only when Carbo drew level with the shrine's entrance that he was able to appreciate the imagery beneath which the offerings had been placed. His eyes widened. Under the area covered by the roof, the garden wall had been plastered and then painted. Wreathed by lines of green ivy, one of Dionysus' favored emblems, were three large panels. On the left was a bucolic scene of the grape harvest. In the background, men labored, placing the fruit they picked in baskets. Other workers carried loads of the purple fruit to a figure in the foreground, which was reclining on a couch and flanked by attendants holding vine branches. A beardless, nude youth, Dionysus lay holding a *cantharus*, or ritual drinking vessel. Carbo instinctively bowed his head. *I ask for your protection, O Great One. For both of us.*

The middle panel depicted Dionysus as a much older man, bearded and wearing a Greek chiton. Draped over his shoulders was the skin of a fawn. Around him clustered groups of women, some fawning in obeisance, others dancing in ecstatic frenzy, still more coupling with men on the floor. But it was the last image that Carbo didn't like. Here was Dionysus, youthful once more, clad in an undergarment, descending into the underworld to hold hands with its god, Hades. *Is that what you're doing today? Making a pact with Hades? It certainly feels like it.*

His chin firmed. Whatever Dionysus' intentions, the girl should be safe here at least. He turned to find her regarding him.

"I thought it was just slaves and women who prayed to Bacchus. Or foreigners."

"My leader's wife is a priestess of Dionysus. I've learned to hold him in great reverence."

"You're a Roman," she said accusingly. "What are you doing with murderous slaves?"

"That's none of your business," Carbo snapped. He pointed. "That door. Can it be locked from this side?"

"No. Only from inside the kitchen."

Damn it! If he stayed, there'd be no chance of rescuing other children. "Stay under the shrine's roof. No one will bother coming into the garden. Even if they do, you won't be seen," he said bluffly.

"You're going to leave me?" She began to cry again.

"I have to," he muttered awkwardly. In an effort to reassure her, he said, "I'll take a look into the house. See what's going on. Make sure it's safe for you." *Safe?*

She didn't seem any happier, but Carbo didn't know what else to say or do. Hefting his sword, he strode toward the small wooden door. Reaching it, he placed his head carefully against the timbers and listened. The voices he'd heard were still audible, but dim. Carbo waited for the count of fifty heartbeats, but the noise level remained the same. *Good. There's no one in the kitchen.* He placed his thumb on the latch. With a metallic *click*, it lifted. He laid his ear on the door again. Nothing. Carbo's stomach began to churn, but he pulled the door open and looked inside.

The kitchen had been thoroughly ransacked. Broken crockery lay everywhere. Doors had been ripped off cupboards. Bags of flour had been slashed open, strings of onions and bunches of herbs hacked down from the rafters. A yellow sludge of olive oil surrounded a smashed amphora. There was no sign of life, so Carbo took a step inside. Seeing the telltale crimson of blood on the tiled floor, he stiffened. He tiptoed further, finding an old man sprawled in the kitchen doorway. The slave—for that's what he looked like—had been nearly decapitated. His head lay at a crazy, unnatural angle to his body. Carbo had never seen so much blood around one man. *He must have bled out.*

A woman's scream transfixed him to the spot. It was followed by another shriek of distress, also female, and then a burst of loud, male laughter. "Let's fuck them here in the courtyard," roared a voice.

"Good idea," agreed another.

"I'm first," said a third, commanding voice. "I'm not screwing either of these bitches after you filth. My cock would probably drop off with what I'd catch."

There were a few nervous titters, but no one argued.

Crixus! What's he doing here? Carbo crept back toward the door. He had nearly reached it when the first woman cried out again. "No! Please! No!"

Chloris? In all the gods' names, how? Why? Carbo reeled with the shock of it. Her begging began again, and any doubt in his mind vanished. It was definitely her. *Oh gods, what can I do? If I go out there, Crixus will kill me.* He had to do something, however, or he'd never be able to live with the shame.

Gritting his teeth, he turned around. There was no way of getting around the old man without stepping in his blood. Carbo hesitated for a moment before dipping the fingers of his left hand in the sticky fluid, and smearing them all over his face. To have any chance of facing down Crixus, he needed to look as if he'd just slaughtered half the town on his own.

Clutching his sword with whitened knuckles, he stepped out into the courtyard. Like the garden, it was full of fruit trees, but a fountain, ornamental shrubs and Greek statues of the gods also served to decorate the space. It reminded Carbo of his family home. Through the vegetation, he spied Crixus and two other men with long hair about twenty paces away. At their feet, he could see the lower halves of two naked women. Chloris, and someone else. The heavily muscled trio were clad in mail shirts, and bloody swords dangled from their hands. They were all Gauls. *Crixus would have his own countrymen with him.* Carbo's courage began ebbing away. He felt as Iolaus, Hercules' nephew, might have felt if he'd been asked to tackle the Hydra on his own. *How to play this? Threatening them won't work.* He was racking his brains for an idea when events took on a life of their own.

"We've got company," one of the men shouted, dropping into a fighting crouch.

The others spun around, snarling with anger.

"It's all right. I'm one of you!" Carbo did his best to swagger up to the trio.

"Trying to distract me from my fuck?" shouted Crixus. His heavy brows lowered, and then he sneered. "Well, well, well. It's Spartacus' little Roman arse wipe. You look to have killed someone at least. What are you doing sneaking around here?"

"Looking for valuables, same as everyone," Carbo lied.

"Well, you'll find sod all here. The family savings are ours. They were under a flagstone in the atrium." Crixus jerked his head at the two women. "These two pretty bitches were hiding in a cupboard in one of the bedrooms. Finding them was a real bonus. The gods left the best for us until last, eh?" He rubbed his crotch and his men sniggered.

Carbo took another step forward, as if to appreciate the women's bodies. *Is it really Chloris?* His heart clenched with horror. It was. There was no mistaking her delicately boned face and the dimple on her left cheek, both now streaked with tears. Or her scars. Seeing Carbo's blood-covered features, she screamed.

"She doesn't like you," said Crixus with a cruel chuckle. "Seeing as I'm in a good mood, I'll let you have her anyway—after we've finished. How does that sound?"

"Good, thank you." Carbo feigned sudden surprise. "Gods!" He kicked Chloris with his sandal. "Chloris, is that you?"

She didn't reply, so Carbo kicked her harder. "Answer me!"

"Y-yes." There was still no trace of recognition in her terrified eyes.

"Ha! I was right." He threw the Gauls a broad smile. "Imagine that."

A sudden scowl creased Crixus' face. "The useless whore was crying about being one of us. I thought she was lying."

Carbo shoved the words out of his mouth before his fear made him swallow them down forever. "She wasn't. Chloris is my woman." At the edge of his vision, he was aware of her reaching out an entreating hand. "The silly cow must have wandered into town after us. Let me take her. I'll find you a replacement. Or two of them! Better-looking ones too."

Crixus' right fist bunched, and he jabbed his gladius at Carbo's face, forcing him to take a step backward. "Cheeky little bastard! Do you really think you can take a piece of cunny from me that easily? I don't give a shit whether she's yours or not."

Carbo flushed deep red. "I—"

"Piss off!" Crixus glanced down at Chloris. "So you belong to this shitbag, eh? I must remember to cut your throat when we're done."

"No!" roared Carbo. He half drew his blade.

The point of Crixus' sword swung back to prick him under the chin. "You're testing my patience, Roman. Want to die right now?"

If I die, Chloris does too. "No."

"You have some brains then. I'm going to count to three. If you're still here when I finish, I'm going to let my friends here carve you up. One—"

Carbo shot Chloris what he hoped was an encouraging look, before he turned and fled. As he ran, his ears rang with the Gauls' mocking laughter. He expected Chloris to call out, begging him not to leave her, but she didn't.

That hurt far more.

Carbo hurdled the corpse in the kitchen doorway with a single leap. Throwing open the door, he sprinted into the garden. He was vaguely aware of the girl emerging from the shrine, her mouth opening in a question. "Get back under there!" he hissed. "The bastards have no reason to come outside."

"Where are you going?" she wailed.

"To get help." Trying not to think about how he was leaving a defenseless child, Carbo ran for the back gate.

Spartacus. He had to find Spartacus.

If he didn't succeed, and fast, Chloris would be dead.

†

The period that followed was the longest of Carbo's entire life. Never had he had a task more urgent, and never had he been so foiled at every turn. On every street, he found nothing but death, destruction and the men who delivered it. There was no sign of Spartacus anywhere. Carbo struggled even to recognize many of the armed men he came across. Fortunately for him, the opposite did not apply, and he received little in the way of open aggression. They even answered his demands for their leader. Carbo didn't know why, but the killing seemed to have eased, and with it the blood lust. Now the slaves and gladiators were in search of wine, food and women—not necessarily in that order.

Men sat on huge amphorae, bending to guzzle the wine that poured unchecked on to the stony ground. They passed around joints of meat, tearing off chunks with their teeth. Lumps were sliced from round wheels of cheese with knives still covered in blood. By some soldiers' feet, Carbo saw open-necked leather bags full of coins. All that he expected. What surprised him, and nearly unnerved him, were the women's screams. They shredded the air in a dreadful chorus of terror and pain. Everywhere he looked, Carbo saw women being raped. Usually it was by men, lots of them, but sometimes the violations were even worse. How anyone could shove a spear or a sword blade inside a living person, Carbo had no idea. It wasn't long before the remains of his meager breakfast came up. Mesmerized, dazed by the violence, he wandered from house to temple, shop to stable in search of Spartacus.

When he found him, it was by complete chance. Glancing around, he found one of the Scythians glowering at him from the doorway of a nondescript house. "Have you seen Spartacus?"

"He's inside," came the growled reply. "Why?"

Carbo was already shoving past, his desperation greater than his fear of Atheas. "Where is he?"

"In office . . . off courtyard."

Carbo broke into a trot. He skidded across the tablinum, catching sight of several imperious death masks of the owners' ancestors before he plunged into the spacious central square. Spartacus was slouched on a stone bench, surrounded by piles of rolled parchment. Taxacis was sitting on the ground nearby, drinking wine from a delicate glass flute. Both men looked up as Carbo pounded over. Taxacis scowled. "By the Rider, what happened to you?" asked Spartacus.

Carbo rubbed absently at the blood caking his face. "It's not mine."

"I'm glad to hear it." Spartacus cocked his head, his eyes as inquisitive as a bird's. "You look scared. What is it?"

Carbo told his tale in a gabble of words, scarcely stopping to breathe.

Spartacus leaped to his feet, silently cursing this bad fortune. To avoid trouble with Crixus, he could have—should have—refused to do a thing. After all Carbo's loyalty, however, that would seem the ultimate betrayal. Crixus was in the wrong, plain and simple. *The damn hothead won't see it that way of course.* Would it do any harm to intervene? Spartacus grimaced. *We shall soon see.* "Let's hurry, or it will be too late."

Carbo felt as if a massive ball of lead had just filled his belly. *It probably is already.*

"Taxacis! Atheas!" Spartacus turned to Carbo. "Which way?"

Numbly, he headed for the door. The three men followed.

Let her be alive still, Dionysus. Please. Her companion and the girl too.

†

It didn't take them long to reach the house. Carbo made to enter, but Spartacus pulled him back. "Let us go first."

Resentfully, Carbo stood aside.

"Where are they?"

"In the courtyard."

"And there are three of them?"

"That's all I saw."

Spartacus' sica came thrumming out of its scabbard. The long, curved blade was covered in telltale, dark red stains. *Whatever many others have done, I have killed no women today.* He glanced at the Scythians, who were fingering their weapons. "I want no bloodshed unless it's absolutely necessary."

They grinned evilly at him.

"Come on." Spartacus took a careful step into the atrium, then another. The Scythians went next, cat-soft on their feet. Carbo was last. He crossed the threshold, seeing for the first time an image of a snarling black dog on the mosaic floor. It was most lifelike. A chain round its neck was all that held it back from springing up at Carbo. Under it were the words *"Cave Canem."* Beware of the dog, he thought warily. I didn't hear it when I was in the courtyard. Why not?

The reason became clear half a dozen paces further on. The body of a large black dog filled the hallway. A snarl still twisted its lips, but its eyes had the glassy look that only death can bring. Its body was covered in hack wounds, and purple strings of intestine had slithered out of its belly. They lay in the creature's blood like fresh sausages in a red wine stew. "It wasn't much of a match for Crixus," whispered Spartacus. "Not much is."

New fear clawed at Carbo. He couldn't hear a sound. Had they come too late?

The low moan—a woman's—that reached his ears a moment later had never been more welcome. The sound was accompanied by a man's loud grunting. *Let Chloris be alive.*

Spartacus made a quick gesture. At once, one Scythian went to stand at his left shoulder, the other to his right. Sweating profusely, Carbo took up the rear. Another signal, and they sped into the tablinum. Moving around the *impluvium*, the pool that collected rainwater from the roof overhead, they came to the doors that opened on to the courtyard.

Dreading what he would see, Carbo peered over Spartacus' shoulder. Only one Gaul was on his feet. He was idly picking his nails with a dagger and watching Crixus and the third man pound away at the two women. Carbo wiped away the tears of fury that sprang to his eyes. This was no time for weakness.

Spartacus' lips framed the word "Perfect" at each of them. Then his left hand chopped forward in a clear command to move. He and the Scythians darted forward like arrows released from hunters' bows. Carbo scrambled to keep up.

They silently covered the twenty strides in perhaps four heartbeats. By the time the Gaul who was standing realized anything was wrong, he had Atheas' sword tickling his neck. He dropped his dagger with a soft *clunk* into a flower bed. Spartacus lifted a finger to his lips, and the frightened warrior nodded. Crixus and his companion were oblivious, still thrusting into their victims with wild abandon. Unsurprisingly, the women had their eyes closed. Chloris had a fist in her mouth, and was biting down on it.

Carbo's rage began to consume him utterly. It was no longer just about rescuing Chloris. He wanted to kill the Gauls too. *That's why Spartacus put me at the back,* he realized. *He knew how I'd react.*

"Crixus!" shouted Spartacus.

The big Gaul's head turned. Shock twisted his features. Cursing, he pulled out of Chloris' companion and clambered to his feet. His friend hurried to do the same. Both men had left their mail shirts on, but they were naked from the waist down. Carbo could see blood on their pricks, and now his fury boiled over. "You fucking animals!" he screamed. He tried to shove past Spartacus, but the Thracian's iron-hard arm blocked his way.

"I thought you'd go running to your master. Damn coward," growled Crixus at Carbo. He eyeballed Spartacus. Unlike his comrades, there was no fear in his face. He had the sense not to reach for a weapon, however. "What business have you here?"

"Carbo asked me to come," said Spartacus. "One of these is his woman."

"I doubt he'll want her any longer," said Crixus, leering. "She's got my seed and Lugurix's in her already. Segomaros was giving her a good pounding too." The man beside him smiled, and Carbo strained furiously, uselessly, at Spartacus' arm.

"That's as maybe," snapped Spartacus. "But it ends here. The girl is coming with us. So is the other one."

"I am one of the leaders of this whole damn rebellion," Crixus thundered, the veins on his neck bulging. "I can do what I like."

"Not here, you can't. Chloris has been Carbo's woman since Amatokos was killed. You know that."

Crixus took a step toward Spartacus. "What are you going to do—kill me if I try to stop you?"

"If I have to, yes," came the calm reply. Spartacus' sica hung by his side, but Carbo knew that if Crixus so much as moved toward his sword, which lay five paces away, he'd be a dead man. The others would meet the same fate at the Scythians' hands.

The Gauls realized the same thing.

Crixus stared at Spartacus with obvious loathing for a moment before grunting, "As you wish. I wouldn't want to blunt my blade on the bitches anyway." He looked to his men. "After all that rutting, I have a raging thirst on me. Let's find some wine, if it hasn't all been drunk by now." Chuckling, he reached for his licium.

With an effort, Chloris sat up. Wanting to help her, Carbo pushed against Spartacus' arm. "Wait," the Thracian hissed. "Let them leave first."

Grudgingly, Carbo obeyed. He marked the faces of Crixus' companions. *Gods help me, I'll kill you both if I ever get a chance. Crixus too.*

No one could have predicted what happened next.

Swaying, Chloris got to her feet.

Carbo's heart ached to see what had happened to her. Even with cuts to her face and with blood running down her thighs, she was still beautiful.

Chloris staggered forward a step, and her fingers grazed the plants that decorated the bed beside her. Then, suddenly, she was gripping a dagger. Segomaros, who was nearest to her, was busy shoving a leg into his undergarment. He didn't see Chloris rush forward. Too late, he felt the blade ramming through his mail and into the flesh of his back. An unearthly scream tore free of his lips, and he staggered with the force of her blow. Snarling like a dog, Chloris stabbed him several more times, punching through his armor with ease. With a loud groan, Segomaros sank to his knees. "The bitch has killed me, Crixus," he said in surprise, before falling on to his face. He kicked once or twice and was still.

A heartbeat later, Chloris toppled on top of him in a dead faint.

"You whore!" roared Crixus, scooping up his sword. "I'll kill you!"

"With me, Taxacis!" Spartacus sprang forward, sica at the ready.

The Scythian bounded to his side. So did Carbo. Together, they stood between Crixus and Chloris. Off to one side, Atheas threatened Lugurix.

"Get out of my fucking way!" shouted Crixus.

"Leave now," ordered Spartacus. "You're not having her."

Crixus' face went purple with fury. "The life of a stinking slave is worth more than one of my warriors?"

"On this occasion, yes."

"Can the bitch fight, as Segomaros could?"

"No."

"What damn use is she then? I demand her life! It's no less than she deserves for stabbing a man in the back."

"A man who had just raped her," said Spartacus acidly.

"I want her dead regardless."

"Carbo wishes her to live."

"Who cares about him? He's a filthy Roman! This is about what I want," bellowed Crixus.

"Carbo is one of my men. He's loyal too, which is far more than I can say for you."

"So that's how it is." Crixus' slit eyes were like two piss holes in the snow.

"That's right," said Spartacus coldly. *It had to come out sooner or later.*

Crixus hawked and spat at Spartacus' feet. "We're not wanted here, Lugurix," he growled. "Let's go."

Silence reigned as Crixus and Lugurix withdrew to the doors of the tablinum.

"This isn't over by a long shot, Spartacus! I won't forget whom you favor over me," the huge Gaul shouted. "That whore should watch her back from now on. Your catamite better be on his guard too."

It was only when Crixus was gone that Carbo realized he'd been holding his breath. Dropping his sword, he ran to where Chloris lay. He rolled her over gently. "Chloris? You're safe now. Can you hear me? It's me, Carbo."

She moaned, and her eyelids fluttered. "You came back. Thank you."

"Of course I did."

"I'm very tired. I think I'll sleep now." Her eyes closed.

"I'll find you a bed," said Carbo with new determination. His gaze scanned the rooms that surrounded the courtyard. Then he remembered Spartacus. Red-faced with embarrassment, he spun around. "I cannot thank you enough. You saved her life."

"I'm glad we came in time. Do you understand why I wouldn't let you kill Crixus?"

"Because he leads too many men. You need him still."

"That's right. For the moment, I need him, the same way I need Castus and Gannicus and their men." A wry smile crooked his lips. "Those two are a trifle easier to keep in line, however."

"They are." Curse Crixus to Hades and beyond, thought Carbo.

"Fortunately, the big bastard needs me too. It suits him to stay." Spartacus glanced around the courtyard. "You can manage now? I'll leave Atheas to help." And to protect you, was the unspoken meaning. "Ariadne will come as soon as I can find her."

"Yes. Thank you." It was a dangerous game that Spartacus had played, Carbo realized, watching him leave. Gratitude filled him that the Thracian should go so far for him. While Atheas made the house secure, Carbo went in search of the girl. She could show him where the best bedroom and the baths were. He hoped too that Ariadne would arrive quickly. Chloris needed all the care that he could get for her.

Spartacus' mood as he walked away from the house was a good

deal darker than Carbo's. For all his menaces, Crixus had not threatened to leave. Yet.

But the cocksucker will. I'd wager my life on it.

What he somehow had to do, thought Spartacus grimly, was bind Castus and Gannicus to him. So that when the split came, they would stay with him.

†

Carbo was careful to cover up the dead bodies of the girl's father and brother before she saw them. He was relieved that giving her things to do seemed to take her mind off what had happened. She hurried to and fro, fetching water from the well, tearing strips of cloth into bandages and helping the second woman to a bedroom. The same could not be said of Chloris. She smiled vacantly at Carbo as he carried her into another room but the moment he laid her down on the bed, she began to sob again. "It hurts. It hurts so much."

Carbo glanced down and had to bite back a curse. There were fresh scarlet stains below the waist of her dress. She was still bleeding. Feeling totally helpless, he sat on the edge of the bed, stroking back the strands of hair that had fallen over her face. "Hold on. Ariadne will be here soon. She'll give you something for the pain." *She'll know what to do.*

Her lips twitched, but instead of a smile, she grimaced.

Aesculapius, please help her, Carbo begged silently. He didn't normally pray to the god of health, but this was no ordinary occasion.

He tried to get Chloris to drink some wine, but she wouldn't. Even persuading her to swallow a mouthful of water was an effort. Much of the time, she seemed unaware of his presence. He was grateful, therefore, that when he stopped caressing her head, her eyelids opened. "That's nice. Please continue."

"Of course." His throat closed with emotion as he obeyed her request. "What were you doing here, Chloris?"

Shame crept across her face.

He waited.

"I was looking for money. We both were."

"Why? I'd give you money if you wanted it."

Silence.

The realization hit Carbo a moment later, making him feel numb. "It was so you could run away, wasn't it? Chloris?"

Without opening her eyes, she nodded.

"You could have said," he muttered. "I'd have just given it to you."

"Really? I wanted to return to Greece."

"I wouldn't have stopped you."

"I'm sorry. I misjudged you." Her lips twisted. "Tell me some stories, please. It will help me to forget the pain."

Swallowing his grief, and his shock at her revelation, Carbo began. Wanting to lift Chloris' spirits, he related every humorous episode he could think of. How he'd once fallen into a dungheap on the family farm. The time he had raided a beehive for honey and been pursued by the angry bees for a quarter of a mile, to the river. To save himself from being stung repeatedly, he'd had to drop his stolen prize and jump into the water. He even told her about when he'd been caught by Paccius spying on the female slaves as they dressed in the morning.

She smiled at that. "Boys will be boys. It's not much to be ashamed of, especially after you've saved my life."

"I didn't save you," he said bitterly. "Spartacus did."

"What were you going to do—take on three warriors? They'd have chopped you into little pieces. Where would I be if that had happened?"

Carbo didn't answer. His heart swelled with a mixture of emotions as he stared down at her. Impulsively, he bent forward and planted a soft kiss on her waxen forehead. There was another little smile. He resumed stroking her hair, and studying her face. The face that he'd learned to treasure. He cared for her still, even if she'd wanted to leave him.

Carbo was in the same position when Ariadne arrived. Startled out of his reverie, Carbo stood up. "You came."

"Of course. As soon as Spartacus found me." Ariadne's gaze moved down, taking in the huge red stain on Chloris' dress. There was a sharp intake of breath. "Gods above. She was raped, I presume?"

"Yes. By Crixus and two of his men," he hissed.

"The filthy dogs. How long since?"

"I-I don't know."

"Did she lose much blood at the time?" Ariadne placed the fingers of one hand on Chloris' left wrist. Her lips moved silently as she counted the thready pulse.

Catching Ariadne's tone of urgency, Carbo threw his mind back to the courtyard. "No, I don't think so."

Frowning, Ariadne began peeling the sodden fabric of Chloris' dress upward.

Carbo averted his gaze. His eyes shot back, however, when Ariadne gave a tiny gasp. "What is it?"

"This." Ariadne pointed.

Carbo forced himself to look. Between Chloris' thighs, there was a black-red gelatinous clot. It was as big as his two fists placed together. The bedding underneath her was also saturated in blood. Dread filled him. "What does it mean?"

Ariadne's face was full of sorrow. "She's lost too much blood," she murmured. "There's nothing I can do."

"She's going to die?"

"She is very near death already," said Ariadne quietly, pulling down Chloris' clothing.

Carbo regarded Chloris' features, which were even paler than before. "No," he whispered, placing a finger under her nostril. It was several moments before he felt the faintest movement of air. A sick feeling filled his belly and he knew that Ariadne was right. Who could lose that much blood and survive? Waves of bitterness bathed his heart. "How can the gods be so cruel?"

"It is very hard, I know."

Carbo's shoulders hunched. "How long does she have?"

Ariadne placed her lips against his ear. "She'll probably have slipped away by sunset. I'm sorry."

Carbo thanked Ariadne, who nodded and withdrew. The instant that he was alone again with Chloris, he was seized by a savage, black despair. During the previous few months, she had become increasingly important to him. In the blink of an eye, all his happiness had been turned to ash. An image of Crixus and his grinning cronies filled Carbo's mind. He shoved it away. *Fuck them. What time I have left with Chloris is too precious.*

He began stroking her hair again. Not knowing what else to do, he spoke of their time together, and of the magic that he'd felt being with her. How he would treasure the memories forever. Then he began to speak of Athens, mentioning every little detail that she'd ever told him. The rich, tree-lined quarter, within view of the magnificent Parthenon, where she'd grown up. The noise each dawn of the priests at their prayers. Chloris playing with Alexander, her younger brother. The regular trips she'd made into the city, to help the kitchen slaves buy provisions, and with her mother to visit their relations. Watching the oiled athletes in the nearby gymnasium wrestling, sprinting and throwing the discus.

Carbo talked and talked, filling the air with tender words. Finally, when his throat was so dry that he could no longer continue, he fell silent. He studied Chloris' face. It had relaxed, and he realized that he hadn't seen her breathe for a long time. She's dead, he thought calmly. In a way, he was relieved. At least her end had been peaceful. Carbo gave her a last kiss on the lips, and then, lifting a clean sheet from the floor, he covered her body.

A cold fury consumed him. All he wanted to do now was murder Crixus and Lugurix. It was a Herculean task to set himself. Even if he managed to slay Lugurix, the big Gaulish leader was an entirely different proposition. Carbo knew that, in reality, he wouldn't stand a chance. He didn't care. Death was preferable to the pain he was currently in. Of course it wasn't that simple. Few people would care if Lugurix died but the entire rebellion would be jeopardized if, by some crazy intervention of the gods, he did succeed in killing Crixus. Could he do that to Spartacus?

Carbo wasn't sure.

✝

Spartacus would have preferred to have slept in their camp, but the still-fluid situation in Forum Annii had persuaded him to spend the night in the town. By being present, he could prevent the worst atrocities from happening. At least, that was the theory. In reality, he couldn't be everywhere at once, but his presence in the central forum, where thousands of the slaves had gathered to celebrate, would be a moderating one. And that, he thought, surveying the general mayhem, could only be a good thing.

Huge fires burned all around him, fueled by an endless supply of furniture from the surrounding houses. Dozens of sheep and cattle had been dragged from their pens and slaughtered on the spot, hacked into pieces of meat that could be skewered on lengths of wood and roasted over the flames. A number of musicians—men who had been freed during the attack?—played drums and lyres, reminding Spartacus of Thrace. The pounding rhythm had crowds of enthusiastic gladiators and slaves on their feet, dancing, swaying, stumbling from side to side. Guzzling down wine, they bellowed out songs at the tops of their voices. The differing tunes clashed to provide a jarring cacophony of sound, but they couldn't conceal the animal noises of lust and pain coming through the darkness from every direction. Spartacus took a small swallow of wine. Much as he would have liked to blank out the dreadful sounds by drinking himself senseless, he would not do so. *I need to stay alert. Rape is part of war, and war is what I am engaged in. I could not stop it all, even if I tried.*

"There you are," cried a voice.

"Gannicus." Spartacus smiled as the moon-faced Gaul wove toward him. In one hand, he gripped a small amphora; in the other, a half-eaten hunk of meat. "Enjoying yourself?" he asked.

"Yes, by Belenus! This is far better than freezing my arse off in a tent in the middle of nowhere." Gannicus belched. "You?"

"It's good to sit by a fire and drink some wine," replied Spartacus evasively.

Gannicus didn't notice. He slumped down beside Spartacus with a great sigh. "The men needed this. Too much marching in the mountains with no damn food and they'd have started deserting, eh?"

"True enough," admitted Spartacus ruefully.

Gannicus gave him a hard nudge. "But now even more will come flocking to join us!"

"Which means we have to keep moving. More men means that more provisions will be needed."

"Where to? South again?"

"Yes. The coastline along the Ionian Sea is said to be incredibly fertile. It has plentiful small towns for us to attack. The area was good enough for Hannibal for a decade or more, so it should be fine for us."

"Sounds excellent." Tearing off a piece of meat, Gannicus sat chewing contentedly.

"I thought I'd find you two together," boomed Castus' voice from the shadows. He emerged into the light, adjusting his belt.

Dirty bastard. I know what you've been doing. "Welcome!" said Spartacus.

Wordlessly, Gannicus held out his amphora. Castus held it up to his mouth, letting the ruby liquid within pour down his throat. Much of it spilled over his face and neck, but he didn't stop until he'd downed a good amount. "Gods, that's tasty," he declared, wiping droplets from his mustache. "I have a thirst on me tonight like I've never known."

"Find your own then," growled Gannicus, reaching out a meaty hand. "You're not finishing mine."

With a filthy look, Castus passed it back.

"Here." Spartacus handed over his vessel.

Castus took it with a grin.

"Where do you think Varinius is?" asked Gannicus out of the blue.

Castus' face soured. "Who cares? He's nowhere near here."

"He'll be looking for us. Be sure of that," said Spartacus.

The Gauls sucked on the bitter marrow of that, pleasing Spartacus. *They need to know that the Romans won't ever forget about us.*

"Another secret meeting without me? This is becoming a habit," sneered Crixus, swaggering in from a side street.

Castus and Gannicus bellowed with laughter. "Come and have a drink."

Grumbling, and throwing sour looks at Spartacus, Crixus approached. "If I didn't know better, I'd say that you preferred to meet without me."

Spartacus wanted to smash his amphora over the big Gaul's head, but he held his peace.

"Shut up!" cried Castus. "You're the one who avoids our company."

"Aye," growled Crixus. "Well, you know the reason for that."

"Peace," said Gannicus, but Crixus was having none of it.

"Not only does he tell us what to do all the time, but he interferes in business that isn't his. Isn't that right, Thracian?"

Spartacus felt a throbbing anger in his chest. He noted that Crixus' tone was more belligerent than ever. *The prick hasn't forgotten what happened earlier. This is no time to be sitting.* He stood carefully, pretending to smooth his tunic down. "We all agree on our tactics, and where we march. Don't we?" Gannicus nodded, Castus grimaced, and Crixus spat with contempt. *As I expected.* "You talk of business that isn't mine. Care to explain?"

"You know exactly what I mean!"

"But the others don't."

Crixus grunted angrily. "Me and a pair of my lads were searching a house earlier, and we chanced upon two fine bits of stuff. Both slave girls. We were just starting to have fun with them when that little sewer rat arrived—what's his name?"

"You know what he's called," said Spartacus icily.

"*Carbo.* Carbo burst in, telling some bullshit story about how one of the whores was his woman. I told him to piss off, so he scuttled off and came back with his master. Spartacus. With his two hunting dogs, the Scythians, in tow. They caught us hard at it, with our trousers down, and forced us to back off the women." Crixus glared as Castus chuckled. "Next thing, Carbo's bitch somehow picked up Segomaros' knife. She stabbed him to death with it! I wanted vengeance, but Spartacus was having none of it. This, when I'm one of the fucking leaders of the whole damn army!"

Castus' and Gannicus' expressions soured. "Is this true?" demanded Castus.

"In a manner of speaking," said Spartacus calmly. "Except Carbo wasn't telling lies. One of the girls was his woman. Chloris, her name was. She used to be Amatokos' lover, before he was killed. Since then, she'd been with Carbo. Which meant, after Carbo asked for help that it was *very* much my business." He eyed them all. Crixus was the only one to look defiant. *Prick.*

Gannicus frowned. "Her name *was* Chloris?"

"Yes. She's dead. The poor creature bled to death after what they'd done to her."

Crixus laughed, and Spartacus felt his anger go white-hot.

Gannicus blinked. "Well, that's an end to it, surely? The bitch who killed your man is dead. Stop thinking about it. Have another drink," he said bluffly, offering Crixus his amphora.

The big Gaul dashed it out of his hand. "So what if the whore did belong to Carbo? I had every right to fuck her if I wanted to! Carbo is nothing. A speck of shit on the sole of my sandal!"

"Carbo is my man, and he's loyal."

"Which is more than you can say for me," hissed Crixus.

"That's right," said Spartacus.

"Screw you!" roared Crixus, tugging his sword from its scabbard.

Discarding his wine, Spartacus drew his sica. And so it comes to this, he thought. Fine. The whoreson has it coming to him. He's going to split from the army anyway.

The two others scrambled out of the way. "There's no need for this," cried Gannicus.

"Piss off!" shouted Crixus, thrusting his blade at Spartacus.

Spartacus parried the blow. The Gaul spun around, carried by the force of his swing and Spartacus brought his sword back down. His intent was to slice open the back of Crixus' sword arm, but the sica met only thin air.

"Think you can hit me with something that simple?" Crixus danced away, out of range. Instantly, he was on the offensive again, his gladius probing back and forth like the tongue of a metal snake. They traded several massive blows, and Spartacus grew wary. The Gaul's iron blade was thicker than his weapon, and if he wasn't careful, the sica could shatter. If that happened, he'd be dead meat. He slid his feet backward, forcing Crixus to pursue him.

"Scared?"

"Of you?" retorted Spartacus contemptuously.

His needling worked. Crixus snarled with fury and darted forward, swinging his gladius overhead like a Gaulish longsword. If he'd had a shield to take the impact of Crixus' attack, Spartacus would have risked it and tried to run him through the armpit, but without protection, he risked losing his head. He shuffled back a few more steps and Crixus followed, grinning with delight. "Ready to die?"

Spartacus' answer was to pick up his amphora and hurl it under-hand at Crixus. As the Gaul ducked, he was charging forward, hacking sideways with his sica. He grinned with satisfaction as the blade sliced open Crixus' upper left arm.

"Bastard!" Dodging out of range, Crixus eyed the flesh wound with contempt. "Think that's going to stop me?"

"It's just a start," Spartacus replied coldly.

"Yes? Well, how about this?" Moving surprisingly fast for a man of his size, Crixus thundered forward. Spartacus thrust his sica at him, and the Gaul smashed it out of the way. Rather than withdrawing, Crixus plowed on, crashing into Spartacus and delivering an almighty headbutt. Only Spartacus' lightning-fast reaction—turning his head— saved his nose from being split in two like a ripe plum. As it was, Crixus' forehead smacked into his cheekbone, sending him reeling backward. Then Crixus punched him in the side of the head, making his ears ring. The Gaul leered in triumph and raised his gladius. Great Rider, help me, thought Spartacus. The next blow won't be from a fist, but a blade.

Blind inspiration struck him. He dragged the strings of spittle in his mouth together and spat the lot into Crixus' face with all his might. "Fuck you!" he shouted.

Shock and utter outrage twisted the Gaul's features, and Spartacus thrust his sica at him, forcing him to parry rather than attack. Regaining the initiative, Spartacus launched a savage offensive. It was time to kill the bastard. *My blade won't break. The Rider won't let it.*

"One. Two. Three!" roared Gannicus. Together, he and Castus hurled the contents of two amphorae over Spartacus and Crixus.

Spluttering with indignation, the pair separated. "What in the name of Hades is that for?" roared Crixus.

Both Gauls advanced, their swords at the ready. "This has gone on long enough," said Gannicus. "You're going to kill each other."

"I'm going to fucking kill him, you mean!" snarled Crixus.

Spartacus barked a scornful laugh. "In your dreams."

"Stop this bullshit!" shouted Castus. "If you start again, we'll stab both of you in the back."

Cold reason overtook Spartacus, for which he was grateful. *The Rider is at work here.* "Why?"

"Why? Because you're both too damn valuable to lose," said Gannicus. "The army needs you. Not one slain, and the other so badly injured he can't fight. And that's what would probably happen if we left you to it."

Crixus' eyes narrowed.

Gannicus is right, thought Spartacus. *And only the gods know which of us would be the one lying dead on the ground by the end of it.*

"Have a drink, and forget about it!" Castus produced another amphora and tossed it at Crixus. The big Gaul caught it one-handed. He looked at it for a moment, and Spartacus prepared to duck. Instead of throwing it, however, Crixus laughed. He eyed Spartacus balefully. "We can do this another time, eh?" Throwing back several mouthfuls, he proffered the amphora.

Castus and Gannicus gave each other a relieved look.

Gauls! They're fucking crazy. Without dropping his guard, Spartacus took the vessel and drank. "To finding Varinius, and wiping him off the face of the earth!" he cried.

Remarkably, even Crixus joined in the roar of approval that followed.

Yet everyone who had witnessed the confrontation knew that the matter had not been settled.

Merely postponed.

XVIII

In the days that followed, Carbo did his best to avoid all human company. He fulfilled his duties as second-in-command of his cohort, marshalling the men together and ensuring that they were all ready to leave the smoking ruins of Forum Annii behind. He followed Egbeo's orders, keeping the slaves in line as they marched and supervising them as they set up camp each evening. He even persisted with the training of the new recruits, hundreds of whom were joining them every day. But Carbo did it all automatically, because he had to. Inside, his anger and grief knew no bounds. Navio was the one person he confided in, and that was just once, the day Chloris had died.

Navio had gripped his shoulder in sympathy. "I know how hard it is," he'd said.

Aware that his friend had had terrible things happen to those he cared about, Carbo had nodded and turned his rage further inward. Locking it deep inside was all that allowed him to continue functioning. Only the sight of Crixus or Lugurix caused his volcanic emotions to overflow. It was fortunate that Navio had been present on each occasion he'd spotted the Gauls. He'd physically held Carbo back. "You'll end up dead."

"So what?" Carbo had hissed. As long as he gained vengeance, he didn't care. Thoughts of death occupied his every waking moment. Each night, his dreams were the same. Yet some small part of him had retained its sanity, because he'd let Navio restrain him, although he ground his teeth in frustration and rage. He was grateful that the army's large size now meant that seeing the Gauls was quite a rare occurrence. All the same, the knowledge that they were alive and unpunished ate away at his soul.

One evening some three weeks after the sacking of Forum Annii, he was startled to see Spartacus approaching his tent. Carbo's memories of the stand-off with Crixus flooded back, and he ducked his head down, hoping that the Thracian was looking for someone else.

"Carbo."

Unwillingly, he looked up. "Spartacus."

"Can I sit?"

"Of course," he replied guiltily. He gestured at the rock where Navio, who was checking on his men, sat. "I'd offer you some wine, but I don't have any. A piece of bread?"

"I've eaten, thank you." Spartacus' gray eyes regarded Carbo keenly. "I haven't seen you for a while."

"No. I've been busy." Carbo cursed his poorly chosen words even as they left his lips.

Spartacus smiled. "I know how it is."

Blushing to the roots of his hair, Carbo looked down.

"I have some news for you."

Carbo's gaze rose slowly. "Oh?"

"Lugurix has had a nasty accident."

His heart filled with a dark joy. "Really?"

"Yes. This morning, he slipped off a narrow section of the path. He fell about two hundred paces and landed on a ledge just above the river at the gorge's foot. He didn't die from the initial fall. From the look of it, he'd broken his back, because he was screaming like a man gut-shot by an arrow. Rescuing him was out of the question, so we had to leave him there. If he's not dead yet, he will be by morning. A terrible way to die," said Spartacus casually.

Carbo's head was pounding with rage and happiness. "He fell?"

Spartacus winked. "Well, he had a little help from Atheas. No one else saw, naturally. Crixus won't suspect a thing."

Carbo stared at Spartacus, uncomprehending.

"I understand what Chloris meant to you. I also wanted you to know that I hadn't forgotten about Lugurix, or what he did. He was always going to be punished. The time had to be right, that's all."

A pulse hammered in Carbo's throat. "And Crixus?"

"I told you before: he's too important to the rebellion. For now anyway. Can you live with that?"

Carbo swallowed. He was overjoyed that Lugurix had suffered a lingering death, but the sweetness of that knowledge was soured by what Spartacus was asking of him. "You want me not to kill him?"

"That's right," replied Spartacus gravely. He was very aware that while Carbo had little chance of achieving his aim, the desperate, or those who have little desire to live, sometimes succeeded where others failed.

Carbo, unaware of his leader's perceptiveness, was grateful to be shown such respect. He sat for some moments, thinking. He was conscious that Spartacus couldn't be kept waiting, but he wasn't going to agree unless it felt correct. "You said 'for now' when you mentioned me getting my revenge on Crixus. What do you mean by that?"

The pup has real balls, thought Spartacus wryly. He wouldn't tolerate this from anyone else, but Carbo had brought him Navio, whose efforts had worked wonders on his men. Because of that, this once he was prepared to be less hard on the lad. "If the day ever comes when Crixus decides to break away on his own, you can do what you want." *When* it comes, Spartacus added silently.

"Very well," said Carbo, looking satisfied. "I swear that I will stay my hand until then."

"Good." Spartacus stood.

"Thank you for killing Lugurix," Carbo blurted, also rising.

"It's Atheas you want to be grateful to."

"You know what I mean," protested Carbo. "It means the world to me."

"I know it does." Spartacus clapped him on the arm. "The hurt lessens with time. You'll see."

Awe filled Carbo as the Thracian walked away. *He knows just what to say.* Somehow the idea of leaving Crixus unharmed now mattered less than it had. Carbo felt much better for it. Sitting down by the fire, he began to whistle a happy tune that he and Paccius had both been fond of.

†

Spartacus sat on an open area of the wooded hillside, looking out over the glittering turquoise of the Ionian Sea. Ariadne was beside him. On the flat plain some distance below them, and adjoining the shore, was their camp. It was enormous, sprawling over more ground than that occupied by eight legions, or even ten. There was order to it too, thought Spartacus proudly. The tents were in reasonably straight lines. A stout earthen rampart and deep ditch ran around the perimeter; sentries walked to and fro, patrolling the fortifications. Outside the walls, thousands of men were being trained by their officers: marching up and down in formation, making shield walls and sparring with one another. Slingers stood in lines, firing stones at straw targets a hundred paces away. Squadrons of riders on shaggy mountain horses wheeled and turned together, their spears shining in the bright sun.

"It's an army now," he said with satisfaction. "A damn big one." *And nearly as good as any I might have raised in Thrace.*

"It is," replied Ariadne. "And all thanks to you."

He pulled her to him. "You've had a hand in it as well. Men flock to hear Dionysus' priestess speak. They long to hear the god's words."

She smiled her thanks. "Maybe. But the forty thousand men who've joined us in the months since Forum Annii didn't come to listen to me. They came to follow you. Spartacus the gladiator. The man who dares to defy Rome. The man who gives slaves hope."

"Hope can be a dangerous thing," said Spartacus with a frown.

It had been clear that there was something on his mind since dawn. *He's ready to talk.* "Why do you say that?"

"On the surface, things couldn't be better. Our numbers have quadrupled. We've given Varinius the slip, and found somewhere remote to live for the winter. It's fertile here, in the 'arch of Italy's boot,' and the farms and towns to raid are plentiful. Metapontum alone provided us with two months' worth of grain. Heraclea was just as rich. Thurii is ours for the taking if we want it. Hundreds of wild horses have been captured and broken, to use as cavalry mounts. Pulcher has more than a score of smiths making weapons from dawn until dusk. Slaves are still coming in their hundreds to join us." He gave her a brittle smile. "Even Crixus has been quiet of late."

"Ever since the fight at Forum Annii, he's done his own thing, hasn't he?"

"The shitbag is probably recruiting supporters so that when the time comes, as many men as possible will follow him, but at least he's not constantly looking for a fight. Despite that bonus, we're still living in a dream world."

Ariadne was no longer enjoying the warm sunshine. "Rome hasn't forgotten us, you mean."

"That's right," he said grimly. "This might seem like paradise, but it won't last much longer than the snow on the mountains to the north. Sure as the melt comes in spring, the legions will come in search of us." His lips gave an ironic twist. "Hannibal survived in this area for more than a decade. He was perhaps the finest general in history, and he outwitted Rome at every turn. But the stubborn bastards didn't ever admit that they'd been defeated by him—even after Cannae. They simply recruited more men and fought on. It took nearly a generation, yet Hannibal was defeated in the end." Spartacus sighed. "And he had professional soldiers. I have slaves."

"They are no longer slaves," said Ariadne sharply. "They are free men. All of them."

"True enough," he admitted. "But they are not legionaries."

"They have been trained mercilessly for months—as recruits to the legions are," she countered.

"Maybe so. Yet most of them didn't come into the world with the warlike attitude that is every Roman's birthright. They're not combat veterans either. When Rome sends its finest men against us, as it inevitably must, will my soldiers stand and fight? Or will they run?" Weirdly, he felt relief at having voiced his greatest worry.

Ariadne pointed at the myriad of figures on the plain below. "Those men love you!" she cried. "They would follow you to the ends of the earth."

Pride filled Spartacus' eyes. "You're right. I do them a disservice. But the outcome will be the same. Even if we beat the Romans another time, and another, they will not have been defeated. A man cannot kill all the ants in a colony. It's not possible." His expression grew calculating. *Yet this is also the hard path that I would have chosen in Thrace.*

Ariadne felt her heart begin to race. They hadn't spoken about leaving Italy since their conversation months before, but it was filling her mind right now. His too, from the look of it. But she would not be the one to mention it first. Spartacus did not yet know that she was pregnant. He mustn't believe that she was trying to influence him.

He cocked his head at her. "What are you thinking?"

"I was wondering what was in your mind to do," she said evasively.

"I do not fear dying in battle," he said thoughtfully. "But if there was another path to take—a path that did not avoid confrontation with our enemies—then I would strongly consider it."

Ariadne waited. *Please guide him, Dionysus.*

"It's not as if the Romans will stand by and let us march past to the Alps," Spartacus said with a harsh laugh. "They'll place every damn legion they have in our way." That image made Ariadne feel physically sick. "If our army can pass those tests, well . . ." Spartacus hesitated before saying, "Outside Italy we can truly be free."

Ariadne wanted to cheer.

"Crixus will not follow me, of course. He was never going to anyway. But when they hear what I have to say, I think that Castus and

Gannicus will. They have learned that I am a better general than their fellow countryman."

"After the way you've organized the army, only a fool would think otherwise."

He glanced at her quizzically. "You've said little about my suggestion, yet you were the one to mention it some time ago. Do you still think it's a good one?"

She smiled. "I do. Rome is far too great a quarry for us to bring it down. I also think that you are destined to return to Thrace. That's why you were pointing east in your dream." *That's what you want to think,* chided her conscience. Ariadne harshly quelled the thought.

He looked pleased.

I must tell him now. Ariadne squeezed his hand. "There is something else."

He raised an eyebrow.

"I have missed my cycle for two months." She made a tutting noise at Spartacus' incomprehension. "I'm pregnant."

His face lit up. "Pregnant?"

Ariadne smiled as she leaned over to kiss him. "That's what I said."

"That's wonderful news. Praise the Rider!"

"I'd be more likely to commend your keeping me in bed each and every morning," Ariadne replied archly. Her dancing eyes belied her scolding tone.

"A man has his needs," he said with a lopsided grin. "Is it to be a son, as you said?"

She caressed her belly. "Yes, I think so. Your firstborn would have to be male, wouldn't he?"

"I'd like that." Spartacus did a quick mental calculation. "He'll be born around harvest time."

"That's my thinking."

"Good. It will be warm and sunny then, and he'll have grown strong by the winter," said Spartacus with satisfaction. "It gives us time to head north as well."

"When will you speak to the other leaders?" *The sooner the better.*

"Now," he said, getting to his feet. "Spring is nearly here. I want to be ready to move the moment it arrives."

A flicker of movement caught Ariadne's eye. She glanced down, seeing a horse and rider galloping toward the camp from the west. The frantic whip strokes being delivered by the horseman told their own story. *The gods always place something in the way.* She tried not to worry. "Your conversation might have to wait."

Spartacus' gaze followed hers. His jaw tightened at the sight. "Maybe so. I'll still be needing to talk to the others, though."

"What is it, do you think?" she asked softly, suspecting what he'd say.

"Varinius," grated Spartacus. "He's found us."

†

"The prick has had a few months to lick his wounds and recruit more men," said Spartacus. The rider had been carrying just the news he'd expected. The man was standing off to one side now, sweat-stained and weary, and watching Spartacus confer with Castus, Gannicus and Crixus. "It's not that surprising that Varinius has been looking for us. He can't go back to the Senate without some kind of success to report. They'd hang him up by his balls."

"So far all he's had are defeats," said Gannicus with a predatory smile.

"He's soon going to have another one," rumbled Crixus.

"The messenger says that Varinius has over six thousand men now," warned Castus. "He's been busy recruiting at Cumae."

"Is that all? That's a drop in the ocean compared to our forces!" scoffed Crixus.

"All the same, let's not underestimate him," said Spartacus. "That's more than a legion."

"Lost your appetite for a fight with all this easy living?" taunted Crixus.

Spartacus' eyes went flat and hard. "What do you think?"

"I—" Crixus began.

Spartacus cut him off. "I agreed before that we would fight Varinius, and I'm a man of my word. But we need to be wary of that many legionaries. We might outnumber the whoresons eight or nine to one, but on more than one occasion, I've seen Roman armies take on worse odds than that—and still come out victorious."

Castus' expression turned wary. Gannicus rubbed his nose and said nothing.

"That's not going to happen to us!" replied Crixus furiously.

"Damn right it's not!" Spartacus caught the messenger's eye. "How far from Thurii did you say they were?"

"About two days' march, sir."

"Two days . . ."

Gannicus pounced on Spartacus' thoughtful expression. "What have you in mind?"

"I think that we should lay a little trap for Varinius. Something that he won't expect from slaves."

"Sounds interesting," said Castus, looking more cheerful.

"Spit it out then," muttered Crixus grudgingly.

"Carbo's made friends with one of the guards on the main gate at Thurii," Spartacus revealed. "He brings him fresh venison and boar now and again. If Carbo asks him to open the gate late at night for some more, the fool will do it."

Castus' eyebrows rose. "You mean to seize the town?"

"Why not? There can't be more than a few hundred defenders. Most of them will be old or out of shape. If we move tonight, the place will be ours by dawn."

"Why would we do that?" demanded Crixus.

"Come a little closer and I'll tell you," said Spartacus with an evil grin.

†

Publius Varinius shivered and pulled his cloak closer around his bony shoulders. He shuffled nearer to the brazier that stood in the center of his sleeping quarters. The damp wood in it sputtered, giving off little heat. Wiping his streaming eyes, Varinius cursed. Since leaving the comforts of Cumae, it seemed he had been cold all the time. Nothing he did, or wore, could take the chill from his bones. It wasn't surprising. Every damn day was a repetition of the one before. Wake up to a freezing tent. Eat a cold breakfast. Break camp. Send out the scouts. Follow in their wake, riding through the winter rain and sleet in steep, muddy, inhospitable terrain. Find nothing. Make a fresh camp. Eat half-cooked, half-burned meat and porridge for dinner. Sleep the sleep of the exhausted—or the dead. Wake the following day and do it all over again. A fresh bout of coughing racked him.

Fucking Spartacus. He and his men had spent weeks following rumor here and gossip there. To Varinius' extreme frustration, every single lead had turned out to be a wild-goose chase. Although the name Spartacus was on everyone's lips, there was no sign of the runaway gladiator in all of Campania. So far, Lucania had been no different. It was worse than trying to find the center of the maze without a ball of string, Varinius thought sourly. At least they would reach the town of Thurii the following day. There he'd be able to commandeer a house. To lie under warm, dry blankets and a solid tile roof. If he never had to sleep in a tent again, it would be too soon.

He eyed the scroll on his table with a jaundiced eye. It had reached him by messenger earlier that day. No doubt Marcus Licinius Crassus, the man who'd written it, was at this very moment comfortably tucked up in bed. *If the smug bastard could see me now, he'd probably laugh until he cried.* Varinius didn't have a good feeling about receiving a personal letter from one of the men who guided the Republic's course. If he'd already met with some success, he'd have hurried to open it, but since leaving the capital, his whole damn mission had seemed doomed to failure. Varinius didn't like to dwell on this, but he made himself, because Crassus would have heard of his woes by now. His vague, misleading reports thus far would not have pulled the wool over the eyes of an imbecile, let alone the richest and one of the shrewdest politicians in Rome. Worryingly, his misfortune couldn't all be put down to bad luck on his and his officers' part. In retrospect, reflected Varinius, it had been a bad idea to split his forces.

After their startling successes against first Lucius Furius and then Lucius Cossinius, Spartacus' men had had the effrontery to raid two of Varinius' encampments, inflicting numerous more casualties, and stamping his soldiers' weakened morale into the glutinous Campanian mud. Disease had thinned his troops' ranks further. It was a miracle that more hadn't deserted, thought Varinius morosely. When word had come that the slaves had withdrawn from Glaber's former camp, there had been no question of leading an assault on it, or of pursuing Spartacus into the hinterland. It might have looked cowardly, but withdrawing to Cumae to regroup, and to bolster his force with new recruits, had been the only sensible option. Anything else, and he'd have had a mutiny on his hands.

Of course that's not how Crassus or the Senate would see it. Roman commanders did not withdraw beyond the enemy's reach. Particularly when the enemy was nothing more than a rabble of escaped gladiators and slaves.

With a muttered oath, Varinius snatched up the letter. Cracking the wax seal with a thumbnail, he unrolled the parchment.

"To Publius Varinius, praetor of the Republic of Rome: Greetings. I trust that this letter reaches you hale and hearty, and that the gods continue to show you favor?" Varinius scowled. The sarcasm starts already, he thought. His eyes flickered across the neatly written words: the mark of a professional scribe. "It has been some four months since you and your fellow officers set out from Rome on the glorious mission to which you were appointed by the Senate." That's right, rub it in.

The news that has reached me here in the capital has been troubling, to say the least. It was surprising enough to hear of the calamitous ambush on Lucius Furius, but the tragic death of Lucius Cossinius and so many of his men was truly shocking. I believe that the slaves also achieved further success with attacks on your camps. Aside from the troubles during the civil war, the likes of these outrages have not been seen in Italy for generations. They cannot be allowed to continue. While I am personally in no doubt that your withdrawal to Cumae was made for the best of reasons, others in Rome do not look upon your actions in such a benign light. Such caution will not bring about the destruction of those who have dared to defy the Republic so flagrantly. It must not happen again. It pains me to do so, but I feel that I must remind you of the fate of Caius Claudius Glaber, your predecessor. I have every faith, however, that your future is a brighter one than his.

The idea of having to fall on his sword made Varinius break out in a cold sweat. He forced himself to continue reading.

May your resolve remain strong. I ask that Diana the huntress guide your path as you hunt down Spartacus. Let Mars keep his shield over you and your men! Success will soon be yours, and peace will return once more to Campania. I look forward to greeting you upon your victorious return to Rome.

With brotherly concern, I remain your fellow praetor, Marcus Licinius Crassus

So there it was, as if he hadn't known it already. Varinius' shoulders bowed under the pressure. Succeed, die in the attempt, or be ordered to commit suicide by the Senate. That's what Crassus' honey-eyed words told him. *What have I done to deserve this fate? How has a straightforward task become so treacherous?* Crumpling the parchment, he tossed it into the brazier, watching with some satisfaction as it blackened and then began to burn.

Its message was engraved in his mind, though.

A discreet cough distracted him from his misery. "Sir?"

Varinius turned. "Ah, Galba!" He made a show of being pleased to see his most senior centurion, a balding veteran with bandy legs and a mean aspect. "What is it?"

"Some good news, sir."

He had Varinius' attention now. "Really? Well, come in, come in. It's blowing a gale out there."

Galba entered, letting the tent flap fall behind him. "I sent a rider ahead to Thurii this morning as you asked, sir. He's just returned."

Disappointed, Varinius frowned. He'd known that there would be a warm welcome for him and his men in the town. What use was there in reminding him now, when he was cold and miserable? "Is that all you've come to tell me?"

"You don't understand, sir. He didn't manage to enter the town. It's under siege, from Spartacus' men."

Varinius could hardly believe his ears. "Vulcan's balls, really?"

"So he says, sir. He's a good lad too, served more than five years in the army."

"Is Thurii still ours?"

"Apparently, sir. There are plenty of defenders on the walls."

"Ha! A band of sewer rats could never take a town. What are the fools thinking?" cried Varinius, his confidence soaring. "How many of them were there?"

"Hard to say, sir. He couldn't exactly hang about. Upward of a legion, he said. Six, seven thousand, maybe more."

"Spartacus has been busy then," mused Varinius, his eyes narrowing. "But they're only slaves, eh?"

"They'll be no match for our lads, sir," said Galba stolidly.

"Any catapults or siege engines?"

"No, sir."

"Of course not," said Varinius dismissively. "What's the lie of the land around Thurii?"

"It's mostly flat, sir. As you know, the sea is some miles to the east of the town. A large area of woods lies to the north, which is probably where Spartacus attacked from. The main road approaches from the west, through heavily cultivated farmland, more of which lies to the south."

"So they can only retreat the way they came?"

"That's right, sir."

"Excellent!" Varinius punched his right hand into his left. "If we leave at dawn, we should arrive there when?"

"The messenger says it's about fifteen miles, sir."

"Early afternoon then. Plenty of time for a battle. I will lead the troops in a frontal assault to relieve the town, and our cavalry can cut off their escape route. We'll slaughter the whoresons."

"They won't know what's hit them, sir," agreed Galba, leering.

"The trumpets are to sound an hour before dawn. I want every man ready to leave by the time the sun hits the horizon. Weapons and one day's food only," said Varinius crisply.

"The catapults and ballistae, sir?"

"We won't need them."

"And the baggage train, sir?"

"Leave it one cohort as protection. It's to follow on behind us. One other thing, Galba. Spread the word about how easy it's going to be tomorrow."

"Very good, sir." Grinning, Galba saluted and turned on his heel.

Varinius' spirits hadn't been so high for many weeks. He reached for the jug and poured himself a large cupful. The wine tasted far better than it had done just a short time before. *That prick Crassus will have his doubts quashed in royal style. He'll fall over himself to be my friend.* Varinius began imagining exactly how he would phrase the letter informing the Senate of his victory. '"Spartacus is dead?"' he mused. "That would be a good start."

†

Varinius slept like a baby. His day also began well. Even as the horizon tinged rosy-pink, his soothsayer, a buck-toothed ancient from Latium, had slit a chicken's throat and read its entrails. To Varinius' delight, the omens had been pronounced extremely auspicious. The day would end with a resounding victory for Rome. The slaves would be driven from the field, with huge losses. Spartacus himself would be captured or killed, and the citizens of Thurii would shower Varinius and his men with rewards. Most importantly, his continuing journey along the *cursus honorum* would be secured.

To the eager Varinius, the fifteen miles to Thurii seemed no more than five. Pleasingly, the mood among his men was also good. Over the previous months of misery, he had grown used to their sullen expressions and mouthed curses whenever they saw him. Desertions had soared; so too had the numbers of malingerers. Now, for the first time in an age, Varinius heard his legionaries singing instead of complaining. It couldn't just be because their heavy yokes had been left behind, he thought. They were marching with real enthusiasm. They looked like men who actually wanted to fight. Varinius made a mental note to thank Galba. This was but the latest example. The veteran officer had proved himself indispensable since the campaign had started.

Varinius was so eager to reach Thurii that he had dispensed with usual protocol and was riding before the front ranks of his troops rather than in the commanders' normal position, some distance to the rear. Only his cavalry, four hundred experienced German auxiliaries, were in front of him and his senior officers. The Germans had been patrolling ahead since the column had set out, reconnoitring the terrain and reporting back to Varinius at regular intervals. Pleasingly, there had been no sign of any enemy scouts whatsoever. *The ignorant fools. They won't even know that we're coming.*

The fertile farmland bordering Thurii to the west resembled any other in the south of Italy. Large fields bounded by trees and hedges had been set aside to cultivate either wheat or vines. The crops of both had long since been harvested, and now the wheat fields stood plowed and empty. Gaggles of rooks cawed angrily as they were disturbed from the trees' bare branches by the marching soldiers. On either side of the road stood countless lines of leafless vines, sadly shrunken from their autumn glory. Varinius, a keen oenophile, had sampled enough of the local vintages to consider buying a farm in the area. The eye-watering prices had put him off until now. *That won't be an issue after today,* he thought triumphantly.

A dozen Germans appeared on the road, and Varinius' stomach twisted. He pretended to ignore the approaching riders, chatting idly to Toranius, one of his quaestors. Soon, however, the thunder of galloping hooves could no longer be denied.

"Ah. Some news, perhaps," said Varinius casually.

Spotting his scarlet cloak and horsehair-crested helmet, the Germans clattered to a halt in front of him. The lead rider made a perfunctory salute. "Praetor," he greeted in heavily accented Latin. "We have sighted the slave army."

"They're not a bloody army!" cried Varinius. "A rabble, more like."

The German inclined his head in recognition. "Indeed, sir."

"Where are they?"

"Arrayed around the town walls. I could see no troops facing to their rear at all, sir."

"Were you seen?"

"There were a few sentries, sir, but we rode them down." The German ran a finger across his throat. "As far as I can tell, the rest are oblivious to our presence."

Varinius could taste his success already. It was sweeter than he could ever have imagined. There would be no more slogging through the mud, enduring the bitter weather. Just a short, sharp battle, with a foregone conclusion. "Very good," he said. "You know what to do."

"We circle around to the north, and wait near the tree line for the slaves to begin retreating. Then we fall on them like the hammers of hell," replied the German.

"Give no quarter. None! I want your men to kill until their right arms can no longer hold a sword," instructed Varinius.

"Yes, sir." The German grinned eagerly. Repeating Varinius' words in his own tongue, he wheeled his horse back toward Thurii. His men followed.

"What are your orders, sir?" asked Toranius.

"I want a *triplex acies* formation the moment that the town walls come into sight." Varinius could see no reason not to use the method of attack that had been tried and tested by generations of Roman generals. "We'll advance on the dogs at walking pace, and charge them from a hundred paces."

"Will they fight, sir?"

"I doubt it very much! On flat ground, no one can master the

Roman legionary. Especially not a band of fucking slaves." Varinius smiled happily. "Mark my words, Toranius. They will run the instant that they clap eyes on us. We probably won't even get close enough for a volley of pila."

†

Half an hour later, Varinius' blood was well and truly up. He'd finally withdrawn behind his men—after all, there was no need to be stupid—but from the back of his horse, he had an excellent and central view of the battlefield. Toranius and the four tribunes stayed close by, ready to relay his orders during the fighting. Running off to Varinius' left and right were the neat ranks of his twelve, full-strength cohorts. Five were arrayed in the front line, four in the second and three in the rear. Short gaps separated the three maneuvering lines. Trumpets blared as the men assumed their final position. Pride filled Varinius. *Gods, but they look good.* The centurions were blowing their whistles and bellowing orders from the front rank of each cohort; near every officer, the unit's gilded standard was being held aloft for everyone to see. The *optiones* stood behind the last rows of soldiers, their vine staffs at the ready. Their job was to beat any man who tried to back away, or retreat. *That won't happen today.*

Content that his forces were ready, Varinius looked toward Thurii, which lay perhaps half a mile away. The messenger had been correct in his estimation. The black stain around the walls told him that the slaves had surrounded the entire town. Just to do that meant that they outnumbered his legionaries by a considerable margin. What of it? he thought scornfully. There was no visible order to the seething mass of men before him. Far from it. Instead of battle cries, the sound of frightened shouts wafted through the air from Thurii. *Excellent.* "They've seen us. Sound the advance!" Varinius shouted.

The musician beside him raised his instrument to his lips and blew a short series of notes. This was taken up at once by the other trumpeters. Then, with measured tread, the lines of legionaries began to march forward. *Tramp, tramp, tramp.*

With his excitement growing, Varinius walked his horse some twenty steps to the rear.

"Hold the line, men," bellowed a centurion. "Have your first pilum ready!"

"Steady," ordered Galba. "We want to hit the bastards all at the same time."

"Revenge for Lucius Furius and his lads!" roared a voice.

"And for Lucius Cossinius," added another.

"REVENGE!"

The cry began echoing up and down the line, drowning out the slaves' noises of distress.

"SI–LENCE!" screamed Galba, clattering the flat of his blade on the helmets of the men around him. "We close in on the fuckers in silence!"

It took some time, but the centurions and junior officers regained control eventually. An odd quiet fell over the legionaries. Varinius had not fought many battles, but he recognized the atmosphere well. The air was laced with the smell of leather and men's sweat. The dominant sound once more was the heavy tread of his soldiers' studded *caligae* on the muddy ground. Interspersed with this was the clash of pila shafts off the sides of shields and the metallic jingle of mail. Everywhere, men were hawking and spitting. They muttered prayers to their favorite gods and surreptitiously rubbed at the amulets hanging from their necks. Varinius felt his own stomach tighten with anxiety. He took a deep breath and let it out again. *Think of the effect this will have. It's absolutely terrifying to have an enemy advance in complete silence. That's why we do it.*

The distance between them and the slaves closed to perhaps 250 paces. Varinius' anticipation grew. They were still well beyond javelin range, but close enough to mean that battle was likely. Sensing the slaves' fear, his men were growing keener by the moment. But the seasoned centurions stayed calm, ensuring that no one broke ranks.

At two hundred paces, the legionaries were ordered to begin smacking their pila rhythmically off the metal rims on the tops of their scuta.

Clack. Clack. Clack.

It was an unnerving sound. A sound designed to send fear darting into men's hearts. To promise the kiss of death from javelin tip or gladius blade. To ensure a trip to the River Styx, there to meet the ferryman.

Few enemies could take the terror of its approach.

A wall of incoherent shouts rose up from Spartacus' men, and then, before Varinius' very eyes, the main body of slaves broke in two. Half began running to the south, and the rest broke and fled for the trees to the north.

Varinius stifled a cheer. "Two cohorts wheel to the left, three to the right!" He waited while the trumpeter sounded his commands, before directing the four cohorts in the second line to split equally and follow their comrades, and the final line of three to halt and hold the center. "Toranius, I want you to lead the chase to the south. It's open farmland, so the sheep-fuckers will have nowhere to go but face down in the mud. Chase them hard. Kill them all if you can!"

"Yes, sir." Toranius' teeth flashed white in his swarthy face.

"You stay here," said Varinius, glancing at two of his tribunes. "The rest of you, follow the cohorts to the left. I want you to run them right on to the Germans. They'll charge when it's time and smash the whoresons against your shield wall." To his trumpeter: "Sound the charge. Javelins at will."

He watched with great satisfaction as his orders were rapidly obeyed. The charging legionaries began to roar battle cries, and this time the centurions did nothing to stop them.

"Kill! Kill! Kill!"

The air to Varinius' left darkened as hundreds of pila were thrown after the retreating slaves. They soared up in graceful, lethal arcs and he counted his heartbeat. One. Two. Three. Four. Five. The missiles' tips turned to point earthwards. Six. Seven. Eight. The screaming began, and Varinius stopped his count with a smile. *There's nothing like javelins to create panic in a fleeing mob.*

Varinius glanced to his right, seeing the same scenario unfold. Toranius would do a good job. He was young, but steady.

His gaze casually returned to the front. The town's main gate was opening. The defenders are making a sally, he thought with some amusement. The sluggards best hurry if they want a piece of the action. Or maybe they've come to thank me for saving their miserable hides.

Hundreds of armed men swarmed out of Thurii. Dressed in Roman mail shirts and wearing typical plumed bronze helmets, they ran with their shields close together. In total silence. Straight at Varinius' three cohorts.

Varinius blinked. "What in Jupiter's name are they doing?"

He glanced around, but Toranius and the tribunes were all long gone.

When he looked back, the men were twenty paces nearer. Varinius was startled to see that some of them had long hair and mustaches. His eyes flickered across their lines and his heart nearly stopped. There was a Nubian in the front rank too. And a man with facial tattoos who could only be a Scythian, or similar. "T-they're not Romans! It's a trap!" he screamed.

With an anxious look, his trumpeter half raised his instrument. "What are your orders, sir?"

"Close order," bawled Varinius. "A volley of javelins at fifty paces."

Tan-tara. Tan-tara-tara.

The legionaries' shields slammed together almost as one. "Right arms back," yelled the centurions. "Pila ready!"

Dismounting, Varinius threw his reins to his orderly, who began to lead his horse out of harm's way. He took up his shield and drew his sword. Varinius had wielded the weapon in battle just once before, but he took comfort from the firmness of its carved ivory hilt. "All right, men. Let's show the scumbags the meaning of courage. FOR ROME!"

"FOR ROME!" they roared back. "FOR ROME!"

Varinius' courage rallied. "Is this all you can throw at me, Spartacus?" It wasn't.

His eyes widened in horror. The tide of men issuing from the town gate had not stopped. Instead, it had grown even denser. Now his three cohorts were outnumbered, and the balance was fast tipping further in the slaves' favor. Moreover, the men running at his legionaries looked every bit as determined as the most hardbitten Roman veteran. They still hadn't uttered a word either. Fifty paces separated the two sides now, no more. Right on cue, orders rang out from the centurions and a tide of Roman javelins flew up. The slaves slowed in response, and sent a volley soaring in the opposite direction. Then, to Varinius' complete amazement, they raised their scuta to protect themselves.

"Raise shields!" went the cry from the centurions.

Foolishly, Varinius looked up. Seeing something flashing toward him, he ducked down behind his scutum. The movement saved his life. There was a sharp, whistling sound, and a pilum flew through the space where his head had been. It sank more than a handspan into the dirt. Two more thrummed down to his left, and a sickening scream behind him told Varinius that his orderly had been hit. He shook his head like a drunken man trying to find his way home. "This can't be happening."

But it was.

XIX

A nother shower of javelins was exchanged, and then the two sides struck each other with a sound like a giant thunderclap. Varinius' legionaries reeled with the impact, the sheer fury of it. At least two score soldiers went down, or were knocked from their feet. They never got a chance to stand up. Gladii lanced down, thrusting into their flesh with a terrible hunger. Normally, the gaps left by such casualties would be filled immediately. Not this time. With froth spraying from their lips, the Gauls that Varinius had spotted thrust themselves, uncaring, screaming, into the breaches. Punching with their shield bosses and stabbing with their swords like men possessed, they drove the legionaries of the second rank back several steps. A centurion who jumped into their path was hacked to pieces in a storm of vicious blows. A *signifer* was killed and his standard raised into the air by a triumphant Scythian.

Varinius' troops, so sure of success just a few moments before, quailed at their enemies' sheer ferocity. This was a world away from what they'd been told to expect. These were no frightened, easy-to-kill slaves. They were more like ravenous, indestructible beasts.

The legionaries fell back another step.

Baying for blood, Spartacus' men pressed forward with renewed strength.

"Hold the line," roared Galba. "Hold the line, you fucking dogs!" With contemptible ease, the veteran centurion lopped the sword arm off a short slave with a rusty helmet. Smashing him aside with his scutum, Galba ran the next man through the chest. He pulled out the blade, laughing as blood spattered all over his face. "Is this all you can do, you miserable sacks of shit?"

There was a momentary pause, and the nearest legionaries glanced at each other.

Listen to him, prayed Varinius. Listen to him!

"Come on, you scumbags," screamed Galba. He leaped forward, using his shield to drive a big Gaul backward into the arms of his fellows. Galba slipped his gladius around his scutum, running it deep into the man's belly. An agonizing scream split the air, and the legionaries took heart. Locking shields, they advanced toward Galba, whose heroic attack had left him alone.

"FORWARD!" shouted Varinius. "FORWARD!"

But someone else had also realized that Galba's position was vulnerable.

A figure emerged from the enemy ranks. Those around him held back, and Varinius' breath caught in his chest. The man was of average height, but his magnificent Phrygian helmet marked him out at once as someone to be reckoned with. He was clad similarly to his comrades, in a mail shirt, and he carried a scutum. Instead of a gladius, however, he bore a sica. *A Thracian. He has to be.* Without a word, the newcomer pointed the bloodied weapon at the senior centurion.

Galba's lip curled. "Think you can take me? Come on, then!" He glanced over his shoulder. "Stay where you are, lads. I want to carve this piece of dirt a new asshole."

Grinning with newfound confidence, the legionaries did as they were told.

Snap! The Thracian's sword clicked into its scabbard. He stretched out his right arm. "Javelin!"

Stepping forward, a fierce-looking Scythian slapped one into his palm.

"Scared of sword work?" Galba sneered. "Slave scum!"

"Not at all," replied the Thracian in accented Latin. Hefting the weapon, he drew back and hurled it with all his might. It covered the distance to Galba in less than a heartbeat. Punching through his scutum, the pilum ripped a hole in his mail shirt and sank deep into his chest. Galba's eyes bulged with the agony of it; his mouth opened in shock. Froth poured from his lips in a bloody spume. He staggered and fell on to his back, his shield still pinned to his body.

"It's just that I'm better with a spear," said the Thracian mildly.

Varinius goggled. He'd never seen a throw like it.

Nor had the watching legionaries. Dismay and fear rippled across their faces, as when a stone lands in a pond.

With a savage grin, the Thracian drew his sica and aimed it at the Romans.

"SPAR-TA-CUS!" roared his men. "SPAR-TA-CUS! SPAR-TA-CUS!"

Acid-tipped claws of fear ripped at Varinius. *Gods above. This is no half-wit rabble-rouser.*

By now, the nearest legionaries were looking terrified. Their heads began to turn, seeking a way to retreat. The men in the front rank pushed back against those behind them. There was little resistance.

With a maniacal yell, Spartacus threw himself forward.

In a devastating surge, the slaves followed.

Varinius was struck dumb with shock. Mesmerized, he watched as the structure of his central cohort disintegrated before his eyes. Some legionaries fought desperately against the wave of attackers, but theirs was a hopeless cause. Once the line of shields was broken, and men presented their backs on the enemy, there was no way back. The soldiers at the front—the first to have turned to run—were also quickest to die. They were hacked down, like rotten branches torn off a tree by a gale. In the time it took Varinius to drop his shield, grab his horse's reins and swing up on to its back, scores of men had been slain. The ground was carpeted with mangled, bloody bodies. Uncaring, the slaves trampled over the dead to reach their next victims. The slaves' swords rose and fell in a dreadful, hypnotic rhythm. Their job couldn't have been easier. Riven by fear, the legionaries were shoving and fighting with one another to get away. The screaming was absolutely deafening.

Despite himself, Varinius quailed. *This cohort is finished.*

Then he glanced to either side, and his desperation reached new levels. Seeing, hearing, sensing that their comrades had broken, the legionaries of the other two cohorts were also in full retreat.

A hand pulled at his leg, and Varinius glanced down in horror at a blood-spattered legionary. He had neither sword nor shield. "Help me, sir!"

Without thinking, Varinius smashed the hilt of his sword into the man's face. He heard the crunch as the soldier's nose broke, and then he was dragging his horse's head around and drumming his heels into its sides. Not liking the chaos, it took off willingly.

What of the other cohorts? Varinius wondered. To the south, he could see Toranius' units engaging with the slaves, who looked to have turned and formed up. Toranius wouldn't be coming back to help any time soon. *Damn it all to Hades!* Varinius' worst fears were confirmed when he looked toward the woodland to the north. Hundreds of horsemen—far too many to be his Germans—were swirling gracefully around a large cluster of armored men. Varinius struggled to make sense of it. How could Spartacus have cavalry? It wasn't possible that his riders had been driven off.

Was it?

He felt the *thump* as something struck his mount hard in the haunch. He shot a look over his shoulder. *A javelin!* Even as Varinius took it in, his horse reared up in pain, throwing him free. He landed on the flat of his back. All the air was driven from his lungs, and for a moment Varinius lay there, looking dazedly up at the sky. It was completely cloudless, he saw.

"Are you hurt, sir?"

Varinius squinted. An optio whom Galba had praised was stooping over him. "Eh?"

"If you want to live, sir, get up!" A filthy hand was shoved in his face.

Varinius took it, and the optio heaved him to his feet. They had to brace themselves against the tide of men who were shoving past, blind to their commander's presence.

"All right, sir?"

"Y-yes," muttered Varinius.

"You go first, sir. I'll guard your back."

"Where to?"

"Anywhere, sir." The optio actually gave him a shove. "Quickly!"

Normally, Varinius would have been incensed by such audacity and had the optio punished on the spot. Now he was happy to turn and run like everyone else. It was that option, or die. Varinius was very aware, however, that fleeing did not guarantee his survival.

Mars, the Bringer of War, forgive my poor judgment. Let me live.

†

By mid-afternoon, the battle was over. It was a spectacular victory for the slaves. The Romans had been completely driven off, suffering massive casualties in the process. Spartacus estimated from the bodies littering the field that more than two-thirds of Varinius' force had been killed. Several senior officers were among the slain. No doubt hundreds more enemy soldiers would die before nightfall. Crixus and his men were pursuing them northward on the Via Annia. Then there were those who would die of their wounds in the following days. *Serves the bastards right.* Grim satisfaction filled Spartacus as he surveyed the field from one of the wall towers.

Grinning with exhilaration, his men descended on the town like a cloud of locusts. In their eyes, it was now time for the pillage that they'd been denied the previous night during the successful assault on Thurii. The defenders had been cut down then in their scores, but Spartacus had prevented any killing of the city's denizens, who had been cowering in their houses ever since.

He was waiting for his troops at the main gate. Half a dozen Thracians surrounded him, carrying the fasces that had been dropped by Varinius' lictores as they fled.

The slaves greeted Spartacus like a conquering hero, roaring their approbation until their throats were hoarse.

"You did well," he cried to the first arrivals. "I'm proud of you. The fat senators in Rome will tremble when they hear of your deeds."

"SPAR-TA-CUS!" they bellowed delightedly.

He held up a hand, and silence gradually fell. "Two things, though, before you go inside the city to claim your just rewards."

"What are they, Spartacus?" yelled Pulcher, the smith.

"I want no killing of children or babes. Enough of them were slain in Forum Annii." Spartacus stared from face to sweat-grimed face. Many could not meet his hard stare. "Any man seen harming a child or an infant will be executed on the spot. There will be no exceptions. Clear?"

An uncomfortable silence fell.

"We hear you," said Pulcher, glaring all around him. "Don't we, lads?"

Men grunted in assent, or shook their heads.

Spartacus nodded, satisfied. "The second thing is to remember that Rome will not regard this loss as anything more than a spur to raise new armies. We have not won a war today. We haven't even won a campaign. To those parasites in the Senate, this will be little more than a nasty shock. They will send far more soldiers next time, and not under the command of a mere praetor. I'd say it would be fair to expect a consul, at the head of an entire army."

"What are you saying?" asked Pulcher with a scowl.

"We can't stay in this area forever. Think on that as you celebrate tonight."

Spartacus was glad to see that many men bore sober expressions as they passed by into Thurii. They might forget his words in the haze of wine that would undoubtedly follow, but the seed would have been planted.

He stood by the gate, receiving the adulation of his men, and repeating his words until night fell, and Crixus returned. Like his men, the Gaul was spattered in blood from head to foot. Seeing Spartacus, he raised a fist. "You should have come with us. The hunting was good, eh?"

Several of his men howled like dogs.

"The Romans won't forget Crixus in a hurry."

"Why's that?" asked Spartacus.

"The last twenty legionaries that we captured had their eyes gouged out, and their right hands amputated," revealed Crixus with a cruel smile. "I ordered them to carry my name to Rome, and to warn the Senate that the same fate would befall every soldier they sent against us."

A loud cheer went up from his men, and Crixus glared at Spartacus.

So now he makes his move to take control. Spartacus was even more glad that he'd spoken with the slaves as they entered the city. "A powerful message," he conceded.

Crixus grinned triumphantly.

"I've done similar things myself, in Thrace. What it does is to make the Romans come back in even greater numbers."

Crixus' brows lowered. "Is that right? Always bloody know better, don't you?"

He's never going to agree to my plan. This final, stark realization unleashed Spartacus' anger. "Not all the time, no," he replied sharply. "But when it comes to fighting the Romans, I've forgotten more than you'll ever learn."

"We'll see about that," bellowed Crixus, the veins on his neck bulging dangerously. "Won't we, boys?"

His voice was lost in the torrent of shouts that followed.

Spartacus waited until the noise died down. "I'm going to assemble the army tomorrow. Make an announcement."

"Which will be?" demanded Crixus.

"I'm going to head north, to the Alps. Leave Italy."

Crixus' eyes widened. "Do Castus and Gannicus know about this?"

"Not yet." *I think they'll stay with me rather than go with you, the hothead.*

"So you're going to ask the men if they want to follow me, or you?"

"That's right," replied Spartacus. "Unless of course you want to come with me."

"Eh?" Crixus threw him an incredulous look. "Why would I want to leave behind the riches that can be plundered here? Why would anyone? Everything in this land is ripe for the plucking."

"Not everything," warned Spartacus. "Two full-strength consular armies will stop you in your tracks."

But his words were drowned by Crixus' men's jeers and catcalls.

Spartacus shrugged and stood aside. He watched as the Gaul led his followers into Thurii. *Each man chooses his own fate. It's not for me to try and change their destiny.* Yet a trace of unease tickled the back of his mind. Who would listen to him tomorrow? How many would cleave to Crixus? What would Castus and Gannicus do? Maybe it had been premature to bring the matter to a head.

Spartacus clenched his jaw. His words could not be unsaid. *Now is as good a time as any.* He glanced up at the darkening sky. *Great Rider, you have my thanks for what happened here today. I ask for your help again tomorrow.*

†

Spartacus waited until late the following morning before having his order to assemble on the ground outside Thurii put about. Thanks to the amount of wine that had been consumed during the night, it took several hours to rouse everyone from their stupor and force them outside the walls. Egbeo, Carbo and their troops were the unlucky ones to be given this duty, and it won them no friends as they scoured the city's houses and alleyways for their sleeping comrades. Curses rained down on their heads, as well as helmets, cups and plates. Even the occasional amphora was lobbed at them. The former slaves had changed markedly over the previous months, Carbo decided. They had discovered their bark, and with it, their bite. Before, he would have been frightened of such a sea change. Now, it thrilled him. Spartacus had really forged an army.

No one actually put up a fight and gradually the bleary-eyed, filthy men were chivvied on to the open area before the main gate. Few had bothered to wash the previous day's blood from their arms and faces. The reek of sweat and stale wine hung everywhere. Mixed with it was the first faint smell of decay from the hundreds of Roman bodies that lay among the slaves. High above on the battlements, Spartacus' nostrils were filled with the sickening miasma. It was fortunate that spring was only starting, he thought. If it had been summer, the stench would already have been unbearable.

He had picked the position because it meant that everyone could see him. Crixus was there too, of course, glowering like an angry bull. Castus and Gannicus stood alongside, looking irritated. Spartacus cursed silently. He'd gone to tell them about his plan the previous evening, but Crixus had already got to the pair. *I could have managed that far better*, he reflected, giving them a confident grin anyway. He was heartened somewhat by Gannicus' nod, but Castus looked away rather than respond. Spartacus' doubt grew. *Great Rider, help me. Do not let them turn from me now.*

Carbo came clattering up the nearest set of stairs. "That's just about everyone. There are probably a few stragglers sleeping it off somewhere, but we couldn't find them." He threw a hate-filled glance at Crixus, but the Gaul didn't notice.

"Well done." Giving a signal to the trumpeter beside him, Spartacus turned to face the thousands of men below. Pride filled him at the magnificent sight. *May the gods let them follow me*, he prayed.

Tan-tara-tara-tara.

An expectant hush fell over the assembled troops.

"Friends! Comrades! I salute you!" Spartacus shouted. He waited as his words spread through the watching host.

"SPAR-TA-CUS!" It began as a low, rumbling cheer, but soon grew in volume until the very walls of the city rang with it. "SPAR-TA-CUS!"

Spartacus ignored Crixus, who was glowering at him. He began to speak, and men quickly fell silent. "Yesterday, we won a famous victory. Our first in open battle against the Romans! Much of it was thanks to Castus, Gannicus and Crixus." He indicated the Gauls beside him. Castus and Gannicus were quick to raise their arms in acknowledgment. Crixus looked furious as he did so, however.

Nonetheless, a huge cheer went up from the slaves.

Directly below the leaders, Pulcher stood forth from the crowd. "But we owe most of our thanks to you, Spartacus," he shouted.

"SPAR-TA-CUS! SPAR-TA-CUS!" A sea of weapons was borne aloft. Men hammered their swords off their shields, making an unbelievable din. Crixus' face grew even more sour, while Gannicus' grin grew a little strained. Castus didn't bother to hide his scowl. Spartacus nodded and smiled, waving in acknowledgment. *This augurs well.* Eventually, the racket died down.

"I asked you to be here today because we have a choice to make. Staying in this area is not an option."

"Why not?" yelled a voice. "Look at the cities we've sacked. Metapontum, Heraclea and now Thurii. Why give up on a good thing?"

Many men shouted in agreement. "Good point," shouted Crixus.

"Three reasons," answered Spartacus. "The first is that here we have our backs to the sea. If the Romans block off the way to the north, we would be trapped."

At this, there were unhappy grumbles.

"Trapped? Ha!" growled Crixus.

"And the second?" asked Pulcher.

"At the last count, the army numbered more than fifty thousand men. After yesterday's victory, thousands more slaves will come to join us. Soon there will not be enough grain to feed us all. That is serious enough, but the last reason is the most important." Spartacus paused. "Rome does not suffer defeat lightly. When those who rule in Rome receive word of what happened to Varinius and his men, they will be furious."

"So fucking what?" roared Crixus. "That's good!"

His men whistled with delight.

"The soldiers who have been sent against us are but a drop in the ocean that is Rome's manpower. When the consuls take to the field, as will surely happen now, they will lead four legions. That's twenty thousand legionaries. The Republic's best units may be abroad, but that many men in armor, and carrying good weapons, cannot be discounted. Only a few thousand of you are that well equipped."

"Are you saying we'll lose?" challenged Crixus belligerently, waving his arms to encourage the jeering that had started.

"No. What I'm saying is that after those soldiers, more will come. The veterans in Iberia and Asia Minor will be recalled. Six, eight, ten legions of solid men who have fought together for years. Will we be able to defeat those too?" The taunts died down, and Spartacus could see doubt writ everywhere on faces now. *Good.*

Carbo's heart was heavy. He'd heard this dozens of times. This was Navio's favorite topic when he'd been drinking.

"Who's to say we won't win?" blustered Crixus. "And even if we fail, we fall in battle, winning a glorious death for ourselves."

A muted cheer rose up from his men, but many more of the slaves looked unhappy.

"Every man who has seen me fight knows that I am not scared of dying," said Spartacus. "But there is another way. A way with honor!"

A ray of hope lit up Carbo's heart.

"What are you suggesting?" Pulcher called up.

"That we march north. The Romans will try their damnedest to deny us the passage, but I tell you that if we stick to the mountains, we can reach the Alps by late spring. Never fear, if we have to fight, we'll fight. After any battles, I would lead you out of Italy—away from the land that enslaved you. To a freedom that can *never* be taken away!"

Pleased muttering broke out. Faces lit with expectation.

"Where would that be—in Gaul?" asked Gannicus loudly.

"If that's where you want to go. I am sure that your ancestral people would welcome you," answered Spartacus with a smile. "Everyone will be free to do as they wish. Some will want to travel to Germania, Iberia or Scythia. I myself will return to Thrace." *Where I will give Kotys the shock of his life, before killing him.*

"What of the Alps? They are perilous to cross," shouted a man.

"Yet Hannibal crossed them with more than twenty thousand men and his elephants. So too did Brennus the Gaul with his armies—twice. More mountains will not stop us! Besides, if we leave now we will reach them when it's still summer."

A confused clamor broke out below as his words spread.

What will I do if that day comes? wondered Carbo uneasily. He had never imagined leaving his homeland.

"I say that you're a fool and a coward, Spartacus!" cried Crixus furiously. "Italy has everything we need. Grain, money, women and countless slaves to swell our numbers. Why in all the gods' name would we leave it? Why run away?"

"CRIX-US!" yelled a Gaul. His voice was quickly joined by others. More men took up the cry.

Motherless cur, thought Carbo angrily. He longed to draw his sword and attack Crixus, but he couldn't. He'd given his word.

Spartacus' supporters began shouting his name in reply.

I knew it would come to this. Spartacus was saddened by the numbers who appeared to support Crixus. It was more than a third of the army. *Can they not see further than the riches he offers them? Clearly not.* He glanced at the Gaul again. Crixus was stalking toward him, stiff-legged. Castus and Gannicus shuffled backward, out of the way. Spartacus tensed, and let his fingers trail across the hilt of his sica. *So it comes to this again. Great Rider, stay with me now, as you always have.*

"I'm sick of this shit. I ought to stop pissing about and kill you now," snarled Crixus. "That would sort the argument once and for all."

"CRIX-US! CRIX-US!" shouted his men.

BEN KANE

"You tried to beat me once before, and failed. If you want to try again, go ahead," challenged Spartacus, raising his voice so all could hear. "Your last memory of this world will be of my blade opening your throat, and sending you to Hades."

"I don't think so," hissed Crixus. The knuckles of his right hand went white on the handle of his gladius.

"No? Come on, then." Spartacus dropped into a fighting crouch. This was going to be a tricky fight. The top of the ramparts was only six paces wide. One false step for either of them and they'd end their lives by having their brains dashed out on the cobbles far below. He was grateful for the small advantage of having his right arm against the wall. With each blow, he had the chance of throwing Crixus off balance, and over the edge.

"You dare to speak of the gods, Crixus, yet you have not been chosen by one!" Ariadne's tone was commanding. She'd been at the foot of the steps from the beginning, waiting for an opportune moment to appear and speak in Spartacus' favor. This wasn't what she'd had in mind. Her heart was thumping off her ribs with fear. *Dionysus, do not let them start fighting. Please!*

Spartacus stared in astonishment as Ariadne glided past to stand between him and Crixus, who had been shocked into momentary silence. Castus, Gannicus and Carbo were little different. Grim delight pulsed through Spartacus at the sight of her.

Ariadne looked magnificent. She was clad in her finest dress; her black hair was held up by a filigree of gold decorated with pieces of blue glass, and around her right arm she carried her snake. The sight of it had already caused superstitious muttering to break out below them.

"I——" Crixus began, but Ariadne cut him off.

"I am a priestess of Dionysus. You——you are nothing!"

Crixus glared, and took a step toward her.

"Beware Dionysus' serpent! One bite, and you'll die in screaming agony." She brandished the creature at him and the Gaul fell back.

Spartacus rejoiced inside. So did Carbo. Crixus looked like a chastised boy.

Ariadne moved forward to the edge of the rampart, and raised her arm so that the snake was visible to all. "This serpent is the proof that I have been anointed by the god."

"Dionysus! Dionysus! Dionysus!"

Ariadne smiled. "He thanks you for your devotion."

"What would Dionysus have us do?" echoed a voice from the ranks.

"Tell us!" demanded another.

"I had a dream last night," said Ariadne.

Men shouted for quiet, and a hush fell over the army. Spartacus kept a wary eye on Crixus, but the Gaul no longer looked as if he wanted to fight.

"Dionysus wants you all to be free! Truly free! Crossing the Alps is not something to be afraid of. As many of you know, the god was born in a range of mountains far to the east. He will watch over us as we journey out of Italy, to lands that are unconquered by Rome. This I have seen. This I have been told!" cried Ariadne. She held up her arm, and the snake partially uncoiled itself, lifting its head to stare disdainfully at the slaves.

A loud, reverential *Ahhhhh* rippled through the throng.

Carbo was also trembling with awe.

Ariadne gave Spartacus a look and he moved to stand beside her. "Remember the vision that Spartacus had of the snake?"

There was an almighty roar of "YES!"

"He too has been marked by Dionysus. He too is a chosen one."

"SPAR-TA-CUS!" boomed the slaves once more.

She took a step back, allowing Spartacus to assume center stage.

He cupped a hand around his lips, and the slaves fell quiet again. "Who will follow me north, to freedom?"

"I will!" roared Pulcher.

"And I!" cried Carbo passionately. His doubts had vanished. After all, their future had just been determined by a god.

The air filled with the noise of those shouting their allegiance to him, and Spartacus' spirits soared. The great majority of men he could see were now roaring in support of his plan. He gave Ariadne a grateful look before glancing at the others. "Well?"

"You've led us well so far," said Gannicus. "I reckon I'll stick with you on this one."

Spartacus nodded his thanks. "Castus?"

"You've got a point about the Romans not leaving us be." There was an eloquent shrug. "Why not leave Italy? I've always wondered what Gaul looked like."

"Excellent," said Spartacus fiercely. He glared at Crixus. "And you?"

"I'm going nowhere with you," growled the big Gaul. "Thousands of men will be happy to follow where I lead too. You know that."

Spartacus' tension eased as Crixus spoke. At last there was no need to try and keep him on board. Their fight wasn't going to happen either. *Why not acknowledge him?* "It's natural that they would. For all that we do not see eye to eye, you are a great warrior." He glanced at Carbo then, and gave him a tiny nod. He's all yours, the gesture said.

Carbo's muscles froze. This close to Crixus, the man's strength and power were all too obvious. If he attacked the Gaul, he'd be committing suicide. *Is that what I want? Is that what Chloris would have wanted?* No, his heart answered. She'd have wanted me to live. I want to live.

Spartacus saw his indecision. *I gave him his chance.* "May the gods make your road easy," he said to Crixus, "and grant you victory over every Roman army in your path."

Crixus' eyes widened with surprise. A half-smile tugged its way on to his face. "Fuck me, I never thought I'd say something like this, but may they grant the same to you."

May they indeed, prayed Ariadne, trying to ignore the worry in the pit of her stomach. She'd seen no bad omens, but none of the details of her "dream" were true. She had made it all up for Spartacus, to prevent a fight with Crixus, and to help win the slaves over. *Forgive me, Dionysus. I meant no disrespect. You have no more loyal devotee than I.*

As Spartacus and Crixus nodded grimly at each other, she redoubled her prayers.

Only time would tell, however, if the god had been angered by her fabrication.

†

Crassus was eating a breakfast of bread and olives when Saenius came sloping into the courtyard. Wiping his lips fastidiously, Crassus waited for the other to approach his table. "What is it?"

"Publius Varinius is here."

Before he has even explained himself to the Senate? This I had not expected. Crassus hid his surprise by dabbing at his mouth again. "What does he want?" he asked offhandedly.

Seeing through his master's charade, Saenius chuckled. "He's here to see if you can save him!"

"The man needs help, all right." News of the disaster that had overcome Varinius' troops had taken barely three days to reach the capital. *Varinius now follows in its wake—like a lost dog finds its way home, expecting a beating.*

"Shall I send him away?"

"No. I want to hear what happened from his own lips."

Saenius hurried off. He soon returned with a sheepish-looking Varinius in tow. "The praetor Publius Varinius," he announced.

Crassus waited for several moments before even acknowledging Varinius' presence. When he did, it was with frosty surprise. "Ah, praetor. You have returned to us."

"Yes."

"Thank the gods. It's a great shame that so many of your men did not also survive," Crassus added in a tone of great sorrow.

"Their deaths hang around my neck like a millstone," said Varinius miserably.

"And so they should! Along with the loss of Furius' and Cossinius' men," Crassus snapped. "Virtually everything I have heard of your actions against Spartacus smacks of utter incompetence!"

Varinius did not dare to reply. He hung his head in shame.

"Tell me what happened at Thurii. I want to understand it for myself."

The words fell out of Varinius in a veritable tide. His withdrawal to Cumae after the surprise of Spartacus' disappearance. The long hunt for new recruits. Issues with desertion, near mutiny, disease and finding enough equipment for his men. The search for Spartacus during the foul weather of autumn and winter. After weeks of fruitless marching, the unexpected good news that Spartacus had besieged Thurii. Varinius' plan to crush the slaves between his infantry and cavalry. The shock of the ambush. The slaves' overwhelming numbers. Galba's charge, and his death at Spartacus' hands. The rout that followed. The incredible appearance of enemy cavalry. Varinius' attempts to rally his men for a counterattack, and their total refusal to do so. Somehow pulling together the survivors. Organizing treatment for the wounded and maimed, and then his return to Rome. Varinius looked exhausted by the time he'd finished.

He's not a complete fool, thought Crassus with a twinge of conscience. Who could have predicted that the town was already in Spartacus' hands? Naturally, he wasn't going to admit that to Varinius. "Clearly, you are here to report this sorry tale to the Senate. I expected to see you there later this morning," Crassus said, softening his tone a fraction. "Why have you come to me before doing your duty?"

Varinius looked up. There was a desperate expression on his long face. "I am a loyal servant of the Republic. Whatever punishment is handed down to me, I will accept."

"I'm glad to hear it," replied Crassus acerbically.

"I thought—I wondered, after your letter, if you might see a way to lending me some support."

"Some support?" Crassus' voice was silky-smooth.

"The senators will be out for my blood. If you were to speak for me, they could be swayed..." Varinius went to say more, but stopped himself.

Crassus considered his options. Did he need the fealty of a failed fellow praetor? No. Would it look good to back a man who had lost repeatedly to a runaway gladiator? Most certainly not. He eyed Varinius sidelong, feeling a modicum of sympathy for the wretch. Was there any benefit at all in defending him? It only took Crassus a heartbeat to decide. "You have failed utterly in the mission entrusted to you by the Senate. Why in Hades' name would I utter a word in your favor?"

"I—"

"I am not without heart, however. If, in the wake of your passing, your family needs a loan to carry them through the lean times ahead, I will be happy to oblige. I charge very little interest."

A nerve twitched in Varinius' cheek, and he swallowed hard. With an effort, he composed himself. "Thank you, but that won't be necessary."

"Very well. If that's all, then . . ." Crassus picked up an olive, and studied it carefully before popping it into his mouth. He did not look at Varinius again.

Saenius materialized at Varinius' elbow. "If you'll follow me, sir?"

"Yes, I . . ." Varinius' voice faltered. "Of course." With slumped shoulders, he followed Saenius from the courtyard.

Crassus watched him go. When he has finished his report, the Senate will offer him only one choice, he thought. Varinius is a dead man walking. That was of little concern. What caused Crassus more disquiet was the fact that Spartacus—the gladiator he'd seen fight and with whom he'd spoken—had turned out to be a formidable foe. Spartacus' successes could no longer just be put down to chance, ill-fortune or poor judgment on the Roman commanders' part. There had been too many defeats, over too many legionaries.

Spartacus wasn't lying when I talked with him, mused Crassus. He is a man to be reckoned with. What a shame he wasn't the one to be defeated that day in Capua. He'd be maggot food now, instead of a thorn in Rome's side.

Crassus hoped that his fellows in the Senate now recognized the danger posed by Spartacus. He would do his utmost to make sure that they did. The insult to the Republic's honor could be tolerated no longer. Both consuls would have to go to war.

Spartacus has to die. And soon.

XX

Typically, it was Atheas who sensed that there was something wrong. Raising a hand, he stopped. Used to their routine, Carbo came to a halt. He was some twenty steps behind the bearded Scythian on a narrow game track that led northward through the foothills of the Apennines, the mountains that formed Italy's spine. Since the army had left the ruined city of Thurii behind them, they had followed similar paths. Carbo had soon grown bored of the drudgery and repetitive routine of marching day after day. Dark thoughts about Crixus, and the fact that he had not tried to kill him, had also dogged his every step. Desperate to shake the gloom that had coated him, Carbo had begged Spartacus to let him join one of the scouts on their solitary missions.

"Why are you wanting to do that?" the Thracian had asked.

"To learn a new skill," Carbo had answered evasively. *And so I can track down Crixus one day.* It might have been pure fantasy, but he still longed to kill the big Gaul. In his tortured mind, for him to have any peace, Chloris had to be avenged.

"There are no better trackers than Atheas and Taxacis," Spartacus had said. "But they won't be interested in letting you tag along." Seeing the anger in Carbo's eyes, he'd relented. "I'll ask for you."

To Carbo's surprise, Atheas had agreed. Whether it was because Spartacus had insisted, he didn't know. Nor did he care. Naturally enough, he had been very wary the first time the Scythian had led him from the camp. Since the time of the confrontation over Navio, their relationship had been one of extreme suspicion. Although Atheas had killed Lugurix, Carbo still feared his blade, and it seemed that despite all that Carbo had done for Spartacus, the Scythian distrusted him. Unsurprisingly, their relationship had got off to a difficult start.

Wanting to make as good a fist of his opportunity as possible, Carbo had aped Atheas' every move and obeyed his orders without question. He was given no recognition for this; indeed Atheas had run him ragged, often covering upward of twenty-five miles a day. The Scythian ate and drank sparingly, making Carbo wonder where he got his incredible stamina from. Biting his lip, he'd learned to get by on similarly small quantities of food and water. They lived in virtual silence, only talking when absolutely necessary.

Time passed, and Carbo became skillful at lighting campfires and gutting game. He could even bring down a deer with an arrow more times than he missed. To his surprise, he also gained some proficiency at the difficult art of tracking. Carbo wasn't sure how or why, but he had eventually won Atheas' approval. A nod here, a proffered piece of meat there, were the little indications he'd had, but those gestures had meant the world to him. Atheas' tiny smile when Carbo had thanked him for killing Lugurix had meant even more. Fortunately, the hard scouting life had also lessened his grief over Chloris. Now it was just a dull ache, rather than the stabbing pain it had been before.

"Pssst!"

He blinked and came back to reality.

Atheas was beckoning him closer.

Sliding his feet over the ground as he'd been taught, Carbo advanced until he was at the Scythian's shoulder.

Atheas pointed through a gap in the trees that lined the side of the track. Carbo peered between the leaves, down the steep slope that led to the bottom of the wooded valley, which ran in a north–south direction. At its floor was a small road, which led to Mutina, some twenty miles away. It was the flash of sunlight on metal that caught his eye. Adrenaline pumped through Carbo's veins as he focused in on a large group of horsemen in bronze helmets, barely visible through the forest canopy. "Cavalry," he whispered.

"Yes," hissed Atheas. "They . . . looking for us."

Since word had come a month before that G. Cornelius Lentulus Clodianus, one of the consuls, was pursuing them with his two legions, Carbo had been expecting this moment. That didn't stop a tide of bile washing up his throat. He'd hoped against hope that Spartacus would lead them straight to the Alps without encountering another Roman army. Of course that had been nothing but a foolish dream, he thought. The horsemen's presence was proof that Lentulus' legionaries must have caught up with and overtaken them. It wouldn't have been hard. The progress of the fifty thousand slaves had been painfully slow. "What do we do?"

"Can't . . . fight." Atheas glanced at Carbo with an evil grin. "Unless . . . you want . . . die still?"

He hadn't hidden his misery that well then. Carbo grimaced. "No. It would be a complete waste. Spartacus needs to hear about this."

"He does. But first . . . we head north. Search for . . . main force."

"There could be enemy scouts on these paths."

"Yes. We must be . . . ghosts. Or we end up . . ." Making a low, guttural sound, Atheas drew a finger across his throat.

Carbo's eyes flashed in the direction of their camp.

Atheas pounced on his reaction. "You want . . . go back? Tell Spartacus about . . . cavalry?"

"No." They'd seen nothing for weeks. He wasn't going to miss out on this.

"Sure?" Atheas' voice had gone hard.

"Yes," replied Carbo firmly.

A curt nod. The Scythian unslung his bow from his back. Bending his knee, he slipped the gut string into place. Carbo copied him at once. When he'd nocked an arrow to his own string, he looked up. "Follow me," whispered Atheas. "We go quick."

Then they were off, trotting down the path, passing through the strips of sunlight like two dancing shadows. The game path looped and twisted its way along the side of the valley for some four or five miles, and they followed its undulations as fast as was humanly possible. The pair traveled in silence, maintaining a keen eye out for enemy scouts. Through great fortune, they did not come across anything for upward of an hour. When they finally did, it was not another human, but a wild boar. Startled by their rapid approach, the creature squealed and fled in the opposite direction, its tail raised high with indignation.

Carbo smiled at its reaction, but Atheas frowned and came to a halt. "We move slow now."

Carbo's lips began to frame the word "Why?" when he realized. "If someone is on the track, they'll wonder what scared the pig?"

"Yes." Atheas pulled back his bow to half-draw and jabbed the arrow tip around him. "Look everywhere. If you see something . . . don't ask. Just loose."

"All right." Suddenly, Carbo's mouth was as dry as tinder. He wasn't going anywhere, though, except forward. Spartacus had placed his trust in him, and he could not betray that.

They crept along the path, around a bend and then another, without seeing a thing. Atheas paused, and Carbo readied himself to let fly. But the Scythian indicated a freshly trampled way off into the scrubby vegetation that lined the forest floor. "Boar went . . . this way. Good."

Carbo nodded.

A few moments later, Atheas suddenly stopped dead again. Before them, the track burst out of the cover of the trees, on to a huge area filled with blackened stumps and charred branches. This in itself was not unusual. Fires commonly swept through the forests in summertime. The aftermath scarred the landscape for years, until the vegetation grew back and concealed the evidence. They moved carefully to the edge of the living trees. It wasn't the vista provided by the gaping hole in the forest that set Carbo's heart thumping in his chest, but what he could see because of it.

The valley broadened at this, its northern end, revealing an area of flatter farmland that spilled down toward Mutina. The road here was wider, and it was filled as far as the eye could see. With legionaries— thousands of them, marching in line like so many ants. Here and there in the column, Carbo could also see groups of horsemen.

"The consular army. It can't be anything else." There was a sickening feeling in Carbo's gut. "They outflanked us."

"How many men?" Atheas' gaze was flickering to and fro like that of a hawk on its prey.

"Ten thousand legionaries. Six hundred cavalry, maybe more."

"You're sure?"

"Yes. Each consul commands two legions. That force isn't big enough for Gellius, the second consul, to be here as well." A black mood took Carbo. "He's probably on our arse."

Atheas threw him a rebuking look. "Taxacis seen . . . nothing. With gods' help . . . other whoreson . . . hunting Crixus."

"Let it be so," breathed Carbo. *May Gellius find him and shred the bastard into little pieces.* What of the rest? his conscience screamed. Fuck them, his rage shouted back. Their fate is their own. They followed Crixus, not Spartacus.

Atheas touched Carbo's arm, bringing him back to the present. "No need . . . see more. We go back. Fast." With that, he'd pushed past and was off down the track as if Cerberus were after him.

Carbo followed, a surge of adrenaline giving him extra speed. The sooner Spartacus knew about this, the better. *What will he do?* Carbo wasn't sure. One thing was for certain, though. They couldn't march around Lentulus and escape. The legions were capable of covering up to twenty miles a day. A battle was inevitable now, and when it came, it would put all their previous clashes in the shade.

Carbo felt traitorous for again asking Jupiter to support Spartacus against his own kind, but he did so anyway. Even with their superiority in numbers, they would need all the help they could get. Facing a full-strength consular army was a very different proposition to every other force they'd come up against. Despite the fact that the troops were only newly raised, this would be Rome close to its deadliest.

Carbo felt uneasy at the mere idea of it. Have faith in Spartacus, he told himself. He'll have a plan. What, though? *Most of our men won't stand up to a line of armored soldiers two legions wide. They will turn and run.* Gritting his teeth, Carbo concentrated on keeping up with Atheas.

But the horror of what could easily happen kept flashing into his mind.

†

By the time they reached the rebel camp, which sprawled over several large clearings in the forest, the sun was falling in the sky. When they were spotted, questions flew at the pair thick and fast. Atheas pretended not to understand. Carbo just ducked his head and kept walking. There was no way he was saying a word to anyone but Spartacus. News like this could cause panic.

They found their leader sitting with Ariadne and Taxacis by a small fire in front of his tent. An iron tripod suspended a pot over the flames, and a delicious smell laced the air. Carbo's stomach grumbled. He hadn't eaten since the morning. *Forget about it. There'll be time for food later.*

Spartacus smiled as he saw them approach. "Perfect timing. The stew is ready."

"We bring . . . urgent news," Atheas began.

"It can wait, surely?"

"I—" protested Carbo.

"When was the last time you ate?" interjected Spartacus.

"Dawn," admitted Carbo.

"Then your stomach must be clapped to your backbone," said Ariadne. "Come. Sit." She produced a blanket.

Shrugging, Atheas sat down opposite Spartacus. Still worried, but silenced by Spartacus' insistence, Carbo joined him. Spoons, bowls of steaming stew and lumps of flat bread were handed out, and a silence fell that was broken only by the sound of chewing and appreciative grunts.

Ariadne watched Carbo and Atheas with a keen eye and tried hard not to let her worries consume her. *It's got to be bad news. Why else would Carbo have a face like thunder?* Atheas was harder to read, but the tension in his shoulders was unmistakable. Ariadne wanted to shake Spartacus and tell him to ask them what they'd seen, but she held back, instead smiling and offering more stew. *He'll have his reasons.*

When Carbo and Atheas were finished, Spartacus lifted a small amphora that had been lying by his side. "Some wine?"

"Yes," Atheas growled happily.

Carbo nodded. He was burning to reveal their news, but he had to wait until Spartacus ordered them to speak. He swilled the wine around his mouth, enjoying it despite himself.

"So it's true! They're back," cried Gannicus, closing in on the fire. Castus was two steps behind him. Both men's faces were set with worry. "What news?" He threw the question at Spartacus, not Carbo or Atheas.

"I don't know yet," came the reply.

"Eh?" barked Castus. "Why ever not?"

"Look at them. They're filthy. Tired. They haven't eaten for twelve hours or more. I fed them first. Looking after my men comes before anything else."

Respect and a little awe flared in both Gauls' eyes. "Of course," muttered Castus.

Ariadne nearly laughed out loud at the beauty, and simplicity, of it. Spartacus had known all along that the other leaders would hear of the scouts' return, and come hurrying to hear what they'd seen. No doubt he wanted to know just as much as they did, but waiting was real proof that he was cool under pressure. That he was not frightened of what was to come. She glanced at Carbo, seeing he had come to the same realization.

Spartacus carefully poured wine for Castus and Gannicus, and re-filled Carbo and Atheas' cups, Ariadne's and his own. He raised it in the air, and waited until everyone else had done the same. "To the victories we have won! To the bonds of comradeship we have forged! To Dionysus and the Great Rider!"

"Dionysus and the Great Rider!" They all drank deeply.

"Now." Spartacus fixed Atheas with a gimlet stare. "Tell me everything."

There was a reverent silence as the Scythian began to speak. He threw an occasional glance at Carbo for confirmation, which pleased the young Roman greatly. Despite Atheas' accented words and poor Latin, he drew a vivid picture of the legions blocking their path. When he was done, he simply folded his hands in his lap and waited for Spartacus to speak.

"So there can be no doubt," said the Thracian, raising an eyebrow at Carbo.

"No."

"What of the other consular army?" asked Gannicus at once.

Atheas shrugged. "We did not see it."

"Maybe it's already behind us," said Castus uneasily, "and they're planning on squeezing us between them."

"No. Our mounted scouts are always some twenty miles behind the main force. Taxacis has been busy too. We would have had word by now if we were being followed. Who knows where Gellius is, but he's not immediately to the south of here." Spartacus eyed Carbo again. "The legions are how far ahead of us?"

"It's as Atheas says. Four or five miles."

"We'll come upon them tomorrow then," said Castus with a curse. "I knew we wouldn't reach the Alps!"

"It was always going to be a long shot for us to do that," reproved Spartacus. "We've done well to get here without having to fight." He did not voice the dark joy that had flared within him. All his life, he had dreamed of taking on a consular army. Of avenging his dead brother while teaching Rome a bloody lesson. Now the gods had granted him that opportunity.

"So near, and yet so far!" moaned Castus. "The damn mountains might as well be a thousand miles away."

"Peace," said Gannicus. "Things aren't that bad. We have nearly five men for every Roman, and these legions are brand new. They're untested in battle."

"Aye, but our soldiers aren't Roman citizens, who are weaned on stories of war and conquest. They're not all wearing a mail coat. Barely half of them have decent swords, and even fewer than that possess a shield." There was a discernible note of fear in Castus' voice. "D'you really think they'll stand against a legionary shield wall?"

"Of course they will," Gannicus grumbled, but he couldn't hide his uncertainty.

Ariadne wanted to speak, but she held her tongue. This was down to the men. To Spartacus.

Carbo tried to ignore Castus' unsettling words. Yet the Gaul had a point. He worried that the slaves' newfound confidence would not be enough. *We can't get away, and we can't fight them in open battle.* He glanced at Atheas, but got no reassurance there. The Scythian's face was a cold, unreadable mask; Taxacis' features were a mirror image of this. Carbo wished that he could be so inscrutable.

"The men might not have the martial background you describe, Castus. They aren't as well equipped as the Romans either. But what they do have"—Spartacus looked at each of them in turn—"is the burning desire to be free! They won't suffer the ignominy of being enslaved again. Am I not right?"

"You are," said Gannicus.

"Yes!" cried Taxacis.

"Anything . . . better than ludus," growled Atheas. "I . . . die before go back . . . that shithole."

"I suppose you could be right," Castus admitted.

"That is our secret weapon," said Spartacus, feeling encouraged. "That is what will win the day for us."

"But we can't take on two legions in open battle. Can we?" cried Carbo, desperate to believe.

"No one asked you to speak." Spartacus' tone was stern. Carbo colored. "For myself, I think that we *could* fight the whoresons face to face. However, I've got a far better idea than that."

"Tell us," urged Gannicus.

"Do you want to know, Castus?"

"By Taranis, I do!"

"While Atheas and Carbo were making their way back, I was checking out the lie of the land around the camp." Spartacus winked. "It's a little habit that my father taught me."

"What did you find?" asked Carbo eagerly.

"A spot where the road narrows as it passes between two sheer rock faces. At the southern end of the defile is a flattish area that is large enough to hold at least ten thousand troops. I'm going to position our best men there. Another fifteen thousand, under Egbeo and Pulcher, will be hidden in a pair of side valleys. When the enemy scouts arrive in the morning, as surely they must, they'll go haring back to tell Lentulus the good news that their forces 'equal' ours. When the Romans return, we'll let their cavalry and one legion pass through, but then the men who are waiting on the cliff tops will roll down boulders, killing as many of the scumbags as they can. Their main purpose, however, will be to split Lentulus' forces in two. Once that happens, the remainder of the army and all of our cavalry will fall on the second legion from behind." A feral grin creased Spartacus' face.

"Where will they hide?" asked Gannicus.

"In the broken ground on either side of the road. There are hundreds of places to stay out of sight."

"By all the gods, that sounds good!" bellowed Gannicus. "We'll give those bastards a surprise they'll never forget."

Carbo was thrilled. *Spartacus always has a plan!*

Even Castus looked slightly less dubious.

Ariadne's smile was bright, but her nerves were in tatters. The trap was decidedly risky. What if the Roman cavalry got wind of the hidden slaves, or spotted those lying in wait above the defile? Even if the ambush worked, the fighting on either side of the blockage would be absolutely savage. Thousands of men would die. She closed her eyes, asking for Dionysus' protection, and feverishly hoping that her previous transgressions would continue to go unnoticed. Unpunished. *Let Spartacus survive at least.*

"Where will you stand?" inquired Gannicus.

"I shall lead the men who serve as bait for Lentulus," answered Spartacus.

The Gauls looked unsurprised, but a little disappointed.

"Destroying the second legion is just as important as taking on the first. Would you do me that honor?"

Pride restored, they grinned their acknowledgment.

Spartacus glanced at Carbo. "I need a reliable man to take charge of rolling down the rocks."

Carbo couldn't hide his disappointment that he hadn't been selected to fight. "If you're sure . . ."

"I am," observed Spartacus firmly. "It's critical that the pass is entirely blocked. Think you can do it?"

"Of course," replied Carbo fiercely. "I'll do it if it kills me." He felt a tinge of panic. "When do you want me to begin the barrage?"

"As soon as half the Roman force has come through."

"How will I know that?"

"Do a rough headcount as they pass below you."

"Right." Carbo's stomach twisted. The task before him was huge.

Spartacus appeared not to notice. He gave each man an encouraging smile. "Then we have a plan. May the Great Rider ensure its success."

As the men drank a toast, Ariadne threw up a fervent prayer, for the favor of one god was not enough. *May Dionysus lend his aid too.* Even when Ariadne had finished, she felt little better. The deity she followed was renowned for his capricious nature. One tiny slip-up in the morning and the whole ambush could fail.

For some reason, she couldn't put that possibility from her mind.

†

When Carbo retired that night, he barely slept a wink. The day he'd entered the ludus, he could never have imagined that his path would involve following a runaway gladiator. Yet fate had led to that very end. Since their dramatic escape, events had taken on a life of their own.

Spartacus' growing trust in him had engendered in Carbo a fierce loyalty. It had enabled him to override his worries about fighting his own countrymen. Nonetheless, the idea of ambushing a consul—one of the two most powerful men in the Republic—was still shocking. Carbo tossed and turned on his blanket, trying to reconcile the irreconcilable, and failing. In the dark before dawn, he finally confided in Navio, with whom he was again sharing a tent. "If I do this, I can never return to normal life. To simply being a Roman."

"Eh?" Navio glanced at him as if he was mad. "You can never do that anyway. No more than I can!"

"Why not?" Carbo didn't want to admit that he'd already gone too far.

"Think about it."

He knew that Navio was right. Nothing would ever be the same again. Even the idea of traveling to Rome in search of his family had palled. His parents would be overjoyed, but he would never be able to reveal to them what he'd done. How could he now become a lawyer, like his self-important uncle? Returning to civilian life anywhere in Italy, which was not that appealing, would also be laced with danger. If anyone got the tiniest whiff of what he'd got up to with Spartacus, he'd be exiled, or worse. Carbo frowned. Where else could he go, but with Spartacus? He gazed at Navio through the gloom. "What would we do in Thrace?"

"Who knows? Serve Spartacus. It wouldn't take him long to carve out a kingdom for himself. I can think of worse things than being part of something like that. It'd beat being ground down by those whoresons in Rome."

"Leave Italy?" It felt strange questioning it, given that that had been their aim for months. Yet it was only now beginning to feel real.

"Why would I do anything else?" hissed Navio. "There's nothing left here for me!"

"I'll never get my revenge on Crixus."

"Come on. You knew that when you didn't attack him at Thurii."

Carbo tried to come up with another argument in favor of staying, and failed. "You're right. I'll go with Spartacus, wherever he leads us."

"Don't count your chickens before they're hatched," warned Navio, punching him on the shoulder. "We have a battle to win first! So while there's time, get some more sleep." Pulling up his blanket, he rolled over and was snoring within moments.

Carbo was envious of Navio's ability to fall asleep no matter what was going on. There was still little light visible through the leather, but he knew that he wasn't going to get any more rest. It wasn't just him, though. He could hear noises from other tents: coughing, snuffling, men whispering to each other. Carbo threw off his blankets. He might as well check over his equipment one last time. No doubt his sword could do with an even keener edge. Tugging up the flap, he was startled to see a figure standing by the remains of their fire. He blinked in surprise. It was Spartacus. He raised a finger to his lips, and so Carbo approached without saying a word.

"Can't sleep? Neither can I," said Spartacus in a low voice.

"What brings you here?"

"I wanted to talk to you."

Carbo smiled as if it were the most normal thing in the world for his leader to come to his tent in secret. "About what?"

"I need to ask you a favor."

A favor? Carbo's heart began to pound.

"There was a reason that I picked you to be in charge of the stones."

"You think I'm a coward," accused Carbo hotly. "That I won't stand and fight."

"No!" Spartacus gripped his shoulder. "That is *so* far from the truth. I have seen your courage enough times not to doubt it. And I trust you as I do few others." *Yet he's a Roman.* The irony was not lost on him.

"Really?" Carbo's eyes searched his leader's.

"Yes. I want you to do something for me. A thing that I would ask no one else. Will you do it?"

"Of course," replied Carbo instantly.

"If we lose today—"

"We won't," Carbo burst in.

"Your faith in me is encouraging, yet my plan is full of risk. So many things have to fall into place. If just one detail goes wrong, everything will fall apart. If that happens, defeat will lie around the corner. I know this."

The truth of Spartacus' words hung in the air like the stink of a rotting carcass.

Carbo couldn't bring himself to argue, so he just nodded.

"If the worst happens, it will be very clear. The moment that you're sure the battle is lost, I want you to leave your men and return to the camp. Go to my tent, and find Ariadne. Atheas will be there, guarding her. He knows that you're to take charge. You're to lead her away from here. To safety."

Carbo was awestruck by the responsibility he'd just asked to accept. Grief thickened his throat at the mere idea of it. If this duty ever came to pass, Spartacus would be dead. *Dead. Like Chloris.*

"Here."

Numbly, Carbo accepted the heavy leather pouch Spartacus handed him.

"There's enough in there to keep you all for a year, maybe longer."

"Where do you want me to go?"

Spartacus gave a bitter chuckle. "Anywhere, as long as it's safe. Find a little town on the coast of Illyria, or maybe in Greece. Live a quiet life. I want to know that my son grew up under your guidance and Atheas' protection."

"Your son? Ariadne is . . ."

"Yes, she's with child. Do you understand now why your task is so important?"

"Yes," Carbo whispered.

"So, will you do it?"

Carbo was staggered by the tone of humility in Spartacus' voice. This was no order, but a heartfelt request from one man to another. "Of course! If the worst happens, Ariadne will be saved. I swear it!"

"Thank you. That makes my load lighter." Spartacus squeezed his shoulder once, hard. "Tell no one of this, obviously."

"I won't."

"Good." His teeth flashed in the darkness. "Now, we'd best get ready, eh? There will be many thousands of Romans to kill. I'll see you when it's all over."

"Yes."

With that, Spartacus was gone, slipping off into the gloom like a wraith.

Gods, let us meet again.

"Who was that?" Navio's head popped out of the tent.

"Egbeo," Carbo lied. "He wanted to know how many men I was taking to the cliffs."

"Rather you than me," grunted Navio. "It's more bloody, but I'd rather stick a sword in a man's guts than crush him like a beetle underfoot."

Carbo smiled, but all his thoughts were on his secret mission. By choosing him, Spartacus had shown him great honor. Yet it was a duty that he did not want, because if it came to pass, the man he idolized would be dead. Jupiter, Greatest and Best, he prayed desperately. *Whatever happens, let us win. Grant us victory!*

Carbo was used to the silence that met his requests of the gods, but this time it resounded in his head like the emptiness of a stone dropped into a bottomless well.

†

They moved out soon after, while the sun was still below the horizon. Clouds of exhaled breath filled the cold air as Carbo's troops tramped through the darkness. It wasn't more than a mile to the spot that Spartacus had ordered them to, which lent a palpable air of anticipation to the march. Although there was no pressing need yet to remain quiet, the men's conversations were held in muttered tones. Working from the description he'd been given, Carbo led his force, some two hundred strong, northward up a slope between groups of twisted junipers and sturdy holm oak trees. The vegetation gradually died away, leaving exposed great slabs of rock that were covered in rosettes of gray-green lichen.

They had climbed a short distance when the stone opened up in a gaping chasm. It stretched from left to right for some distance and was about twenty score paces across. Carbo walked up to the edge, and looked down. The drop was precipitous. Cursing, he took a step backward. The wind that gusted to and fro here could easily sweep a man to his death. Lying down, he crawled to the lip with a great deal more caution. The view was breathtaking. At least five hundred paces below, the thin ribbon that was the road threaded its way along the valley floor. The only sign of life was a pair of ravens that were chattering noisily to each other as they banked and turned on the early-morning air currents.

Carbo's gaze flickered from side to side, assessing the best spot for the ambush. Unsurprisingly, his eyes focused on the narrowest part of the gorge. There the two sides were little more than a good spear's throw apart. He made his mind up at once. Anything that was dropped from that point could not fail to strike anyone on the road. A roseate glow to the east told him that dawn was approaching. Time was of the essence. Carbo began issuing orders.

The physical labor that followed filled him with relief. Finally, he was able to put what he'd been asked to do from his mind. Even the thought of killing hundreds of his fellow countrymen was better than thinking about Spartacus lying bloodied and still on the field below. If he died, Carbo did not know how he would bear it.

XXI

S partacus eyed the sky, which was filled with dark, lowering thunderclouds. It wouldn't be long until the heavens opened. At this altitude, it wouldn't be surprising if the precipitation fell as hail, or even snow. He wasn't the only one to have noticed. Men were casting nervous eyes upward, and whispering unhappily to one another. *Damn it all. The weather's been fine for weeks. Why does it have to change now?* Spartacus refused to countenance what his troops were thinking: that the gods were angry. *The plan is good. It will work.* Those were the words that Ariadne had whispered in his ear as he'd left her in the camp.

All the same, their fates hung by the slimmest of threads. He would have to move among the men now or panic would spread. And the damn rain had to hold off, or there might be no battle. The enemy scouts had been and gone some time before. By now, Lentulus knew where they were. Yet if the ground was going to be reduced to a mud-soaked swamp, he'd probably choose not to advance. Only a fool chose to fight in such treacherous conditions, and Spartacus doubted that a man who'd become consul fell into that category. *Let's hope that Lentulus is possessed of the same arrogance that I saw in Crassus.* Spartacus was relying on that overweening Roman sense of superiority: that despite hearing of his successes, Lentulus would refuse even to entertain the notion that he, a renegade gladiator, would be capable of more than the most primitive battle plan. With his men in plain sight, what else could he be trying here but a full-blown battle?

It will work, Spartacus told himself. Carbo will succeed in blocking the gorge. His men would hold before the savagery of the Roman assault. Pulcher and Egbeo would fall on the Romans like Vulcan's hammers. Castus' and Gannicus' forces would also prevail. Squaring his shoulders, Spartacus strode out in front of his troops. They bellowed their love for him, and he raised his arms in recognition of it. As the noise abated, he told them of their bravery in following him from the ludus or in running away from their masters. He praised their efforts during the arduous training, the sweat they'd shed and the hardships they had endured beneath Navio's iron discipline. "For a Roman, he's not bad," Spartacus shouted, and they roared with laughter.

The tension eased a little, and he paced to and fro, reminding them of each incredible victory that they'd won. How, despite being betrayed, he and seventy-odd men had broken out of the ludus. How the impossible task of defeating three thousand soldiers had been achieved by climbing down a cliff and causing panic in Glaber's camp. How they'd repeated their success against first Furius, and then Cossinius. As if that wasn't remarkable enough, they had given Varinius the slip, and when he had finally found them at Thurii, they had virtually annihilated his entire command. Although the fool had survived, the Senate had ordered him to fall on his sword when he'd brought the news of his disgrace to Rome.

The yells of delight grew louder and louder with every detail.

Spartacus encouraged his men with fierce waves of his arms. They'd need every scrap of self-belief possible in the fight to come.

The clamor abated gradually, and he glanced up. Miraculously, the black clouds had moved on without drenching them. The rain or hail would now fall on the peaks to the south, he judged. *Thank you, Great Rider.* He drew his sword and pointed it at the sky. "Look! The gods' favor is still with us! The storm is passing."

"Is there anything you can't do?" cried a voice.

"I try my best, Aventianus," Spartacus replied with a wink. Hoots of amusement rose from his men. *What perfect timing. I must thank Aventianus afterward.* Instantly, doubt flared up in his mind. *Don't tempt fate. I'll tell him if he survives. If I survive.*

A man nearby cupped a hand to his ear. "What's that?"

A hush fell over the slaves.

For a heart-stopping moment, there was silence. Then the unmistakable blare of trumpets carried down the wind.

"They're here!"

A visible tremor passed through the ranks.

Spartacus' misgivings, however, vanished like dawn mist beneath the rising sun. This was his purpose. To fight Rome. It was not in his homeland, as he'd wished, but that didn't matter. He had been granted the chance to take on a Roman army commanded by one of its consuls. What more could he ask for? *Victory,* he thought. *That's what I want. Nothing else is good enough.*

Spartacus filled his lungs. Throwing back his head, he cried, "There are only ten thousand of the whoresons. How many are we?"

"Fifty thousand!" Aventianus called out.

"That's right! FIFTY THOUSAND!" Spartacus bawled. "Five of us for every stinking Roman! We will have VICTORY—OR DEATH!"

There was the slightest delay, and then his men echoed the refrain until the very cliffs resounded with it. "VICTORY OR DEATH! VICTORY OR DEATH!"

Spartacus picked up his scutum and began to hammer his blade off its iron rim. "Come on!" he shouted. "Do the same. The Romans must take our bait, and march into the gorge without thinking."

There were fierce grins from those who heard. At once they began to emulate him. More slaves joined in. The noise spread through the army like wildfire. For the moment at least, the fear that the thunderclouds had engendered was gone. So too was the uncertainty of facing a full-strength Roman legion. Battle rage took some men, who screamed until their faces went purple. A mad euphoric feeling descended on others. Cracked laughs rang out, and the front ranks swayed forward a few steps until their officers chivvied them back into line.

Spartacus had never heard a racket like it since he'd first ridden with his tribe to war against Rome. An age ago, in Thrace, when the Maedi had lost. Pride filled him now, however. For all that these men were slaves, they had the courage of true warriors. If a battle began, they *would* stand and fight. Spartacus felt the certainty of that in his heart. Today perhaps the bloodstained shame of the previous defeat would be erased once and for all.

A series of angry trumpet blasts echoed through the defile.

Spartacus smiled with satisfaction. Lentulus *did* want a fight.

Now it was down to Carbo to spoil the consul's party.

†

High on the cliff tops, Carbo heard the Roman *bucinae* too. He was lying on his belly at the northernmost end of the gorge, observing the first legion emerging around a bend in the road. Before it rode several squadrons of cavalry, the scouts who had brought the news of the slave army to Lentulus. As he watched, a large group of horsemen broke away and rode forward into the defile. Carbo stared at them in alarm. *What in Hades are they doing?* He was grateful that his common sense kicked in. They're going to ensure that Spartacus hasn't blocked off the exit. That's it. So Lentulus isn't a fool, Carbo thought, glancing around uneasily. Maybe that's not all he wants checked out.

Rock scraped off rock, and Carbo craned his neck to see over the edge. He'd never been more grateful to be lying down, not to be profiled against the sky. Climbing up the scree-covered slope from the direction of the legions were four—five—six dark-skinned, bearded men. Barefoot, they were clad in short-sleeved tunics. Their only weapons were the slings draped around their necks. Carbo had seen Balearic slingers once before, in Capua. They were fast-moving skirmishers

who also acted as scouts. Clearly, these men had been sent to recon-
noitre the cliff top. Carbo's mouth went bone dry with fear.

They had to be killed, and fast, or Spartacus' whole plan would
fall apart, and Carbo's task of saving Ariadne would become a dreadful reality.

Carbo rolled away, out of sight, and jumped to his feet. Sprinting to
the nearest of his soldiers, he explained what was going on. Alarm filled
their faces, and a new urgency filled Carbo. "None can escape, or we're
all fucked! Get it?"

They nodded grimly.

"The dogs will see what's going on the moment they reach the
top, so they have to be taken down instantly. Out of sight of the legions too."

One man picked up a hunting bow. "I can deal with two, if not
three of them."

"Good," said Carbo. *If only I had more archers!* "Make it two, so you
don't miss. The last ones to come up as well." He pointed at three other
slaves in turn. "We'll hide behind the last piles of stones. You take the
first man; you the second; and you the third. I'll take the fourth. None
of you make a damn move until I do. Clear?"

"Yes," they muttered.

Quickly ordering everyone else to conceal themselves, and to remain silent, Carbo ran back to the piles of stones nearest to where he
thought the slingers would emerge. There was precious little cover for
all of them. Carbo prayed it would be sufficient. A heartbeat later, the
next shortcoming of his plan hit him like a hammer blow. What if the
first scout who got to the top realized what the mounds of rocks meant,
and turned to flee? They'd have to pursue the slingers down the slope
in full view of Lentulus' army. All hopes of surprising the Romans
would be lost. Acid washed the back of Carbo's throat, and he had to
swallow it to prevent himself from retching. The only way his spur-of-
the-moment ambush would work was if the enemy scouts decided to
investigate the cliff top properly.

His entreaties to Jupiter grew frantic. *I will build an altar in your honor.*

In front of it, I'll slaughter a bull—the best I can find. I will do the same every year, as long as I am able.

Guttural whispers set Carbo's pulse racing to new heights. Steadying his nerves, he squeezed the hilt of his sword as hard as he could. With great care, he peered around the rocks. Nothing. *Where the fuck are they?* Carbo waited. And waited. Every moment lasted an eternity, but he could not move even a step from his position. The slightest sound would alert the scouts to their presence.

When he finally saw a mop of black, curly hair emerging not fifteen paces from where he stood, Carbo blinked with shock. He watched with bated breath as a tanned face poked over the edge and glanced carefully from side to side. There was a short delay, and then the slinger scrambled up and on to the cliff top. He was soon followed by two more. Crouching low, they began padding toward Carbo's hiding place.

Where in Hades are the rest? Waiting until their comrades give them the all clear?

Carbo was afforded no chance to give thanks as the remaining scouts climbed into view. The first three were almost upon him. "NOW!" he roared, and threw himself around the mound of stones. He had a brief impression of startled faces and shouted curses before, miraculously, he was past, charging for the top of the slope and the trio of slingers there. They took one look at him, and turned to run. *Zip!* An arrow flashed past Carbo, burying itself deep in one man's back. He went down with a loud groan. "Take the one on the right!" Carbo bellowed. Praying that the archer had heard him, he aimed for the figure to his left, a short man with prominent cheekbones.

Luck was on his side. The slinger was so desperate to escape that as he spun, he tripped and went sprawling to the ground. Carbo was on him like a wild beast on its prey. He hacked down with his gladius, slicing open the man's back from his shoulder to his waist. Blood flew up in great gouts, and a bubbling scream of agony left his victim's lips. It was cut brutally short as Carbo plunged his blade between the slinger's ribs, shredding one lung and piercing his heart. Instantly, the man slumped down; his arms and legs kicked manically and then relaxed.

Frantically dragging free his sword, Carbo whipped around to see what was happening. The bowman had not been exaggerating about his ability. Another corpse lay on its back beside the first, an arrow jutting from its open mouth. Carbo's gaze flickered to the rocks where he'd hidden. Two slingers were down, but the last had killed one of his men, and was now armed with a sword. Spinning on his heel, he pounded straight toward Carbo, shrieking at the top of his lungs.

Carbo's vision narrowed. If he didn't stop this man, he would be to blame for everything.

Zip!

An arrow shot over the slinger's shoulder. It nearly took Carbo's eye out. "Stop shooting!" he cried, stepping into the other's path. He raised his sword.

But the scout had no interest in fighting him. Skidding to one side, he angled around Carbo, aiming for the top of the slope.

He'd misjudged, thought Carbo, cursing silently. "Take him down! Quickly!" Ducking, and praying that the archer didn't hit him instead, he sprinted forward. There was a rush of air over his shoulder, and an arrow struck the slinger in the back. He staggered, but then righted himself. Dropping his sword, the man tugged free one of the two strips of cloth that was draped around his neck. He wove closer to the edge, waving the black fabric over his head.

The grim realization of what the scout was trying to do hit Carbo at once. The banner meant "Enemy sighted," and if anyone in Lentulus' army saw it, he would have failed.

Carbo covered the last few steps at breakneck speed. Ramming his gladius into the man's back, he reached up and grabbed the cloth with his left hand. Somehow he threw his arm around his moaning victim's neck, and dragged him backward, all the while shoving his blade deeper. The slinger's cries quickly dropped to a low whimpering. A heartbeat later, he'd become a dead weight, so Carbo let him fall. Pulling out his sword, he thrust down twice, adding another blood-spattered corpse to the others lying nearby.

Carbo scanned the area. All the scouts were down, dying or dead.

His men gave him victorious grins, but he did not return the smile. They had not necessarily succeeded. Someone might have seen the fighting. He dropped to his belly and wormed over to the edge. With churning guts, he studied the massive Roman column, his eyes roving to and fro for any indications of alarm or disquiet. To Carbo's immense relief, he saw nothing.

"Were we seen?" It was the bowman's voice.

Carbo moved back a little. "No. I don't think so." *Thank you, Jupiter.*

The bowman let out a long sigh.

"Good work," said Carbo.

"I should have taken the last bastard down with one arrow."

"He was strong and desperate," replied Carbo. "Anyway, he's dead now." His eyes strayed to the slinger's body and took in the second strip of cloth around his neck. It was red, the same color as the *vexilla* flags used by the legions. A new wave of panic swamped him. The banner could have only one purpose. It was to signal that there was no danger on the cliff tops. If it wasn't seen, more Roman troops would be sent to investigate. Carbo glanced down and cursed. His tunic was saturated in blood. Unbuckling his belt, he pulled the sodden fabric over his head and threw it down. "Quick! I need the tunic with the least blood on it."

The bowman gaped at him.

"So I can wave the red cloth at the Romans and not arouse suspicion."

At last the bowman understood. Together they checked the dead. It didn't take long to see that the cleanest tunic was the one belonging to the slinger who'd been struck in the mouth. They stripped the corpse and Carbo shrugged on the sweaty garment. Then, grabbing the red strip of cloth from the last man's neck, he strode to the top of the slope. With his heart thumping like a drum, he raised it over his head and waved it from side to side. "Nothing here!" he shouted in accented Latin. "Not a soul to be seen!"

There was no response from below.

Carbo was glad. It made it more likely that the slingers' fight for survival hadn't been spotted. He redoubled his efforts, cupping a hand to his lips so that his voice carried further. A last his efforts paid off. Followed by a signifer, an officer in a cohort near the front shoved his way out of the ranks. A moment later, the standard was raised and lowered a number of times. Without even waiting to see how he responded, the officer returned to his position. Sheer exultation seized Carbo. "We did it!" he hissed to the bowman.

"Well done, sir."

Unused to being addressed in such a manner, Carbo blinked. Then he squared his shoulders proudly. "We'd best keep a good watch in case any more of the bastards come poking around. You stay here with the others. If you see as much as a rock fall, I want to know about it."

There was a fierce grin of acknowledgment.

Carbo inclined his head and began calling his men together. They'd need strict orders not to move until he told them to.

†

Spartacus' two biggest concerns as Lentulus' forces spilled out of the defile were that Egbeo and Pulcher would attack too soon, and of how much damage the Roman cavalry could do. The enemy riders pulled off to one side, allowing their foot soldiers to maneuver into position, a process that took considerable time. Sitting calmly on their horses some three hundred paces away, they looked quite harmless. From bitter experience, Spartacus knew otherwise. It had been a calculated decision to afford himself no horsemen. He'd decided to leave his riders with Castus and Gannicus. They had been training solidly since their formerly wild mounts had been captured in the mountains around Thurii, but unlike the slaves who fought as infantry, Spartacus' riders had never been tested in battle. As one great bloc, they'd be more confident, and more likely to succeed.

Besides, he wanted the cream of his men—those around him—to learn the taste of a victory that they'd won alone against the most invincible of enemies: the legionary. He was pleased by the barrage of insults that they were already hurling at the Romans. Naturally enough, one or two overeager fools had thrown their javelins, but the rest were holding their lines in good order. It was proof that the training he'd started, and which Navio had continued, had paid off. Proof that they'd shed their slave mentality.

He had a calm confidence that Carbo would play his part well. The young Roman was as loyal as any of his men—even Atheas and Taxacis. *Great Rider, I ask that Carbo never has to do what I asked of him.* With that request, Spartacus closed his heart. It was time to ready himself for battle. He deliberately filled his mind with the graphic images of Thracian villages that had been overrun by the Romans. The mounds of mutilated bodies. The sheets of gore and hacked-off limbs that had coated the ground. The grinning, empty-eyed heads on pila that had been stabbed into the mud. Old men who had been crucified on the gable ends of their own houses. Countless women who'd lain motionless, like dolls discarded by children. The pools of blood spreading from between their thighs that had given the lie to any such innocent notion. The tiny crumpled forms that turned his stomach still: babies who'd had their brains dashed out against walls. And his brother Maron, wasted to little more than a skeleton, dying in screaming agony.

A swelling rage began pulsing through Spartacus. His very eyeballs throbbed; his chest felt as if iron bands were strapped tightly around it. He felt angrier than he'd done in years. This was the moment he'd dreamed of. Longed for. *Vengeance will be mine.* All he wanted to do was kill. Slash, hack, chop into little pieces every motherfucking Roman who came within reach of his sword.

He called for his trumpeters. "Remember the arranged signal. Act the instant I give you the command. Mess it up, and I'll cut your balls off. Understand?"

The trio nodded dumbly. Fearfully.

Spartacus waved them away, to the safety of the ground behind his men. He surveyed his troops for the final time. He'd ordered three lines, and arrayed them in cohorts, as the Romans did. Nearly all the soldiers were armed with pila. Most were armed with a gladius and a scutum, and wearing a bronze crested helmet, as the legionaries did. They were a magnificent sight.

"I see you!" Spartacus shouted. "I see you, my soldiers, and my heart is filled with pride! Do you hear me? PRIDE!"

They cheered him for that until their throats were hoarse.

"Today, you are going to fight a full-strength Roman legion for the first time. It is an occasion to be grateful for. To rejoice in! To thank the gods! Why? I hear you ask. Because we are going to take on the legionaries and tear them into bloody shreds!" Spartacus barked a triumphant laugh. "The moment that Carbo blocks the defile, the battle will begin. When the bastards hit our lines, our trumpets will summon ten thousand of our comrades from their hiding places. They will fall on the Romans' left flank, and sweep all before them. We shall do the same from our position. By the end of the day, I swear to you that this field will be littered with the enemy's dead! Every man of you will have slain until his sword arm is shaking with weakness. Every one of you will be properly equipped. There will be more grain and wine in the Roman camp than we can eat, enough silver to fill all your purses, but best of all," and Spartacus pointed his sica at the silver eagle that stood proudly above the center of the Roman line, "we will have two of those in our possession. What more proof of the gods' favor can there be?"

"SPAR-TA-CUS!" they roared. "SPAR-TA-CUS!"

Keeping rhythm, Spartacus began to hammer his blade off his scutum.

Clash! Clash! Clash!

Roman soldiers advanced in complete silence, a tactic that intimidated most opponents. Fuck that, thought Spartacus, and redoubled his efforts. Let Lentulus hear my name, and the thunder of my men's anger, and tremble in his britches. Let his troops soil themselves with fear.

"SPAR-TA-CUS! SPAR-TA-CUS! SPAR-TA-CUS!"

Spartacus smiled grimly and resumed his place in the midst of his men.

The deafening noise went on and on and on.

Spartacus squinted at the enemy lines. *Good. There must be nearly five thousand Romans in view. Carbo will act any moment now.*

†

The waiting that Carbo had had to endure before previous ambushes paled into insignificance beside that morning. Every fiber of his being was screaming at him to heave the first rock over the edge. To add to his own concerns, his men were on tenterhooks. The immensity of their task and the dreadful effect it would have were all too clear now. They were desperate to start the fight, and Carbo had his job cut out to maintain discipline. "Spartacus told me when to attack, understand?" he growled over and over. "We *must* split the legions in two. Too soon, and we'll leave Castus and Gannicus with all the work to do. It's all down to us, and we have to get it right."

Eventually, his message seemed to sink home, and the men relaxed a fraction. However, the knot in Carbo's belly did not go away. For upward of half an hour he watched the legionaries marching steadily through the defile. Although they were the enemy, it was a magnificent sight, and a tiny part of his heart ached that he had never been able to join the legions. *The pricks wouldn't accept me,* he thought savagely. *Only Spartacus was able to see something in me.* He glanced at the piles of boulders, some of which were larger than ox carts. *Those will be their punishment.*

The sound of shouting and metallic clashing rang out, and Carbo's head went up. He couldn't discern any words, but it had to be Spartacus' men who were making such an immense amount of noise. *The gods be with them.*

When he looked down again, Carbo saw a break in the Roman column. Deep in the ranks of the next units he also saw the glint of an eagle standard. This was the second of Lentulus' legions, and it was about to pass directly below his position.

"All right," he said in a low tone. Abruptly, he grinned. There was no need for silence now. "At the count of three . . ." he shouted. "Spread the word." He waited as his order passed down the lines of men. A moment later, the men at the far end lifted their hands in acknowledgment. Carbo licked his lips, and placed his palms against a rock nearly the same size as himself. Then he cried, "ONE! TWO! THREEEE!"

With a great heave, he pushed it over the cliff. Awestruck by the speed it instantly gained, Carbo glanced to either side, watching as his men did the same with scores of other stones, slabs and chunks of rock. Dust sheeted the air as the missiles bounced and pounded off the sheer faces, setting off mini-landslides. The earth shook with a terrible, ravening thunder.

Carbo didn't look to see what effect their barrage was having. He didn't need to. It could only result in utter devastation. Great swathes of legionaries were a heartbeat from being wiped out of existence. Unsurprisingly, his men were peering down with macabre interest. "Don't stop!" he shouted. "More! I want more rocks going over! We have to block the defile completely."

"Kill them all!" roared the bowman. "Every last pox-ridden whoreson!"

"Kill! Kill! Kill!" answered the slaves, renewing their attack with a savage, disquieting glee.

Carbo closed his eyes briefly. *The gods have mercy on the poor bastards down there. Let them die quickly.*

Then he got back to work like everyone else.

†

When the rocks started rolling from the cliffs, virtually all sound was blocked out on the flat ground beyond. The slaves' mouths opened and closed in silent mime, their javelins and swords moved innocently up and down off their shields. What would follow, however, thought Spartacus grimly, would be far from innocent.

A huge dust cloud rose into the air above the defile. Romans and slaves alike stared in either horror or delight. A fierce glee gripped Spartacus. The almighty din meant that Carbo was doing exactly as he'd been asked. "Steady!" he roared. "Let fear tear at the enemy! The dogs know now that they're on their own." He glanced at the mouth of the side valley where Egbeo and Pulcher lay in wait with their troops, but could see nothing. *Good. Their discipline is holding.*

The rumbling of the rockfall died down. It was replaced by a terrible, new sound: that of the men who had been mashed or trapped beneath the stones, but not killed. The gorge rang with their screams and wails. Most were begging for death, an end to the agony of crushed limbs, pelvises or broken backs. Spartacus' soldiers whooped with elation, and clattered their weapons off their shields with renewed vigor.

Lentulus acted fast. Aware that the noise would soon spread panic among his legionaries, he had the bucinae sound. His soldiers marched forward in good order, and his cavalry cantered off to the right, no doubt charged with wheeling around to fall on the slaves' rear.

Although he'd expected this, Spartacus cursed silently. He hoped that the men at the back remembered their orders. They'd been trained to thrust their javelins out together, forming a network of iron points that most horses wouldn't approach. Of course being shown how to do it and having to do it when being charged by the enemy were two very different things. Placing his trust in the gods, Spartacus ordered his trumpeters to signal the advance.

"Stay in line! Move together!" His words were repeated all along the front ranks, and the slaves began tramping forward in one great mass. "SPAR-TA-CUS! SPAR-TA-CUS! SPAR-TA-CUS!" they yelled.

They were too far away to see the expression on the men's faces, but Spartacus fancied that there was already some wavering in the enemy ranks. In contrast to the neat appearance of his own forces, he could see gaps here and there among the legionaries. *We can do it! Great Rider, grant me the might of your right arm to smite the whoresons, and smash them into the mud where they belong.*

They closed to within a hundred paces. The air crackled with tension, and it was flavored with a slick tang of fear. For all the bravado that had gone on in the moments prior, this was the time when men were about to begin dying. The slaves' faces were taut; their jaws were clenched; they muttered prayers or growled encouragements at one another. Yet their shouting did not die away. If anything, it increased in volume.

"SPAR-TA-CUS! SPAR-TA-CUS! SPAR-TA-CUS!"

Spartacus was revelling in it. *They want to fight. They want Roman blood, as I do.* "Front three ranks, ready javelins!" he cried.

All around him, thousands of arms went back, and a forest of barbed metal tips pointed upward at the sun.

"Hold! Hold!" He counted the paces as they drew nearer to the Romans. Ten. Twenty. Forty. At last Spartacus could see the individual legionaries. Like his men's, their faces were twisted with emotion. Rather than tension, however, it looked like pure fear. The only exceptions were the legionaries around the silver eagle, who looked grimly prepared. Dimly, he heard the enemy officers shouting encouragement, ordering a volley of javelins. *Now!* "One! Two! Three! LOOSE!" he shouted in response.

There was a loud humming noise as his order was obeyed.

The same command rang out again from the Roman lines.

In graceful arcs, two separate clouds of pila shot upward. For several heartbeats, they darkened the sky between the two armies. It was a beautiful but dreadful sight, thought Spartacus. This was when the men's training would really become evident. "Shields up!" he roared, raising his left arm. "Shields up!"

Clatter, clatter, clatter. A wall of scuta presented itself to the sky.

With heavy thumping sounds, the Roman javelins landed in a torrent of deadly iron. Inevitably, some found tiny gaps between the slaves' shields or ran through the layered wood to pierce an arm. Roars of agony and savage curses went up from those who'd been injured, manic laughs and shouts of thanks to the gods from those who hadn't.

Spartacus was unhurt. A quick glance over both shoulders told him that their casualties were reasonably light. He studied the Romans, coming to the same conclusion about them. As usual, the javelins' primary effect had been to lodge in men's scuta, rendering them unusable. "If anyone in the front two ranks needs a shield, get the men behind you to pass theirs forward," he shouted. "Advance!"

As they marched on, those without protection hurriedly demanded their comrades' scuta.

Another exchange of javelins took place, causing a few score more casualties, and then the two sides were only thirty steps apart. Spartacus raised his whistle to his lips, and saw a centurion opposite do the same. Instead of sounding the charge, however, Spartacus blew an odd series of notes that had his men frowning in surprise. But not the trumpeters. They blew their instruments with all their might, a sharp *tan-tara-tara*. Twice they repeated it, and as the sound died away, it was replaced by a long shrill from Spartacus' whistle, which was echoed by those of his officers.

Their call was met by the indignant shrieking of the Romans' whistles.

"Shields together," roared Spartacus. "Forward!" He began trotting toward the enemy, his gaze roving over the legionaries he'd be most likely to clash with. One was a youth of about nineteen or twenty, whose eyes were already wide with terror. The other was a man in his twenties, hard-faced, jaw clenched, probably a veteran. Instantly, Spartacus aimed for the second soldier. He was the more dangerous; killing him first was imperative.

An inanimate roar—the sound of thousands of war cries melding as one—ripped through the noise of battle, dragging men's attention away from the fight. It came from Spartacus' right, and the Romans' left. *Thank you, Great Rider.*

Egbeo, Pulcher and their men were attacking.

Understanding the noise's significance, the slaves cheered at the tops of their voices. "SPAR-TA-CUS! SPAR-TA-CUS!"

"Stay close!" cried Spartacus. "Watch out for each other!" They were the last commands he gave. From now on, no one would be able to hear. The world closed in around him as Spartacus rushed the last few steps to the Roman front rank. All he was aware of was the close proximity of a man on either side, and the wild eyes of the enemy soldiers over the tops of their scuta. His heart pounded in his chest; sweat stung his eyes and he blinked it away.

Roaring a war cry, he smashed his shield boss into that of the hard-faced legionary. The force of the strike rocked the man back on his heels, and before he could retaliate, Spartacus' sica went skidding over the top of his scutum to take him through the neck. The iron grated through muscle and cartilage to lodge in the Roman's spine. Spartacus ripped it free, and the other's mouth opened in a terrible scream. The sound was cut short by the tide of arterial blood that sprayed from the back of his throat.

There was a flicker of movement at the corner of Spartacus' vision. Instinctively, he ducked his head. Instead of taking out his eye, the young legionary's gladius rammed into the crest on the top of his bronze helmet. It punched Spartacus backward, momentarily stunning him. The iron blade stuck in the torn metal, and Spartacus' head was dragged from side to side as the Roman frantically tried to free it. There was no chance of untying the leather chinstrap that held his helmet in place. With a screech of metal, the legionary ripped his gladius half out. His lips peeled back in a snarl of satisfaction. Utter desperation filled Spartacus. His opponent pulled his arm back again, so he shoved forward instead of trying to fight it. The Roman staggered, and his grip on his sword weakened. Spartacus screamed like a lunatic, and the startled young legionary let go.

Spartacus brought up his sica and thrust it into the other's left eye socket. There was an audible *pop*, and aqueous fluid spattered on to the front of his shield. The legionary jerked with agony as the blade sliced through bone and into his brain. He juddered and shook, a dead weight on the weapon's tip. Spartacus tugged it free, letting the corpse drop to the ground. It was immediately stamped underfoot in the press.

There was a heartbeat's pause in the fighting. Quickly, Spartacus undid his chinstrap and let his ruined helmet fall. "Come on!" he roared at the legionaries in the next rank. "Hades is waiting for you!"

"SPAR-TA-CUS! SPAR-TA-CUS!" boomed the men around him.

With dragging feet, the Romans shuffled closer. A few rows back, Spartacus spotted an officer using his vine cane to beat men forward. He exulted in the sight. It was an ominous sign so early in a battle. "The cocksuckers are scared!" he shouted. "They're fucking terrified!"

Then his eyes fixed on a standard some thirty paces off to his left. He levelled his sica at it. "Take the eagle!"

With loud cries, the nearest slaves shoved onward, slamming their scuta into those of the legionaries and driving them back a step. Shield bosses smacked off each other and gladius blades sank deep into flesh. Men got close enough to head butt their enemies or ram a dagger home into their necks. They spat in the Romans' faces, screamed insults and called down the fury of the gods on their heads. Stunned by the slaves' sheer fury, the legionaries withdrew another pace.

In that instant, the world changed.

There was a noise like a striking thunderbolt, and the Roman lines shook with a massive impact. It was Egbeo and Pulcher, thought Spartacus. "NOW! PUSH THEM!" he roared. Bare-headed, spittle flying from his lips, he threw himself at the nearest Romans. Like a pack of baying hounds, his men followed.

"SPAR-TA-CUS! SPAR-TA-CUS!"

The legionaries could take it no more. Their faces pinched with overwhelming terror. Desperate to flee from the madmen who were bearing down on them, they shoved at one another like trapped animals. In the space of a dozen heartbeats, the center of Lentulus' line turned about and engaged in a full-scale retreat. Shields and weapons were flung down. The wounded, and those who were simply weaker, were knocked to the ground where they were trampled to death.

The slaves advanced, slaying all before them, showing mercy to no one.

The *aquilifer*, the soldier carrying the legion's eagle, and the men charged with protecting him, were the only ones to hold their position. A tight little bloc of shields and swords, they roared and cursed at their comrades, calling on them to stand and fight.

It made no difference. Like a wave ebbing from the shore, the legionaries melted away from the front line.

Then Spartacus charged forward, bellowing like a rogue bull.

Too late, the aquilifer realized that his fate was upon him. Too late, he saw that the precious eagle was about to fall into enemy hands. "Retreat," he cried. But Spartacus and a score of slaves surged in, and they had to fight. The standard-bearer and his comrades went down in a vicious blur of hacks and slashes. The standard fell from his slack fingers, but before it could hit the ground, Spartacus snatched it up.

"Look, you shitbags," he bellowed in Latin.

Amid the mêlée, a few terrified Roman faces turned around.

"The eagle is ours. The gods are on our side!" Spartacus shook the standard defiantly at them. "Cowards!"

No one answered him, and his men yelled with delight.

He took a quick look around. The legionaries on the left flank were also in full retreat. Those on the right, who until that point had held their position, were wavering. It wouldn't be long until they also broke, thought Spartacus with certainty. He had no idea where the Roman cavalry were, but they couldn't have made much of an impression because the ranks to his rear were still solid. The battle on this side of the defile was as good as won. He had a hunch that with the advantage of all their horsemen, Castus and Gannicus would be achieving the same on the other side.

Let it be so, Great Rider.

†

Ariadne's worries about Spartacus had consumed her from the moment he'd left. She'd spent hours praying and making offerings to Dionysus, but typically, had seen nothing that remotely reassured her. She knew better than to get angry with the capricious god, so she funneled her frustration into marshalling the camp's women and preparing them for the inevitable influx of wounded after the fighting was over. Even that supposition was disquieting. If the slaves lost the battle, there'd be no need for bandages, dressings and poultices but that,

like Spartacus' death, didn't bear thinking about. And then there was
Atheas, who'd been shadowing her every move. Ariadne found it unnerving. Before Spartacus had left, she had asked him what would
happen if things went against them. He had touched a finger to her
lips, saying, "That isn't going to happen." Ariadne had insisted, however, and so he'd told her of how the Scythian and Carbo would escort
her to safety.

She glanced at Atheas. His attempt to reassure her, a smile full
of sharp brown teeth, made her feel worse. Yet interacting with the
Scythian was preferable to talking with the other women. Every sound
that reached them from the direction of the battlefield was either
met with tears or wails of dismay. Even when, as now, the noises died
away, the lamentations went on. Ariadne peered at the sky. How long
had it been since Spartacus had set off with the army? Four hours?
Five?

"What do you think has happened?" she whispered to Atheas. "Is
it over?"

He cocked his head quizzically. "Impossible ... say. Maybe they ...
rest ... before fight again."

The agony of not knowing was suddenly too much to bear. "I'm
going to the cliffs to see what's going on."

Atheas was on his feet before she'd even finished speaking. "That ...
very bad idea."

Ariadne gave him a frosty glare. "You will stop me?"

"Yes," he said with an apologetic look.

She wasn't surprised by his answer, but felt the need to argue anyway. "I'll do what I want."

"No." Atheas' tone was firm. "Too dangerous. You ... stay here."

"Your women fight, do they not?"

He grinned, sheepishly. "Yes."

"Why should I not even go to watch the battle then?"

"Because Spartacus ... said so." Atheas hesitated for an instant.
"Because of ... child."

"He told you."

"Yes," replied the Scythian awkwardly.

A poignant image of Spartacus giving Atheas his final instructions filled Ariadne's mind, and her breath caught in her chest. *The gods bless him and keep him safe forever.* "Let us hope that you and Carbo are never called on to fulfill the duty that he asked of you."

"I also ask . . . my gods . . . that." There was a gruff, unusual note to his voice.

Tears pricked at Ariadne's eyes. In the chaotic months after they'd escaped the ludus, the unswerving devotion that he and Taxacis had showed to Spartacus had gone unacknowledged, by her at least. Until that very moment, she hadn't realized how much she'd come to take it for granted, and of how dear the grim, tattooed warrior had become to her. "Why do you follow him?"

His thick eyebrows lifted. "Spartacus?"

She nodded.

There was a tiny smile. "No one . . . ever ask me."

"I'd like to know."

"When Taxacis and I . . . captured . . . other slaves refuse . . . talk with us. Think all Scythians . . . savages." Atheas spat his contempt on the ground. "But Spartacus . . . different."

"Go on," encouraged Ariadne.

"In ludus . . . he act like . . . leader." He shrugged. "No chance . . . return . . . Scythia, so we decide . . . follow him."

"He is grateful for your loyalty. I want you to know that I am too."

Atheas dipped his head in acknowledgment.

"You chose wisely," said Ariadne. "When we cross the Alps, you will be free to travel to Scythia once more."

He grinned fiercely. "I look forward . . . that day."

"And so do I." May Dionysus grant that it happens, thought Ariadne, doing her best to ignore the pangs of concern that were tearing at her heart.

✝

By trotting from one end of the cliff tops to the other, Carbo was able to monitor the fight on both fronts. He had a bird's-eye view of the battle, and so it was patently clear when the tide turned not just for Spartacus, but for the Gaulish leaders as well. Smashed apart by the slaves' cavalry, Lentulus' second legion was then slaughtered by Castus' and Gannicus' men. At least a third of its legionaries fell on the field, and the rest were harangued as they fled, losing countless more men in the process. The story was little different on Spartacus' side of the defile.

As the scale of the victory became clearer, Carbo's men grew more and more ecstatic. They danced and sang, praising every god in the pantheon for the interventions on their behalf. He, while also delighted by the victory, was struck by the shame of the Roman defeat. He was furious with himself for even feeling that emotion, but it couldn't be denied. The sooner they crossed the mountains and left Italy, Carbo thought, the better. There at least he would have no regard for their enemies. He would be able to follow Spartacus without feeling in some way disloyal to his heritage. Perhaps, too, he could forget Crixus, and what he had done to Chloris.

Yet if it ever came to it, Carbo also knew that he would follow the Thracian into battle against the legions again. Too much water had gone under the bridge since he'd left home. Too much blood had been shed for there to be any going back.

He was Spartacus' man, whatever the future held.

And that, despite all the uncertainty, was a good feeling.

†

More than two hours passed. Finally, the noise of loud cheering carried into the camp. Ariadne's heart jolted in her chest. She raced with everyone else to the track that led north, and waited. Shivers racked her body, but they weren't caused by the cooling mountain air. Just because the slaves had won didn't mean that Spartacus had survived. She saw the same fear mirrored in every woman's expression. They all had loved ones in the army's ranks, but it was likely that many of them would never return. Guilt suffused Ariadne at the very thought of it, but she hoped that others had died rather than Spartacus, that she would not be the one to be left alone forever.

She stole a glance at the pinched faces around her. Even Atheas looked concerned. *They're all thinking the same thing.* That realization made her feel fractionally better.

"SPAR-TA-CUS! SPAR-TA-CUS! SPAR-TA-CUS!"

The loud cry filled Ariadne with an unquenchable joy. She was running before she knew it, her feet pounding along the track. A disorganized mass of slaves rounded the bend, and she scanned them frantically. It was impossible not to notice the dozen standards that were being brandished aloft. Despite her worries, Ariadne's eyes widened at the sight of two silver eagles among them. Then, recognizing Spartacus, bloodied from head to foot, without a helmet but walking without help, she let out a yelp of happiness. A moment later, she had reached him, and thrown herself into his arms.

His men's cheering redoubled. "SPAR-TA-CUS!"

"You're alive, you're alive," she murmured.

"Of course I am," he replied, squeezing her tight. "Were you worried about me?"

Shocked, Ariadne pulled back to stare at him, and saw that he was joking. She didn't know whether to laugh, to cry, or to kiss him. In the event, she did all three, in that order. She didn't care that he stank of sweat and other men's blood, that everyone was watching, that a priestess of Dionysus was not supposed to act in such a manner. All Ariadne cared about was that the man she loved had not died that day on the battlefield. That the child growing in her belly still had a father. Those two things were enough.

There were shouts of delight as the other women arrived and were seen by their men. The slaves streamed forward to be reunited with their loved ones, leaving Spartacus and Ariadne like an island in a river, oblivious, locked in each other's arms.

"You won," she said at last.

"We did," he declared. "Everything went according to plan, thank the gods. Lentulus took the bait, and advanced into the gorge. Carbo split the legions apart, and shook their confidence. The moment the battle began, Egbeo and Pulcher emerged with their men to take them in the left flank. The bastards never knew what had happened. They broke and ran like a flock of sheep with a wolf among them."

"And Castus and Gannicus?"

"They fared just as well."

"Where are they?"

"Pursuing the Romans. Butchering every man they find, and making sure that they can't regroup. Not that there's much chance of that. The rest of the men are stripping the Roman dead of their weapons and equipment, or ransacking their camp for supplies."

"Was Lentulus captured or slain?"

"Unfortunately not. When he saw that the battle was lost, he fled on horseback. Not that it matters!" His scowl was replaced by a smile. "He can carry the news of this defeat to the Senate himself. You've seen the eagles we took. The shame of that disgrace will be a far greater sting to Rome's pride than the men who were killed today. Lentulus will be lucky to survive with his head."

She kissed him happily on the lips. "You are a great general. Truly, Dionysus favors you."

"The Great Rider was here today too. He lent me his strength," he said reverently. Joy filled him. *Maron has finally been avenged.*

Silence fell between them as they both offered up thanks to the gods.

"What next?" asked Ariadne. Her pulse quickened with new fear. "You're not tempted to go in search of the second consular army?"

"Tempted? Of course I am! Crixus might even welcome the help!" He saw her concern, and his fierce expression gentled. "No, the Romans are like locusts. There's no end to their armies. If Gellius appears, we will fight him, but my plan is still to head north, to the Alps."

"They are not far now." Ariadne let her mind wander. "Our son could be born in Gaul."

"Maybe," said Spartacus, wary of tempting the gods, wary because life had previously handed him so many harsh lessons. "Let us reach the mountains first, and cross them before making any assumptions." He grinned at her, keen to dispel his worries. "Today, though, let us rejoice in our victory and the knowledge that Rome has learned a lesson."

"What's that?" she asked, smiling.

"That slaves can also be soldiers. That they can take on the might of a consular army, and win. I knew it could be done, and today I proved it."

A man could die happy knowing he'd accomplished that.

AUTHOR'S NOTE

I know that I am not alone in finding Spartacus' life compelling. Along with Hannibal Barca, he is one of the most iconic figures I can think of. What's not to love? His is the story of a man who was wronged and sold into slavery, who is forced to fight for his life for the amusement of the mob. Escaping captivity with a few supporters, he won incredible victories against totally overwhelming odds, gained the support of tens of thousands of escaped slaves, won more amazing battles, and planned to escape from Italy completely. As most of you know, things for Spartacus started to unwind after that, but the tragedy of his tale only adds to the drama.

Capturing people's imagination in the 1950s, Howard Fast's book *Spartacus* sold five million copies. It spawned a blockbusting film starring Kirk Douglas, which just about everyone in possession of a television has seen. Consequently, Spartacus has become a name recognized by all. The man's renown may have dimmed of recent years, but in the last eighteen months he has been portrayed anew. I was delighted when the series *Spartacus: Blood and Sand* screened on TV here in the UK. From the two episodes I have allowed myself to watch, it seems to play fast and loose with historical detail, but few can deny that it makes for dramatic and exciting viewing. In September 2011, few people were left untouched by the tragic death from cancer of Andy Whitfield, who brought Spartacus so vividly to life in the series. Recently, word has come of a new Hollywood version of the tale. I only hope it can live up to expectations. Naturally, I wish the same of this book. I have done my very best to do justice to the incredible story of the man who took on the might of the Roman Republic and nearly brought it crashing down. I sincerely hope that you think it brings Spartacus the Thracian to life.

It is a tragedy that little more than four thousand words about Spartacus survive from ancient texts. No one truly knows why this is. I like to believe that the Romans didn't want a man who trounced their armies on multiple occasions remembered or glorified. After all, it's the victors who write history. The losers generally get demonized or forgotten. Not Spartacus, thankfully. Perhaps this was because the Romans actually held him in some regard—we're told that "he possessed great spirit and bodily strength"; he was also "more intelligent and nobler than his fate." While the dearth of information means that much detail about Spartacus and his rebellion has, tantalizingly, been lost forever, it also offers the novelist a huge gift: being able to fill in the gaps. It also allows less room for criticism—hopefully! A wealth of knowledge survives from the Roman Republic of the first century BC, which allows the background to be described, and the tapestry of the story to be woven richly around Spartacus. As always, I have stuck to historical detail whenever possible in this tale. Where I deviated from it, I will explain why.

Spartacus (Latin for Sparadakos, which can conceivably be interpreted as "famous for his spear") is usually understood to have come from Thrace, a region covering much of modern-day Bulgaria and beyond. However, this is not a definite fact. He is described in one ancient text as a nomadic "Thracian" of the Maedi people, but this does not completely prove his racial origins, because other texts simply record him as a "Thracian." In other words, he may have been forced to fight as a Thracian gladiator in the arena. Yet the Thracians were recorded as being a fierce, warlike people. Many of them also served as mercenaries with the Roman legions, so in my mind it fits that Spartacus came from Thrace.

We know that for a time, he fought for Rome (as a noncitizen, this would have been in the auxiliaries). It was common for Thracian auxiliaries to fight as cavalry, and it is generally thought that Spartacus may have done so as well. We do not know why Spartacus was enslaved, so my account of his return to his tribe, his encounters with Ariadne and the treacherous Kotys, and his purchase by Phortis are fabricated, but his innocence is not. He really was a gladiator in the ludus in Capua. While Kotys and Phortis are fictional characters, Lentulus Batiatus did exist. So did Spartacus' woman/wife, who is stated to have been a priestess of Dionysus. History has not honored us with her name, so I picked the name Ariadne, who in legend married no less a figure than the god Dionysus.

Spartacus' dream about the snake and its portent is recorded. In these secular days, it is hard to imagine how important the details of his vision could have been to his followers. Two thousand years ago, people believed in a multitude of all-powerful gods. They were superstitious in the extreme and lacked our understanding of science and nature. Random events such as the way a flock of birds flew, whether sacred chickens ate or not and where lightning bolts struck could have immense significance, and determine people's actions and deeds. In my mind, for Spartacus to have a priestess of Dionysus—a god revered by slaves—as his wife could only have added to his appeal.

It was my decision not to allow Spartacus to fight as a Thracian gladiator. I felt that it was a way for his resentment to increase even further. In the late Republic, there were just three classes of gladiator, which I have detailed. Life in a ludus was much as I have described, but Crassus' visit to the school is fictional. So too are the scenes in Rome, although Crassus' manner of purchasing burning buildings is documented, as is his wealth, astute political ability and his rivalry with Pompey. Restio is a product of my imagination, but Spartacus' escape attempt *was* betrayed, which is probably why only seventy-odd gladiators escaped. He didn't have a young Roman follower called Carbo, but Crixus and Oenomaus were real men who got away with him. Oenomaus was killed soon afterward; it was my decision to make this in the first battle. Castus and Gannicus are mentioned later in accounts of Spartacus' life, but I felt that they would add to the story by being present from the start.

The fighters marched to Vesuvius, where they were besieged by Glaber and his men. The astonishing account of how they abseiled down cliffs using vine ropes and put three thousand soldiers to flight is true. Glaber's fate is unknown, but we know that Varinius, Furius and Cossinius were next to be sent to deal with the insurrection. In the meantime, Spartacus was recruiting strong, tough slaves to his cause— farm workers and herders were natural candidates for his army. The rebel Sertorius is known to have sent military advisers to another enemy of Rome, Mithridates of Pontus. It's not impossible then to think that men like Navio became involved with Spartacus.

There are few details of the battles that followed in the autumn of 73 BC other than that the slaves won them decisively, and that Cossinius was disturbed in a swimming pool, pursued and killed in his camp. The precise details of that priceless scene are my doing. As far as I know, there is no evidence for the use of whistles by Roman officers to relay commands. Trumpets and other instruments were used for this purpose. However, whistles have been found in sites all over the Empire, including in the proximity of the legionary fortresses at Chester in the UK and Regensburg in Germany. It's not too much of a jump after that for me to have them in the hands of centurions during a battle. A whistle could have been very useful in getting the attention of men who were only a few steps away.

The manner of Spartacus' withdrawal from Varinius' forces in the dead of night is as the texts describe. Mention is made of his desire to march north to the Alps, but apparently his men thought of "nothing but blood and booty." Whether Crixus and the other Gauls were at the center of the argument over what the slaves should do at that point is unknown, but given the later schisms in their army, it seems likely that they were. Little information survives about what the slaves did next, but details of the atrocities of the attack on Forum Annii remain. Other towns and settlements met the same fate. Intriguingly, some archaeological discoveries from the "heel" of Italy may date to the time of Spartacus. A warehouse portico discovered in the ruins of Meta-pontum was destroyed during this period. A small gray vase was found buried under a house in Heraclea and dated to the same timeframe. It was filled with over five hundred silver coins and a gold necklace. Most of the coins can be dated to between 100 and 80 BC, and many are of low denomination, which is unusual for such finds, and may mean that the trove was buried in haste.

Setting the location of Varinius' defeat at Thurii is fiction; how-ever, he was beaten decisively, losing his horse and many of his standards to Spartacus' forces. His fate is unknown. Crixus split from Spartacus' main army eventually—I made it after the clash with Varinius. Twenty to thirty thousand men followed him. As I mentioned before, we don't know when Castus and Gannicus joined the rebellion. In my version of the story, they were there from the days in the ludus and stayed with Spartacus when Crixus left. The slaves' journey north through Italy is shrouded in mystery, but they marched along the Apennine Mountains and had their path blocked by the consul Lentulus. Scant details of the battle that followed survive: Lentulus was defeated; his men fled the field, leaving their baggage train; many standards were lost.

By the time I'd got to this stage, it was clear that Spartacus' story wasn't going to fit in one novel. I punted the idea of a second book to my editor, who responded with huge enthusiasm. It's going to be writ-ten back-to-back with this novel, and is scheduled for release in late 2012. My mind is in overdrive thinking about it already.

The list of references for Spartacus is shorter than normal, because of the aforementioned lack of material. Apart from my Roman his-tory texts, the main books I used were an excellent book on the whole rebellion called *The Spartacus War* by Professor Barry Strauss; *Spartacus and the Slave Wars: A Brief History with Documents* by Brent D. Shaw, which details every little scrap of ancient text about the man; *Spartacus and the Slave War 73–71 BC*, an Osprey book by Nic Fields; another Osprey title, *The Thracians* by Chris Webber, was recently added to in a fantastic way by his textbook *The Gods of Battle*, which I recommend highly. The brilliant website www.RomanArmyTalk.com has to be mentioned too—it's a wonderful place to find out anything and everything about the Roman army, and its members are always quick to answer any queries. Going to the RAT conference in York this year was extremely enjoyable; the lectures were excellent, and it was great to put faces to so many names.

As ever, I am hugely grateful to a large number of people. Rosie de Courcy, my editor, and Charlie Viney, my agent, are fantastic people to work with, and I deeply appreciate all that you do for me. Thank you very much to everyone at Preface, Cornerstone and other departments of Random House: it's all your hard work that helps my books to do so well. I'm grateful to Leslie Jones, a reader of mine, for his input on Sertorius and his intelligence officers. Claire Wheller, you're an incredible physio, and thank you for keeping my RSIs at bay. Arthur O'Connor, an old veterinary friend, has to get a big mention too. He is the "wall" off which I bounce my ideas and finished manuscripts. He invariably comes up with great ideas as well as lots of "homework." I am always immensely appreciative of them. Thanks, Arthur!

Cheers and good wishes to all of you wonderful readers out there. It's because of you that I am able to keep writing. Please pop by my website www.benkane.net any time. You can also look for me on Facebook or Twitter: @benkaneauthor. And last but not least, thank you to Sair, my lovely wife, and Ferdia and Pippa, my wonderful children. I love you all very much.

GLOSSARY

Abella: modern-day Avella.

acetum: sour wine, the universal beverage served to Roman soldiers. Also the word for vinegar, the most common disinfectant used by Roman doctors. Vinegar is excellent at killing bacteria, and its widespread use in Western medicine continued until late in the nineteenth century.

alopekis: a typical Thracian cap made of fox-skin. It came in two styles, pointed or with a low crown.

amphora (pl. *amphorae*): a large, two-handled clay vessel with a narrow neck used to store wine, olive oil and other produce.

aquilifer (pl. *aquiliferi*): the standard-bearer for the *aquila*, or eagle, of a legion.

as (pl. *asses*): a small bronze coin, originally worth two-fifths of a *sestertius*.

Asia Minor: a geographical term used to describe the westernmost part of the continent of Asia, equating to much of modern-day Turkey.

atrium: the large chamber immediately beyond the entrance hall in a Roman house. This was the social and devotional center of the house. It had an opening in the roof and a pool, the *impluvium*, to catch the rainwater that entered.

Attic helmet: a helmet type originating in Greece, which was also widely used elsewhere in the ancient world.

auctoratus (pl. *auctorati*): a free Roman citizen who volunteered to become a gladiator.

aureus (pl. *aurei*): a small gold coin worth twenty-five *denarii*. Until the time of the early Empire, it was minted infrequently.

auxiliaries: Rome was happy to use allied soldiers of different types to increase their armies' effectiveness. For most of the first century BC, there was no Roman citizen cavalry. It became the norm to recruit natural horsemen such as German, Gaulish and Spanish tribesmen.

ballista (pl. *ballistae*): a two-armed Roman catapult that looked like a crossbow on a stand, and which fired either bolts or stones with great accuracy and force.

Belenus: the Gaulish god of light. He was also the god of cattle and sheep.

Bithynia: a territory in northwest Asia Minor that was bequeathed to Rome by its king in 75/4 BC.

Brennus: the Gaulish chieftain who is reputed to have sacked Rome in 387 BC. (Also a character in my book *The Forgotten Legion!*)

bucina (pl. *bucinae*): a military trumpet. The Romans used a number of types of instruments, among them the *tuba*, the *cornu* and the *bucina*. To simplify matters, I have used just one of them: the *bucina*.

caldarium: an intensely hot room in Roman bath complexes. Used like a modern-day sauna, most also had a hot plunge pool. The *caldarium* was heated by hot air that flowed from a furnace through pipes into hollow bricks in the walls and under the raised floor.

caligae: heavy leather sandals worn by the Roman soldier. Sturdily constructed in three layers—a sole, insole and upper—*caligae* resembled an open-toed boot. Dozens of metal studs on the sole gave the sandals good grip.

Campania: a fertile region of west central Italy.

Campus Atinas: modern-day Vallo di Diano.

Campus Martius: part of the Tiber flood plain to the northwest of Rome. It was here that men exercised, armies were mustered and votes taken.

cenacula (pl. *cenaculae*): see *insula*.

censor: one of a pair of senior Roman magistrates whose primary function was to maintain the official list of all citizens.

centurion (in Latin, *centurio*): the disciplined, career officers who formed the backbone of the Roman army. In the first century BC, there were six centurions to a cohort, and sixty to a legion. See also entry for cohort.

Cerberus: the monstrous three-headed hound that guarded the entrance to Hades.

Cilician pirates: sea raiders from a region in southern Asia Minor who, in the second and first centuries BC, caused severe problems to shipping in the eastern Mediterranean.

Cinna, Lucius Cornelius (d. 84 BC): Little is known of the early life of this four-time consul. An ally of Marius and an enemy of Sulla, he was killed in a mutiny by his own troops.

cohort: a unit of the Roman legion. There were ten cohorts in a legion in the 70s BC, with six centuries of eighty legionaries in every unit. Each century was under the command of a centurion.

consul: one of two annually elected chief magistrates, appointed by the people and ratified by the Senate. Effective rulers of Rome for a year, they were in charge of civil and military matters and led the Republic's armies into war. Each could countermand the other and both were supposed to heed the wishes of the Senate. No man was supposed to serve as consul more than once. But by the early decades of the first century BC, powerful nobles such as Marius, Cinna and Sulla were holding on to the position for years on end. This dangerously weakened Rome's democracy.

Crassus, Marcus Licinius (*c.*115–53 BC): an astute Roman politician and general who joined with Sulla after Cinna's death and whose actions at the Colline Gate on Sulla's behalf helped to take Rome. He lived modestly but was reputedly the richest man in Rome, making much of his fortune by buying and seizing the properties of those affected by Sulla's proscriptions. To reveal more about him would ruin some readers' enjoyment of the next book, so I will stop here.

Cumae: modern-day Cuma.

Curia: the building in Rome in which the Senate met.

denarius (pl. *denarii*): the staple coin of the Roman Republic. Made from silver, it was worth four *sestertii*, or ten *asses* (later sixteen).

Dionysus: the twice-born son of Zeus and Semele, daughter of the founder of Thebes. Recognized as man and animal, young and old, male and effeminate, he was one of the most versatile and indefinable of all Greek gods. Essentially, he was the god of wine and intoxication but was also associated with ritual madness, *mania*, and an afterlife blessed by his joys. Named Bacchus by the Romans, his cults were secretive, violent and strange.

editor (pl. *editores*): the sponsor of a *munus*, a gladiatorial contest.

familia: by taking the gladiator's oath, a fighter became part of the *familia gladiatoria*, the tight-knit group that would be his only family, often until death.

Fortuna: the goddess of luck and good fortune. Like all deities, she was notoriously fickle.

Forum Annii: a farming settlement in the Campus Atinas that has been lost to history.

frigidarium (pl. *frigidaria*): a room in Roman baths containing a cold plunge pool.

fugitivus: a runaway slave—a fugitive.

Gaul: essentially, modern-day France.

Getai: a Thracian tribe.

gladius (pl. *gladii*): little information remains about the long "Spanish" sword of the Republican army, the *gladius hispaniensis*, with its waisted blade. It is not clear when it was adopted by the Romans, but it was probably after encountering the weapon during the First Punic War, when it was used by Celtiberian troops. The shaped hilt was made of bone and protected by a pommel and guard of wood. The *gladius* was worn on the right, except by centurions and other senior officers, who wore it on the left.

Great Rider: almost nothing is known about Thracian religion. However, more than three thousand representations of one mysterious figure survive from Thrace. These depict a deity on horseback who is often accompanied by a dog or a lion. He is usually aiming his spear at a boar hiding behind an altar. Invariably, there is a tree nearby with a snake coiled around it; often there are women present too. Other carvings depict the "hero" god returning from a successful hunt with his dogs or lions, or approaching the altar in triumph, a bowl held in his hand. No name for this heroic deity survives, but his importance to the Thracians cannot be understated. I have therefore given him a name I thought suited quite well.

Hades: the underworld—hell. The god of the underworld was also called Hades.

Heraclea: modern-day Policoro.

Hercules (or, more correctly, Heracles): the greatest of Greek heroes, who completed twelve monumentally difficult labors.

Iberia: the Iberian peninsula. In the first century BC, it was divided into two Roman provinces, Hispania Citerior and Hispania Ulterior.

Illyria (or Illyricum): the Roman name for the lands that lay across the Adriatic Sea from Italy, including parts of modern-day Slovenia, Serbia, Croatia, Serbia, Bosnia and Montenegro.

impluvium: see *atrium*.

insula (pl. *insulae*): high-rise (three-, four- or even five-story) blocks of flats, or *cenaculae*, in which most Roman citizens lived.

Iugula: "Kill him" in Latin.

Juno: sister and wife of Jupiter, she was the Roman goddess of marriage and women.

Jupiter: often referred to as *Optimus Maximus*—"Greatest and Best." Most powerful of the Roman gods, he was responsible for weather, especially storms.

Kabyle: Thracians did not live in large urban gatherings. Kabyle was the only settlement that *may* have looked like a town as we would nowadays describe it.

kopis (pl. *kopides*): a heavy Greek slashing sword with a forward curving blade. It was normally carried in a leather-covered sheath and suspended from a baldric. Many ancient peoples used the *kopis*, from the Etruscans to the Persians.

lanista (pl. *lanistae*): a gladiator trainer, often the owner of a *ludus*, a gladiator school.

lararium: a shrine found in Roman homes, where the household gods were worshipped.

Latin: in ancient times this was not just a language. The Latins were the inhabitants of Latium, an area close to Rome. By about 300 BC it had been vanquished by the Romans.

latifundium (pl. *latifundia*): a large estate, usually owned by Roman nobility, and which utilized large numbers of slaves as labor. *Latifundia* date back to the second century BC, when vast areas of land were confiscated from Italian peoples defeated by Rome, such as the Samnites.

latro (pl. *latrones*): thief or brigand. However, the word also meant "insurgent."

legate: the officer in command of a legion, and a man of senatorial rank.

licium: linen loincloth worn by nobles. It is likely that all classes wore a variant of this.

lictor (pl. *lictores*): a magistrates' enforcer. *Lictores* were essentially the bodyguards for the consuls, praetors and other senior Roman magistrates. Such officials were accompanied at all times in public by set numbers of *lictores* (the number depended on their rank). Each *lictor* carried *fasces*, the symbol of justice: a bundle of rods enclosing an axe.

Lucania: modern-day Basilicata, a mountainous region of southern Italy.

ludus (pl. *ludi*): a gladiator school.

machaira: another word for *kopis*.

Maedi (also spelled Maidi): a Thracian tribe from which Spartacus may have originated.

maenads: women inspired to *mania*, or ritual ecstasy, by Dionysus. Euripides reported that they ate raw meat, handled snakes and tore live animals apart.

manica (pl. *manicae*): an arm guard used by gladiators. It was usually made of layered materials such as durable linen and leather, or metal.

Marius, Gaius (*c.*157–86 BC): another prominent Roman politician of the late second century and early first century BC. He served as consul a record seven times, and was a very successful general, but was outwitted by Sulla's march on Rome in 87 BC. Marius was also responsible for extensive remodeling of the Roman army. He was married to Julia, the aunt of Julius Caesar.

Mars: the Roman god of war.

Metapontum: modern-day Metaponto.

Minerva: the Roman goddess of war and also of wisdom.

Mitte: "Let him go" in Latin.

munus (pl. *munera*): a gladiatorial combat, staged originally during celebrations honoring someone's death. Their popularity meant that by the late Roman Republic, rival politicians were regularly staging *munera* to win the public's favor and to upstage each other.

Mutina: modern-day Modena.

Neapolis: modern-day Naples.

Nubian: a person from Nubia, a region in the middle Nile valley.

Nuceria: modern-day Nocera.

Odrysai: the most powerful of the Thracian tribes, and the only one briefly to unite all the others.

olibanum: frankincense, an aromatic resin used in incense as well as perfume. Highly valued in ancient times, the best *olibanum* was reportedly grown in modern-day Oman, Yemen and Somalia.

optio (pl. *optiones*): the officer who ranked immediately below a centurion; the second-in-command of a century.

palus (pl. *pali*): a 1:82-m (6-ft) wooden post buried in the ground. Trainee gladiators and legionaries were taught swordsmanship by aiming blows at it.

peltast: a light infantryman of Greek and Anatolian origin. Thracian peltasts were feared because they were fierce fighters as well as expert missile-throwers. Apart from a shield, they usually fought unarmored and, depending on their nationality, carried javelins and sometimes spears or knives. Their primary use was as skirmishers.

pelte: the most distinctive feature of the peltast, a crescent-shaped shield most probably invented by the Thracians.

phalera (pl. *phalerae*): a sculpted disc-like decoration for bravery that was worn on a chest harness over a Roman soldier's armor. *Phalerae* were commonly made of bronze, but could be made of more precious metals as well.

Phrygian helmets: these originated in Phrygia, a region in Asia Minor. They had a characteristic forward curving crest.

pilum (pl. *pila*): the Roman javelin. It consisted of a wooden shaft approximately 1.2 m (4 ft) long, joined to a thin iron shank approximately 0.6 m (2 ft) long, and was topped by a small pyramidal point. The range of the *pilum* was about 30 m (100 ft), although the effective range was probably about half this distance.

Pisae: modern-day Pisa.

Pompey Magnus, Gnaeus (106–48 BC): son of a leading politician, he fought at a young age in the Social War. He led three private legions to Sulla's aid in the civil war, helping Sulla to gain power. In 77 BC, he was sent to Iberia as proconsul, his mission to defeat the rebel Sertorius.

Pontifex Maximus: the leading member and spokesman of the four colleges of the Roman priesthood.

praetors: senior magistrates who administered justice in Rome and in its overseas possessions such as Sardinia, Sicily and Spain. They could also hold military commands and initiate legislation. The main understudy to the consuls, the praetor convened the Senate in their absence.

Priapus: the Roman god of gardens and fields, a symbol of fertility. Often pictured with a huge erect penis.

Rhegium: modern-day Reggio di Calabria.

rudis: the wooden *gladius* symbolizing the freedom that could be granted to a gladiator who pleased a sponsor sufficiently, or who had earned enough victories in the arena to qualify for it. Not all gladiators were condemned to die in combat: far from it. Prisoners of war and criminals usually were, but slaves who had committed a crime were granted the *rudis* if they survived for three years as a gladiator. After a further two years, they could be set free.

sacramentum gladiatorum: the solemn vow taken by gladiator recruits, which was more binding than any other oath in the Roman world. My version is very close to that given in historical texts.

Samnites: the people of a confederated area in the central southern Apennines. A warlike people, the Samnites fought three wars against Rome in the fourth and third centuries BC. They also backed Pyrrhus of Epirus and Hannibal against the Republic. Their fight against Sulla in the civil war was their last gasp. The large number of Samnite prisoners of war is thought to have given rise to the gladiator class.

scutum (pl. *scuta*): an elongated oval Roman army shield, about 1.2 m (4 ft) tall and 0.75 m (2 ft 6 in) wide. It was made from three layers of wood, the pieces laid at right angles to each other; it was then covered with linen or canvas, and leather. The *scutum* was heavy, weighing between 6 and 10 kg (13–22 lbs).

Scythians: a fierce, nomadic people who lived to the north of the Black Sea. They were tattooed, warlike and superlative horsemen, who were widely feared, and whose women are reputed to have given rise to the legend of the Amazons. By the first century BC, however, their heyday was long gone.

Senate: a body of six hundred (historically, it had been three hundred, but Sulla doubled its number) of senators, who were prominent Roman noblemen. The Senate met in the Curia, and its function was to advise the magistrates—the consuls, praetors, quaestors etc.—on domestic and foreign policy, religion and finance. By the first century BC, its position was much weaker than it had ever been.

Sertorius, Quintus (*c*.126–73 BC): a prominent noble who allied himself to Cinna. He was given control of Spain in 83 BC, but proscribed a year or so later. His campaign against Rome was initially very successful, but his own defeats and those of his lieutenants in

76 BC cost him dearly, reducing his activities from then on to guerrilla warfare.

sestertius (pl. *sestertii*): a silver coin, it was worth two and a half *asses*; or a quarter of a *denarius*; or one hundredth of an *aureus*. By the time of the late Roman Republic, its use was becoming more common.

sica: a large curved sword used by Thracian cavalry in the first century BC. Sadly, little is known about this weapon, and it may have been similar to the *kopis*, or the traditional Thracian curved sword.

signifer (pl. *signiferi*): a standard-bearer and junior officer. This was a position of high esteem, with one for every century in a legion. Often the *signifer* wore scale armor and an animal pelt over his helmet, which sometimes had a hinged decorative face piece, while he carried a small, round shield rather than a *scutum*. His *signum*, or standard, consisted of a wooden pole bearing a raised hand, or a spear tip surrounded by palm leaves. Below this was a crossbar from which hung metal decorations, or a piece of colored cloth. The standard's shaft was decorated with discs, half-moons, ships' prows and crowns, which were records of the unit's achievements and may have distinguished one century from another.

Silarus, River: modern-day River Sele.

Social War: this conflict took place between 91 and 87 BC, waged by Rome's Italian allies against her supremacy. Many disgruntled Samnites took part. The war ended largely through the political concession of granting Roman citizenship to the enemy.

Styx, River: the river of the underworld, Hades.

subarmalis: a garment worn under armor to protect the body from chafing. The singular term may actually be *subarmale*, but there is controversy over this.

summa rudis: the official who maintained order in the gladiatorial arena.

Stygian: infernal, hellish—as of the River Styx.

Sulla Felix, Lucius Cornelius (*c.*138–78 BC): one of the most famous Roman generals and statesmen ever. He was a ruthless man who made himself dictator, caused civil wars and ultimately helped to weaken the Republic, yet he also strengthened the position of the Senate, and retired from public life rather than remain in power.

tablinum: the office or reception area beyond the *atrium*. The *tablinum* usually opened on to an enclosed colonnaded garden.

Tanager, River: modern-day River Tanagro.

Thrace: an area in the ancient world spanning parts of Bulgaria, Romania, northern Greece and southwestern Turkey. It was inhabited by more than forty warlike tribes.

Thurii: modern-day Sibari.

tiro (pl. *tirones*): a gladiator recruit.

titurium: the name given by the Greeks to the Thracian war cry; it supposedly mimicked a cry to the Titans, the gods who preceded the Olympians: Zeus, Artemis et al.

Toutatis: a Gaulish god who is thought to have been worshipped as the protector of tribes.

Triballi: a Thracian tribe renowned for their savagery.

tribune: a senior staff officer within a legion; also one of ten political positions in Rome, where they served as "tribunes of the people," defending the rights of the plebeians.

trireme: the classic Roman warship, which was powered by a single sail and three banks of oars. Each oar was rowed by one man, who was freeborn, not a slave. Exceptionally maneuverable, and capable of up to eight knots under sail or for short bursts when rowed, the trireme also had a bronze ram at the prow. Triremes had very large crews in proportion to their size. This limited their range, so they were mainly used as troop transports and to protect coastlines.

triumph: the procession to the temple of Jupiter on the Capitoline Hill of a Roman general who had won a large-scale military victory.

Venus: the Roman goddess of motherhood and domesticity.

Via Annia: a Roman road in northern Italy; also an extension of the Via Appia, which ran from Capua to Rhegium.

Via Appia: the main road from Rome to the south of Italy.

vilicus: slave foreman or farm manager. Commonly a slave, the *vilicus* was required to make sure that the returns on a farm were as large as possible. This was most commonly done by treating the slaves brutally.

Vinalia Rustica: a Roman wine festival held on 19 August.

virtus: a much-respected Roman virtue, associated with courage, honor and manliness.

Vulcan (or Vulcanus): a Roman god of destructive fire, who was often worshipped to prevent—fire!

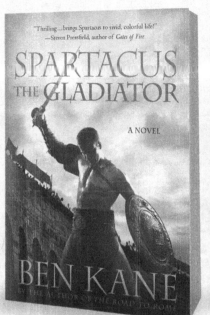
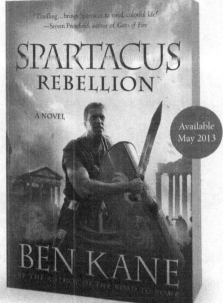

"Kane is a natural storyteller, merging suspense
and intrigue with graphic battlefield scenes
and historical color into a ripping story that
will please series fans and new converts alike."
—*Publishers Weekly*

ST. MARTIN'S PRESS   St. Martin's Griffin